Death Becomes Them
By Adrian Cousins

Prologue

2016

Acting Sheriff Hank Peterson killed the engine and silenced his radio after skidding his police cruiser to a halt on the edge of the muddy dirt track. Hank slugged down the remains of his coffee whilst peering through the trees towards the trail leading to the lake shore. After a particularly heavy session whilst watching the ball game with the boys at Marty Bride's beer house, he'd hoped today would pan out to be a quiet one. Unfortunately, after a panicked call from Jake, his rookie deputy, it appeared that wasn't going to be the case.

The strobe lights emanating from Jake's cruiser, parked a few yards ahead, danced through the dense grove of pine trees that encircled and tightly cloaked the eastern tip of Lake Ozark. Hank grabbed his heavy metal flashlight from the passenger footwell. Although a bright morning, he knew ten feet into the thick undergrowth, the tall pines transformed the vista down to the lake into a dark tunnel.

Whilst wincing at the strobe lights and hoping the more-than-suggested dose of Advil would soon dull his hangover, the acting sheriff shoved open the door and heaved his sizable bulk out into the spring sunshine. The cruiser's suspension creaked with relief as he somewhat ungainly alighted.

As he threw the door closed, Hank spotted Jake lumbering through the trees towards him. Jake had radioed through earlier, stating he was scooting this way after a bunch of kids had apparently discovered a body. This was all he needed today. Hank was all for an easy life, which involved sipping coffee and shovelling cinnamon rolls down his throat at the diner over on Bagnell Dam Boulevard, not dealing with stiffs by the lake.

This particular area covered by the Miller County Police Department rarely dealt with situations of this sort. No, this low-crime part of Missouri wasn't like Palestine West, a horrendous neighbourhood in his home city of Kansas where he'd spent many years in his long career dealing with drug-related violent crimes and homicides. Despite that, whilst his heavily perspiring deputy hauled himself up the incline towards him, Hank knew he was in for one hell of a shit day.

"Jake, what we got?"

Jake, panting and wheezing like Rocky, Hank's twelve-year-old Labrador, halted and puffed out his cheeks before resting his hands on his knees. Although twenty years Hank's junior, he seemed to model himself on the acting sheriff if his gut-straining shirt was anything to go by. Jake rarely crossed the threshold to the local gym, preferring to accompany the acting sheriff when savouring the artery-clogging delights of a cinnamon roll and a couple of ring doughnut chasers at the local diner.

6

Hank glanced around the glade, waiting for his deputy to catch his breath. Although the track, a mixture of soft earth and pine needles, lay muddy from recent rains, he presumed the forensic boys would fail to identify any tyre tracks now their cruisers had obliterated the evidence. Hank knew he was out of practise when it came to managing crime scenes. Also, it appeared his clueless rookie deputy hadn't given any thought to the fact that dumping a body up here would require transport.

As Hank flipped the trunk to grab a roll of police tape to secure the area, Jake straightened up.

"It's some limey. He's down near the water's edge."

Hank glanced up as he grabbed the blue and white roll of tape. "Oh, crap, a tourist. I hate tourists," he huffed. "This Brit got a name?"

Jake patted his pants pockets, then glanced around at his feet, stepping back while searching the bed of pine needles and frantically patting his pants and shirt pockets some more. "Err … oh," he stuttered, before offering up an opened-mouth-frowning expression and sporting a worried look.

Hank threw the truck lid down. "Well, if you know he's a Brit, I'm kinda guessing you have his ID."

"I did."

"You did? Hell, what does that mean?"

"Ah, sorry. I checked the guy's pockets and found a wallet. He had a few bills and one of those funny looking European driver's licences in it. I assumed he's a limey 'cos that licence got that fancy union flag printed on the front, but I've forgotten the stiff's name." Jake restarted his pocket-patting routine when clocking Hank's somewhat bemused look.

7

"You tellin' me you've managed to lose the god-damn thing?"

Jake nodded, realising he must have dropped the dead man's wallet somewhere along the trail.

Hank lowered his head and heavy-footed thumped his way towards his hapless deputy. Jake backed up a pace as Hank raised his head and pursed his lips. "So, let me get this straight. We've got ourselves a stiff by the lake, and you've rummaged around whilst tramping your boots across a potential crime scene." He pointed over Jake's shoulder towards the lake. "You hook out his wallet and then lose it in the two minutes it's taken you to get back here."

Jake winced.

Hank slowly shook his head. "I guess we better find it then."

Jake nodded as he turned, preparing to scoot back down the trail.

"Hey, ease up. Hold those wild horses of yours. No need to shoot off like a spooked rattlesnake." Jake skidded to a halt, glancing back at Hank. "I take it he's dead and not some drunk sleeping off a heavy night."

"Hell, yeah, he's dead, alright. I reckon he's been in the water for a couple of days. Reckon he's just washed up … the stiff's definitely dead."

Hank nodded, flipped on his flashlight and strode forward, closely followed by his hapless deputy.

"As I said. I guess he's been in the lake for a while. It ain't a pretty sight. Made my stomach flip like a pancake, it did," blurted Jake.

Hank lumbered forward, his heavy boots causing the mat of dead pine needles to dance with each step. "Say we look for this wallet and quit the yakking."

"Yeah, sure. You know, he kinda looks like one of those zombies from *The Walking Dead*."

Hank didn't respond, only offering a slight shake of his head. If Jake put as much effort into police work as his tongue did with talking, Hank thought the boy would make Commissioner before he reached thirty.

Hank's earlier career gave cause for him to witness the aftermath of many a homicide which could haunt a man. So, some stiff by the lake wasn't going to worry him, despite Jake's insistence that the corpse resembled a zombie.

Although they scoured the trail in the few minutes it took to traverse the steep decline to the lake, neither man discovered the missing wallet. That said, Hank wasn't looking that hard because he focused all his efforts on keeping his footing whilst cursing his pounding head.

After assessing the corpse for a few seconds, Hank clicked off his flashlight and, with creaking knees, squatted to grab a closer look.

"Well, I've seen enough dead bodies in my time. Stabbin's, shootin's, strangulations, and a few bludgeoned to death," he glanced up at Jake. "But this one don't seem to have suffered anything like that."

"You reckon he just drowned?"

"Yup, reckon so. That lake has taken a few over the years, and will again if these dumb-ass tourists don't respect the water." He groaned and rubbed his lower back as he straightened up. "You better go find that wallet. Presumably, someone's missing him, and it would be good to know his name."

"Sure thing. You don't think he was murdered, then?"

"Hell, no. The medical examiner will have to confirm it, but I reckon this jackass probably fell in the water after too many beers. This is just some unfortunate accident."

Or was it?

Part 1

1

1984

Newton's Cradle

Sidney squatted down on his haunches in the corner of his office, assessing the shattered picture frame which, only a few moments before, he'd unceremoniously lobbed at the wall when sat at his desk.

The framed picture of his wife wasn't the only object he'd flung when in a fit of rage, but it was the most poignant, considering the blazing row he'd just endured with the woman whose picture now lay amongst the splintered wood and slivers of glass.

He carefully extracted the picture from the debris, shaking off the vicious-looking slivers, before clasping the photo with both hands. The gorgeous Deana Statham, depicted in her wedding dress, smiled back at him. It was fair to say that was a significantly different expression to the one she'd offered just before marching out of his office, a nanosecond before he'd snatched up the picture and hurled it in the direction she'd just vacated.

Deana Beacham, as she was called when they met eight months ago, had stolen his heart. That drab January day, when she'd waltzed into his car lot whilst eyeing up a Ford Escort, the vivacious woman had wooed him. For Sidney, it really was love at first sight. Of course, deep down, Sidney had always known she was out of his league, and the fact that she was pregnant when they met always played at the back of his mind as to why a woman like that would be interested in a man like him.

However, love is blind. So, despite the warnings from his friends and family that she was a black widow and it would inevitably all end in tears, Sidney married the woman before the spring bulbs bloomed and her tummy swelled. He'd been warned, but he'd not taken heed – Deana had spun her web and reeled him in. Now, six months after they'd married, she'd discarded him, leaving him crumpled like the cigarette packet he'd crushed and lobbed after pelting the picture frame at the wall.

Sidney pinched his nose and tightly squeezed his eyes closed as he tried to hold back the tears. Not tears for lost love, but for what an idiot he'd been. Although in his heart he knew this day would come, he never imagined it would happen so quickly.

"Sid. Sidney, you okay in there?"

His office door cracked open, nudging against his leg, thus stopping Joanna from being able to step into his office.

"Sid?" she called out again, shoving the door harder, trying to peek in.

14

"Err … yup. I'm fine." He dragged his shirt sleeve across his nose whilst using the back of his hand to dry his dampened eyes before standing and allowing his dependable assistant to fully open the door.

"Don't, Joanna. Just don't," he mumbled, as he padded back to his desk.

He knew she must have heard the argument, along with the ensuing office trashing which followed. However, he really couldn't swallow the hefty helping of 'I told you so' that was surely about to be delivered by the woman who'd not only been his trusted assistant for two years but also held an extremely diminutive view of his soon-to-be ex-wife.

Sidney and Joanna locked eyes before she set about clearing the mass of projectiles that liberally covered the carpet-tiled floor of his Portakabin office. Sidney extracted a cigarette from a packet that he hadn't crushed during his fit of rage, lit it with his engraved Zippo lighter and collapsed in his swivel chair whilst watching Joanna attempt to restore some order.

"Did you hear it all?" he asked, spinning the lighter around in his hand before rubbing his thumb across the engraving of his name – a present from Deana.

Joanna met his eyes as she set his Newton's Cradle back on the desk – every aspiring entrepreneur's desk sported an executive ball clicker. Although Statham & Hunt Car Sales was only a second-hand car dealership nestled in the shitty end of town, Sidney harboured big plans for the future.

"Well?"

"Yes," she nodded. "I know you don't want to hear this, but you're better off without her."

Sidney leaned forward and pulled the first ball back before releasing it, thus allowing the conservation of momentum to begin. For a few moments, they both watched the balls rhythmically collide. Sidney likened the slowing of the swinging balls to how his life seemed to be grinding to a halt – an ever-decreasing momentum.

"She said she never really loved me."

Joanna placed a stack of car brochures on the desk and hesitated, unsure what to say to that comment. 'I told you so' seemed appropriate, but based on the events of the last week and the pandemonium she'd just witnessed, Joanna thought that was a comment for another day.

"You're better than her."

Sidney shrugged his shoulders before leaning forward and flicking ash in the already full ashtray – the only item that remained on the desk during his fit of rage. "It's a bloody mess; I know that much."

"Your life or this office?" She raised an eyebrow before retrieving yesterday's newspaper and plonking it on top of the stack of brochures.

"Huh … both!"

"What about Damian? Will you still be able to see him?" Joanna knew that his adopted son meant the world to Sidney. Although she was pleased, at last, that bloody woman was out of her boss's life, she knew losing Damian would crush him.

Sidney lifted his cigarette from his ashtray before halting the slowing balls. "Although he's not my blood, he's my boy. She can rot in hell if she thinks she can take him away from me."

"Good. Stay strong, Sidney." She leant forward and patted his hand.

"I can't believe the bloody mess I'm in. What with Dennis and now that bloody woman. She really did take me for a ride."

"Well, that should put things into perspective." Joanna thumped her forefinger on the newspaper, just below a picture of the bombed Grand Hotel in Brighton next to the headlines – *Cabinet survives IRA hotel blast* – "It could be worse. You've only got a failed marriage and an arrested business partner to worry about."

"Hmm, Thatcher was lucky to survive that. They'll get her eventually, you know. While they're trying to get her, they can stick a bomb up Deana's arse if they want."

"I don't think it's a joking matter. A bomb killed my mother in '41, I'll have you know."

"Yes, alright. But I presume your mother wasn't the most unpopular woman in the world, unlike Thatcher and that bloody wife of mine. You know, those two make a good pair," he chuckled. "Perhaps the bloody IRA can get them both next time."

"That's a wicked thing to say."

Sidney held up his hands and nodded. "Look, sorry, Jo. It might have escaped your notice, but I'm having a bit of a shit day."

Joanna grimaced.

"What?"

"Look, I'm afraid your day's about to get worse. Those two police officers are back. They arrived just as Deana left. I asked them to give you a moment, but I'd better let them in."

"Bollocks," he muttered.

"What do you think will happen? Will the business survive?"

"Jo, don't worry. We'll be okay. Dennis is going down for this, but he's not taking me with him. Deana can skip off with her lover, but I'm not letting her and Dennis rip my life apart."

Joanna rubbed the back of his hand that lay on the desk, offering a reassuring smile. "Good. Right, I'd better let them in. It's that rather rotund woman and her sidekick again."

"DI French?"

"Uh-huh," she threw over her shoulder as she opened the office door. "This way, please."

Sidney stood and stubbed out his cigarette before fastening both buttons on his double-breasted suit jacket as DI French barrelled her way through the door, her expression suggesting she wasn't too chuffed about being kept waiting.

This would be the second time Sidney had the pleasure of her company. At their first meeting, he found the woman somewhat formidable. A cross between Miss Marple and Jack Regan, although the vision of Miss Marple chasing armed blaggers in a Ford Consul with a blue light slapped to the roof, was difficult to formulate.

"DI French, take a seat." Sidney waved to the chairs to the left of his desk.

"We'll stand," she barked, causing her sergeant to hop up from where he was about to nestle his backside into one of the plastic moulded chairs.

Sidney fiddled with his suit-jacket buttons, not knowing whether to sit or remain standing. Also, a little unsure if the rotund DI's bark demanded they all stand or if he was free to sit.

"It appears you have a temper, Mr Statham." DI French glanced around the office, her eyes coming to rest on the smashed frame by the door.

"Look, sorry about that. My wife was just informing me she's leaving me for her lover … the framed picture of her bore my frustration."

"Quite," nodded the DI as she aggressively folded her arms. "Okay, I'm here to advise you we've charged your business partner, Dennis Hunt. However, we're satisfied that you are not involved and believe Mr Hunt acted alone."

Sidney heaved a sigh of relief before slumping into his swivel chair. "Thank you." He reached for his cigarettes, surprised that his voice seemed to have shot up a few octaves and how his hand appeared to tremble.

"Please refrain from smoking whilst I'm in the room, Mr Statham."

Sidney's hand hovered above the packet.

"Of course, following your statement, you will be called to give evidence for the prosecution."

"What? You want me to turn on my business partner?"

"You're a key witness. I might add that I could be landing a charge of perverting the course of justice at your door, so I suggest you could regard yourself as fortunate. You were fully aware of what Dennis Hunt was up to, but you chose to ignore it, which in turn has put vulnerable people in danger." She turned to her silent partner. "Would you agree, sergeant?"

"Ma'am," he nodded.

"But he'll know I've provided the evidence to put him away … where does that leave me?"

DI French slapped the palms of her hands on his desk as she leaned forward. "We're expecting your full cooperation. Of course, my sergeant here could riffle through those filing cabinets and check whether any of those cars on your forecourt are displaying, shall we say, dubious mileage? I reckon we might discover some interesting documents, and I could perhaps add to that charge of perverting the course of justice which is hanging over you like a dark cloud."

"DI French, are you suggesting that I have clocked my fleet of motors?"

"Mr Statham, I'm not suggesting anything. However, if I felt so inclined, I could have each car checked to establish whether anyone has tampered with those odometers … is that something you would feel comfortable with?"

Whilst locking eyes with the austere officer, Sidney swallowed hard, his Adam's apple bouncing as the audible noise filled the void in the conversation.

"Well?"

DI French won the staring competition when Sidney glanced at her sergeant, who still held his notebook and pen at the ready.

"No, that won't be necessary."

"Good. We see eye to eye on the matter, then?"

Sidney nodded, accepting that a rummage through those files would highlight some irregularities he'd prefer were kept under wraps. Not that he was involved in criminal activity as such, but the turning back of a few odometers by a few thousand miles always made his cars a tad more saleable. The second-hand car business was a tough one, and Sidney knew he needed to take every advantage to ensure he stayed ahead of the competition.

"Look, do you think we can keep my car business out of this? I'm a little worried that the court case will damage my reputation."

DI French straightened up, returning to her previous pose of arms folded across her tray-of-beer chest. "Your car lot is of no interest to us … as long as you cooperate."

Sidney nodded.

"Mr Statham, if I were you, I'd be more concerned about your business partner's associates than your grotty second-hand car business. Unfortunately, because of your association with Dennis Hunt, you've flirted with the wrong sort, and I'm not referring to the woman who appears to have just given you the good old Spanish archer."

2

2016

Desperate Housewives

Fred Hallam's Private Investigations, a one-man band type of affair with offices in the less salubrious end of town, had enjoyed better times. Back in the good old '90s, he prided himself on conducting discreet investigations, delivering effective results with a reputation for discovering the truth.

Back then, Fred Hallam was the go-to man for any spouse looking for evidence of their partner's infidelity – desperate housewives, mainly. He'd regarded himself as a Jim Rockford type character, although he didn't own a Pontiac Firebird Esprit or live in a trailer on Malibu Beach. That said, he owned a rather tired sports jacket and a half-decent pair of slacks, but that's where the likeness to the Californian private-eye character ended.

Twenty-odd years on, and along with his hair, business had all but fizzled away, probably due to rarely being in a state of sobriety and a propensity to screw up any assignment offered to him – and those were few and far between. Now he resembled the incompetence of Inspector Gadget, without the regular dose of good fortune which the hapless cyborg detective benefited from.

So, when a man who wished to remain nameless offered an assignment of, shall we say, somewhat dubious ethics, Fred considered two things. First, the realisation of how low he'd sunk by even considering the offer, and second, the five-thousand-pound payment couldn't be turned down. Well, a man has bills to pay, doesn't he?

Whilst hunkered down in his rust-decorated, pre-millennium Ford Transit van, parked on the Broxworth Estate near the drug den that back in the day used to be a thriving community centre, Fred surveyed the group of working girls. Tonight's sortie into this hideous place involved trying to pick one who he thought might fit the bill and thus be up for making a fast buck.

"Christ, they're a bit rough," he muttered, whilst surveying the 'talent' on offer. He watched the girls as they strutted up and down, occasionally leaning through car windows of some kerb-crawling desperadoes, leaving little to the imagination as their short skirts rode up whilst negotiating the price of sexual relief.

With his wily old detective eyes, he focused on one particular girl with ample boobs who paraded about in a dangerously short leather skirt. Although not perfect, Fred thought she'd do and was undoubtedly better than the rest of the tarts milling about in this squalid end of town.

He'd selected the Broxworth Estate to find an appropriate girl based solely on keeping the price down. He suspected some rough dog of a bird with a decent chest might not be too concerned about his somewhat dubious suggestion and would therefore be satisfied with a few hundred quid stuffed down her cleavage.

Fred slid out of the driver's seat and flung the door shut, not turning to lock it because there was no point – not even the residents of the odious Broxworth Estate would consider stealing his old rust bucket.

"Excuse me, love," Fred waved his arm at the tart in the leather skirt as he trotted towards the row of dilapidated shops. The stench of overused cooking oil that wafted from the Chinese takeaway assaulted his nasal passages as he scuttled past the open door.

The blonde in the miniskirt, whilst swilling gum around her open mouth, turned around and thumped her hands on her hips. "You looking for a bit of business?"

"Err … kind of."

"Well, you are, or you ain't. Which is it?"

"Err … sort of. Look, I may have a proposition for you."

"You have, or you haven't … what's this, some bleedin' guessing game?" she fired out between a couple of chewing gum-swilling revolutions.

Coupled with her apparent lack of diction, as Fred approached, he assessed she might not be what he was searching for. That said, he wasn't looking to employ her services for stimulating conversation purposes and didn't require her to recite poetry. As long as she could get her kit off and wrap herself around the body of his target, then he'd be the best part of five grand better off.

"Oi. What you staring at, tosser? You're not one of those weirdo-type nutters, are you? This ain't no free peep show, y'know. If you're gonna just gawp, you can piss off."

24

The gum-swilling tart bore down on him, her high-heeled boots affording her a good few inches height advantage above Fred's modest five-foot six-inch frame.

"No, I'm sorry." Fred flashed his best grin and defensively raised the palm of his hands. "I was just—"

"I know," she chuckled. "You were just checking me out, right? Well, you ain't going to get any better than me around here, I can tell you. But I ain't cheap, mind, and—"

"No. It's not like that," Fred interrupted her before she had the chance to trot out the entire menu on offer.

"Oh, I get it. First time, is it, mate? Had a falling out with the missus, have you?"

"No—"

"Hey, don't worry … I do virgins all the time."

"I'm not a virgin."

"Well, I should think not, at your age," she chuckled, again swilling her gum around and letting it rest in her front teeth before continuing. "Listen, short-arse. A virgin is a first-timer with a tom."

"Oh, of course." Fred ignored the comment regarding his height or lack of. Although a common comment thrown at him, this wasn't the time to lob insults back and forth. Also, assessing this particular tart, he could think of many. Anyway, after over fifty years of suffering references regarding his low physical stature, he'd grown – no pun intended – tired of retaliating.

"Right, what is it then? Blow, or you want the full English?"

"Full English?" Fred frowned, his tone moving his statement to a question.

"Christ! Full English is you shoving your d—"

"Alright, I get it. I don't need a geography lesson."

She nodded and swilled her gum. "But listen up, I don't do it up the bum, so don't even ask."

"Look, sorry. This isn't what I was proposing. What's your name?"

The aggressive tart closed the gap and laid her hand on his chest. "Anything you want it to be, big boy."

Fred copped an eyeful of her well-chewed gum as she offered a saliva-filled display of her cement mixer impression. Now close up and personal, Fred considered he'd made a mistake. Perhaps he should scoot back to his van and call up some escort agencies that might offer up a bird with slightly more endearing qualities. However, that would increase costs, so he bashed on despite her less-than-polished persona.

"Is there somewhere we could talk? You know, privately."

"Talk. You wanna talk?"

"Err ... yeah. As I said, I have a proposition for you."

"Oh, shit me, you the Old Bill? Christ, how many times are you lot going to try to get us girls to turn, eh?"

"What?"

"I ain't ratting on no one, and I ain't seen nuffin!"

"Seen what ... about what?"

"Whatever you're trying to get information on. I didn't see it happen, and I don't know who did it?"

"No." Fred stepped back a pace, a smidge frustrated with how difficult this was to offer a working girl a monkey for a quick assignment. "I'm not the police, okay? I just what to employ your services."

Whilst thrusting her barely covered chest at him, she thumped her hands on her hips and eyed him up and down before nodding, presumably satisfied he wasn't the Old Bill. She fished out a handful of brightly coloured condoms, holding them up in a fan formation. "Pick a colour, or I've got extra-large available if you're well-hung, although they only come in black."

Fred glanced at the rainbow on offer, realising he was just going to have to come straight out with the proposal rather than holding a discreet conversation, which he would have preferred. "Look, you up for earning a quick monkey for one night's work?"

"Fuck me! You really do want a full English, don't you? I'll throw in a blow for that. Cash up front, mind." She raised a finger as if enforcing her financial demands. "And nothing near my arse, not even a finger."

"No, I don't want that."

"Well, what the bleedin' hell do you want?" she spat back whilst securing her rainbow collection in her bag. "I guess you ain't throwing a monkey my way for nuffin. You some perv? One of those weirdos that go around beatin' up women?"

"Babe, you alright?" called out a voice from behind Fred.

"Yeah, fink so."

"Where's Leroy? You need this tosser sortin' out?"

Fred swivelled around to assess who was suggesting some Leroy fella needed to get involved. Whilst frustrated that the operation appeared to be going south and rueing his decision to pick up a girl from the estate, he spotted a blonde dressed in a pink hoodie aggressively marching towards him.

Again, he defensively held his hands up. "Look, ladies, I'm not looking for trouble."

"Well, you give her any shit, and you'll find it, alright?" the blonde barked, before turning to the girl in the leather skirt. "Trace, get Leroy."

"Woah, I'm going, I'm going." He backed up a couple of paces as the leather-skirt tart shot off towards a dark alley situated at the side of the Chinese takeaway, leaving him in the company of the blonde sporting a rottweiler persona.

"Go on then, piss off, you twat."

Before hot-footing back to his van, Fred assessed the blonde, giving her the once up and down. Now, this girl fitted the bill. Apart from baring her teeth and appearing to chew a wasp, she was nothing short of stunning.

"Oi, twat, I said, piss off. I'd get going before Leroy cuts your saggy sack off."

Although not relishing castration from their pimp, he held his ground when recognising this was an opportunity too good to miss. "Look, you working?"

Although not flashing the flesh, dressed in a hoodie and jeans, she seemed to know the lie of the land, so Fred assumed she must be a working girl. He considered the blonde may be enjoying a night off or on a fifteen-minute unpaid tea break if they benefited from such a thing. Although Fred had never dabbled, being more of an internet porn and a packet of Kleenex type of guy, he thought he could make an exception for this girl. If she could lose the aggressive attitude, she might just be the girl he was searching for – stunning and potentially inexpensive.

"Me?"

"Shit," he muttered. "Hey, sorry, love. I just thought—"

"Look, I don't do that no more, so no, I ain't working. I've moved up in the world, I'll have you know. I do films and a bit of internet live show stuff if you're interested." The blonde seemed to take on a more conciliatory tone, appearing to soften as she altered the conversation towards a sales pitch. "So, I don't go sucking punters off in crappy Transits no more."

"Okay. No problem." Fred grabbed the door handle to his van, keeping half an eye on the alley, fully expecting some baseball-bat-wielding heavy to come barrelling through.

"I done you before?"

"No, love," he chuckled, yanking the squeaky door open. "I think I'd remember." Fred hopped onto the driver's seat and stabbed the key in the ignition whilst praying this attempt to start the engine would fall into the ten per cent of first-time starts.

The blonde tapped on the driver's window.

The alternator clicked. "Bollocks," he hissed. "Come on, you piece of shit."

She tapped again, cranking her hand around to suggest he should lower the window.

Fred huffed and complied. "What?"

"Look, I take it you're not a pervert or some serial killer."

"No, love."

"Alright. If you fancy a bit of business with Trace, then I'll get her back 'ere. You treat her right, though. Otherwise, you'll have me to deal wiv, an' all." She enforced her threat with a pointing finger but kept the rottweiler persona under wraps.

"Nah. I'll leave it. Anyway, I'm not looking to hook up with a girl."

"What the fuck you doing, then?"

Three more attempts and the starter motor complied. However, the engine failed to fire. As Fred twisted the key around again, a giant of a man accompanying the tart in the leather skirt exited the alley. Although he wasn't wielding a baseball bat, Fred considered this might be a good time for the gunk-filled fuel lines to inject a dribble of fuel; otherwise, he feared for his health.

The blonde stepped away to meet the not-so-welcoming party whilst Fred repeated his attempts to start the engine. As the battery protested and slowed, the starter motor whined, causing Fred to panic. He was on his own, in the middle of one of the country's most notorious estates, with a hefty-looking thug just ten feet away who appeared ready to remove his body parts.

Fred wiped his sweating hand down his slacks before winding up the window and locking the door. Not for one moment did he believe these security measures would protect him, but it was all he could do. He turned the key again – nothing – he was doomed.

"Oh, thank God for that," he mumbled, as he watched the thug-man and the tart walk away before the blonde tramped back to his van. Fred wound down the window.

"Look, geezer, I've done you a favour. I told Leroy to do one, but I suggest you piss off before he changes his mind."

"Cheers, thanks."

"I take it you know you're on the Broxworth?"

"Yeah."

"Right, well, you'll know then that it ain't safe around 'ere."

"Look, how do you fancy five hundred quid for a couple of hours doing a bit of escort work for me?"

The blonde narrowed her eyes. "What sort of escort work? I told you I don't do that kind of stuff no more."

"Hey, no sex, just whipping your kit off for a few minutes."

"Who the hell pays five hundred for a gawp? You ever heard of internet porn? You can get all that for free … and right dodgy stuff if you're into all that."

Fred leaned through the window. Unusually for him, holding the higher ground and peering down to talk. "Look, it's a simple setup job. All you have to do is turn up at some geezer's hotel room and knock on the door. Then, you dive on him when he opens up, and I get some snaps of the event."

The blonde thumped her hands on her hips, pondering the offer.

"You up for that?"

"Is this a joke?"

"No, straight up. I just need a fit bird to pull a job off."

"And you reckon there's no sex, and you're not a rapist."

"No. You interested?"

"What's your game, eh? This don't sound like proper escort work. And how do I know you're not some weirdo?"

"Christ, how can this be so difficult? Do I look like some deranged nutter?"

The blonde smirked. "Nah, alright. I've known many of them in my time, and you look fairly normal, I suppose."

"Thanks, I'll take that as a compliment."

"So, who's this bloke?"

"That doesn't matter."

"Go on," she shrugged.

"So, I've got a job which requires this bloke to be caught in a compromising position. All I need is a few snaps of him with another woman, and we both get paid. The geezer in question will be staying in a hotel in Birmingham tomorrow night. You get yourself all dolled up, and rock up to his room in the buff with just a coat on. Drop the coat and pounce on him when he opens up, just long enough for me to capture a few shots."

"How much you getting paid?"

"What?"

"Well, you're giving me a monkey, so how much you getting?"

"Enough."

"Well, as I see it, you're running out of time. If I say no, you ain't gonna get no one else now, are you? So, I wanna grand."

"Jesus!"

"Well?"

"Seven hundred."

"Nine."

"Eight hundred, but that's—"

"Deal!" the blonde interrupted.

"Christ, you drive a hard bargain," he huffed. "Right, I'll pick you up tomorrow at six from the Beehive Pub car park."

"Nah … not near here. Pick me up in town. I'll be at the Carrow Road Bridge at six. But listen, I want a ton now, four hundred before we leave and the rest on the way back."

Fred nodded as he reached for his wallet. "What's your name?" he asked as he thumbed out a wad of twenties and handed them out of the window.

The blonde raised her hand to take the cash, but Fred snatched his hand away. "Name."

"What's yours?"

"Fair enough," he chuckled.

"You'll turn up? You're not going to run off with my cash and then leave me waiting on that bridge?"

"You'll have to risk it, won't you," she smirked.

Apart from her stunning looks, Fred thought there was something about this girl that suggested honesty. Perhaps he was being naïve, a trait he would regularly accuse his clients of displaying. However, if she didn't show, he'd be more concerned about finding a replacement than the forfeited hundred quid.

"I'll risk it."

"Cool. Right, I suggest you piss off before Leroy changes his mind or some other wanker decides they don't like the look of you. I'll see you tomorrow at six, and remember, four hundred upfront or the deal's off."

Fred nodded.

"The poor bugger we're setting up. What's his crime?"

"Who cares? We do the job, and we get paid. I just guess the poor sod is in the wrong place at the wrong time."

The blonde nodded. "Pick me up in somefink better than this mobile skip. You'll have to hire a car or somefink."

"Yeah, I'll borrow a mate's car. Reckon this thing's given up the ghost."

"You flooded the engine when you shit your pants with Leroy 'ere. Try it again. I reckon it'll start now."

"I doubt it." Fred swivelled the key, and the engine fired, almost purring or more growling like a Ferrari. "Bugger me," he chuckled.

The blonde made a fist and flexed her biceps. "Girl power."

3

Three weeks later

Apocalypse Now

"Piss off. I ain't your naffin' keeper!" she boomed.

"Christ, who the hell was that?" asked Rob, lifting his beer bottle to his lips, now sporting a shocked expression. He peered past me, attempting to spot the woman who'd launched the barrage of abuse that pulsed through the kitchen window of my squalid shithole of a flat.

"That, my old friend, is the dulcet tones of the next-door neighbour screaming at her boyfriend. Look, there he goes, stomping off up the landing." I pointed to the nondescript bloke wearing a hoodie as he whizzed past the window after receiving a mouthful of abuse from his girlfriend.

"She sounds a delight."

"Not really. She's some rough slag, like the rest of the inhabitants of this bloody estate. I think she's a hooker. Well, I assume she is, going by the way she dresses and the noises that come from her flat."

Rob raised his eyebrows and chuckled. "Blimey."

"You should hear it. She's either got blokes in there all day long like some knocking shop, or the bloody woman enjoys talking dirty to herself."

"And you can hear all that through the walls?"

"Yep, right down to every fake moan."

Rob puffed out his cheeks and shook his head. "Entertaining then?" he chuckled.

"Not really, mate," I whined. "I've not clapped eyes on her yet, but she shouts at him all the time. All I know is her name is Courteney because the geezer she lives with bellows it out when she doesn't buy the correct quantity of beer that he deems enough for him to get shit-faced before he slaps her about after a hard day selling drugs."

"He's a drug dealer?"

I nodded before taking a swig of my beer. "Yep. Every night, it's the same routine. Although tonight is a tad quieter because he's pissed off down the landing instead of giving her a good thrashing."

"Christ, mate. Sorry, but this is one hell of a dump."

"Don't I know it!" I somewhat aggressively spat back at Rob.

Although, to be fair to Rob, since being kicked out by my girlfriend a couple of weeks back, he and Lee were the only mates who'd stood by me. They say you only know who your true friends are when in times of crisis. My current situation, as in renting a two-bed hell-hole of a dump on the Broxworth Estate with a drug dealer and his prossy girlfriend as neighbours, could be described as a crisis – or worse. However, as I stood in my grubby flat nursing a beer bottle, I couldn't think of a better word to describe my dire predicament.

Rob held his palm up and nodded, accepting my apology for biting back. Although I hadn't apologised, we'd known each other for that long, he knew I was sorry for snapping.

"What's another word for crisis?"

"I don't know. Why d'you ask?"

I shrugged before taking a swig of beer.

"Alright. What about disaster or calamity … catastrophe? Armageddon, perhaps? What about in the shit? Or perhaps apocalypse?"

"Apocalyptic." I waved my bottle at him. "That's the word. My life is apocalyptic."

"Oh, mate, I'm sorry. You know I'd suggest you could billet at my place for a while, but I think Laura would throw a hissy fit if I suggested it."

I nodded – she would. It's safe to say Laura was not my number one fan.

"Anyway, I think she would side with your missus. You're not exactly at the top of her Christmas card list if you get my drift."

"Ex-missus."

"Yeah, okay. She's not going to forgive you then?"

I shook my head before tipping the bottle back and savouring the dregs.

"Thought as much. Anyway, why are you renting this place? Not exactly the bloody Ritz, is it?"

I thumbed towards the bathroom where Lee had shot off to a few minutes ago, claiming he needed a dump, as he put it. "You know Lee's dad is the landlord? He wangled me a deal because it's just become vacant last week when some woman moved on."

"Yeah, I know. Lee said as much on the way up here."

"It's good of Lee, really. We've only known him for a little while, so he didn't need to step in and help."

"I don't think it was out of the kindness of his heart. His old man is still getting rent money from you."

"Yeah, I know, but I'd be royally fucked without this shithole to lay my head in."

"Sorry, mate. I would ask Laura, but—"

"Hey, forget it. I understand."

"But anyway, I mean, why here? I know Bridget has kicked you out of the flat, but surely you could rent something better than this?"

"I'm broke, mate."

"What? No, come on. Just sell a few of those fancy cars on your forecourt and rent a house in town."

I shook my head and glanced out of the window. "I can't."

"Christ, that bathroom of yours is a bloody health hazard. I reckon you could catch Ebola in there. If I'd shat on the floor, I doubt you'd notice. The place is disgusting," announced Lee, as he wandered back from clearing out his bowels before plucking up his beer bottle.

"Well, I expect it is now after you've splattered it with whatever. Anyway, your dad owns this dump, so getting the decorators in is down to him."

"A catering-size bottle of bleach might be a start. Anyway, my old man is doing you a favour by letting you have this place."

"I know." I waved my beer bottle at him as a gesture of apology.

Lee grinned before taking a swig of his beer. "I'd give it a wide berth for a couple of hours. That ruby-murray I had last night seems to have worked its way through at last."

"Oh, lovely!"

"Anyway, what were you saying? What is it you can't do?"

"Oh, yeah. Look, I was just saying to Rob that I'm a bit strapped for cash."

"Damian, I don't get it." Rob blurted after swigging a mouthful of beer. "You must have hundreds of thousands of pounds tied up in the business. Take some cash out and rent a flat that doesn't put you in danger of getting stabbed. There's a murder up on this estate nearly every day. Stay here much longer, and you're liable to get knifed." Rob glanced at Lee, who seemed focused on filling the room with a sulphurous vapour, now pulling a pained expression as he released a fart. "Your dad can vouch for that, I'm sure."

"Yeah, Dad's got a few flats up here. There's been a few stabbings and murders in them over the years," Lee confirmed, as he released more gases and simultaneously burped.

I dismissively shook my head. Since Bridget kicked me out, I hadn't told anyone what I'd done, not my father and certainly not anyone who I regarded as a mate. They all thought I'd been stupid enough without divulging my utter naïvety.

"Come to think of it, why don't you stay in your showroom? You could stick a camp bed in your office. It's a damn sight better than this place." Rob waved his free arm around the kitchen, which sported clumps of mould and dubious-looking fungus that could culture a penicillin farm. "This entire estate could benefit from an enema."

I closed my eyes and dropped my head.

Rob continued. "Anywhere is better than this shithole. It was in the paper last week; did you see it? They found a bloke hanging in one of the stairwells with his kneecaps broken. They reckon it's the Albanians dealing with a rival gang. The whole place is like living in a bloody war zone."

I shrugged, momentarily avoiding informing my mates of the other issue that significantly trumped the break-up with my girlfriend. Of course, I was upset about Bridget; she'd broken my heart. However, notwithstanding my lost love, I had significantly more devastating problems to deal with.

"Damian?"

I glanced up at them both. Rob, with his palms open, awaiting my reply, Lee just necking his beer. "I've been stupid … I've done something really fucking dumb."

"Err, yes, mate. You got caught with another bird—"

I held my hand aloft. "I'm not talking about that. I've done something far worse. And, as I keep telling you, I have no idea who that bloody woman was or why she came to my room."

"Look, mate. I'm just asking as a friend. But you were set up? You definitely didn't know that woman in those pictures?"

My jaw dropped as my eyes bulged at his suggestion – perhaps Rob wasn't the friend I thought he was. I glanced at Lee, who just shrugged, seemingly more interested in swilling beer and filling my squalid flat with repugnant gases than jumping in to defend me. Only these two mates had stood by my side throughout this complete debacle, and now it appeared Rob was swapping sides, probably persuaded by that overly pompous, somewhat prissy wife of his.

Rob, probably clocking my bug-eyed expression, tried to dig his way out. "Hey, look, mate. No one could blame you. If a fit bird bundled her way into my hotel room and got her kit off, I think I might have struggled to push her away."

"Are you for real? How many times do I have to say it, for Christ's sake?"

"Alright, alright. Calm down."

"Calm down! You're as bad as Bridget and that poncy wife of yours, as well as every other bell-end that seems hell-bent on ruining my life. I told you what happened."

"Alright!"

"Look, I've told you before, but just so you're both clear, I'll bloody repeat myself. I'd just returned to my room after chatting with a couple of the guys in the bar who I'd met at the motor show earlier. I pulled off my shirt, getting ready for a shower, and there's this knock on the door. I whipped it open, thinking it would be housekeeping bringing up an extra pillow that I'd requested. But no … some bird dressed in a mac, bundles in and shimmies out of the coat. So, there I am, with my top off and this naked woman all over me, snogging my face off when I realise some bloke is standing in the doorway capturing the entire episode on his mobile!"

"Okay, okay. I'm just saying it's a bit odd that you were apparently in some embrace with the girl. If it's, as you say it is, a setup, why didn't you push her away?"

41

"I did!"

"Well, the pictures looked like you had your hands on her tits," chuckled Lee.

"I was trying to push her away, not there to have a grope!"

"Alright. But look, don't bring Laura into this. I know you've never liked her, but she's not the one who's been caught with her pants down."

"I didn't have my bloody pants down! I was set up. Someone must have paid her to do that so they could capture the pictures. Some bastard is trying to ruin me and, so far, they're doing a pretty neat job of it."

I glanced at Lee. "You believe me, don't you?"

Lee just shrugged before taking a swig of his beer.

"Sake," I muttered, as I turned away from them both, royally pissed off by their lack of support.

"Look, Damian—"

I swung around and jabbed my beer bottle at Lee. "Hang on, Rob," I interrupted him as I focused on Lee. "You said the pictures suggested I had my hands on her tits."

Lee shrugged, losing eye contact.

"How would you know that?" I narrowed my eyes at him. "You haven't seen the pictures … you can't have."

"No, course not. You *said* you had your hands on her tits."

"You did, mate," threw in Rob.

I glanced at Rob, who nodded to affirm his statement. Now I couldn't remember what I'd said and to who. However, something felt off. "Some bastard set me up, and it would be good if you could believe that."

Rob nodded. "Alright, if you say so."

"I do!"

"Okay. So, someone set you up. But I don't understand why. I mean, what could anyone gain from it? Yeah, alright, Bridget kicked you out, and you're gonna split up, but so what? You've only been together a few months. It's not as if you were married, is it?"

"Someone is hell-bent on ruining me. That much I do know."

"You reckon it's an old boyfriend of Bridget's? You know, jilted lover type thing?"

I huffed. "Rob, I don't know, but there is more to it than just a ploy to split us up."

"What d'you mean?"

"I don't know. It just doesn't feel right. There's something off about the whole thing."

"Who was the bloke who took the snaps?"

"Don't know that either. One minute the bird's all over me whilst he snaps away, capturing the evidence before they both scoot off as quickly as they arrived. To be honest with you, I thought they'd got the wrong room and nothing more would come of it. They'd realise their mistake when they looked at the pictures and see that I wasn't the bloke they were after."

"What, you think the setup was meant for someone else?"

"Yeah, the hotel is huge. There are hundreds of rooms full of blokes attending the motor show, so I presumed someone was planning to blackmail some poor sod with the mucky snaps."

"You!"

"No, that's my point. I've not been blackmailed by anyone. The pictures were sent to Bridget, and that was it. She confronted me and booted me out."

"You can't blame her."

"No, I know. But, look, she wouldn't listen to reason. You don't think you could have a word with Laura? Perhaps she could persuade Bridget I was set up."

"Err … you're having a laugh, mate. Laura's convinced that you're bang to rights. She's not going to swallow your version of events. Also, I thought you said Bridget has disappeared?"

"Yeah. Since booting me out, I haven't heard from her. She seems to have vanished."

"Anyway, you were saying. Why can't you kip at your office? What else have you done?"

I winced.

Rob shot a look at Lee, who appeared to have taken a back seat and become more concerned with his bowel movements.

"Shit, I need another crap," he announced before nipping back to the bathroom.

"Open the window in there," I bellowed, as he disappeared down the corridor.

"Damian. What's going on?"

"Rob, I don't know how to tell you this, but I've been a complete idiot."

4

Minder

Rob raised his eyebrows, probably thinking getting caught in a hotel room with another woman was foolish enough, so how the hell could there be anything else worse to tell – well, there was – a lot worse.

"Damian, what the hell have you done? You'd better spit it out, mate."

"Christ. You're not going to believe this."

Rob's eyebrows held their lofty position, awaiting my revelations. "Anything's possible where you're concerned," he chuckled. "It can't be worse than that time you shat yourself on the school coach when Mackey laced your drink with laxatives."

For a brief moment, I recalled the incident on the school trip when I'd defecated in my school trousers. The driver had to pull the coach onto the motorway's hard shoulder whilst Miss helped clean me up. I suffered the rest of the journey perched on a plastic carrier bag with my lower half wrapped in a towel. What I'd give to repeat that embarrassing episode instead of my current predicament.

I shook shit-splattered school trousers from my mind. "About a month ago, I put the business in Bridget's name."

Rob blinked as his head seemed to sink forward, synchronised with his slowly gaping mouth.

I held my hand up. "I know. You don't need to say it."

"Fu … fucking hell! What the hell for?"

"Look, it seemed like a good idea at the time."

"Err … sorry, mate, you're gonna have to run that by me again, I'm afraid. What part of signing over your car dealership to your girlfriend seemed like a good idea?"

"It wasn't like that."

"Jesus, Damian. You've only been together a few months. What on earth possessed you?"

"Well, last month … I proposed."

"Marriage?" Rob somewhat incredulously blurted.

"Why not?"

"You're besotted with the girl. You only met her back in January. You give up your flat and move in with her, and now you're telling me that you've gifted the woman your bloody business!"

"I didn't give her the business … just spreading tax liabilities … sort of."

"Sorry, what's tax got to do with this?"

"Well, her brother's an accountant, see. He suggested we could benefit from reduced tax when we got married if the business was in her name."

Rob shook his head, appearing somewhat bemused by my stupidity. "And what tax dodge exactly? Because, my old

46

mucker, I can't see any tax benefit by putting the business in her name."

"It's not a dodge, as such. Her brother sort of explained it, but it was all a bit complicated."

"You'll have to tell her you want it back. Presumably, you're no longer getting married, so it will have to be signed back over to you."

"I've tried. But, as I've said, I can't get hold of her."

Rob questioned my statement with open palms and a shrug of the shoulders.

"I turned up to work on Friday, only to find the place closed up. I rang one of my sales team, and they said Bridget had given them all notice and was selling up. When I bombed around to my old flat to confront her, the place appeared empty. It looks like she's cleared out and done a runner."

"Christ, Damian. You tit!"

"I know, but I don't need reminding, thanks!"

"You fall for it every time, don't you? This is just like that time when that bloke conned you into buying a timeshare, and your dad had to bail you out. You really are the most gullible tosser I know."

"Well, thanks, mate! I'm in the shit, so a bit of support wouldn't go amiss, you know. I'm fully aware what a total prick I've been, and I really could do without you ramming down my throat what a total twat I am!"

"Alright. Where is she, then?"

"I've no idea. Barry, my guy in my sales team, reckons she changed the locks and has already agreed to sell the fleet to a rival dealer at a knockdown price. Thacker's, over near the Bowthorpe Estate."

"Shit, really? I'm surprised Thacker's has taken on your cars. That place is a bit of a crummy, run-down, second-hand sort of place. My dad bought a car from there a few years back. He reckoned it was like an Arthur Daley set-up."

"Who?"

"Oh, I dunno … it's that spiv-type bloke in that old '80s TV show."

"Well, whatever. I expect she sold them at a loss … my loss!"

"I take it you haven't informed your father about this latest debacle you've landed yourself in?"

"Err … no. Anyway, he's all loved up and shacked up with that girl who's my age whilst gallivanting around California. I'm not sure he's going to give two shits. Dad sold his house for a tidy sum. Although worth a fortune, the business wasn't his main asset."

"What about your mother? She's got a few quid, ain't she? Could you ask her for help?"

"My actual mother?"

"Yeah … look, I know you and her don't have much to do with each other, but she is your mother. Perhaps it's time she stepped up to the plate."

"Rob … she's dead."

"Oh … I'm sorry, mate, I didn't know."

"Nah, don't worry. She died a couple of weeks back in a car accident. Look, it's no skin off my nose because she was never a mother to me."

"Jesus, Damian, I don't know what to say."

"As I said, don't worry about it, mate. Look, I know what you said about your missus, and I get it after that embarrassing episode at your wedding. So, I understand I'm not exactly in her good books, but d'you reckon she can try to find out where Bridget's gone?"

"Damian, I can't even mention your name without her going off on one. Your best-man speech was a disaster. You might recall it caused an all-out brawl, and Laura's father had to pay the hotel compensation for the damage to the ballroom."

"Okay, okay." I held my palm up, accepting I'd not thought before blurting out my ill-chosen jokes. "Look, Rob, I need some bloody help here. The least you could do is grow some backbone and tell that bloody woman of yours to stop being such a prissy cow. Anyway, I thought the story about her and the two ski instructors was funny."

"Jesus, mate, it was. But blurting it out during your speech at the wedding breakfast wasn't the greatest idea, was it? Bloody hell, Damian, you really are a complete dick!"

"Well, thanks a lot. Jesus, when you're in the same shite as me, I'll remember this."

"Well, that's not going to happen. Even Homer Simpson couldn't make such a mess of things. Ever since our bloody school days, you've gone from one crisis to the next. Then your father gifts you the car dealership and, within a couple of months, you've managed to cock that up as well. My Laura might be high bloody maintenance, but she has a point when she refers to you as a dickhead—"

An aggressive thumping on my kitchen window halted Rob's rant.

"Oi. Keep the noise down in there. You're making enough racket to wake the bleedin' dead. I'm trying to work, you know."

Rob and I peered at the woman bellowing through the window from the outside landing.

"Is she for real?" I blurted. "Right, I've had enough." I flung open the kitchen window, which offered a view of the landing that served as access to the twelve flats on the second level of Belfast House – one of three blocks that made up the odious estate that I now rather dubiously called home.

"I live next door, and you're making too much bleedin' noise." She reinforced her point by aggressively shoving a finger at me.

"What? Are you taking the piss? I have to listen to your racket every night! You and that boyfriend of yours do nothing but shout at each other."

"That's got bugger all to do wiv you. If you don't like it 'ere, you can piss off back to where you came from."

"I wish I could."

"Well, go on then! My Karl will happily throw you out if you carry on making that racket."

"Damian, leave it, mate."

Ignoring Rob's sensible suggestion, I pushed on. "Oh, yeah? Well, I'd like to see him try. Anyway, I don't need some bloody hooker to tell me to keep my voice down." My vulgar accusation regarding her career seemed to stop her in her tracks as if my words had slapped her across the face.

"Oi, twat, what I do has got piss all to do with you!" She thrust that finger at me. "Men! You look down on the likes of me, but you're all quite happy to wank off watching a bit of porn when it takes your fancy."

"Damian! Just leave it!"

I huffed, my mate's sensible suggestion hitting home. "It's Courteney, isn't it?"

"Yeah. How d'you know that?"

"A lucky guess, you could say."

"Have I done you?"

"Done me?" I quizzed.

"Yeah, you know, are you a punter I've done? You look kinda familiar, I guess."

"Oh, no … never," I affirmed, keen to make it quite clear I was not the sort to pay for sex. That said, the girl with the potty mouth was not what I'd expected. The slag persona didn't fit the face – she was stunning.

"Well, I reckon I know you from somewhere. You into live porn?"

"What? What kind of question is that?"

"Damian, I said leave it, mate."

"Hey, pretty boy, no need to get arsey!"

"Okay, okay." I dropped my aggressive tone. "Look, for the last week or so, I've been your neighbour, so you've seen me come and go, I expect."

She nodded and hovered by the window but seemed to have run out of conversation.

"Look, I'll keep the noise down, and perhaps you could as well? What d'you say?"

"Yeah, alright. Look, I'm warning you, though. That Karl of mine is a right tosser and a dangerous one at that. Keep well clear of him."

I nodded. "Thanks for the tip; I'll bear it in mind."

"Look, as I'm your neighbour, I'll give you a discount on my live web shows if you like?"

My mouth gaped. I'm a man of the world, but this offer from my neighbour was somewhat of a shock.

"Don't worry. If you're a bit shy, you can turn your webcam off if you prefer to wank in private." Courteney offered a winsome smile as if she just suggested coming around for afternoon tea rather than discounted access codes to some dodgy website depicting live porn.

"Thanks, but I'll take a rain check if you don't mind."

Courteney nonchalantly shrugged. "Alright, but don't wait too long, 'cos I ain't going to be doing this game forever, you know. As soon as I've got enough cash, I'm out of here." With that, she spun on her heels and disappeared into the next-door flat.

"One seriously fit bird!" chirped Rob, as I closed the window.

"Rob, she's a sex worker!"

"Well, I would! I wonder if she'd offer me a discount on the account that I'm your mate."

"Well, you need to start acting like one first. Perhaps believing my story about what happened in that hotel room would be a start, and not siding with that bloody wife of yours."

Rob held his palm aloft and nodded. "I do, mate. I just had to ask, sorry."

"I know." I nodded toward Courteney's flat. "I'll have a word if you like … anything has got to be better than your Laura."

"Leave it, mate. I know she's high maintenance, but that's my wife you're slagging off."

"Like she doesn't slag me off. I really have no idea why you married the woman … well, apart from the fact that her family are loaded."

"That helped, along with her dad paying off our mortgage. Anyway, that Courteney is bloody fit, ain't she?" he winked.

"You!" I scoffed. "I can just imagine what Laura would say when discovering you with your pants around your ankles and tugging at your old-chap whilst Courteney talks dirty to you."

"Yeah, you're right. Christ, that don't bear thinking about," he chuckled. "Anyway, it's a pity you didn't run a mile when that bird grabbed you in that hotel room. You might not be forced to live in this shithole. And," he wagged his finger at me. "It's a pity you didn't see through Bridget because I reckon she saw you coming."

"Leave it, Rob. I can't listen to any more 'I told you so' comments."

"Fuck, that's better," muttered Lee, as he re-emerged from destroying my bathroom. "Did I miss anything?"

I shook my head, wondering if I would ever be able to use the toilet again. "Just my neighbour offering a discount on a wank."

"Really!"

"Some tart next door who's on those dodgy porn sites, that's all," Rob interjected before finishing his beer.

"I'd think carefully before waving your todger at some tart online if you don't want the piss taken. By all accounts, I heard you're not that well-endowed," he chuckled.

"What?"

"I'm not surprised that bird done a runner in that hotel room when she copped a glimpse of your little wiener." Lee wagged his little finger, offering a knowing smirk.

"What? How the hell d'you know the size of my manhood?"

Lee, clearly embarrassed, waved his hand dismissively. "Forget it. Just a joke."

"Well, not funny. And, as I've said to both of you … I've been set up!"

It seemed whatever I said, no one would believe my version of events in that hotel on that fateful night, which led to losing my girlfriend and my business.

Someone had set a honey trap.

Someone seemed hell-bent on ruining my life – I needed some answers.

5

Licence To Kill

"Adrian, Alan. Or should I say 005 and 004?" chuckled Mark, as he nodded at the two gents nursing schooners of sweet sherry whilst awkwardly hovering away from the main throng of mourners.

Although Mark, or 003, to use his Bond analogy, knew both men, they couldn't be described as acquaintances as such. However, attending his ex-wife's wake felt somewhat awkward. So, rather than mingle with some of her relatives, who he recalled not particularly warming to when married to the woman, he thought two of her other ex-husbands might provide better company. At least the three of them had something in common.

Adrian offered a slight nod to acknowledge Mark. "Her sixth husband should have been her seventh."

Mark and Alan shot a quizzical look at Adrian, presumably both confused by his odd statement.

"Well, Alex Bond was her sixth husband. He should have been 007, if you see what I mean?"

"Oh, I see," chuckled Mark. "Well, 007, Dickie Burton, was married to the woman longer than the rest of us. I think he deserves credit for lasting that long."

Alan smirked and mockingly raised his eyebrows. "Ha, yes, I think they actually made five years together; what an achievement! I'm surprised Deana hadn't got bored with the poor bloke long before then."

All three men nodded before Mark took a swig of his beer whilst the other two disappointedly assessed their glasses of sherry.

"Dickie was a fair bit younger than the rest of us … perhaps that's why she hung onto him. She wasn't getting any younger, and you know how the woman liked to bounce around. Like any man, I'm up for an active relationship, but the woman used to wear me out," babbled Alan, attempting to break the awkward silence.

"I know! I watched you, remember!" retorted Mark.

Alan raised his palm, offering an apology for the memory of being caught with Deana when Mark was still married to her.

"I must say, this all feels somewhat awkward," Adrian waved around his glass, indicating the gaggle of mourners. "I almost feel like a vicar in a brothel," he chuckled.

"A rather apt analogy, considering we're in Deana's house, don't you think?"

"Oh, Alan. Come on, man. I know we've all got some murky history with the woman, but show a bit of respect," retorted Mark, before taking another swig from a bottle of Peroni.

"Really, Mark? The woman was a hussy! I was having an affair with her for nearly eight months before you divorced the bloody woman." Alan glanced down at his sherry, wondering where Mark had discovered a beer.

Mark nonchalantly accepted Alan's statement as he recalled the scene in his bedroom when arriving home, a day early from a business trip, to find his Deana in bed and her head rhythmically bobbing up and down under the covers whilst the naked Alan lay back grunting with pleasure.

"And two months after that, Deana and I started an affair," Adrian raised his eyebrows at the two men, husbands numbers three and four.

"Maybe you're right. I think our wonderful Deana *was* a bit of a hussy," chuckled Mark. "So, here we are all together … husbands number three, four and five. I don't suppose numbers one, two and six are here as well. Not sure all seven of us have been in the same room together before."

"Well, number seven, Richard, is dead, of course," Alan pointed his undrunk schooner of sherry at Mark and nodded.

Mark shrugged his agreement. "Yes, of course. Decent sort was Richard."

Alan sipped his sherry, wincing as he swallowed the liquid. "According to Ben, or Ziggy as he now calls himself—"

"Who?" interjected Adrian, as he placed his schooner down beside a plant pot after deciding the sweet sherry wasn't his thing.

"Oh, that's Richard Burton's son, Deana's stepson, I guess. Anyway, I was chatting to him at the service and apparently Sidney, that's husband number two, or 002 if you prefer, now lives in California, shacked up with some young floozy half his age, the flukey git."

"Didn't Deana have a son with Sidney?" Adrian chipped in as he scanned the room, trying to spot a bottle of beer like the one Mark sipped.

"Blimey Adrian, you were married to the woman. Didn't you ever meet the boy?"

"No, I believe Deana wasn't that close to him. Anyway, we were only married for three months, remember? She ran off with Alex, who became husband number six soon after we returned from our honeymoon."

"Oh. Well, yes, the lad is called Damian. Well, he's in his thirties now, I guess. Sorry, I'd forgotten that Deana quickly binned you off for another."

Mark struggled to contain his laughter, wiping his mouth and nose from where he's snorted his beer. "Christ, that ex-wife of ours was something else!"

Alan smirked at Mark's comment before turning to Adrian. "Where's Alex, then?"

"No idea. Apparently, after Deana buggered off and took up with Richard, I heard he'd shot back to Canada."

"Oh … she certainly had an effect on all of us, one way or another. Anyway, as I was saying, her son, who stayed with Sidney when she left him for you." Alan nodded at Mark. "Has apparently got himself in a bit of a pickle. The word on the street is he's lost his business, his girlfriend has chucked him out, and he now resides in some squalid flat on the Broxworth Estate. The boy's hit rock bottom."

"Really?" Mark necked the last of his beer before placing the empty bottle next to Adrian's discarded schooner of sherry.

"I only met him a few times. Deana wasn't what you'd call the maternal type."

"You'd think his father, Sidney, would step in and help him, wouldn't you? He might be shacked up with some floozy whilst soaking up the sun in California, but you'd think he would support his son." Adrian threw in as he parted from the group and headed for a table where he'd spotted bowls of peanuts and a collection of beers.

"Adrian, grab me one, there's a good chap," Alan called after him, spotting the beeline Adrian was making.

"Me too," barked Mark, before turning to Alan. "You know Sidney wasn't Damian's real father, don't you?"

"Oh, yes. I was aware. I presume Ian, her first husband, was his father?"

"Who?" quizzed Adrian, as he handed out the beers before tipping a handful of nuts into his mouth.

"Cheers, Adrian, good health," Alan clinked his beer against the other bottles. "Ian, Deana's first husband, is Damian's father, not Sidney … even though Sidney brought the boy up."

Mark shook his head. "No, that's not right. Ian divorced Deana when she was caught having a fling with some bloke at a work conference. Deana said Ian wasn't the father but never said who was."

"Bloody hell. Jesus, the woman was insatiable. I know I was only married to the woman for a few months, but I never knew all this. So, who d'you reckon is the father, then?"

Mark leant forward, performed a furtive sideways glance, and lowered his voice. "I'm led to believe the bloke she copped off with at the work's conference is the father."

"Christ, really?" Alan blurted. "Whatever happened to him?"

"Well, here's the thing. Deana killed him."

"What!" exclaimed Alan and Adrian in unison. Presumably, both were somewhat shocked to discover their dead ex-wife had murdered someone.

Still keeping his head forward and in hushed tones, Mark continued whilst enjoying the shocked expressions on their faces. "Don't look so shocked. She didn't poison the man or cut him up and stuff his body parts under the patio. No, whilst she and this chap were getting it off in the hotel bedroom, the bloke shot his load then had a heart attack, would you believe?" he chuckled.

"Died?"

Mark nodded to Adrian, affirming his answer.

Alan pulled a face before taking a swig of beer. "She never mentioned this to me."

"Well, it's the truth. Now, all of us can attest to what a rampant little minx our girl was, God rest her soul, but mark my words, our ex-wife gave the poor chap such a workout that his heart gave in."

"Hell of a way to go … I take it he was an older chap, then? Deana was never that fussy," Alan chuckled, raising an eyebrow when glancing at Adrian, the older of the three men.

"What the hell are you insinuating?" belligerently barked Adrian. "I'll have you know Deana left you for me because you couldn't keep up with her. She reckoned you didn't have the stamina!"

"Gents! Keep it down," hissed Mark. "Come on. She caused all sorts of mayhem when she was alive. Don't let the woman create havoc when she's dead."

Adrian and Alan offered each other a nodded apology.

"And no, the poor chap who snuffed it in her bed was only in his thirties, apparently."

"That's assuming he is the father. You could perm anyone from ten, where our Deana is concerned … I'd be surprised if she knew who it was."

"Adrian, never a truer word said." Alan chinked his bottle against his, keen to avoid getting embroiled in an argument. Although, in the back of his mind, he now wondered if Deana had made that comment, remembering a few frustrated accusations Deana had thrown his way about premature ejaculation.

"So, I presume he's here today, this son of hers?"

Both Adrian and Mark swigged their beers, awaiting Alan to answer as he seemed to be in the know.

"Apparently not. As I said, I'm aware he's in a bit of a mess, but he hasn't turned up to his own mother's funeral. I'm led to believe that Damian and Deana's relationship wasn't exactly cordial, and Damian wanted nothing more to do with his mother."

"You reap what you sow. That ex-wife of ours couldn't expect any sympathy from the boy if she was prepared to cut him free from her life."

Both Alan and Adrian nodded agreement at Mark's comment.

"So, Alan, how do you know all this? Y'know, about Damian's recent fall from grace?"

Alan copied Mark by furtively glancing around the room to ensure their gossiping wasn't overheard. "Carol, that's my third wife, has her hair done every Saturday morning at that swanky place on the High Street. Bloody ridiculous what she spends each week if you ask me. I told her we have to be careful now I live on a pension. How can a quick snip and blow-dry cost nearly a hundred pounds?"

Neither Adrian nor Mark commented or offered their opinion regarding Alan's assessment of hairdressing charges.

Realising he'd shot off on an unnecessary tangent, Alan continued after another quick glance around. "Anyway, the stylist also does one of Damian's old neighbours. As you can imagine, they gossip—"

"Women!" tutted Mark.

Alan nodded his agreement. "I know. You wouldn't catch us blokes gossiping. As I said, the neighbour reckons that Damian's girlfriend booted him out and took the business from him after someone anonymously sent some rather tricky photos to their home, showing Damian in a rather compromising position with some woman in a hotel room."

"Like mother like son," chuckled Adrian.

"Quite."

"Hang on, how come the girlfriend wrestled the business from him?"

"Well, that neighbour reckons Damian stupidly put the business in her name as some tax dodge. So, he gets caught with his trousers down and, not only is he out on his ear, the poor boy has lost his livelihood as well. The crazy thing is, he'd only been living with this girl for a few months!"

Adrian let out a low whistle. "Silly boy. He really is a chip off the old block, what with Deana's antics and Sidney skedaddling off with some young floozy."

"Indeed. To add to this juicy story, the business he lost is Statham Cars."

"What? As in Sidney Statham Cars?" blurted a surprised Mark.

"Yes! A year back, Sidney sold a swanky Aston Martin to this American woman who was over here on a year-long contract working in the film industry. Anyway, one thing led to another, and good old Sidney ended up dating her."

"Oh, right. And Sidney upped sticks and shot off back to the States with her?"

"No. Listen to this. Sidney ran off with the woman's daughter, who's half his age. Apparently, he was so besotted with the girl he gifted the car business to Damian, sold his big house, and buggered off."

"And now Sidney's prestigious car dealership is run by Damian's ex-girlfriend?"

"Well, sort of. Damian's ex has already put the place up for sale. It's all closed up, and the word is she's looking for a quick sale to make a fast buck."

"Well, if you're going to play away from home, you have to take the consequences. I seem to recall when your first wife caught you banging Deana, she threw you out on your ear."

"She did. But let's be quite clear, my first wife didn't catch me out because I seem to recall that you told my wife when *you* caught us the day you returned early from your business trip!"

"Oh … yes. Sorry old chap."

Alan chuckled. "Don't worry, that's all water under the bridge, as they say."

"Oh! Did you see that?" Adrian hopped to his left and glanced down at the carpet.

"What?"

Adrian pointed to the upended schooner and the double helping of sherry soaking into the carpet pile.

"Christ, man. You need to be more careful."

"It wasn't me," retorted Adrian. "I didn't touch it."

"You must have. Alan and I are nowhere near it," hissed Mark.

"Gents, forget it. Ziggy isn't going to give two shits about his dead father's carpet. I think this might be my cue to sneak out. I've paid my respects to my ex-wife and, to be honest, Carol wasn't too chuffed about me coming in the first place."

"You're not wrong. It's time I was going too."

"Did you see that?" Adrian pointed to the second schooner, which appeared to, by its own volition, shift an inch towards the edge of the table.

"What?" asked Mark and Alan in unison as they stared at the nearly full glass.

"That glass moved!"

"Are you drunk—"

"What the—"

All three men stood mesmerised as the schooner shifted again, then tipped off the side of the table, smashing against the already prone glass on the carpet.

"My God! D'you reckon there's a ghost in here?"

"Maybe it's Deana; come back to haunt us. Perhaps she's not too chuffed about our conversation." Alan raised his eyebrows and smirked.

"Very good, very good, Alan," chuckled Mark, as all three stepped away from the mess on the carpet. "You know I wouldn't put it past our Deana to come back and haunt us. It's just the sort of thing she would do."

Adrian offered his hand for the two gents to step forward towards the door. "You know, I reckon the Grim Reaper escorted that bloody woman to the gates of hell and the demons took one look at her and sent her back. I reckon even the Devil would find her too much of a handful."

Alan turned and playfully grabbed the forearms of the two gents. "You know, it's no bloody surprise she called her son Damien. She's the mother of the anti-Christ!"

"My son's name is Damian. It's spelt differently, you idiot! Christ, I can't imagine what I saw in you three. What was I thinking!" muttered Deana, as she turned away from her trinity of ex-husbands before deciding who else's conversation to earwig. For sure, wandering around your own wake wasn't as much fun as she'd thought it might be, now wishing the mourners would all bugger off and leave her alone.

6

Welcome to the Pleasuredome

"Terry. Terry, darling, can you hear me?"

Terry held Deana's mobile to his ear, uncertain which way to hold it. "Hello."

"Ah, good, you can. You can come back now. They've all gone."

"Oh, right. Oh, hang on, how do I end the call on this thing?"

"Push the red button."

"There are no buttons."

Deana huffed. "Terry, don't worry, just come back."

Terry held the phone away from his ear and watched as the screen confirmed the call had ended before hot-footing back from the churchyard, where he'd been for nearly an hour after Deana's wake started to fizzle out. Deana thought, although Terry had attended her wake when the house was packed with mourners, as the congregation thinned out, it would be better that he made himself scarce in case anyone questioned who he was.

Two weeks had elapsed since he awoke after being dead for thirty-odd years. And nearly a week had passed since Deana revealed Terry had a son. Now her funeral was over, he was keen to glean some answers to the questions which Deana avoided whilst distracted by her stepson coming back to the UK earlier in the week to attend the funeral of his father and Deana.

Being dead with no fixed abode was super tricky. Of course, it was far easier for Deana because she was invisible. However, Terry wandered about in plain sight like some doppelgänger, although reasonably confident he didn't have a living double. So, as he was visible to all, Tuesday morning had been somewhat tricky when Ziggy entered Deana's home whilst Terry lay in bed chatting to the invisible Deana. Fortunately, Deana's stepson hadn't ventured into his parents' bedroom, choosing instead to rest after a long flight.

Faced with this somewhat awkward situation, Terry crept out of the house to avoid detection. Although not a particularly difficult operation because he'd previously experienced many similar when enjoying extracurricular activities in some woman's bedroom when her husband unexpectedly arrived home. No, fleeing a woman's home in a state of undress wasn't an unusual situation for Terry. If fact, you might say he was well-versed in performing impromptu shimmies down the odd drain pipe.

So, after three nights in a seedy dump of a hotel, he, at last, could move back into Deana's home. Terry had questioned why he couldn't stay in something less hideous than the dump he'd eventually booked into. However, it appeared that thirty-odd years after his death, you needed ID for everything and cash seemed to be a thing of the past – his past.

So, a run-down B&B where the landlady appeared to be the sort who preferred cash, judging by the smirk on her face when securing the roll of notes Terry offered into her ample cleavage, and wasn't bothered about seeing ID or requiring an address, appeared to be his only option. Bored witless, he'd spent three days in the company of five other men, who all looked as desperate and lost as he did. Although, presumably, they weren't dead like he was.

"Ah, there you are, darling." Deana hovered by the back door as Terry skulked in, trying to avoid detection from any curtain-twitching neighbours.

"How d'you know Ziggy or anyone else won't come back?"

"Ziggy had a catch-up with my darling Dickie's solicitor when that rabble of mourners eventually left. Unbeknown to them, I perched between them on the sofa and listened in to what they had to say—"

"Of course you did," he chuckled.

"Yes, well, Ziggy is flying back to Australia tonight, and Henry, that's Dickie's solicitor, will handle things this end. But basically, as far as they are concerned, the house is all closed up and Henry will deal with probate. So, we've got the place to ourselves for some time yet. We just have to ensure you're not spotted by any of the neighbours and definitely avoid that bloody Drake woman."

"Okay. Well, someone could have tidied up a bit before they left. The house looks like a bomb site."

"Yes, never mind. Not our concern now."

"What about all your belongings? What is Ziggy planning to do with those?"

"He just instructed Henry to sell it all off to a house clearance company, which is disappointing because Dickie and I collected some nice pieces together."

"Oh, that's odd. Why on earth would he do that?"

"Ziggy finds possessions all too pretentious."

"Bloody weirdo."

"Terry, I've told you before, please don't be so prejudicial. Not everyone has the same values as you. We're all different."

"Good job!"

"I beg your pardon? If you're referring to the fact that it's good that others are not like me, then I'm quite offended, I'll have you know. Yes, I accept I'm a ravenous sex goddess with an insatiable and somewhat voracious desire for male company, but I have a good heart … albeit a dead one."

Terry opened his mouth to defend himself.

"And don't attempt to interrupt me when I'm in full flow. I'll have you know that Ziggy, dear boy, has a bohemian attitude to life, where his surfboard is his only valued possession, and the commune he lives in is his family. I think it's a rather healthy attitude to harbour and one that many could benefit from."

"Alright, alright. If you say so."

"I do so."

"What about your husband's watch collection?"

"Oh, I expect Henry will arrange for the sale of valuable items prior to the house clearance."

"You don't reckon I could have another one of his watches, do you? It's just he's got a Patek Philippe which I rather like and had my eye on."

"Oh, Terry. If you must," Deana dismissively waved her arm in the air. "Help yourself. Ziggy's inheritance will run into millions, so I guess another missing gaudy-looking watch won't be a problem."

"Oh, great."

"Although, as you're dead, I really can't see the point of wanting another watch. It's not as if time holds any relevance anymore."

"No, well, whatever. But I can tell you, there's nothing gaudy about a Patek Philippe watch," he chuckled.

"If you say so. They're all the same to me, Casio, Timex, Rolex or Philip-whatever; they all just tell the time. Now, if we're talking handbags, that's a very different matter altogether. There's something special about a Hermès or Louis Vuitton to carry a few essential items about. One of those hanging off your arm shows real class."

"A supermarket carrier bag is just as effective," he muttered.

Deana tutted and shook her head. "Heathen! Anyway, carrier bags are the scourge of society."

"What? How can a carrier bag be regarded as a scourge?"

"Plastic, darling. Plastic is destroying the oceans, causing climate change and the melting of the polar ice caps. Basically, destroying the planet we live on. That is a scourge if ever there was one. Ziggy has been an anti-plastic activist for years, and good on him."

"Blimey. Times have changed. I'm slightly amazed the humble carrier bag can be accused of causing all those issues. I recall everyone was pleased when they replaced paper bags so we could stop felling trees."

"Yes, well, it's all gone full circle. Paper bags from sustainable sources are very much in vogue."

"Sustainable?

"Terry, it's been a long day. What with attending my own funeral, having to suffer the indignity of watching my own body being dumped in the ground and then listening to all those wittering relatives and ex-husbands at my wake, I'm too exhausted to discuss plastic bags and the ethics or operational processes of the Forest Stewardship Council."

Terry opened his mouth to speak.

"Put a sock in it, darling," Deana interrupted. "You ask too many questions. Now, I suggest you be quiet unless you intend to make a dead woman happy by whisking me off for a little excitement under the covers."

Terry nervously grinned.

"No, I thought not."

"I presume you behaved yourself and didn't play any more games after I left?"

"Games? What are you on about now, for heaven's sake?"

"Well, get up to any funny business, like tipping over any more sherry schooners."

"Oh, I see. No, not at all; I was a good girl. Although, did you see the look on my ex-husbands' faces? What a hoot that was," she chuckled, as she extracted a cigarette from a packet on the kitchen worktop and expectantly raised her eyebrow at Terry.

"What?"

"Light my cigarette, darling."

"You do it."

"Terry, come on. A man should light a woman's cigarette. Etiquette, darling."

Terry complied with her request, deciding he would join her. Well, why not, he thought. When dead, that negated the need to worry about the long-term health implications of smoking.

"Were you pleased with the turnout? I thought it was rather decent of some of your ex-husbands to turn up, even though you tried to spook them."

Deana pondered that thought for a moment as she dragged on her cigarette. "Well, I suppose so. Although, there was a lovely turnout at the church, the service was a bit of a bore, but I thought perhaps more of the congregation would have returned for the wake."

"I'm sure you had far more than mine."

"Oh, yes, yours was a right sorry affair."

Terry frowned. "Oh, did you go to mine?"

Deana nodded as she inhaled from her cigarette. "Yes, darling," she blew a plume of smoke to the ceiling. "I snuck into the back of the church. Although, of course, I didn't attend the wake because that would have been rather awkward. Can you imagine me turning up at your parents' home and saying I was the last person to see you alive when you lay naked in my bed?" she chuckled.

"Oh, no, I suppose that could've been a bit awkward."

"That's an understatement, darling. Christ, the atmosphere at the church was bad enough, what with your family and Sharon's at loggerheads. It was like a scene from Frankie's *Two Tribes*. So, I can't imagine that the wake was exactly

72

detente, and if I'd stuck my nose in, that would have been like throwing a hand grenade into the party."

Terry removed his cigarette to speak, but Deana stepped forward, placing her index finger on his lips.

"Don't ask, darling. Let sleeping dogs lie. It's not healthy to dwell on the past." She removed her finger, holding his stare.

"Frankie? Two tribes?" quizzed Terry.

"Relax, darling," she quipped, before taking a long drag on her cigarette and smirking at his confused expression.

"What?"

"Forget it … as I said, it's all in the past."

"On that subject of the past. Are you going to start answering my questions?"

"Darling?"

"My son! That little bombshell you landed on Friday."

"Oh, yes, of course. Look, sorry, sweety, but I've been a little preoccupied with Ziggy coming back and my funeral."

"Well, now you're stuffed in that box six feet under, can we discuss my son, who I know sod-all about? Christ, I'm only just getting the hang of having a daughter, let alone a son."

"Yes, darling, of course. I must say, I don't like the idea of my body being unceremoniously lobbed into that box and buried. And I'm a little disappointed at the casket they chose. Did you see all that gold decoration and the ornate handles? Far too garish for my taste."

"Deana! Stop avoiding the subject."

"Yes, of course. Now, regarding little Kimmy, that seems to have panned out rather nicely, so we just have to repeat the operation with Damian."

"Damian … that's his name?"

"Uh-huh."

"And I presume he's not Kim's twin brother, so who's the mother?"

"Can't you guess?"

Terry frowned.

"No, I presume that may be too difficult. I'm sure there were many women you bedded in the latter half of 1983."

Terry pondered that statement. Fair point, he thought. Of course, as far as he was concerned, 1983 was only a couple of weeks ago. So, remembering his conquests of around that time wasn't that difficult. He could easily conjure up three.

"Has the penny dropped, darling?"

"Penny! No, surely not her?"

"Oh, my. Dear, dear, you and Penny Pincher, your old HR manager?"

Terry shrugged.

"I thought you couldn't stand the woman?"

"It just seemed to happen one day."

"What on earth do you mean … it just seemed to happen? Copping off together doesn't just happen!"

"You can talk! Well, anyway, it just did."

"Good grief, Terry. And there was I thinking I was the one into free love."

Terry felt a little awkward. For sure, he'd always enjoyed a little luck with the ladies. However, now dead and missing his wife, Sharon, he viewed his conquests a little less triumphantly.

"So, no, it wasn't Penny Pincher. Who else do you think is Damian's mother?"

"Oh, no. Not that neighbour of mine who we met last Saturday. Marjory Price?"

"Old twinset and pearls," she giggled. "No, darling, not her."

"Who then?"

"Have another guess … I'm rather enjoying myself. Come on, play along. It's my funeral day. Now I'm dead, I don't get birthdays anymore, so my funeral could be classed as my special day."

Terry huffed.

"Come on, darling, indulge me."

"Well, there were a few others in the last few months—"

"Thirty-three years ago, darling. Come on, keep up. You must remember you've been dead a long time."

Terry nodded and pointed his cigarette at her, acknowledging the correction.

"There was Paula, one of the checkout supervisors at work. We got it on a few times in the store cupboard behind the work's canteen."

"Oh, Terry, how sordid," she chuckled. "Having a bunk-up whilst surrounded by catering-sized tins of beans and peaches in syrup."

"It was more of an electrical services cupboard, actually."

"Yes, I'm sure your little tryst was electrifying … any sparks fly?"

"Hilarious. It was quite intimate, I'll have you know. Paula was going through a difficult time with her boyfriend, and I was just comforting her."

"What, banging her brains out, type of comfort?"

"Sort of," he smirked.

"Deary me, at least my dallying was in the full knowledge of my darling Dickie, not holed up in some broom cupboard in the back end of a supermarket. And no, Paula isn't the mother. Have another guess."

Terry shook his head. "I can't think of anyone else. There was only you … the night I died."

Deana laid her hand on his chest and longingly looked into his eyes. "We can repeat the event if you like … not the death bit … if you get my drift," she purred.

"Oh, Christ, woman, give it a rest. They've only just buried you, and you're already gagging for it."

"A woman has needs, darling," she pouted. "I'm sure Paula didn't have to beg you between running up and down the checkout line whilst answering bells to those little checkout girls."

"Yes, well, that may be so. But if not Paula, Penny or Marjory, who."

"Me, silly!"

"Wha—"

"Yes, darling. That night of passion put me in the family way. We had a son, Terry. A true love child."

7

Hot Fuzz

Rob hadn't offered up much in the way of help. Also, he'd blankly refused to ask his prissy wife to step in and assist. However, I needed to keep him as a friend. Although I'd not known Lee for long, he'd also rallied around. That said, his comment about the photos was odd. As far as I knew, Bridget hadn't shown them to any of my mates.

Anyway, since the revelations of the night in that hotel room circled around my friends and acquaintances, I'd become somewhat lonely. So, keeping Rob and Lee close was important.

Of course, Rob was quite right regarding his statements about my ability to land myself in tricky situations. I figured I was just the unlucky sort, and the often-dire calamities that bestowed my life were not really my fault. That said, I could often leap in without thinking things through, and I guess Bridget was an example of that.

Laura, Rob's wife, had always held a diminutive view of me, and I guess relaying the incident with her and two ski instructors in that cable car during my best-man speech at their wedding didn't help. But that was me – open my trap and dive headlong in without thinking about the consequences.

Until now, apart from the occasional cock-up and embarrassing situation, I'd muddled through. Unfortunately, a couple of girlfriends had binned me off due to my inability to do and say the right thing, and I'd never enjoyed what you could call a long-term relationship. So, when I met Bridget, a woman about a thousand ladders worth of rungs above me, I thought my luck had finally changed.

Six months before the vivacious Bridget dropped into my life, my father embarked on his midlife crisis, or perhaps old-age crisis would be a more apt description based on the fact he was now past sixty. Anyway, he buggered off with a woman half his age, gifting me his prestigious car showroom and thus allowing me the opportunity to dump my shite job in a call centre where I'd spend all day informing distraught claimants that the small print of their insurance policy negated the company's liability to pay out. My role as a claims handler, which consisted of spending all day shattering claimants' hopes, didn't exactly deliver job satisfaction.

Now I'd managed to lose my father's business, my first task in the morning would be to traipse back with my tail between my legs and beg my old boss to re-employ me. However, that may be a tricky path to tread because I recall telling him exactly what I thought of the company on my last day. Also, advising the smelly bastard that everyone in the office calls him Halitosis Harry, or sometimes referred to as *Stinkor,* in reference to those of a certain age who grew up with the characters from *He-Man and the Masters of the Universe,* due to his repugnant oral odour that wafted around whenever he trawled the open-plan office checking up on us all, may not help my quest. So, I guess that burnt bridge might be a somewhat tricky path to traverse.

Anyway, there I was, at the start of the new year, the proud owner of a car showroom, with eleven employees selling swanky cars to the middle classes and a gorgeous woman hanging off my arm to boot. At the age of thirty-two, at last, I'd finally made it.

Now, a few months later, I'd lost everything. As acts of stupidity go, placing my business in Bridget's name and getting caught in a hotel room with a nameless, but from what I can remember in that brief moment, a gorgeous woman, has to top any previous calamity bestowed upon me.

Gullible, that's me. A trait I inherited from my father, who not only got sucked in by my mother when she conned him into marrying her after she found herself pregnant, divorced and jobless, but also had now fallen for a woman half his age. *Idiot.*

I suspected that the young American woman my father had run off with would soon bin him off when it dawned upon her that he wasn't the sugar daddy she originally had him pegged for.

So, like my father and my grandfather before, I had the propensity to be easily taken in. Of course, that unlucky trait had to be the product of nurture, not nature, because my father adopted me from birth. That said, I really couldn't moan about him because Sidney Statham had been good to me, unlike my mother, who'd upped sticks and sodded off when I was still in nappies.

That succession of gullible idiots flowed through the Statham men, generation to generation, handed down like some precious heirloom. Apparently, my grandfather fully believed the BBC Panorama programme about spaghetti growing on trees. Also, my father was totally taken in by the Smellovision joke about the next generation of TVs that would allow the viewer to savour the nasal senses whilst enjoying the pictures. For sure, that would have put the kibosh on *Countryfile*. Of course, I kept the tradition of credulous dickheads alive when believing the flying penguin story and deriding my mates for their lack of knowledge of the natural world.

The only positive I could take from these calamities – April 1st had already passed for this year. So, although I was clearly a fool, I wasn't an April fool. Well, maybe I would be in eleven months, but for now, I was just a fool. I guess, with my heritage, namely a line of ancestors with the propensity to be easily duped, I shouldn't be too astonished that my life has turned to shit.

Flipping the top off another bottle of beer, I opened my front door, stepped out onto the stale-piss-smelling landing and leaned on the steel railing whilst surveying my new neighbourhood – what a dump.

As the sun sunk behind the tower block opposite, it appeared the warm spring day had decided it was time to draw to a close. The dark shadow cast by the tower blocks cloaked the central square of the Broxworth Estate in semi-darkness, morphing the vision below me into some vista of hell – quite a metaphor for my life.

I raised myself on tiptoes and peered over the edge. Although my flat is located on the second level and not a significant distance from the ground, I figured I would suffer death if I tipped forward and allowed myself to drop. However, knowing my bloody luck, I suspect I'd end up with every bone broken and then live until I'm a hundred as a paraplegic.

I settled my feet back on the firm concrete landing and surveyed the graffiti-covered concrete buildings that faced me. As I pondered how impressive it was that the street artist covered the building that far off the ground whilst I also tried to avoid contemplating jumping over the balcony, a now familiar voice dragged me back from my catatonic state.

"Hiya."

I swivelled my head to spot my neighbour stepping out of her flat. Although Rob had jested about taking Courteney up on her earlier offer, I had to agree this woman was not how I expected a prostitute to appear. That said, I probably held limited knowledge of what a sex worker actually looked like. I guess their portrayal in films was open to interpretation, but I couldn't recall any of them looking quite like this girl.

I smiled back and raised my beer bottle, acknowledging her greeting. Although I wasn't in the mood to chat with my new neighbour, at least she wasn't shouting, an unusual situation going by my previous encounters when in her or that druggy boyfriend's vicinity.

Despite her rough persona, the blonde-haired Courteney could stop traffic with her impossibly long legs and radiant smile. She'd undoubtedly give Vivian Ward a run for her money, and her high-heeled, thigh-length stiletto boots drew my eye.

As she rummaged around in her handbag, I caught myself giving her the once over, now focusing on her thighs – specifically the six inches of flesh between her head-turning short skirt and the top of her boots. She was young, maybe only twenty, and I wondered how such a radiant beauty ended up doing what she did for a living.

"Like what you see, do ya?"

"Oh, sorry," I embarrassingly blurted, before shooting my hands up and closing my eyes. "Look, I'm sorry, I wasn't … you know." I opened my eyes to find her standing with her hands on her hips, smirking at me.

"Yeah, you were. You were checking me out. I look alright, don't I?" In one well-practised move, she flicked her blonde hair around her shoulder and pouted, pointing all the right body parts in my direction.

Now I was embarrassed.

"Well? When a girl asks you how she looks, you're supposed to compliment her."

"Oh, yes, of course … you look … nice, very nice."

Courteney snorted a laugh. "You're cute, you know. I see you've stopped shouting at that fella. Is he a mate of yours?"

"Rob. Yeah, he's a good mate."

"Oh, right. Well, if I had a good mate who wouldn't help me out, I think I'd ditch him. He didn't sound like much of a friend to me."

I straightened up and leaned my back against the balcony whilst Courteney locked the steel mesh gate that covered her front door.

She'd made a good point. Although Rob and Lee were my only friends standing by me, apart from listening, they hadn't offered any help.

Rob, my mate of twenty-plus years, had just been happy to tell me what a prat I was before swanning back to his semi-detached box and prissy wife – although she most definitely wasn't when in that cable car – and his humdrum life in suburbia. As for Lee, well, yes, his father had helped me out, but all he could offer up was that he thought my penis was on the small side. However, unless he'd checked me out when at the urinals on some night out on the town, I was reasonably confident I'd never waved my manhood at him. So, I'd dismissed that comment as a crap joke.

Courteney dropped her key in her bag, checked she'd locked her front door and swivelled around. "Anyway, where d'you come from, then? No one moves to this estate unless they're hiding from the fuzz or in the shit. Which is it then?"

I smirked, quite tickled by her choice of words. Now all I could conjure up in my mind was Sergeant Angel as he attempted to hunt the cloaked figure. However, the Broxworth Estate was a far cry from a delightful Gloucestershire village.

"Gone all coy, have ya? Lost your tongue?"

"I'm in the shit. Not on the run."

"Thought as much."

"Yeah, and to be honest with you, it's the sort of shite I can't see me being able to crawl out of."

Courteney swished her long blonde hair around her neck again. Not that I'm an expert on these things, but I thought I detected some bruising around her right eye, and she'd gone to great lengths to cover it with concealer makeup.

"Yeah, well. You better learn the rules sharpish, d'you 'ear. Step out of line around 'ere, and you land yourself in far worse shit, I can tell ya."

I nodded whilst further assessing the girl in front of me. Rob was right. This girl was one fit bird, as he put it – as stunning as my Bridget and Julia Roberts.

'Not your Bridget, dickhead, remember? You blew it, and she's done a runner with your business.'

I chose not to answer my mind talk, knowing full well the accuracy of the statement – especially the *dickhead* part.

"You off to work, then? You don't look like a hooker."

Her glare suggested my choice of words was ill-thought-through. "Oi, you twat. I ain't no tart … not anymore."

"Sorry."

"Anyway, what would you know what a working girl looks like? You an expert on the subject, are ya?" she aggressively spat.

"No, sorry. Look, I didn't mean to offend. Unfortunately, I have a habit of opening my trap without thinking."

"Well, you wanna be careful, 'cos the wrong word to the wrong sort around 'ere, and they'll cut your tongue out."

"Right, I'll bear that in mind."

"You do. Don't fink your toffee-nosed attitudes can work around this place." She waved her hand toward the two other monolithic, graffiti-covered, grey tower blocks that constituted the accommodation offered on the Broxworth Estate. "Some of us have no choice but to live 'ere. If you've fucked up, that's your problem, mate."

"Toffee-nosed?"

"Yeah, all posh-like."

"Me?" I chuckled, tapping my beer bottle to my chest.

"Yeah … you talk as if you're on Downton."

"Downton?"

"Yeah, that *Downton Abbey* programme. One of my Karl's little kids nicked the box-set on Blu-ray from the local supermarket. He was gonna sell them on, but we got watching it, and we both love it. Anyway, you talk just like that young bloke in the series."

"Can't say I've ever watched it," I chuckled. Although not a series I would imagine ever tuning into, it somewhat surprised me that Courteney and Karl enjoyed it. I struggled to imagine them slouched on the sofa with a joint and a tin of Stella each whilst engrossed in a period drama.

"Well, you can borrow the box set when we're done if you like."

"No, that's okay. Anyway, I don't have a Blu-ray player."

"Oh, well, Karl can get you one if you like. He'll just get one of the kids to nick one from the shops. He'll probably cut you a deal as you're a neighbour."

"No, honestly, you're fine." This wasn't the time to inform her I didn't own a TV either. "Your boyfriend's got children, then?" I changed the subject, although a little shocked he sent his offspring out on shoplifting missions. I guess a modern-day Fagin-type character, and from what I'd seen so far, the Broxworth Estate was doing a pretty good impression of how I imagined the Dickensian Bethnal Green to look.

"Karl, kids? You taking the piss?"

"You said he sends his kids out to steal for him."

"Not his kids! The school kids that work for him."

"Oh, yes, of course." I wondered if he sent them up chimneys as well.

"Look, I've gotta get going 'cos I'll be late." As Courteney marched past me, I was somewhat impressed by how the girl managed to stride along in those four-inch heels without tottering over and suffering a compound fracture.

"Right. Well, be careful out there," I threw after her, quoting a certain Sergeant Esterhaus from one of my father's favourite TV shows. Although Hill Street Station is set in a nameless city in the States, I figured the Broxworth Estate could rival any no-go area that any US city could offer.

Courteney turned, shooting a quizzical look. "Of what? Be careful of what?"

I awkwardly waved my hands, not knowing why I'd said what I said or how to respond. Apart from suggesting birth control, I really wasn't equipped with how to advise a sex worker to stay safe.

She stepped back towards me. "Look, whatever your prejudice might be, how I earn a livin' has got fuck all to do wiv you."

I nodded, looking away to avoid eye contact.

"If you must know, I'm doing some filming tonight. I know a geezer who makes porn films," she pointed a finger at me and smirked. "That's probably how you recognise me, eh? When you're tugging on your old chap whilst watching a bit of porn on your mobile."

My head shot up, wide-eyed at her bluntness.

"You can catch me at my website if you like. Karl's got a mate who's just set it up. Suzzysuck.com, that's my stage name."

"Oh."

"Yeah, check it out. There's a fee, of course, but there's a little teaser that's free before you enter your credit card."

"Of course, there is."

The stunning woman flashed me a smile and sashayed her way down the landing. I didn't recognise her from any porn site, but she did look familiar. Okay, so yes, like any thirty-two-year-old man, I'd dabbled in watching internet porn, but it wasn't a hobby as such, like knitting, or stamp collecting, which I didn't do either. What was for certain, I wouldn't be visiting Suzzysuck.com, even for the free teaser.

8

The Sting

After cracking open another beer, I searched for a pen whilst rummaging through one of the kitchen drawers that sported a ball of Blu Tack, various rusting paperclips, and a ticket stub for Glastonbury 2004. Along with a tatty copy of *James Clavell's Shogun* that lay on the bedroom windowsill, these seemed to be the only items the previous tenant had left behind.

I set about writing a to-do list with the sixth pen I plucked out of the drawer. The first four I'd tried were all dried up, and the fifth had leaked blue ink on my fingers, which I smeared across the front of a discarded envelope. I'd always been list obsessive; I usually wrote lists of lists. Although after penning, I would rarely consult them.

Notwithstanding my short foray into *Successville* – namely those few months when my life had hit the dizzy heights of everything going my way – my lists had just been something I would do, much like others used the notes app on their phone or the calendar on Outlook. Now I was living in *Shitsville*, I had to change tack and formulate a workable plan of how to crawl out of this mess.

I took a swig of my beer before peering down at the back of the torn-opened envelope where I'd written, *find Bridget*, and *find her brother*. I plucked up the pen and added, *ask Stinkor for my old job back*. After taking another swig of beer, I dropped the pen, struggling to think of what else to write. Instead, I whipped out my phone, opened the Safari app and tapped in Suzzysuck.com.

Courteney jiggled her assets at me whilst inviting me to enter my credit card details with promises of erotic wonder that would ensure instant stiffness and relief. As my neighbour repeated her routine, a red warning box flashed up, advising me my surfing was being tracked.

"Oh, shit." In a state of full-on panic, I randomly thrashed at the screen, desperately attempting to eradicate Courteney. After her jiggling assets eventually disappeared, following my random and frantic finger-stabbing at the screen, I cleared the history and lobbed my phone down on top of my somewhat short to-do list. "Christ, dickhead, why did you look at that?" I momentarily wondered if a detective from the dodgy-porn-site division of Fairfield CID would be knocking on my door, resulting in my name being added to the sex offender's list.

"Get a grip," I muttered. Along with a propensity to land myself in difficult scrapes, I'd always suffered from an over-active imagination with the ability to fear the worst unlikely outcome in every situation.

I plucked up the envelope and perused the list. So, asking *Stinkor* for my job back was a reasonably straightforward task. That would be point one, which I would perform tomorrow morning.

I guess I would have to grovel to levels I'd never reached before. However, I'd previously demonstrated a high-achieving proven track record in my ability to inform distraught claimants that the company didn't give a shit that their house had burnt down and not to expect their policy to pay out due to a clause detailed in the small print. And I'd secured the *Call-Handler of the Month* award seven times in three years, which had elevated me to *Employee of the Year* for 2015. So, with that record, if I swallow a catering-sized slice of humble pie, *Stinkor* might relent.

Points two and three were somewhat trickier. Bridget had cleared out of her flat, and rather stupidly, no shock there, I didn't have any contact details for her brother, Nathan. Bridget had never divulged who the landlord was, and Nathan had always come around the flat with the paperwork regarding the business, so I didn't actually know what company he worked for.

As much as I didn't want to believe it, since the incident in that hotel room and the mysterious hand-delivered envelope stuffed full of the pictures depicting me with some leggy-blonde, who could rival Courteney in the gorgeous woman stakes, I accepted that there was a possibility there was more to Bridget than meets the eye.

I'd been played for a fool, which I guess wasn't that difficult. Yes, I'd fallen for the oldest trick in the book – a seriously hot, beguiling, Machiavellian black widow had used her beauty to suck in a stupid, recently made-wealthy man.

Back in January, when I'd met Bridget, I thought she was too good to be true. Bridget had stated that she'd worked on cruise ships as the entertainment manager, made a pile of cash, and had now come back to Fairfield to search out a career in television, preferring to build her future career on dry land.

Bridget definitely sported that TV presenter look. Although, now thinking about it, Fairfield wasn't exactly the world's media capital, and I don't recall her attending any job interviews. Also, I was somewhat surprised she'd rented a one-bedroom maisonette in town. However, she'd said all her cash was tied up in long-term investments that would pay big later. So, living in a small rental was a price worth paying for long-term gain – it had all seemed plausible.

However, rather than questioning who she was and learning about her family, I'd allowed myself to get sucked in, believing her declaration of undying love and fully accepting that all her close friends were away working at sea. Despite our engagement, Nathan was the only member of her family I'd met. Who were her parents? Well, that was another question I'd never asked.

As I contemplated that Jones probably wasn't her real name, based on the fact during our short time together I don't recall she received any post, my mobile rang displaying *Number Withheld*.

Dodgy-porn-site investigators, perhaps? They would withhold their number, wouldn't they? Could they have tracked me that easily? No, they wouldn't ring. They would surely knock on the door – or would they? I plucked my phone up, dithering on my decision on whether to answer or ignore. My procrastination led to the caller deciding for me. The call ended, with my iPhone informing me I had a missed call.

As I stared at the screen, the *Number Withheld* displayed again, lighting up the picture of Bridget. I made a mental note to change the background. I couldn't face her every time the bloody thing rang. The woman I trusted, I'd loved, who'd now run off with my business. Trusting – a trait of mine that seemed to land me in the shit, with some depressing regularity.

I hit the green button before my mind talked me out of it.

"Hello," I tentatively greeted the unknown caller.

"Damian. Damian Statham?"

"Yeah?"

Christ, the male voice sounded official. Apart from peeking at Courteney's free teaser, I tried to think what else I'd done. Surely I couldn't get in trouble for just checking out my neighbour's mucky website, could I?

"Damian, you don't know me. However, I have some information which you may find interesting."

"Oh. What?"

"This is not a conversation we can conduct over the phone."

"Sorry, who are you?"

"Look, I can't say. However, I guess you're keen to locate a certain Bridget Jones, and I'm not referring to the film character. Would that be correct?"

The unknown caller had piqued my interest. Perhaps my luck was changing.

"I could be." I winked to myself, pleased with how I seemed to be playing it cool.

The caller fell silent.

"Hello, you still there?" Annoyingly, a hint of desperation crept into my voice, which the caller clearly picked up on. Perhaps I'd played it too cool.

"Yes, I'm still here," he chuckled. "So, are you interested in hearing what I've got to say, or shall we end the call?"

"No … I mean yes. I mean, I am interested, not that I want to end the call," I blurted. That nanosecond, when displaying my phlegmatic unflappable demeanour, evaporated and now fearing my only lead in finding Bridget may be lost.

"Okay. Meet me by the public toilets in Eaton Park tomorrow at eleven. Come alone."

"Yes. Err … who are you?"

The caller audibly sighed. "Just meet me at eleven."

"Yes, okay. Is that in the morning?"

"What?"

"The morning or at night?"

Another sigh. "AM."

"Right. How will we recognise each other? Do we need a code word, or perhaps both carry a certain newspaper?"

I think I detected a third sigh from the mystery caller just before the line went dead. I checked the screen, which sported a damp imprint of my ear. The caller had killed the call.

I drained my beer bottle, tipping my head back to lap up the last few drops. Perhaps points two and three on my relatively short to-do list wouldn't be so difficult after all. Whilst pondering the caller's identity, I remembered my bomb-threat training from my time at the call centre.

Every year management insisted that all call handlers repeated certain training modules to ensure we were fully updated with company policy and safety procedures. Apart from the standard training regarding how to wield the policy's small print against claimants, we also completed the fire and bomb-threat training. The latter demanded the immediate completion of a form with specific questions about the caller. If we received a call claiming the building was about to be bombed, said form would supposedly assist the police with their inquiries.

Disappointingly, I couldn't recall the training to any level of detail. Based on the fact that the chances of Al-Qaeda or any other world terrorist organisation would consider the call centre in Fairfield a viable target was slim to zero, I, along with my peers, thought the re-coaching was a complete waste of time. That said, we did piss off a fair amount of policyholders, so maybe there was a possibility a disgruntled claimant would flip, purchase the required amount of fertiliser and detonators, and attempt to blow the call centre to kingdom come.

I grabbed the blue-ink smudged to-do list and pen. So, the caller was male – good start. What about age? Hmmm, somewhere between twenty and sixty, I guess. That narrowed it down. "Accent?" I muttered. Hmmm, nondescript English. He didn't stutter, didn't have a lisp, and laughed like any bloke would in that broad age group. "Oh, hang on he sniffed. Well done, Damian," I praised myself as I penned *sniffer* next to the word *male*. I tapped the pen on my notes, trying to think of the other questions on that bomb-threat form. "Background noise!" I excitedly exclaimed, before a feeling of deflation soon poured chilled water on that. I think I could recall a car alarm going off, but that was it.

Frustrated with my efforts, I lobbed the pen across the worktop. So, tomorrow I was meeting a man, aged somewhere between twenty and sixty, who was probably brought up somewhere in the southeast of England, who may suffer from a cold, or just has a nervous sniffing type tic, and lives or works near a car park or road.

Brilliant.

Deciding my detective skills were lacking, I gave up and padded back into the bedroom, which sported a crappy, pine double-bed, with my sleeping bag from my scouting days laid on top. Along with a lopsided chest of drawers, these were the only pieces of furniture the landlord had provided. I plucked up my recently acquired copy of *Shogun* from the windowsill and flopped on the mattress, ready to dive into chapter two, hoping to while away a few hours and try not to think about the meeting with the mystery man in the morning.

As I folded back the spine of the well-read book, I pondered the thought that it might just be the right thickness to prop up the three-legged set of drawers.

9

In the Best Possible Taste

"We had a child? You and me?" Terry waved his arm between them as they stood in the kitchen. "We had a child after our one session in that hotel room?" Terry incredulously questioned as he struggled to get his head around this latest revelation.

"Yes, darling. A love child."

"Wha … how? What, but how?"

"Terry, darling, you, of all people, should know full well how."

Terry gawped at her, his mouth gaping, delivering his now perfected Hans-Gruber-falling-from-the-Nakatomi-Tower look.

"You seem a little surprised, darling."

"Err … yeah, you could say. But you've never mentioned him. You bang on about Ziggy, that plastic-hating surfer boy, your stepson, but you never mention your actual son. Our son!"

"Well, it hasn't exactly been what you might call a smooth ride, as such."

"And?" questioned a bug-eyed, hand-gesticulating Terry.

"And what, darling?"

"Oh, no you don't. I'm not having an 'it's complicated' conversation about this one." He performed the bunny ears gesture as he took a breath before launching into a rant.

"As far as I'm concerned, just two weeks ago, I was attending my work's annual conference in 1983—"

"Savouring the delights I had to offer," interrupted Deana with a smirk.

"Yes, quite. But anyway, there I was, enjoying life. But now, thirty-three bloody years later, where the world seems to be playing out the script of some H G Wells inspired novel with all the swanky complicated gadgets ruling everyone's life, I discover that in, *for me*, a rather short space of time my best mate married my wife, she then committed suicide, and the rather amazing news that I have a daughter—"

"Whose life we successfully put back on track," Deana again squeezed in, halting Terry's flow.

"Yes, we did, but she won't have anything to do with me because she's not of the mind to believe her dead father can come back from the dead—"

"Which is quite reasonable for her, don't you think?"

"Yes, I suppose so. But … *now*, I discover I also have a son—"

"We have a son, darling. It's we, as in us, not just you."

"Yes, alright we … Christ woman, you keep interrupting me. If I did that to you, you tear me off a strip, so—"

"Yes, well, I'm your elder, and I expect some respect. Also, as a woman, I have the right to interrupt a man."

"What? Who says so?"

"I do, darling. Now, come on, calm down. You're getting so worked up. If you carry on like this, you'll probably suffer another heart attack. Remember the last one you had killed you, so we really don't want a repeat of that performance, do we now?"

Stumped by that rather odd statement, Terry took a breather.

"Now, let's go and relax in the sauna, and I'll bring you up to speed on Damian and our mission."

Terry appeared a little concerned at the mention of the sauna, recalling Deana's previous attempts to get her hands on his body.

"Oh, Terry, don't look so worried. You're giving me a complex with your constant rebuffing of my generous advances. You can wear a towel, and I promise to keep my hands off you. Dyb dyb dyb Scouts' honour." She gave a two-fingered salute, stuck her tongue out the side of her mouth and crossed her eyes Benny Hill style.

Terry was fast learning that certain attitudes and statements, which seemed perfectly alright to him, were no longer fashionable thirty years after his death. Benny Hill chasing scantily clad women, and Kenny Everett's Cupid Stunt character had been assigned to history. That said, he enjoyed watching *Yes Minister* on one of the millions of channels on offer on Deana's almost cinema-screen-sized TV. And apparently, the political jokes of his day were still relevant in this time.

"Anyway, I'm older than you."

"Well, you were born seven years before me, that's true. However, as you've been dead for thirty-odd years, I'm now twenty-five years your senior. However, you saucy boy," she growled and gently ran her long red nails down the front of his shirt. "I have the body of a nubile thirty-year-old, and that's a pleasure you can take advantage of when you're good and ready. Though, I can't wait forever. Despite being dead, I have needs, Terry ... womanly needs," Deana delivered with her trademark purr.

The two weeks together had taught Terry that forcing Deana to divulge information when he wanted it didn't work. Frustratingly, he had to play to her fiddle and wait until she decided to spill the beans regarding the next revelation she had to offer. Also, he knew if he was going to get her to talk, he had to play along with her little games.

So, wrapped in the largest towel he could lay his hand on, Terry sat with his arms folded inches from Deana, who'd selected the tiniest towel to cover her body, which barely covered her front bottom and chest. Terry copped an unwitting eyeful of her bum when Deana stood to throw water on the coals.

Terry, feeling somewhat vulnerable, squeezed tightly against the side of the sauna whilst desperately trying to avert his eyes from Deana's near-naked form. The woman needed no encouragement from him, and he lived in a constant fear she would pounce upon him through the steam.

Not understanding how it all worked and why this had happened to him, dead-Terry was a very different man to how he'd acted when alive. As for Deana, well, there was no denying he'd never seen a woman of that age appear so alluring – almost as good as that day thirty-three years ago when he spotted her across the conference hall and wanted to dip her in honey and lick her all over. The very day he died after performing his wish, albeit without the honey.

After saving his daughter from his evil best mate, Terry had prepared himself for what came next. The afterlife, or something of that sort. Of course, he hoped to see Sharon again, aware that there would be copious amounts of grovelling on his part if his dead wife was to be persuaded to take him back after he'd shagged his way through the 1980s female population of Fairfield.

Like everything else, Deana had been somewhat tight-lipped on what lay ahead after they had finished their missions when roaming the world like a couple of characters from a Shakespearean play. Certainly, Deana acted like some sex-crazed banshee with her constant advances and warnings of the consequences of mission failure.

Although Terry had complied with Deana's demands to get his kit off in the sauna and was ready to push her for answers, he became distracted.

"So, why do you shave?" Instantly regretting the question when Deana smirked and removed her towel. "Cover up! You're a bloody nymphomaniac who's obsessed with parading around naked."

"Well, darling, you asked." Deana flung her towel to her side and crossed her legs.

"Christ," he muttered, trying to avert his eyes.

"Every three weeks or so, I would endure a Hollywood wax. I used to have a Brazilian, but Conrad, my personal trainer, preferred the smooth look. My darling Dickie didn't mind. Of course, now I'm dead and invisible to everyone else, popping into town and having my usual beauty treatments is more difficult. So, I have no choice but to do it myself now."

"A Brazilian?"

"Yes, darling. Au naturale is not really in vogue. And, I'll have you know, Cleopatra regularly removed her hair from down there."

"Did she really?"

"Oh, yes, she did. You're not looking, darling."

Terry stared straight ahead and swallowed hard as he detected Deana uncross her legs. "Can we change the subject? And can you please cover up?"

Deana rested her hand on Terry's lap. "Yes, to the first part, and no to the second."

Terry glanced down at her hand that lay on his towel, millimetres from his manhood. "You promised not to grab me if I came into the sauna."

"Darling, I lied."

"If you can't remove your hand, please stop rubbing."

Deana offered her trademark perfected pout. "Is little Terry-werry getting excited?"

"Little?"

"No, darling. That is something I recall you are not. Nor was Conrad either," she chuckled.

"Damian. Can we discuss Damian and not your opinion on the size of my … well, you know what, or any of your other conquests?"

She patted his towel. "Yes, of course."

Terry shot his head sideways, sporting a scowl, instantly turning his head back when remembering Deana was naked.

"Now, Damian was conceived that evening in the hotel."

"Why didn't you take precautions?"

"Err, excuse me. I don't recall you enquiring about contraception or supplying a condom. Although it was a long time ago, I recall you couldn't wait to point Peter at my pussy."

"A hairy one, I recall, unlike this new bald edition you now parade about."

"Oh, was it? Ha, how revolting. My, my, what was I thinking back then?"

"Look, I really don't want to discuss pubic hair. Can we get back on track and discuss my son?"

"Our son."

"Yes, okay. Our son."

"So, darling. As I was saying … after you died and Freshcom let me go … as you can imagine, the fallout of two married employees discovered copping off at their conference was rather frowned upon. My manager at the time thought it best that I look elsewhere for gainful employment."

"Bellingham? Old Bellingham, the buying director?"

"Oh, yes, that was him, Charles Bellingham. I'd forgotten his name. The randy old sod couldn't keep his hands off me."

"You didn't?" Terry shot a look sideways, again shooting his head back when instructing his mind to remember that he was conversing with a naked woman in a sauna who needed no encouragement.

"Oh, no. Not him! Blimey, the man was older than my father. He was well known for his wandering hands, and it was also rumoured that he would only employ women to his team if they were what he openly stated were 'easy on the eye', to coin a phase. He used to joke that his wife was a blunderbuss, so he deserved to have fit young ladies around him at work because he certainly didn't get that at home."

"I can imagine."

"Yes, it's rather funny, really. Of course, if a manager made that sort of comment these days, he'd be dismissed and face an employment tribunal for sexual harassment."

"Really?"

"Yes, darling. You wouldn't be able to whisk your little checkout ladies off to the electrical store cupboard these days. There are strict laws about sexual harassment. You can't have wandering hands and get away with it now."

Terry glanced down. "Does that apply to women's wandering hands as well?"

"Absolutely!"

"What about yours?"

"I'm allowed. It's my sauna," she giggled whilst patting his towel and raising her eyebrows.

"Damian!" barked Terry.

"Yes, of course. So, as you can imagine, I found myself in a spot of bother. Jobless, homeless because my first husband booted me out, and pregnant. Not a great situation to find myself in at twenty-five, I can tell you. 1983 Britain was a very different place compared to today—"

"A lot better, going by what I've witnessed so far."

"Please don't interrupt. I might get distracted, and I'm aware you're struggling in that department at the moment." Deana squeezed his crotch.

Terry gulped when feeling her touch.

"No, I had to find some accommodation, which wasn't that easy. You couldn't just hop on the internet and trawl around for rooms to rent. No, I spotted a postcard in the newsagent's window, next to the ones selling cars and prams, you know the sort of thing."

"Inter-what? You said hop on the inter-thingy. We've taken the bus and taxis, but what's that? Is that a new public transport system like InterCity?"

Deana's jaw dropped as she stared at him.

Terry turned his head to face her, keeping his sight-line focused on her eyes, determined not to look down. "What?"

"Over two weeks, you've been back alive, and still you say stupid things."

Terry shrugged. "It's not my fault I've been dead for some time and missed out on a few things."

"No, I guess not. The internet is how you find things when searching on my computer and phone."

"Oh, yeah," he nodded. "That engine that makes them work."

"Search engine, darling. But anyway, we digress. Odette Bains had placed an advert looking for a like-minded woman to share a flat, and so that's where Odette and I first became friends. We moved in together, but of course, I needed a job and a husband."

Terry pursed his lips but kept his focus on the opposite wall.

"Back then, being a single mother wasn't in vogue, you could say. I certainly wasn't planning on producing a brood of children, all of various different colours, like some of these celebrities do today. It seems to be in vogue for women to be unmarried with a white and brown child as must-have accessories."

Deana thought Terry looked confused. However, she wasn't a racist, of course not. Her most recent lover, Conrad, was third generation Jamaican, and boy, what a lush he was. However, rather than stoke Terry's outdated attitudes, which he demonstrated an annoying propensity to voice in all the wrong company, she thought it best to move on and avoid more questions.

"So, I met Sidney when hunting down a modest little run-around at one of those tacky second-hand car places. I'm afraid, back then, I had to settle for a car that would be classed as way below my social standing. However, at the time, needs must, as they say."

"He was your second husband?"

"Yes."

"How many did you have in total?"

"Seven."

"Seven! Jesus woman. Seven by the time you were sixty?"

"Terry Walton, how dare you? I'm nowhere near sixty!"

"Yes, you are. What are you, fifty-eight?"

"No! and I've told you before, enquiring about a woman's age is not considered good form."

"Fifty-seven."

"Maybe. Now, stop your interrupting. Let's have a little more steam, shall we? Be a love and drop some water on those rocks whilst I lie here and look all womanly."

"Alright. But can you move on with the story because I'll be shrivelled like a prune if we stay in here for much longer?"

"Oh, darling. I can assure you, judging by where my hand is, there's nothing shrivelled about you."

10

Cruel Sea

I fought my way through another chapter of my newly acquired book. Although Mr Clavell did his best to hold my attention, I struggled with keeping focus and thus started losing the plot due to muddling up the different characters and my mind drifting.

Anyway, after discovering the book wasn't about Mitsubishi's now somewhat outdated Sport Utility Vehicle – and at just shy of twelve-hundred pages, I guess it could have been tricky to write a book that length about a car – but rather a historical fiction saga set in seventeenth-century Japan, suggested this was probably not my typical sort of reading.

I couldn't be described as what you might call an avid reader. However, I would power my way through a few Jack Reacher type thrillers when laying splayed out on some Iberian beach whilst my girlfriend of the time would lay motionless as she worked hard on acquiring the required level of tan that would flatter her temporarily acquired bronzed skin when wearing a white strapless dress. I recall asking one of them, as she performed one of her regular hourly turns akin to a hog on a spit roast, why she kept her finger splayed wide. Apparently, an even tan between hand and foot digits was also essential.

As you can imagine, whilst she invested hour upon hour in significantly improving her chances of developing melanoma skin cancer, that afforded me plenty of time to kill. Apart from the occasional dip in the sea, and a quick ogle at the equally tan-obsessed, half-naked talent laid out in the vicinity of our hemmed-in pitch on the beach, I amused myself with Mr Reacher's latest exploits. At the time, I often wondered how one bloke seemed able to land himself in such exciting, albeit dangerous, situations.

Jack Reacher was just the type of man I needed to help me out of my current predicament. I was the good guy, albeit a right nitwit, but I needed his skills to set things straight.

I allowed my tatty copy of Japanese historical fiction to flop onto the mattress as my mind raced around, flitting from one thought to the next, just like the discarded plastic bags and sweet wrappers that the wind relocated throughout the litter strewn alleyways of the estate that I now rather dubiously called home.

Just like those redundant wind-swept bags caught in hedges and branches, my mind hovered on a thought before whisking randomly away to something equally unrelated. However, my mystery caller was never far from my thoughts, that wind-swept sweet wrapper that circled around in the air only to land in its original position on the carpet of discarded rubbish which the residents of this particular den of iniquity couldn't give two shits about.

The dulcet tones of the star of Suzzysuck.com raised my mind to the surface. Her tone and choice of vocabulary shaking free my thoughts akin to a submarine breaking through the choppy waters – I was definitely living in a *Cruel Sea* – how many more depth charge attacks could I survive, and had I surfaced to surrender?

As I listened to Courteney's and Karl's volley of verbal blows with their repeated choice of vulgar vocabulary exchanged across their flat, I presumed they weren't enjoying another episode of Downton whilst cuddled up on the sofa snorting cocaine. Class A drugs and their shared love of English period dramas aside, I struggled to understand why the two of them stayed together.

I guess from Karl's point of view, he had Miss Broxworth 2016 on his arm. Not that I thought this shithole of a place held a yearly beauty pageant, but I guess she could be regarded as the local stunner. Although, I accept that's in the eye of the beholder. And, of course, her career choice wasn't what most men would find acceptable for their girl to embark upon. However, from what I'd seen and heard from him, he was a loser, a drug-dealing junkie that was surely only treading water before spending most of his life at her Majesty's pleasure.

As for Courteney, well, I just thought the girl could do better than him. Even a nitwit loser like me would be a better option – just. Anyway, she just seemed to have a kind heart and an oddish, pleasant way about her. Apart from the shouting and liberal use of the C word when bellowing at her man, she displayed chinks of a caring, softer side. She'd offered a discount for her services, the opportunity to borrow her dubiously acquired box set of Downton and, even though she didn't know me, offered to secure a stolen Blu-ray player at a knockdown price – a cross between Mary Poppins and Lara Croft, in thigh-high leather boots and a potty mouth, type of character.

Lullabied by the constant bellowing of my brolly-wielding, athletic archaeologist, in the form of my neighbour, I drifted off to sleep only to be rudely awakened by the spring sunshine as it poked its head around the building opposite and streamed through the less-than-blackout curtains. Apart from James Clavell's bestselling novel now lying across the flattened pile of the cheap polypropylene carpet, nothing had changed. Despite my mind's constant whirring, I appeared to have slept well whilst lying spreadeagled on my sleeping bag.

With a mug of coffee in hand, I took up my newly preferred pose of leaning on the balcony wall outside my flat, taking in the sights. Fortunately, this morning I wasn't contemplating suicide.

As I sipped my drink, it reminded me of when I'd padded onto the balcony of our hotel suite when holidaying in Sorrento with my previous girlfriend. Rachel and I had just started dating, and the Sorrento holiday was supposed to be a week away to cement our relationship. Unfortunately, notwithstanding the stunning scenery and the romantic ambience that the Italian resort provided, the holiday only served to confirm to Rachel that I wasn't the right man for her.

Then, a few months later, Bridget stepped into my life. Rachel was no Bridget as far as looks go. Like any idiot male whose brain is controlled by his groin, I quickly forgot Rachel and any attempts to woo her back and took up with Bridget – oh, what a fool.

Of course, the vista in front of me was a far cry from Sorrento. That hotel balcony didn't offer views of grey monolithic '60s-styled concrete tower blocks. High-rise dumps that sported an almost complete covering of modern street art, of the graffiti variety, along with a collection of abandoned vehicles all in various states of decay near the burnt-out community centre, which held centre stage in one of the most run-down deprived areas of the county. I thought even *Shameless'* hapless Frank Gallagher would have found the place below his social standing.

I sipped my coffee and pondered the day as I watched a gang of hoodie-clad youths surreptitiously exchange packages and cash – Broxworth's thriving economy appeared to be up and running even at this early hour.

"You wanna refill?"

I spun around to see Courteney at her door, dressed in a skimpy thigh-length dressing gown with oversized fluffy slippers engulfing her feet as she held up a half-full cafetière.

I glanced at the dregs of my coffee. "Err … yeah, alright," I chuckled, slightly taken aback that my neighbour would make coffee in a cafetière – she didn't seem the sort.

Courteney padded over and filled my cup before skipping back into her flat and then rejoining me with her mug. We leaned over the railing, taking in the sights.

"Where's Karl?" I questioned, a little concerned because he didn't seem the sort that would allow Courteney to fraternise with the neighbours. However, he appeared quite happy for her to earn a living either on the streets or naked in front of a camera.

"Pissed off to one of his mates. We had an argument last night, and he stormed off."

"You don't say."

A mild spring breeze caught her hair and lifted it from the side of her face. With no makeup applied, I could see the faint outline of bruising below her left eye.

"What's your name?" she turned and leant her back against the railings, facing the flats. Either way, the view wasn't much different, although the waft of stale urine seemed a little more pungent when facing inwards. Courteney didn't seem to mind or notice.

"Damian."

"For the love of God."

"Sorry? What's wrong with my name?" I took a sip of coffee, surprised at the wonderfully bitter taste.

"Oh, nuffin. You got the same name as that artist bloke with the skull. You're not called Hirst, are you?"

I frowned, wondering what tangent this conversation had shot off to. "Err … No, I'm Damian Statham."

"Courteney Klein. Pleased to meet you," she held out her hand, not for a handshake as such, but more as a debutante might do when presented to a potential suitor at a ball. The situation seemed almost comical as we stood on a piss-stinking concrete landing and not in court at the palace.

I fist-bumped her, which didn't quite work, and I could tell it wasn't what she expected. "You've been watching too much Downton," I chuckled. "Klein, you say, as in pants."

"Pants?"

"Yeah, Calvin Klein. Most of my underwear is Calvin Klein." I held my hand aloft. "Sorry, way too much detail."

"Oh, yeah. No, it's Danish, apparently. Somewhere back in history, my ancestors must have come over from Denmark.

"Oh, right." That explained her looks. All Scandinavian girls were stunning, weren't they? Or was that just a typical bloke's preconceived notion?

"Show us your pants, then," she smirked.

"Sorry?"

"Look, these are mine. Victoria's Secret," she announced as she parted her dressing gown to reveal her cheese-wire-styled thong, which Courteney appeared delighted to show me as she performed an Anthea Redfern type twirl. Not that I thought for one moment the TV presenter ever would show her butt off on the landing of this odious estate. However, I recall my father constantly repeating the catchphrase when presenting his latest girlfriend, of which there were many.

"Right … lovely," I nervously chuckled.

"Knickers or my arse?"

"Oh, both, I suppose." I detected my embarrassment flush through the two-day stubble.

"Yeah, they're well nice. They cut your arse in half, but as they're well small, they're easy to nick."

"Nick?"

"Yeah, you know. You can get handfuls of them in your pocket if you're careful. It's shit easy, as long as you keep an eye out for the shop assistants."

"Hmm, I'm sure. D'you pay for anything, or do you and your boyfriend pilfer everything?"

"Nah, don't nick from the local shops. You don't shit on your own doorstep, do ya?"

"No, I guess not. What did you mean about for the love of God about my name? Most people think of the Antichrist when I introduce myself."

"The Omen … Damien Thorn," she delivered in a deep, spooky-type voice.

"Yeah," I chuckled, surprised she would know what I was talking about. I didn't have her pegged as a film buff, and that film was even before my time, let alone hers.

"For the love of God. Damien Hirst. You know, the diamond-encrusted skull."

I guess my bemused look suggested I had no idea what she was rambling on about.

"Shit me. And they say I'm the fick one. You must have seen that skull he made with loads of diamonds all over it. It's called, *For the Love of God.*"

"No, I must have missed that art gallery viewing," I chuckled.

"He's done loads of famous stuff. He's the one who put that tiger shark in the tank of formaldehyde. I fink he's also cut a cow in half."

"Oh, yeah, that rings a bell of sorts."

"You into art, Courteney?" This wasn't the sort of conversation I expected to have after our introduction yesterday when she bellowed through my kitchen window or the assault on my eardrums when listening to the slanging matches she and her boyfriend conducted each night. Discussing art with a local prostitute seemed almost surreal.

She shrugged. "Nah … not really. I read a lot, though. When I'm not working, nothing I like better than sticking my head in a book."

"Really?" I chuckled, my facial expression probably conveying I found her statement rather hard to believe. Who the hell was this girl? She had the diction that any self-respecting navvy would be proud of, made her living somewhat dubiously, and resided one rung up from the gutter.

114

However, apart from her kindness, she appeared well educated – oh, and undeniably beautiful, even more so as she playfully grinned at me, displaying her Hollywood smile. Without her war paint and working-girl clothes, Courteney had to be the most stunning girl I'd met. And, considering Bridget, that was no mean feat.

"What?" she quizzed, probably wondering why I sported a surprised look.

"How do *you* know about Damien Hirst and stuff like that?"

"I get it. You mean, how come a low-life hooker, as you called me, has any interest other than sucking dick? That's what you meant, ain't it?"

"No ... no, far from it."

Courteney thrust her hands on her hips and assessed me. I couldn't decide if she was about to slap me, turn on her heels and march those fluffy slippers back into her flat, or flip up one of her long legs and kick me over the balcony, Lisbeth Salander style.

"Okay. But listen, just 'cos I don't talk like one of your posh mates, and I ain't got a nice office job, it don't mean I'm fick."

"Oh, no—"

"You lot are all the same," she interrupted. "Well, tosser, you live 'ere now, so you can forget finking you're above any of us who live in this shithole."

"Courteney, I'm—"

"I have to put on an act, you know," interrupting again and poking a finger at me to force her point home. "If punters fink I'm a cleva cow, they mightn't want to pay for my services.

115

Men think they have to be in control. Some bird with all the answers ain't that attractive."

"Courteney, I didn't mean anything by my question. I'd rather not fall out over this."

"Alright. But watch your mouth."

I raised my palm defensively, more as an apology rather than a concern she might wield any kickboxing skills upon me. "Look, I seem to be losing friends at a frighteningly fast pace. To be honest, the number of mates who are still talking to me is dwindling. So, it's just nice to have a coffee with someone who isn't hell-bent on ruining my life or reminding me what a total bell-end I am."

I decided not to tackle her regarding the 'posh' comment. I presumed anyone who didn't previously reside here might appear posh to those unfortunate enough to have been born and bred in this odious place.

"Okay. Cool."

We both sipped our coffee. I tried to think of something to say to break the awkward silence.

"You don't have any tattoos, then?"

Courteney frowned.

"Sorry, for some reason, I thought of Lisbeth Salander a moment ago, and I noticed when you twirled you didn't have any tatts."

Why the hell I was asking this, I have no idea. However, I'd developed the skill of randomly blurting irrelevant statements or asking totally inappropriate questions. When I was younger, my father always excused my odd way by saying he reckoned I was on a bit of a spectrum, as he called it, blaming it on an inherited trait from my real father.

116

Although how he knew that, God knows, because the bloke died before I was born. As for my mates or ex-mates, they just thought it was Damian being Damian, as in, a bit of a knob.

"Nah, not my fing."

"I've got a couple on my back. Although I regret them now."

"Oh, well, most fellas have them these days. It's just I don't see the point." She pointed her coffee mug at me. "Course, I don't mind them on a bloke, so I don't mean to offend, like."

"None taken. Anyway, you're way too pretty for tatts."

Courteney flashed her smile, seemingly happy to take my sincerely delivered compliment.

"You might want to cover up." I waved my hand at the gaping dressing gown where the cord had loosened when performing her cheese-wire-knicker twirl. That said, from the glimpse on offer, it was easy to see how she'd transitioned into the adult entertainment business because the girl possessed a body most women her age would cut their right arm off for.

"Oh, shit. Sorry. I normally charge for that. You've had a freebie there." She flashed that smile, placed her mug precariously on the metal rail that ran along the top of the balcony, and made herself decent before swishing her long blonde locks around her neck.

"You seen the films? I thought they were pretty good. Although if you're into Downton, maybe that isn't your sort of thing."

"What film?"

"The Girl with the Dragon Tattoo films."

"Oh, yeah, but the books are way better."

117

"I've not read them. I'm more of a Jack Reacher sort of bloke." Based on the fact that I'd only managed a couple of chapters and already struggled to grasp the plot, I thought I'd leave out mentioning my latest read. Starting a book reviewing club with my prostitute neighbour was probably not a good idea. I couldn't imagine sitting in her flat discussing the latest best-seller whilst Karl hoovered up a line of his favourite white powder. Also, as was becoming clear in this short and somewhat surprising conversation, I thought I would be out of my depth. I feared Courteney was significantly better read than me.

"Oi, tosser. Who are you?"

I glanced past Courteney to spot an aggressive-looking thug barrelling along the landing. Wearing a black hoodie and sporting a particularly menacing demeanour, I presumed the man advancing towards me was Karl. However, that description could be attributed to most blokes on the estate, but I wasn't looking forward to meeting my neighbour.

11

Mona Lisa

"Oh, bollocks, the wanderer returns," muttered Courteney. "Where the hell have you been all night? You can naff off back to Fat Larry's place if you're skunked up to your eyeballs. I can't be doing with your shit this morning."

Karl slapped his hand around her cheek, pinching her windpipe as he leaned into her face. Courteney didn't flinch. With her head pushed back, she just held his stare.

Feeling somewhat awkward, well, three's a crowd, as they say, I didn't know whether to offer a polite cough before introducing myself or just bolt back into my crummy flat and avoid the confrontation.

Although Karl appeared to have the physical advantage, it appeared Courteney won the staring game. She shoved him backwards, forcing him to release his hand – the whole dynamics of this confrontation changed.

Typical of the type of chap I had him pegged for, his demeanour and aggressive stance suggested Karl liked to play the bully. However, it appeared he wasn't altogether in control of Courteney, as he liked to portray.

"You have to pay to look at her. Piss off before I cut you." Karl revealed the tip of what appeared to be a Bowie knife he'd concealed up the sleeve of his hoodie as he stepped towards me.

"Leave it! He's the bloke who's taken Kimmy's old flat."

Karl nodded as he slipped the knife point back to conceal the protruding tip.

"Damian. I've just moved in. Well, it's a stop-gap until I sort a few things out," I introduced myself with a nervous laugh. I refrained from offering my hand because something suggested he wasn't the handshake sort of chap.

Karl stepped forward, entering my personal space. Annoyingly, I stepped back, instantly and unwittingly conveying I felt intimidated. His smirk suggested Karl knew that.

Although my old boss stole a march on this guy in the halitosis department, his breath sported a pungent dead-rat aroma. I guess the dark edges of his teeth probably didn't help much. I couldn't decide if he was just one of those guys whose eyes appeared to suggest a deranged mind lurked behind, much like the mug shots on TV of captured serial killers, or his skunk-fuelled evening had dilated his pupils leaving a glassy film across them.

Karl snorted and sneered before jerking his head forward to feign a head butt. I flinched.

"You ain't going to survive up here, you pussy."

"Shit, Karl, just leave it!"

I glanced over his shoulder. Courteney folded her arms and shook her head. Presumably well-versed in watching her man intimidate the residents of the landing. I had no idea who the

120

previous tenant was, this Kimmy woman who Courteney had mentioned, only knowing she probably attended Glastonbury in 2004 and enjoyed reading historical fiction. However, I guess she wouldn't have found Karl too endearing, and I wished I could follow her lead and escape this place.

Karl stepped back and pointed at his girl. "If you're going to do him, make sure you charge the twat. No discount for neighbours and I reckon he's got a few quid." With his instructions delivered, Karl stepped around me and disappeared down the landing.

"You can't let blokes see you're scared. You're gonna have to toughen up 'cos gits like my Karl can sniff out fear like a shark smells blood."

I dragged my hand over my face, detecting a slight tremble. I really wasn't cut out to live in a place like this.

"Where …" I closed my mouth and swallowed, noticing my voice had shot up a few octaves and now resembled a soprano choir boy as if about to bang out a rendition of *Walking In The Air*. "Where's he gone?"

"Don't worry. The git won't be back 'til later. Anyway, why are you 'ere? Karl is right about one thing … you ain't the sort to live in a shithole like this."

"It's a long story," I huffed, ramming my trembling hands into my jeans pockets.

"Come on," she beckoned her head towards her front door. "Karl might be a smackhead and addicted to all sorts of shit, but I can't go more than half an hour without caffeine. I'll make us a coffee, and you can fill me in wiv the details."

I hesitated.

"Hey, forget what that twat said. I ain't offering sex. I don't do that no more; it's all online now, remember?"

I nodded, recalling the offer of a discount code to her website. However, I held my position, unsure whether entering her flat was a particularly terrific idea.

"Oh … I guess it's private. Sorry, I was just lendin' a friendly ear."

"No, it's not that."

"Right … you don't fancy stepping into an ex-prossy's flat. You fink you're too good for that, I guess. Well, mate, you ain't anymore, 'cos you live 'ere now."

"Christ, no. That's not what I meant." I glanced along the landing where Karl had disappeared a few moments ago.

Courteney stepped up and grabbed my hand. "He won't be back for hours. The git will be moving his stash about before collapsing at Fat Larry's gaff with a skunk pipe in his hand."

I nodded and followed her towards her door.

"Oi, your door."

"What?"

"You need to lock your door."

"Oh, don't worry, there's nothing worth nicking in there."

"You need to wise up. Leave that door open, and you'll have a posse of hopheads and squatters in there, and you won't be able to get 'em out."

"Oh, right."

"Jesus, you really are out of your depth."

After accepting the girl's security advice, I settled down on a stool in her kitchen as she bustled about making another cafetière of coffee after grinding some beans. I presumed the plethora of kitchen appliances were all stolen goods, but I guess becoming an accessory to theft by drinking her coffee was the least of my worries. The kitchen appeared immaculate, clean, and orderly. I suspected that had nothing to do with Karl. We stayed silent as the rather odd enigma of Courteney Klein prepared the drinks like a well-trained barista.

I caught myself assessing the girl as she swished about in that dressing gown. I wasn't a lecherous type of guy, you know, the sort that undresses women with their eyes. However, I confess, if I could ignore her profession, she was the sort of stunner that turned heads, and I couldn't help myself taking in her beauty.

"Why are you here?"

She turned, tightening the cord on her dressing gown, which again appeared to have worked loose, showing off her pilfered underwear. "We're talking about you, not me."

I nodded and shrugged.

"Got kicked out of that children's home on my sixteenth birthday and had nowhere to go. Local housing officer stuffed me in some women's refuge place for a few weeks, but I hated it. Then I got caught up with the wrong sort, and that's where I met Karl."

"Oh. Yes, I can imagine."

Courteney placed a mug in front of me. "No, Karl saved me from a gang of nonces that were pimping out young girls. I guess I owe him."

"Oh."

"Karl's ten years older than me. At the time, he was a better bet than those bastards who wanted to pimp me out to those sick bastards into kiddy porn."

"Christ."

I was a little lost for words. She was right – I was out of my depth. I really couldn't imagine how awful that gang could be if Courteney regarded Karl as her knight in shining armour. Although my mother abandoned me as a baby, and my adopted father enjoyed the superfluidity of short-term relationships, I considered, in comparison to Courteney, I should be thankful for my relatively privileged upbringing. Despite many a new stepmother arriving and departing my life, my father had looked after me well.

"What about your parents?"

"Didn't have a dad. Mum gave birth to me when she was fourteen, so I ended up in that bleedin' kids' home. That shithole called Lexton House over on Coldhams Lane."

"Where is she now?" I took a slurp of coffee – my neighbour was a coffee queen.

"Dead. Drug overdose. That's why I don't do it."

"But you live with Karl. Who, by all accounts, is a habitual user."

"As I said, I guess I owe him. Anyway, what is this, some interrogation?"

"No. Sorry."

Courteney stepped closer, her long legs nudging against my knees as she squeezed into the gap between my thighs. She performed that hair swishing routine and smirked at me before sipping her coffee. "It's alright. I like you."

"Ah ... look, I don't really want to—"

"What?" she raised her eyebrow.

"I know I said you're fit ... you *are* fit. But ... I. Look, I don't want to offend you ... but I'm not into—"

"Hookers?"

I didn't know whether to nod or shake my head, confirm her statement or keep schtum.

"You're cute, you know that," she took another sip of her coffee. "As I said, you can watch me online if you like, but I don't do punters no more. So, lose the frightened rabbit look."

I'd not been accused of being cute before. Unlike most girlfriends, Bridget had called me all sorts of endearing names, and I wondered why I hadn't seen through her apparent lies. I guess I'd been besotted and blinded to the truth by a woman who, in reality, would never lower herself to the likes of me unless there was some ulterior motive.

Other girlfriends had been more honest, referring to me as dickhead, or tosser, which at times those terms of endearment afforded a certain accuracy about them. Bridget never called me anything derogatory, presumably keeping me sweet while she reeled me in, preparing for the kill. But cute, well, that was a new one.

"So, let's have it. I reckon you stuck this," she ran her index finger along the fly of my jeans. "Somewhere where your girlfriend wasn't too pleased about. She caught you and slung you out."

"Not quite. But you're right about being booted out."

Courteney raised her eyebrows, holding my eyes as she sipped her coffee.

"It's a bit more complicated."

"So, you ain't played away, but you've done somefink to piss her off that's enough for you to have to rent that shithole next door, which suggests your break up is permanent."

I filled Courteney in on the headlines about Bridget. I left out the part about the blonde in the hotel room but enlightened her about my stupidity regarding the business and my meeting in a few hours with the mystery man in Eaton Park.

"Shit me! It's like something out of a John le Carré novel. Although I still don't get why she booted you out if you ain't shoved your todger where it shouldn't have gone."

"Look, I got caught out, but not as you think. Anyway, you and your books," I chuckled.

"Karl finks books are shit. I bet I'm the only girl on the estate who reads, but it's my way of escaping. When I lived in that home, that's all I did ... read books to forget where I was."

"Why don't you do something else? You've got the brains."

"That's my business."

I held my hands up, only just missing brushing them across her breasts by a millimetre. I'd become so comfortable with this girl close to me that I'd not realised how intimate our position was. As if clocking my thoughts, she nudged back a half-step.

"So, who d'you reckon this geezer in the park is, then?"

"No idea."

"Tell you what. Why don't I come wiv you?"

"What?"

"I'll come wiv you and watch. Y'know, like a lookout. I can keep an eye out whilst you talk to him and see if anyone else is watching."

"Christ, you do like your spy novels," I chuckled.

"Right, that's sorted, then. I'll go over there early and hang around. I can then watch what happens. We can meet up later, and I'll let you know what else I spotted. I'll take a few pics and then can ask around to see if anyone knows him. If he uses toms, one of the girls will know who he is."

"Alright. Why not. Look, before I go to the park, I've got to nip into town and beg *Stinkor* for my old job back."

"By the power of Grayskull!" Courteney triumphantly thrust her arm into the air.

"Bloody hell, girl. Is there nothing you don't know? Even some hardened *Masters of the Universe* fans have never heard of *Stinkor*."

Still holding her superhero pose, my new neighbour placed her index finger to my lips, now holding a pose akin to a referee indicating offside. "Pretty impressive … eh? But, listen up, cute boy, we need to get you off the Broxworth, 'cos you ain't got the stomach for living up 'ere."

"No, shit," I mumbled, with her finger still tight to my lips.

After only a few days in this particular hellhole, Courteney's assessment of my situation suggested a truer statement had never previously been uttered. If a fit, young internet porn sensation was to be my salvation, so be it. I really had run out of options.

An unlikely alliance, you might suggest – my *Mona Lisa*.

12

Flatliners

Terry endured a fitful night's sleep, waking every now and then. Usually, in this new routine, he would wake in the wee hours and pad through to one of the spare rooms, only to discover Deana had joined him sometime later. It's as if they unwittingly played a game of musical beds, with Terry attempting to outfox her, only to find Deana next to him when he awoke, usually cuddled up with her arm across his chest.

Terry would prefer to sleep on his own. However, like a doleful puppy, the attention-seeking Deana followed him from room to room. So, he gave up trying to avoid the woman and accepted his leech-type bed companion would have her way.

Deana was that type of woman who wore you down and, popping the fact that he was dead to one side, Terry didn't possess the energy to fight her. She insisted they slept together, not in the biblical sense, although she spent most of her waking hours trying to force that issue, but just the desire to have a man next to her as she slept.

When alive, Terry couldn't recall turning down any woman's advances. And although Deana had matured to a lady of more senior years, there was no denying the woman still could attract men half her age. He'd heard a term used in a film they'd watched together which Terry had to enquire the meaning of. Deana had enjoyed explaining MILF, and Terry accepted that the woman probably could be the visual representation of the phrase.

However, for some reason unbeknown to him, his desire to roger every female with a pulse just didn't seem to exist anymore. Since dying, it was as if he'd been bestowed with a personality change or anti-androgens had been injected into his veins – bromide in his tea scenario. For sure, Deana could not be accused of supplying the drug because she would be more likely to pop some Viagra in his tea. A new pill that, going by Deana's description of its medicinal properties, Terry thought sounded amazing. He wouldn't have minded his own stash of the drug when, back in the day, entertaining a group of ladies and disappointingly finding his stamina waning.

Watching films was a pastime they both enjoyed whilst holed up in her house awaiting the process of probate to sell the property, a point which he presumed would lead them to the next stage of their journey through this new existence called being dead.

Terry escaped the sauna last evening without Deana getting her way and, following an initial sulk, Deana said she was off to play with her rabbit. An odd statement considering she disappeared to her room, and as far as Terry was concerned, he hadn't spotted any pets in the house. Anyway, whatever she was up to, this afforded Terry some Deana-free time to settle down to watch a film. When flicking through the exhausting list on offer, he'd settled on *Flatliners,* which, as the story unfolded, he thought had a rather aptness to it based on his own somewhat odd situation.

As Terry lay awake, with the naked Deana serenely lying next to him, he mulled over their conversation whilst in the sauna and the film he'd watched. He considered the possibility that he'd flatlined, meaning the last few weeks spent here in the future were actually only fleeting glimpses into the afterlife. Perhaps this span of time, in reality, was only a few seconds and not two weeks. If that were to be the case, any moment now, he would spring back to life, open his eyes, and find a paramedic leaning over him whilst holding a set of defibrillator pads above his chest.

"Deana," he whispered.

Nothing.

"Deana. Wake up."

"What?" she mumbled.

"Deana, wake up. I need to talk to you."

"Terry, unless you're going to make love to me, shove a sock in it and go back to sleep."

"I think I've worked it out."

"At last. Halleluiah."

"What?"

Deana pulled up her pink satin eye-mask. "You've worked out that I'm the fittest woman any dead man is going to have the opportunity to woo and, at last, you want to take me." She flung the bed sheet away, offering herself up.

Terry pulled the cover back over her body. "No—"

"Pity."

"Listen. I've worked out what we can do about Damian."

"Great. Well, unless you want to change your mind." She flung the sheet away again. "As it's the middle of the night, I'm going back to sleep."

"It's half past six."

"Oh, well, it's a bit early, even for me, but how about it then?"

Terry hopped out of bed before hoisting up a pair of boxers.

"I guess that's a no, then?"

"I'll put the kettle on. Then I have some ideas to run through with you."

Terry padded back into the bedroom with a tray holding a teapot and cups. His mother always taught him tea was to be made in a pot, despite in the '80s, his time, tea bags seemed to be the preferred option.

Deana covered her chest with the bedsheet as she shuffled into a sitting position. Terry presumed she'd accepted his boxers were on and wouldn't be coming off despite her best efforts.

"This better be good because unless there's the offer to satisfy my womanly needs, this time of the morning should be solely reserved for milkmen, postmen, and bakers."

"And butchers and candlestick makers."

"Yes, very droll. What I'm saying is any time prior to seven o'clock is the dead of night. People of my class don't need to be awoken so early."

"Yes, M'Lady."

Deana raised an eyebrow.

"Shall I be mother?"

"Well, you're not acting like a man, so I guess so."

"Give it a rest, Deana. We have more important things on our plate than your desire to whip my boxer shorts down."

"What a lovely thought."

Terry tutted. "We have to concentrate on Damian, not sex."

"That may be so. However, as I keep trying to explain to you, I have needs. Despite the fact that we're dead, I really do need to be satisfied. Although my rabbit hits the spot, it's not the real thing."

"Your rabbit?"

"Yes darling, I explained last week … my Rampant Rabbit … my sex toy. I have quite a collection, which my darling Dickie, God rest his soul, I, and a few close acquaintances used to enjoy."

"Why am I not surprised?"

"Come on then. Let's hear it. What amazing plan have you conjured up?"

Terry duly poured the tea before adding the milk, as his mother had taught him.

"So, just to recap. Damian is brought up by your second husband, Stanley—"

"Sidney!"

"Yes, of course, Sidney. It's hard to keep track of the names."

"Ismaaar."

"Sorry? Who's Ismaaar?"

"Ian, Sidney, Mark, Alan, Adrian, Alex, Richard. I-S-M-A-A-A-R … ismaaar."

"Oh."

"See. It's an easy way to remember the names and the order in which I married them. I have a little ditty that goes; *Ian screwed Mark after Adrian analed Richard.* It's a bit like *Richard of York gave battle in vain.*"

Terry shook his head in disbelief. "You're unbelievable."

"I know, darling. You're so lucky to be with me," she giggled, flashing a nipple.

"No, I was talking about your little ditty on how to remember your husbands' names. At least the one for rainbow is clean. Yours is about placing your husbands in some sordid, perverted sex positions whilst playing a game of nude Twister."

"Oh, I've done that! What fun! Although I recall Dickie wasn't too chuffed on one occasion when he ended up with his nose inches from Bernard's arse."

"You've got to be joking."

"No, darling, it was so funny. Of course, although Dickie wasn't too thrilled, the rest of us fell about laughing."

"No, I mean you're joking about playing nude Twister."

"Oh, no. Surely everyone has played that after a few drinks at a dinner party?"

"Deana, I very much doubt that. You're one of a kind."

Deana smirked. "Too true. I am. You are lucky to be with me … any man would be."

"Right, of course. I'll try to remember that."

"You do so. Also, back to my little ditty … if you add up their birth years, adding mine on top, the sum equals 444."

"And?"

"Darling, 444. It's the number of the angel that denotes a sign of love. How apt is that!" she giggled before taking a slurp of her tea.

"Right, okay—"

"This is nice, darling," she patted his thigh. "It reminds me of Saturday mornings when Dickie and I would enjoy breakfast in bed. We had lots of fun."

"Deana?"

"Yes, darling."

"Do you think it's possible for you to think about something other than sex? Just for a tiny moment so we can discuss our son."

Deana snuggled up close, resting her cup on his chest whilst offering her perfected doleful pout up at him. "I'll try, darling."

"Right, Sidney brings up Damian after you left him for Mark—"

"As I said, I know that wouldn't have afforded me the mother-of-the-year-award, but the man was so dull."

"Yes, I'm sure he was—"

"That said, the man demonstrated decent paternal qualities, so I knew he would look after Damian far better than I could. I wasn't put on this earth to look after children. They're so needy and callow, don't you agree?"

"And you're not?"

"Well, that's my point. How could I bring up a baby with all my desires and needs?"

"Yes, I see your point. Anyway, as I was saying—"

"Don't think badly of me, darling. I just couldn't bear it."

"Any chance you could stop interrupting me?"

Deana laid her free hand on his thigh and stroked her hand through his hair, allowing her fingers to slide under his boxer shorts. "Of course, darling. I'm all ears."

"After you left him, Sidney's business goes from strength to strength, his car business growing into a substantial going concern before he gifts the whole thing to Damian when he upped sticks to run off with some woman from the States."

"Uh-huh," Deana slurped her tea.

"Damian then appears to, for some odd reason, follow in Sidney's footsteps and gift his business to some woman who's now disappeared."

Deana nodded.

"Our boy has lost everything. Now, you said he's a bit naïve like Sidney, stupidly got himself in a bit of a pickle, and now his girlfriend has binned him off, taking the business with her."

"Is there a punch line to this, or are we still just recapping?"

"Well, last night, whilst you were entertaining yourself with Bugs Bunny, I watched a film called *Flatliners* that got me thinking. In that story, these medical students experiment with dying—"

"I've seen the film; I don't need a recap. This isn't Barry Norman's film review."

"Does he still present that programme? I used to like that."

"Terry, no. Barry Norman must be in his nineties by now."

135

"Yes, of course. Anyway, as you've seen the movie you'll remember; when they die those students relive an event in their past. So, a sort of recap, although sometimes what actually happened has changed, but the key is their own history."

"Darling, you're boring me."

"Deana, what has happened to Damian is part of *his* history … yours or Sidney's. I don't think some girlfriend of his has stumbled across our boy and just got lucky. I think there's an event in history that may explain why that girl entered his life."

Deana scrambled up on her knees, taking the bed sheet with her. Terry's suggestion now taking precedence over the constant need to try to woo him. "You think his ex-girlfriend purposely became his girlfriend to take his business?"

"I do."

"What does that mean we have to do?"

"Deana, our boy needs his real parents' help."

13

Life Is Like A Box Of Chocolates

I'd been accused of stupidity, unwavering blind faith, and possessing a frighteningly acute lack of common sense on too many occasions for as long as I care to remember. From school through to owning a swanky car showroom, many derided my actions, accusing me of displaying imbecility to inconceivable levels.

I knew I held that label. Although, notwithstanding my often-displayed naïvety, some chose to see the caring side, which, of course, increased my vulnerability. However, rarely had anyone laughed at me, derided me, and enjoyed my suffering as much as Halitosis Harry. The bastard seemed to revel in my misfortune and tearfully roared with laughter at my suggestion about coming back to work for him, despite my plethora of back-catalogue employee of the month awards.

As I slithered away from the offices of my previous employment, the reality of my situation hit home. I was in a quagmire of shit, with no life belt and only a twenty-two-year-old, potty-mouthed internet porn star attempting to throw me a lifeline.

After completing the sixth form and achieving three failed A-levels, I'd worked for fourteen years at that insurance company before leaving when my father gifted me that car sales business. So, I'd never been unemployed. Savings weren't something I'd been particularly good at, always enjoying blowing my monthly disposable income at the weekends like any self-respecting idiot with no plans for the future.

For the first time in my life, I became concerned about what lay ahead. Of course, losing my father's business had been a disaster. However, being a reasonably happy-go-lucky sort of guy, without the luck part, I'd never been that materialistic. Notwithstanding that attitude to life, I needed somewhere to live and the ability to buy food and, of course, beer. Young Courteney was quite correct in stating I wasn't cut out to live on the Broxworth Estate, but at this point, I had no choice. The rent for that shithole was more than I could afford, and anywhere better would be out of my reach, so out of the question.

As I trudged towards Eaton Park, I pondered that maybe after failing to re-secure gainful employment, my luck would change when my mystery caller provided information about Bridget.

I settled on a bench near the public toilets, the one furthest from the children's play area. The spring sunshine appeared to have brought out a gaggle of young mums dragging their children to the park. The last thing I needed was some over-cautious mother to accuse me of watching the children. A sad state of affairs, but I guess with the media constantly whipping up hysteria that weirdo predators lurked at every turn, who could blame parents for their overprotective attitude?

Whilst trying not to look like a pervert, I visually scoured the area for Courteney. With twenty minutes to go before my mystery caller was due to show, I expected to spot Courteney in position. However, no one seemed to fit the bill. And unless she was in disguise, dressed as a bearded rough sleeper camped down near the toilet block, it suggested she hadn't turned up yet.

I repeatedly tapped my phone, checking the time. As the digital clock approached eleven o'clock, the display turned excruciatingly slowly. Now, as time evaporated, the display appeared to be on speed as the minutes shot by at warp-factor acceleration. I presumed Courteney had changed her mind, probably deciding to wash her hair because that was the excuse women used to indicate they weren't interested, wasn't it?

At ten minutes past the hour, I feared my mystery caller would also be a no-show. Apart from the young mums and the shrieking and occasionally crying loud children who repeatedly circuited the multi-coloured plastic play area with its all-weather rubber safety matting, there didn't seem to be anyone hanging around who I thought fitted my mystery man that I deduced was somewhere between eighteen and sixty suffering with a cold or an allergy.

Whilst performing my Forrest Gump impression without the box of chocolates, a man in his fifties appeared from behind me and perched at the other end of the bench seat – this was it.

I played it cool, kept my head forward and waited whilst repeatedly swivelling my eyes in an attempt to see what he was up to. He didn't appear to be holding a folded-up newspaper, so I guessed he hadn't planned to pass me a file containing the information about my ex-girlfriend. Nevertheless, I continued to wait, expecting he would speak at some point.

Without turning and breaking cover, so to speak, I couldn't get a good look at him. However, from my sideways glancing, I assessed a pair of sensible lace-up shoes, albeit well-worn, and a pair of grey trousers, the sort of thing my father might wear and call slacks. Although after meeting his young American lover, my father changed his wardrobe, choosing to shop at *Superdry* for the first time in his life, plus binning off his Y-fronts in favour of something more modern for his young floozy to pull down.

The only other feature I noticed was my mystery man wore a camel-coloured coat. Maybe he had that file tucked inside or suffered from a spring cold because the weather was far too warm for anything more substantial than a light jacket.

Although he fitted inside my relatively wide age group, he didn't appear to sniff, so perhaps his cold was on the way out. Whilst waiting for something to happen, I scanned the park, disappointed that Courteney appeared to have stood me up. Although she had seemed nice enough and had surprised me with her love of books and high intelligence, I guess she was like most people I met, as in a bit false. As per usual, I liked to see the good side of everyone, which often left me feeling somewhat let down.

I clicked my phone. Five minutes had now elapsed, and this man still hadn't made any attempt to make contact – what the hell was he waiting for? I glanced left and turned back to face forward. He appeared clean-shaven but, other than that, I didn't glean any further information during my furtive two-second assessment. Then, I sensed him turn and look at me – I glanced around.

We eyeballed each other. I raised my eyebrows, and he reciprocated – I nodded. He nodded to my nod, nudging his head over his shoulder to where the rough sleeper lay camped out by the toilet block. I nodded, nodding to his nod, now wondering if he was suggesting we should move to a more secluded location so that he could hand over the file.

I considered that all this head movement was becoming slightly ridiculous. Yes, I understand he may want to stay anonymous for whatever reason. However, unless Bridget was a member of the British Secret Service or a spy for the FSB, and this guy was an agent for the CIA, I really thought this clandestine meeting was a bit over the top.

I decided to just ask, so I shifted in my seat and faced him. He followed my movement, then opened his coat by pulling the sides apart by way of parting his hands that he'd stuffed in the side pockets.

I gasped as my mouth dropped.

He grinned, presumably delighted and rather proud of his curved erection.

"Fucking hell! What the fuck …"

As quickly as he exposed himself, he covered up and scuttled away. I jumped up and open-mouthed watched as he scooted across the grass playing field with a somewhat gangly gait. I guess running with an erection wasn't that straightforward; something I'd never tried.

Now fearing some of the over-protective mums might have noticed the whole sordid event, I swivelled around to see if any of them had also spotted that hideous sight.

It appeared one had, as I spotted one mum leave her young child and stride purposefully towards me. I prayed she thought

141

I was a victim and not part of the depraved event that had just transpired. I hovered, not knowing whether to become embroiled in a conversation that could turn into a melee resulting in the police attending or skedaddle like the willy-waving guy who'd now made it across to the park gates.

For sure, if these mums thought I was a willing participant in alfresco exposure, I wouldn't have time to make my escape before the entire fleet of panda cars from Fairfield Police Station were down upon me. So, deciding that running could be construed as an admission of guilt, I waited to see what this advancing woman might accuse me of.

"Bleedin' hell. I take it he wasn't the guy you're s'posed to be meeting? Or was he?"

"Courteney?" I exclaimed, my voice rising into soprano, as my calling out of her name came out as a high-pitched question.

She halted a few feet away and thumped her hands on the hips of her ripped jeans whilst swilling her gum around. "Err … yeah. Who the hell did you fink I was? We agreed I'd be here. Gotta say, though, I wasn't aware you were into cottaging."

"Woah—"

"Look, I ain't 'ere to judge. Whatever floats your boat is fine with me. But I think you and your mate exposing yourselves near a kids' playground is a bit frigging sick."

"No, hang on—"

"If that's what you're into, then I guess that's why you weren't too interested in my discounted offer."

"No."

142

"No, what? You're not into sucking dick in public toilets, or no, you're not into women. Which is it?"

"Christ!" I rubbed my hands across my face. "How do I get into these situations?"

"I get it. You wanted me to come and spy on you, like some sick fantasy where you get off touching other men whilst someone watches. You sick fucker. I'm in a good mind to tell Karl. He'll either cut your dick off or tip you over the landing balcony."

"Jesus, Courteney. Shut up and listen! I'm not into all that," I waved my hand around, gesticulating at nothing in particular, but just felt the need to become animated. "I didn't ask you here. *You* volunteered. *And* I have no idea who that pervert was," I threw my arm in the direction of where the willy-waver had shot across the park. "Or, for that matter, where the bloody bloke, who rang me yesterday, has got to. Christ, I'm not some bloody pervert. And yes, as you asked, I am attracted to woman, especially ones that look like you."

Courteney shifted her stance, leaving one hand planted on her hip whilst pointing at me with the other. The swilling gum didn't halt for one moment as her mouth performed perfectly timed revolutions.

"Got a bit of fight in ya, I see," she smirked.

"Sorry. I've had a shit morning. And I was convinced this bloke would show up after calling me yesterday. I guess it was some sick joke Bridget is playing."

"She's really kippered you, ain't she?"

"I'm beginning to think so. Anyway, who are those kids you were playing with? I didn't see you turn up, although I wasn't expecting you to be with all those mums."

143

Courteney turned and waved to a woman who now held the hand of the same little girl as she guided her down a plastic slide. "I came up with Trace. She's a mate; we used to work the estate togever. I thought we could take her little 'un to the park and, that way, I could watch what was going on without looking suspicious."

"Right. Well, I thought you hadn't turned up. I didn't recognise you in that get-up with your hair tied back."

Courteney assessed her clothing and then smirked at me. "I don't wear PVC thigh-length boots and leather miniskirts all the time."

"No … I guess you don't."

Courteney stepped forward in her brilliant-white Nike trainers and closed the gap between us. The trainers looked new, and I wondered which shop on the High Street had suffered a stock shrinkage issue this week. Again, as she performed in her kitchen, she came to a halt in my personal space, causing me to involuntarily try and take half a step back, only prevented by the wooden bench seat.

As she looked up at me, I became mesmerised by her rotating gum, as if she had perfected the routine to use as some hypnosis technique. "So, which look do you prefer?"

"What?"

"This look, jeans and hoodie, or the PVC boots look?"

"Oh," I nervously grinned, feeling, once again, slightly hemmed in. "I really wouldn't like to say."

"Well, you said you fancied me, so I guess you like one of the looks."

"Did I?"

"Yeah. You just said so when you had your rant and gobbed off about not being a pervert."

"Are you sure?"

She rolled her eyes. "Err … yeah! You said I am attracted to woman, especially ones that look like you. Meaning, as in me."

"I said that?"

"Yup. So, you do fancy me, or were you lying? Which is it?"

A nervous laugh escaped my mouth as my mind whirred around, wondering what game she was playing. Was she touting for business? Could this be her way of securing a transaction, much like other businesses would use social media or TV advertising or stick a flyer through your letterbox? I guess her chosen profession limited her options because all three of those mediums probably didn't lend themselves to that sort of advertising, even after the watershed.

She leaned forward and kissed my cheek. "How old are you?"

Shocked, I scanned the park, half expecting the thug Karl to suddenly appear and stick his fist through my face. The force of the impending punch would result in me taking flight and ending up on the other side of the toilet block.

"Thirty-two," I answered, still warily scanning the park for a thug wearing a black hoodie in need of a visit to the dental hygienist.

"Oh, you don't look it. I had you pegged for late twen'ies."

"Why d'you ask?"

"Dunno. But you are a bit naïve for a bloke in his thirties."

145

"You're not the first to accuse me of that. In fact, *Stinkor* reaffirmed that very point an hour ago when he pissed himself laughing at my suggestion about getting my old job back."

"Oh. As you said, shit day."

"You could say."

"Come on. Let's nip into town. I'll buy you a coffee, and we can get a cream cake."

"I can't imagine you eat many cream cakes, not with a figure like yours. Once on the lips, twice on the hips, as they say."

"You saying I'm skinny?"

"No. Sorry. I don't know why I said that. I told you, I have the propensity to open my gob before engaging my brain. You're not skinny … you're not fat, of course. You're …" I halted before saying something stupid.

"You're cute."

I delivered that nervous laugh, unsure how to respond. "Are we allowed to go into town for a coffee?"

"What you mean, it's illegal? Like the guy waving his cock around, we might get arrested?" Courteney grabbed my arm, mockingly scanning around as if worried about a police swoop.

"No, you know what I mean. Karl."

"That twat. Don't worry about him."

"You said he might castrate me or throw me off the balcony. Sorry, but I don't put those thoughts in the don't worry category."

"That's if you're a nonce. But you ain't, are you?"

"No. You could do better than him, you know?"

"Like you?" Courteney turned and waved to her mate, who waved back before encouraging her daughter to wave. Courteney exaggeratedly waved to the little girl, blowing a string of kisses her way before linking arms with me. "Come on. And you don't have to answer that. I know decent guys like you would never look at trash like me."

I rammed my hands in my jeans, keeping her arm linked in mine. "Don't put yourself down."

"What, like you do yourself?"

"That's different. I'm a bit of a knob. You're not. I think you're ..." Again, I held back from saying something stupid.

"See, you do fancy me," she giggled. "You are cute."

14

Sonic The Hedgehog

"You going to eat all of that?"

"Uh-huh," Courteney mumbled through the sizable chunk of chocolate éclair that protruded out of her mouth, a wispy blob of cream now attached to the end of her nose, affording her the look of a unicorn. As her front teeth clamped down on the cream bun, dissecting a good third of its mass akin to a Great White slicing in half an unfortunate swimmer, she used her middle and index finger's cerise-coloured painted nails to force the confection mixture into her mouth, resulting in her cheeks bulging like a chipmunk or as if she'd just suffered extensive dental surgery with the inevitable swelling.

I shook my head in disbelief as she attempted to move the mixture around her mouth. I feared she would treat me to a vision of mulched choux pastry due to her requiring to open her mouth because, surely, she would either choke to death or suffocate if she attempted to persevere.

She grinned, fortunately not affording me the view. Finally, after rolling it around for some considerable time, she managed to swallow. A vision akin to witnessing a python as it forces a bear-sized creature through its gullet.

"Wha'?" she fired out, somewhat illegibly.

"Nothing," I chuckled. "You've got a quart of whipped cream on the end of your nose."

She performed a cross-eyed motion whilst attempting to reach the blob with her tongue before giggling. Then, somewhat expertly and in one swift movement, she swished it off and into her mouth via the use of one of those cerise fingernails.

"Love éclairs."

"No shit."

"Don't you eat cakes?"

"I'm not hungry. To be honest with you, this morning's events have zapped my appetite."

Courteney had insisted on buying. A rare treat for the retailer, I guess. However, thieving from a coffee shop was probably difficult, as in limited self-service, or self-nicking, in Courteney's case. That said, my coffee date expertly slipped a saucer-sized gold-wrapped chocolate coin in her pocket when distracting the young lad behind the till with a question that forced him to turn around. The oldest trick in the book, which I suspect most children in their time had committed once in their life when visiting the corner shop. I tried it with a tube of *Toffo* sweets when I was about thirteen whilst trying to impress my peers. I didn't even like the sweets; of course, they caught me.

Grounded for a hundred years – that's what it felt like – along with the confiscation of my Sega Mega Drive, I thought my world had ended. At the time, I vowed to hate my father for the rest of his life – without my video game, life wasn't worth living. Clearly, Courteney hadn't suffered such a fate and thus had many years to perfect her craft.

I had offered to buy, you know, the old-fashioned attitude of the gentleman buying. However, Courteney insisted on paying for the drinks, stating she was earning and unwittingly reminding me I wasn't. I chose to ignore the chocolate coin theft; some things are better left unsaid.

"What d'you reckon happened to that bloke, then?" She licked the side of her second eclair, seductively hoovering up the cream that oozed from the sides. I'm no expert, but I guess the confectioner became distracted this morning, as it appeared Courteney's éclair contained at least double the specified amount. As I watched her tongue expertly glide up and down the sausage-shaped bun, lapping up the excess cream, my mind wandered off to where it really shouldn't.

"The bloke who didn't turn up or the one waving his dick around."

Courteney snorted a laugh as she leaned forward, just avoiding firing globules of cream and saliva at me. "Oh, Jesus. Now I've seen a fair few cocks in my time, but bloody hell, never some geezer waving his one-eyed python around in the park like some well-hung stripper at a hen party. Even for me, that was a new one."

"Well hung? Can't say I had that good a look."

"Yeah, it looked pretty hefty, even from where I was standing."

"I'll take your word for it. Now, I take it, before we started talking about the relative size of willy-waver's tackle, you were asking about the mystery man who was a no-show."

Courteney nodded. "You wanna bite?" she offered up the unchewed, although licked, end of her cake.

I held my palm up. "You're alright, thank you."

She shrugged. "You don't know what you're missing."

"I'll risk not knowing."

"What you gonna do now, then?"

"Oh, I don't know. I think it was probably Bridget playing games by getting some bloke to ring me and offer up false hope."

"I don't see why she would do that."

"Well, I guess to rub salt in the wounds."

"But why? If you're right, and she's run off with your business, surely, she'd put as much distance between you and her as possible."

"Maybe. But what else can be the reason?"

"You pissed anyone else off?"

"Loaded question."

Courteney raised her eyebrows as her teeth sunk into her cake.

"Yeah, okay. So, most of my mates have deserted me, but I can't think any of them are twisted enough to start playing games. Maybe the chap got held up and was running late. We left the park at about half past. What if he turned up after we left?"

I waited for Courteney to complete her python impression, her swallowing of the cake and not the one-eyed variety.

"Nah. You had any calls?"

"What d'you mean."

151

"He'd have called you if he showed up and you weren't there."

"Oh."

"I reckon it's a straight-up diversion job."

"What?"

"That call was to get you in that park at that pacific time. Some bloke was never going to turn up and offer up any evidence about that bitch who stiffed you."

"It's specific, not pacific."

"Yeah, I know the difference. You taking the piss on how I speak?"

"No, sorry."

"Fuck me. I'm trying to help you, and all you can do is pretend to be Professor 'iggins."

"Yup, sorry. That was crass."

"Yup, is informal and incorrect. The correct word is, yes."

Surprised by that statement, I scrunched my nose. Courteney smirked and raised her eyebrows before shovelling in the last of her cake. Less than twenty-four hours into our somewhat unlikely alliance, this girl never ceased to amaze me. No woman devours books and classic literature before slipping off to make a porn film – well, maybe one.

"What was that about a straight-up diversion?"

Courteney jogged her head from side to side as she chewed her cake, waving her hand around as if that action would assist her jaw to power through it quicker.

"Right, I reckon you might have been set up."

"I thought you said Bridget would have skedaddled by now."

"No, someone else."

"Christ, who else?"

"You tell me?" She pulled out her phone and appeared to tap away, presumably firing off a text.

"So, someone wanted me in that park at that time."

"Uh-huh." Her thumbs continued to dance across the screen of her phone, briefly pausing before repeating. The whoosh sound of the text message exchange between Courteney and whoever was just about audible above the low chatter coming from the couple on the next table.

"Oh, shit, you don't reckon willy-waver had somehow got my number and lured me there hoping I fancied a quick session in the gents, do you?"

"No. You've been stiffed."

"No pun intended, I guess?"

"Err … what?

"Oh, forget it. What do you mean, I've been stiffed?

"We've got a problem. Well, pacifically, you have." Courteney flipped her screen around, showing me the text exchange with a person called Deli.

"Who's Deli?" After her previous rebuke, this wasn't the time to mention specific and pacific again.

"A mate. She lives in the next flat along the landin'."

I leaned forward to read the text exchange.

Courteney: *'Hey babe. Any bait?'*

Deli: *Yo. bare buki touring. Dissing our landin. Wite geezer long garms bust that new peng flat.*

Courteney: *Shittin.*

Deli: *Na U Chipse him?*

Courteney: *Leave it. When?*

Deli: *Gone def no mandem.*

Courteney: *Cheers babe.*

Deli: Two black thumbs emojis.

I peered past the phone to Courteney, indicating I'd read the texts.

"Guess you don't get 'em."

"If you're suggesting I don't understand, you're spot on."

"Yeah, thought so. Basically, Deli is saying a white bloke who looked out of place because he's not known on the estate bust into your flat this morning."

"What? You're joking!"

"That bloke asked to meet you at eleven to make sure your flat was empty. I'm guessing you ain't given a key to no one else?"

"No. Could it be my landlord?"

"Nah. Deli knows everyone. She's saying this geezer is unknown. Whoever they are, they needed you out of the way so they could break into your gaff."

"Well, they'll be sorely disappointed because apart from my bed and a three-legged chest of drawers, there's bugger all in there." Although a bit pissed off that I'd been burgled, the saving grace was I had nothing worth taking. I guess the thief would have been somewhat pissed about choosing my flat as

154

a target because, as they scoured the four rooms, they would only discover a tatty paperback to lob in their swag bag.

"That's my point. I don't fink they broke in to steal anyfink."

"What then? Squatters? Oh, bollocks, what the hell am I going to do if I have squatters in the bloody place?"

"Damian. Don't be so bloody fick. We need to get going." Courteney stood, raising her coffee cup with her as she poured the remainder down her throat. "Come on. We ain't got much time."

"For what?"

"Jesus, man, you are dumb. Someone got you out of your flat to plant something in there."

"What? Like a bomb."

"No, you donkey. Evidence of some sort. You're being fitted up. If we don't find it before the filth, you're in deep shit."

Courteney's explanation rolled around my head, clanging into the sides of my brain. Like one of those Christmas-cracker Chinese puzzles that, as hard as you try to arrange the pieces, nothing fitted, nothing made sense.

"Damian, shift your arse. We have to go!"

I hopped up and caught up with the gold-coin thief as she reached the door. "What was that thing your friend said about peg and chirping?"

"Peng and chirpse?"

"Yeah."

"It means that you're fit, and am I hittin' on you."

"Oh. Are you?" I trotted to keep up with her as we scooted down the High Street. "Well?"

"I might be. But I fink we need to get back. We can chat about your good looks later, alright?" she threw out without turning to face me or halt her high-speed jaunt.

I picked up my pace, keeping up with Courteney as we hot-footed along. I wasn't quite sure what to make of her comment. Yes, Courteney was every bit as attractive as Bridget, and they both worked in the entertainment business, but that was where the similarity ended. However, perhaps despite her light-fingers, this girl lacked the evil streak I'd recently discovered my ex-girlfriend possessed. That said, I wasn't sure what I thought about a porn star hitting on me, and more worryingly, I probably had more significant issues to deal with if her friend Deli was to be believed.

15

Watch With Mother

"Right, then. What's the plan?" Terry drained his coffee before scooping up the breakfast plates and ferrying them to the sink.

"Darling, dishwasher, remember? Washing up in a bowl is something out of the Victorian times. Even the scummy sort who live in cheap rented housing own dishwashers."

"Oh, yes. I'm not used to all these new-fangled gadgets."

"Oh, Terry, you sound like my grandmother; God bless her soul. You've only been dead for thirty-odd years. Next, you'll be claiming you used a mangle and soaked in a tin bath in front of the fire after sweeping chimneys."

"Well, as a kid growing up in the '50s, I never imagined all these technological advances. I can remember our first television. After watching the Queen's Coronation on a neighbour's TV, my parents decided to save up for one. I can remember it was a bloody great thing made of Bakelite, and my mother kept a white doily on the top. My mother and I used to watch *Andy Pandy* together."

"Watch with Mother."

"Yes, that was it."

"How lovely," she replied with a hint of sarcasm. "This is starting to sound like an episode of *Antiques Roadshow*, with some old crusty reminiscing about the good old days whilst acquiring a valuation on some crummy-old heirloom that's worth bugger-all."

"Well, if I hadn't died in that hotel room in '83, I'd be sixty-five this year. I'd be collecting my pension." Terry turned and pointed at Deana as she sipped her coffee. "Of course, you'll be able to get yours in a couple of years," he chuckled.

"If you're referring to the fact that I'm just over fifty, be very careful."

"You wish. What is it, two years before you start queuing at the post office on a Thursday morning with the rest of the blue rinse brigade after making good use of your free bus pass?"

"Very droll, I'm sure. Now, whilst you've been lying in that grave up at that graveyard for the past thirty years, I might remind you that you missed the odd thing or two. As well as the Cold War ending, the melting of the polar ice caps, and Barkers in Kensington High Street closing, which was a great shame as that left only Harrods as a decent store in London; also, internet banking has changed the way we move money. Cash, my darling boy, is like washing up bowls, a thing of the past."

Terry shrugged.

"As you pointed out a moment ago, we are both dead. So, I think the Department for Work and Pensions won't need to worry about paying out my pension. Also, those stupid idiots who run the country, and it doesn't matter which variety there are as they are as bad as each other, thought it would be a good idea to raise the age that a woman can claim her pension. Us women now have to wait as long as men, can you believe?"

"Well, you lot were all fighting for women's rights with all that bra-burning stuff. So, it stands to reason that you can't get your pension earlier than men. You lot can't have it both bloody ways."

"You lot?"

"Women. Equal rights and all that feminist stuff. They were banging on about it in my day. I remember a posse of till ladies lay siege to my office, claiming we should pay them the same as warehousemen. I put them straight, I can tell you. How could a housewife earning a bit of pin money whilst sitting at a checkout expect to earn the same as a man who has the responsibility of putting food on the table?"

"My God." Deana shook her head in disbelief. "I suppose the only positive I can take from that statement is that it demonstrates how far we've come in thirty-odd years. I suggest, darling, you keep that attitude to yourself because outside of these four walls, you're liable to get lynched! And, dear boy, bra-burning feminists is something that paradoxically never happened. It was a fallacy that men conjured up to put down women."

"Blimey, touched a nerve, have I?"

"Yes, Terry. And regarding equality, some are more equal than others, to quote Napoleon."

"The pig, not the short bloke who rebuffed Josephine?"

"Yes, but I don't think he actually said that. Although you and the short dictator have much in common regarding rebuffing a beautiful woman's advances."

Terry nervously grinned, worried that Deana, only dressed in her thin silk dressing gown, might advance. "Who won the Cold War then?" he asked, keen to change the subject and deflect her Jezebel thoughts. "I take it we did, as we don't have a communist dictator."

"Perestroika, or Glasnost, whatever it was called in the '90s."

"What?"

Deana held her hand aloft. "Oh Terry, this isn't a double-history lesson. I'm not a schoolteacher, so don't start asking questions. When we return from our little jaunt, I'll set you up with my iPad. Then you can surf away to your heart's content learning about the last thirty years' momentous historical events."

Terry raised his hand, just as he would have when at school.

"No. I'm not explaining iPad or surfing at the moment. Now, we have to get going. Referring to your earlier question, I think we have no choice other than talking to our boy, see what has happened and if he can shed any light on the subject."

"Good job you're invisible. Otherwise, Damian might find meeting his dead mother a bit of a shock."

"Yes, indeed. I know we didn't share the greatest mother-son relationship, but I will admit to being slightly put out that he didn't attend my funeral."

"Yes, yes, I'm sure you are."

"I know he attended your mother's last year."

"Oh, really? Did my parents know of him?"

"Oh, darling, do wake up. He tends to their graves, remember. Your parents really took to the boy. Of course, they weren't particularly welcoming to me when I presented myself on their doorstep when eight months pregnant, as I'm sure you can imagine. Our relationship slipped further when I left Sidney, but they took an interest in Damian as he grew up."

"Oh. I don't know what to say. Hang on, do Kim and Damian know each other?"

"No, not as far as I know. Your parents were very keen that Damian wasn't known about. They visited him to give Christmas and birthday presents alike. However, you must remember, he is my son, and I am the scarlet woman who apparently killed you."

"Yes, I can see that could be awkward. So, how do we find him?"

"Good question. My sources suggest our boy now rents a flat on the Broxworth Estate."

"Oh, bloody hell! You've got to be joking. Christ, what is it with my kids and that hideous place?"

"Quite."

"So, his girlfriend conned him out of his business, and now the poor sod has to live there."

"Yes, I'm afraid so. Unfortunately, I don't think we can go back there after last week's rather silly events in that betting shop. However, we could start by asking around in the other shops if anyone knows him. I seem to recall a grubby-looking takeaway and an open-all-hours type establishment. So, shall we start there?"

"Bloody hell. We'd better get our riot gear on if we have to return to that God-awful place."

"Yes, darling. It's a good job I'm dead because being seen there twice in as many weeks would have a rather detrimental effect on my social standing."

~

Transportation for the walking dead is a tricky thing, especially as Deana is invisible to all apart from the dead and some small children who are fully alive. Deana and Terry, whilst on their earlier mission to save his daughter, Kim, which also involved ruining his old mate Sam, previously used various forms of transport to get around town. Although Ziggy, along with everything else, had left Deana's husband's Maserati behind when he returned to his life on the Gold Coast, they knew taking it out for another spin was way too risky.

Ubers and public transport were their only option, and although Deana found the local buses degrading in terms of comfort and other clientele, that had become their preferred way of travelling.

After taking their bus ride and zipping through one of the alleyways from Coldhams Lane to the estate, they headed straight for the open-all-hours convenience store.

"When was the last time you saw Damian?"

"Hmm ... probably his twenty-first birthday."

Terry halted. Deana, who'd carried on walking, turned and raised an eyebrow.

"Darling?"

"Jesus, no wonder you didn't win any motherhood awards. Christ, woman, our son is thirty-two and the last time you saw him was over ten years ago despite living in the same bloody town."

"Darling, I don't think you are in any position to criticise me. Anyway, Damian has his own life, and I had mine."

"Yes, I get that. But bloody hell, weren't you at all interested?"

"Darling, as the years passed, Sidney wasn't that supportive in allowing access. When Damian turned eighteen, he chose not to be too interested in searching out his mother."

"Yeah, but Christ, woman."

"Terry, if you hadn't died in that bed that evening, you and I could have raised our boy together. But no, you decided to have a heart attack and leave me with a child, booted out by my first husband, and jobless after Freshcom's decided that they would like to dispense with my services."

Terry stepped forward. "You wanted to be with me? We only had one night together. Are you suggesting you would have wanted to leave your husband for me?"

"Don't get all above your station. But yes, even though I didn't know I was pregnant with Damian at the time, I think I knew I wanted you." Deana laid her hand on his chest and peered up at him. "Few men have stolen my heart, but you did. I think I could have stayed with you for the rest of my life. But you, you idiot, you had a bloody heart attack and left me."

"Oh."

"Yes, oh."

"Well, you seemed to go through men like a dose of salts. I can't imagine if I had lived, you would have stayed with me."

"We'll never know, will we?"

"No, I suppose not."

"And my darling, you would have faced a dilemma because when you died, I became pregnant with Damian and your wife was already pregnant with little Kimmy."

"Jesus, that would have been a bloody nightmare."

"Yes, can you imagine?" she chuckled.

"Come on, we'd better move. I get the feeling if we stand around for too long anywhere on this estate, we're liable to attract some unwanted attention."

"Yes, quite right. I don't like the look of those youths over by that takeaway. They look rather shifty to me, and I'm not overly keen regarding the way they keep looking at us."

"Well, they can only see me, so I guess they think I'm some nutter or drunk who's spent all night in the pub."

"Oi, tosser, over 'ere," called out one of the youths, as he hefted his shoulder off the front window. The three others remained in position as they slouched against the shop front of the takeaway that appeared, based on the extensive colony of blue-bottle flies buzzing about on the window, to be the sort of establishment that served up a free helping of salmonella or dysentery with each portion of fried rice.

"Oh, hell. Not again," muttered Deana.

The youth exaggeratedly sauntered towards Terry. Deana thought he either suffered from sciatica or was attempting to copy the John Wayne swagger. The crotch of his joggers appeared to hang so low Deana assumed he must have lost his braces or he'd shit himself. Whichever, she thought he needed to hoist them up because she had no desire to look at his underpants that were clearly on show.

A middle-aged bald man cut across his path, causing the youth to slow his advance towards them. The swaggering youth appeared to consider taking the chap to task, which would have afforded them the opportunity to move on. However, Baldy jumped into a rusting Transit van, leaving the path clear for his advance on Terry.

"I know we've dealt with a few of these situations, but there are four of them. So, I think we might need to make a run for it," hissed Terry.

"You dizzy, blud?"

Terry glanced at Deana, who shrugged – like Terry, not understanding what the youth said. Terry thought the heavy gold chain around his neck that swung wildly from side to side as he advanced towards them could cause serious injury. One false move and he'd knock out his gold tooth that appeared as he grinned.

"Sorry, I don't understand."

The youth turned to his mates, raising his chin and nodding whilst holding that gold-toothed grin.

"I said, you dizzy … crazy?"

"Oh. No."

"Us heads not seen your like. Your yard around 'ere?"

"Look, mate. I have no idea what you're on about."

Deana stepped away. "Terry, time to move. I could whack him with my handbag. But as you pointed out, there're four of them. Although we have the advantage of surprise, I really don't fancy our chances."

"Jesus, woman, how the hell do you get me in these situations?"

"Terry, just move!"

"Oi, dizzy. Who you talking to? You dissing me?" the youth, who Terry thought was probably still of school age, appeared to become aggressive.

"Jordan! Get over 'ere," boomed a woman, as she and a bloke appeared from one of the alleyways that served as access to the estate.

The confident boy with the gold tooth nodded to the woman, who thrust her hands on her hips and beckoned him with a nod of her head. From what he could see, Terry thought the woman was way too young to be his mother, but he and Deana grabbed the distraction as an opportunity to scuttle away.

Deana halted near the alleyway from where the woman and bloke had appeared, grabbing Terry's arm. "Oh, surely not?" she blurted, whilst staring back at the couple.

"Deana, don't stop. We need to move."

"Hang on, darling. I think I know that man."

"Really? I can't imagine you know anyone on this bloody estate."

"Hide in the alley and keep watch. I need to check and perhaps listen to their conversation."

"Deana!" hissed Terry, as she jauntily skipped towards the couple, who now stood in a huddle with the youth and his mates who'd joined him.

Terry spotted the man shoot his head around to look at him as he called out Deana's name.

Deana walked straight up to him and inspected his face like a tourist whilst visiting Madame Tussauds, scrutinising the model and looking for inconsistencies and imperfections where the artist had failed to capture the true likeness of the latest superstar. "Oh, darling. I think this is our boy. Although, I must say, if this tarty thing next to him is his new girlfriend, he's sunk far lower than I thought."

16

High Plains Drifter

My head shot around to look at the bloke who, for some odd reason, just blurted out my dead mother's name. He seemed to be holding position slapped against the side wall of the convenience store, which, with its steel mesh covering the door and window, resembled a high-security prison rather than a local store where you'd pick up a tin of beans and a lottery ticket.

The odd chap hovered inside the alley from which Courteney and I had just stepped after she'd paid for a taxi from town. Unfortunately, the Uber driver had refused to drive onto the Broxworth, fair enough, so we'd had to hot-foot our way from Coldhams Lane back to the estate.

Like me, he didn't appear to fit into the typical look of any resident of this odious place, sporting a rabbit-in-headlights appearance. I had no idea who he was or why he'd called out that name to no one in particular. Also, as Courteney had suggested, we were in a hurry, so why she'd called over a bunch of delinquent-looking youths, God knows. I guess she knew what she was doing, so I decided to play along.

As the group of youths gathered around Courteney, who appeared to be holding court, they seemed to have lost interest in the odd bloke who still watched from his position in the alley.

"You seen any strange geezers milling about on my landin' or the estate?"

"Might have."

"Jordan, stop pissing about. You're heading for a slap."

"Don't dis me and my crew."

"Crew? Oh, Jordan, you're still a kid, you little twat. I'll get my Karl to bend you in half so you can shove your dick up your arse if you don't start talking."

"I could do your arse if ya like?" his accent poorly imitating that of someone of West Indian origin, although clearly, Jordan had no such heritage.

The slap that caught the lad's face landed with such speed that he and his mates didn't see it coming. Shocked at the ferocity of Courteney's attack, my jaw dropped, now a smidge concerned about what would happen next. Although of school age, the four youths appeared streetwise and, I suspected, could handle themselves.

"Shit, Courts, that hurt!" A significant change in accent to his earlier suggestion of what he wanted to do to Courteney's bottom.

"Watch your mouth, you shit. Now, start talking, unless you want to explain to Karl why you fink you can dis me."

"Oh, darling, this place is so awful. Can you hear this girl? Did you hear what that boy just said? I can't, for the life of me, imagine what their homes must be like. And what are the parents doing, allowing them to talk like that?"

169

The odd bloke broke cover and stepped towards us. Only I noticed because Courteney had the attention of the youths, who were probably thinking about how Karl might rearrange their body parts. After meeting Courteney's boyfriend earlier this morning, I was in no doubt that he was capable of such an act.

"Terry, stay back. I don't know how this is going to play out."

The chap seemed to slow his advance, hovering about ten yards away. We locked eyes. He seemed familiar, as if we'd known each other for years. His features and facial expression suggested we could be related – a weird feeling because I was reasonably confident that I didn't have a brother and, judging his age, he would have to be a twin brother. We held each other's gaze whilst my potty-mouthed python-impersonating guardian angel, in the form of a brazen lady of the night, quizzed the now obedient youths.

"Deana, is it him?"

I narrowed my eyes and involuntarily glanced around to see who this odd man was addressing, although aware that no one else was in close vicinity. I could only assume he was talking to Courteney because she was the only woman in earshot, so I presumed he'd confused her with someone else. Unless, of course, one of these youths had a rather unusual name. Well, I guess John Wayne was called Marion, and I believe Richard Gere's middle name is Tiffany, so if it's good enough for them, well, maybe. That said, any low-life youth gang member might struggle to get by on this estate with a name like Deana – the same name as my dead mother.

"Terry, for Christ's sake, shut it! You're going to cause a scene. And yes, I'm fairly certain it's him."

"You alright, mate?"

My question halted Courteney's interrogation as all six of us stared at the bloke, who appeared to shuffle nervously on the spot like a naughty boy caught up to no good.

"That's him," Jordan swivelled around, his gold chain launching in flight around his neck as he pointed. "He's the geezer I was telling you about."

"Oi! Who are you?" spat Courteney. "D'you know this geezer, Damian?"

Courteney didn't wait for my reply, which I failed to offer. Instead, she muscled past me and confronted the chap, who hopped back a pace as she barrelled up to him whilst waving an accusing finger. "Oi, I asked you who you are?"

Like an obedient pack of hounds, Jordan and his crew joined Courteney, showing strength in numbers, which I guess was essential when confronting anyone stupid enough to walk about the Broxworth Estate. Two of the boys circled behind him, in what appeared a well-practised pincer movement the pack employed as they homed in on their prey when out intimidating folk, leaving me standing yards away.

Something gnawed at my brain. I felt sure I must know this bloke, which suggested he wasn't a local. Was he the git who'd bust into my flat and, as Courteney suggested, planted something there that was going to make my life a billion times worse? Although, after the last couple of weeks, this morning's failure to secure my old employment and an incident with a pervert in the park, I doubted if that were at all possible.

"Oh, darling, you're a nightmare. Now we've got a situation. I think you better make a run for it, and I'll catch you up."

"Well? Lost your tongue, have ya?"

"Courts, we could shank the git for ya," suggested Jordan, who seemed to have forgotten the slap, now appearing to show his manhood credentials in the way of displaying his gang-culture testosterone. Although not to be confused with his suggestion about sticking it up Courteney's backside, the very reason for receiving the slap in the first place.

"I'm Terry."

"Right, Terry. What you doing 'ere?"

"I'm looking for Damian Statham."

"Darling, I hope you have a plan because as much as I'm pretty nifty with swinging my Hermès handbag around, I can't see this is a good idea. I think we need to gracefully retreat and regroup."

"Who are you?" I called out from behind the melee, causing Courteney and her pack to turn and look at me. This strange character, who glanced to his left and nodded to thin air before returning his attention to me, who'd twice called out my mother's name, rather spookily also had the name of my dead biological father.

"Damian? You are Damian Statham?"

I nodded.

"I need to talk to you about your situation. You know, about what happened with your girlfriend."

"So, you're the bloke who stood me up this morning. Where were you at eleven?" I stepped forward; Jordan and his crew parted, but Courteney held her ground.

"Sorry?"

"Hang on, mate. Don't play games with me, 'cos I've had it up to here today." I tapped my forehead, indicating how tall the pile of shite I'd stepped into since entering Halitosis Harry's office. With my newfound confidence, supplied mainly by my leggy-blonde accomplice, I stepped close to Courteney, just inside this guy's personal space. "You called me to arrange a meet. So, come on, what's the crack? What information have you got?"

"Courts, I could cut him."

"Jordan, piss off and take your puppies with you. You couldn't cut butter, you little twat."

Out of the corner of my eye, I noticed the gang slope away, surprised that Courteney could *dis* them, as seemed to be the word used on the estate, and get away with it. However, as she was with Karl, I guess that afforded her some status amongst the less desirables who made up the vast majority who resided here.

"Oh, well, she's a delight! I'm a little disappointed Sidney didn't raise our boy to keep better company. Although, I suppose she managed to discharge the services of those revolting scoundrels, albeit in a rather vulgar manner."

As was the case when Courteney questioned him, this Terry bloke seemed reluctant to talk, constantly glancing to his left as if suffering with some odd affliction. Moreover, he had a guilty aura about him that suggested he *was* the bloke who'd played me, thus gaining access to my flat.

"You the fuzz? You like, the filth? I think I can smell pig shit."

I glanced at Courteney, as did the man in front of me who raised his eyebrows at her statement, a little taken aback by her vulgarity.

"No, I'm not the police. Look, I don't know anything about a meeting this morning. But I know about Bridget. I'm just here to talk to you because I may be able to help."

"Do we know each other?"

"No, but I know ... knew your mother."

I snorted my disdain in response to the mention of the woman who abandoned me. "Well, she's dead, and I guess about as useless as when she was alive."

"Charming, I'm sure. We could abort? I'll advise the powers that be, that we no longer harbour any interest in this mission if that's going to be his attitude. How ungrateful!"

"Okay, let's leave your mother out of this for the moment."

"Are you her son, the same as me? She shagged her way through most blokes in the town, so I'd be amazed if I don't have a half-brother or sister somewhere." I'd often thought about that very point, knowing what my father, with some regularity, used to say about her. As I assessed his facial features, I deduced we had some similarities.

"Terry, darling, this is all rather unpleasant. Can we go? Because I really don't think I can suffer much more of this character assassination."

Terry glanced left and dismissively shook his head before turning back to face me. Courteney had become uncharacteristically quiet, not even swilling gum. I felt sure

174

her mouth must be wondering what had happened to her with its apparent lack of action.

"I'm not your brother," he dead-pan-faced announced, delivered like the stranger in *High Plains Drifter.*

I momentarily considered this man was here to clean up the estate, just as Clint Eastwood had in the mining town of Lago. That said, I couldn't see his horse, and he wasn't chomping on a cheroot.

Courteney, presumably deciding her mouth had been closed for too long, dragged me from my thoughts. "So, if you ain't the geezer who phoned Damian yesterday and you ain't the filth, how come you know so much?"

Before this Terry bloke could respond, and at lightning speed, Karl appeared between us, forcing Terry back with his hand planted on his chest.

"I don't know you. No one talks to my bitch who I don't know."

"Karl!"

"Shut it, bitch," he bellowed, without turning around.

Now I had a dilemma. I needed to know who this Terry bloke was and what he knew about Bridget. However, now that I had Karl between us, I didn't fancy my chances of persuading Courteney's man to leave us. I thought he might not take it too kindly if I advised him he was interrupting a private conversation.

"Darling, this is our cue to leave."

Terry raised his hands and slowly backed away before turning and scurrying back down the alley.

"Karl, what the fuck?"

Karl snorted but didn't give chase. Instead, turning his attention towards me. "I don't like you," her odious boyfriend calmly delivered, nudging his head at me. Then, as in a re-run of earlier, he feigned a headbutt in my direction, causing me to flinch.

I watched as Karl forcibly dragged Courteney away by the wrist. My leggy-blonde accomplice delivered a torrent of verbal abuse at him, the sort of words that weren't becoming of a lady.

She wasn't a lady, perhaps a lady of the night, but not a lady. However, she had tried to help me, and significantly more than any other so-called friend had since that day those pictures landed in Bridget's lap. Despite all her bluster and confidence, Karl seemed to be able to control this independent, intelligent girl. I guess she felt she owed him.

My mystery man had not shown up, and this Terry bloke, whoever he was, had disappeared into the labyrinth of piss-ridden alleys, presumably ensuring he put significant distance between himself and Karl – who could blame the man.

I glanced up to Belfast House, specifically my flat's front door. If Courteney was correct regarding her fears following that odd text exchanged with Deli, then I should be concerned about what someone had planted there and for what purpose.

Someone appeared hell-bent on ruining me. So far, the only lead I had to whom that may be was a bloke with an odd tic and the same name as my biological father. Now, because of Karl, that lead had disappeared.

I trudged towards the block of flats I now called home, wondering what lay behind my front door and fearing my day was about to implode.

Most people would consider suffering indecent exposure in the park a bad enough event to experience. However, I had the feeling that when I opened the door to my flat, that hideous sight presented to me by willy-waver could pale into insignificance by whatever was bestowed there.

17

A few days earlier

A Fist Full Of Dollars

A month had elapsed since Fred earned the five grand for one night's work. The 'perfect ten' working girl with the long legs performed brilliantly, allowing him to capture the required shots, and his client appeared pretty chuffed with the resulting snaps.

What had happened to the poor sod who he'd set up, he had no idea. It was none of his business; at the end of the day, it's a dog-eat-dog world. His client got what he wanted, and Fred got paid – so all good.

Assignments were slim pickings since that night, just a couple of desperate housewives shelling out a few hundred for reports of their husband's dallying, all run-of-the-mill stuff.

Whilst waiting for his phone to ring, he rechecked his watch. As nothing was doing, and his mobile hadn't rung for two days, Fred thought it was time for a liquid lunch. A couple of pints in his usual haunt, the Murderers Pub, then he'd nip down the bookies for the rest of the afternoon. As he swung his legs off his desk, he heard a set of heavy footsteps as they thumped their way up the metal gantry to his first-floor office.

The man with no name pushed open his office door.

"Oh, you again." Fred swung his legs back onto his metal desk, the thumping of his heels causing the second-hand desk's heavily dented top to clang. "Take a seat," Fred gestured to the lone chair shoved into the gap near the battered filing cabinet.

The man with no name remained standing, pulled out a crumpled envelope from his jacket pocket and lobbed it next to Fred's shoes. "Five grand in there."

Fred raised his eyebrows as he leaned forward to retrieve the envelope. He peeked inside, the content of which appeared to be roughly the sum the man suggested.

"You have another geezer in mind that needs setting up?" Although Fred wasn't overly pleased with himself for taking the last job, the pay was good. Catching cheating husbands was one thing – they risked getting caught with their pants down, so Fred was happy to get paid for providing the evidence. However, setting up potentially innocent blokes was altogether a different ball game.

The man with no name shook his head.

"What then?"

"Same bloke."

"Oh, wasn't the set of pictures I provided enough?"

"Oh, yeah. No, that worked a treat," he grinned, slowly revealing a set of perfect pearly whites.

"What then? Why d'you need a re-run?"

"No re-run ... we're stepping it up a level. I need your help to ruin this bloke."

Fred frowned as he once again eyed up the envelope. Although happy to take the cash, he felt uneasy about another job that clearly wouldn't be classed as ethical and certainly would not fit into the code of conduct to which holding a private investigator licence demanded – not that Fred ever held one, or any legislation required that he did.

"You up for planting a bit of evidence?"

Fred narrowed his eyes, a little concerned about where this conversation was going but kept half an eye on that envelope stuffed full of cash. "Look, I'm happy to sail close to the wind, but full-on illegal I'm not so comfortable with."

No-Name pursed his lips and offered a slight nod before reaching for the envelope.

"Woah ... hang on," Fred hovered his hand above the cash, effectively stopping his guest from grabbing it. "Let's not be too hasty," he nervously chuckled. "Would this job be fully illegal or just slightly illegal?"

No-Name smirked. "Depends on how you view it, I guess." He retrieved a second, thicker envelope from his other jacket pocket and carefully placed it on the desk. Unlike the first, this was sealed with duct tape wound around it.

"What's in there?"

"You don't need to know. However, to stay on the side of only slightly illegal, I suggest you only touch it with gloved hands. No need to have your prints all over it."

"Let's just say, for argument's sake, that I do touch it with a gloved hand. What would I be doing with it? Hypothetically speaking, of course."

"Hypothetically, you'll be planting it where I tell you to."

Fred pursed his lips and pondered what lay before him. The package, which resembled a half-pound pack of butter, presumably contained drugs. If caught with this in his possession, that wouldn't be good from a legal standpoint.

Fred had performed a few investigating assignments along with the hotel set-up for this chap. However, now the stakes had risen, causing Fred to become concerned about the true identity of No-Name and specifically the type of people who employed him. Even if this guy was just some minion sent from an organised crime gang, any further involvement could pull him way too deep into something he should be avoiding. However, taking the first job had surely already dragged him down to the point of no return.

"Why aren't you using your own people for this job?"

No-Name raised an eyebrow, darkness forming around his narrowed eyes hooded by that unbranded baseball cap tightly moulded to his head. "Own people?"

An uneasy feeling of foreboding swept across Fred. The Ghost of Christmas Past now stood before him, his mind recounting the events of his more youthful years when Fred had perhaps favoured his wife and family before spirits of a liquid kind gradually poisoned his mind and any relationships. Fred had hit rock bottom. No longer a respected PI – more of a lackey for some crime syndicate.

Shaking those thoughts from his mind, Fred pushed for more information. "I take it you have people who, how shall we say, fix things? You know, fixers." Fred thought of Ray Donovan, the TV show he enjoyed, probably because he secretly daydreamed that Ray's and his business were similar. Of course, he knew otherwise. But apart from the occasional flit through Pornhub, a man had to indulge in his fantasies – right?

"I think you've got ahead of yourself. You're the fixer, and I'm just a guy who needs a job completing. You're the bloke who I'm paying to do the job. Now, last chance, you gonna do the job, or am I walking?"

Using a pen to avoid touching it with his fingers, Fred scraped the package across his desk, allowing it to drop into the top drawer that he pulled open before plucking up the envelope of cash and placing it securely in his inside jacket pocket.

"I'm your fixer."

No-Name grinned, displaying those pearly whites.

Fred shuddered. Although he was another five grand better off, he'd now crossed a line. What line, who knew, but definitely into the realms of full-on illegal.

The man with no name supplied his instructions verbally: the address, and the exact layout of the flat and where to stash the package that now lay next to a half-full bottle of whisky. Fred had scribbled it all down on the back of a brown envelope, which had initially contained a notice of a speeding fine when caught on a traffic camera on Coldhams Lane driving at speeds in excess of fifty miles per hour in a thirty miles per hour zone. Apart from being amazed his van could reach that speed, disappointingly, some of the cash in his jacket pocket would be required to pay the fine.

~

Now, three days later, although sweating, he felt relieved that he'd completed the job. Of course, illegal entry sometimes was necessary and, although not part of the code of ethics for a private investigator, there had been the odd occasion in the past where entering someone's home uninvited was required to capture evidence. However, planting evidence was a whole new ball game.

As he bolted down the concrete stairwell, Fred removed his baseball hat, sunglasses, latex gloves and jacket, securing them inside his rucksack. As he exited the stairwell into the main square of the estate, his appearance had significantly altered from the man who may have been spotted crouched by the door, fiddling with the lock of flat 121 Belfast House.

Fred, an experienced operator, knew the Broxworth was the sort of place where nothing went unnoticed. The positive about an operation of this sort, in a place like this, was no neighbourhood watch scheme existed, unlike the leafy suburbs. So, if some nosey neighbour spotted him as he worked his picks in the Yale lock, he was confident they wouldn't be calling the police.

Mindful of the speed cameras on Coldhams Lane – the last thing Fred needed was another fine and more points on his licence – he plucked up a new burner phone and called the number provided by the man with no name. The conversation lasted for a few seconds; just Fred confirming he'd completed the job.

As Fred pulled up to the traffic lights near the Beehive Pub, he extracted the SIM card and pinged it out of the window, the last act when covering his tracks on this lucrative mission to ruin the life of Damian Statham.

Part 2

18

1984

One Million Years B.C.

Sidney wrung his sweaty hands as he leaned forward whilst squashed into the end seat of the excruciatingly back-breaking, arse-numbing wooden bench. His head now inches from the highly polished chrome rail that perched on top of the balcony's balustrade, which served as the public gallery of Fairfield's main courtroom.

The interest in the case, stoked by the local media, resulted in every day of the five-day trial affording a packed court of members of the public. Also, members of the press swelled the benches as they either furiously scribbled notes or carefully drew pictures of the defendant, who stood in the witness box for nearly two full days.

Sidney had endured his interrogation on day two. Although the counsel for the prosecution prepared him well, the barrister defending Dennis Hunt shredded him as if he'd been scrubbed vigorously along a cheese grater. Of course, he'd not suffered any physical scarring. However, the mental anguish he'd suffered at the hands of the petite woman as she peered at him over the top of her horn-rimmed glasses left Sidney doubting whether he knew his own name. By expertly employing her viperous tongue, she'd ripped his evidence to shreds, which surely had thrown doubt on the charges against his former business partner, resulting in DI French verbally tearing a strip off him later that day.

As he kept his head low, the chrome bar obscured the sight of the defendant who'd eyeballed Sidney throughout the trial. Of course, Sidney was complicit, as DI French had indicated during his interrogation earlier in the year. However, turning Queen's evidence against Dennis had secured his liberty, thus avoiding the threat of a charge of perverting the course of justice being levied at him. Sidney held all the aces for the Crown as they tried to secure the successful prosecution of Dennis Hunt for people smuggling.

When enduring the cross-examination metered out by the horn-rimmed viper, in the form of the barrister for the defence, the prosecuting counsel frequently had cause to object, stating that Sidney was not on trial and accusations about his complicity were to be struck from the record. Fortunately, the Judge had agreed and, after the fifth objection, Horn-rim had no option but to change tack.

"Will the foreman of the jury please stand."

Sidney bowed his head as a low murmuring swept across the courtroom, although silence speedily returned when the judge raised one eyebrow.

Over the past few days, Sidney analysed the jury and had decided the woman with the purple rinse, doing a reasonable impression of Dame Edna Everage, would be appointed as foreman. She had that authoritarian look about her. However, not to be. The nervous-looking, wiry gent who wore the same blue-and-white-hooped tank top each day now stood. Sidney thought he looked terrified by the ordeal and suspected that a verdict of not guilty was about to be uttered.

"Has the jury reached a verdict upon which you all agree?"

The court held its breath.

A guilty verdict would allow Sidney to make a clean break. His business would be solely his, and he could get on with life. After Deana had given him the Spanish archer – to coin a phrase from the rotund DI – he'd found a new woman. Although not as vivacious as his now ex-wife, she appeared happy to play mother to Damian, so all would be good. Well, good for a few years until they released Dennis. However, that would buy him time to consider his options.

Dennis and Sidney had always sailed close to the wind regarding the legality of their various money-making ventures together. However, as time passed, Sidney had taken a less hazardous course whilst his business partner diversified into riskier sidelines that, if caught, would result in a custodial sentence.

Those ventures afforded Dennis to gain connections with the sort of acquaintances who Sidney wouldn't want to invite for Christmas lunch. However, those dubious liaisons of his business partner weren't on trial. So, a guilty verdict would sever any of those connections to Sidney – all good. However, if a not guilty verdict landed, Sidney feared he'd be left with no choice but to go on the run because his old mate Dennis probably wouldn't be overly chuffed with Sidney's evidence where he'd spilt the beans to save his own arse.

The nervous chap in the blue-and-white tank top appeared ready to shit himself, causing the judge to intervene. Sidney noticed Dame Edna Everage tut and shake her head, suggesting his hunch had been correct. She'd wanted to act as foreman but had presumably lost the vote, resulting in this poor sod with the loose bowels being browbeaten into the position.

"Please answer the Clerk," boomed the judge.

"N-no," he stammered.

More murmurings rumbled around the courtroom that, once again, halted as the judge raised that bushy eyebrow that the former Chancellor of the Exchequer, Denis Healey, would have been proud of. That said, Sidney very much doubted the judge held the same 'redistribution of income and wealth' ideology as the politician. Also, going by his gruff performance thus far, it suggested he didn't benefit from the politician's avuncular manner.

The senior member of the judiciary nodded to the clerk, who accepted the nod as instruction for his next question for the near self-defecating foreman, who Sidney thought appeared to shake.

"Have the jury reached a verdict of which at least ten of you agree?"

"Y-yes."

The court held their breath. If someone decided to drop a pin, everyone would hear it.

"Do you find the defendant guilty or not guilty on the charge of supplying unlawful passage for illegal immigrants into the United Kingdom?"

"G-guilty."

The rumblings shot around the court; a raised eyebrow by the judge now useless in its ability to negate the noise.

"Hang him!" screamed a woman who jumped up behind Sidney.

"Remove that woman from my court," boomed the judge. "I will have silence!"

Dennis, the judiciary, jury and any other hangers-on swivelled their heads to the public gallery as the woman defied the Judge twice more before a couple of burly looking bailiffs muscled in to silence her banshee wail. All witnessed the scene as the two chaps dragged the unrelenting woman from her seat.

As Sidney turned around to face the court, Dennis pointed directly at him before the two prison officers lowered his hands to apply handcuffs. Sidney followed Dennis's gaze as he now focused on Cheryl, his heavily pregnant wife.

Sidney had known her since school. By far the prettiest girl in his class, which afforded her the nickname of Loana, in reference to every boy's dream movie icon, Raquel Welch. If that baby were female, with Dennis's Adonis looks, the baby would have a strong chance of growing up to be a supermodel by the turn of the century.

Cheryl curled her lip at Sidney, suggesting, at the very least, their friendship had reached a conclusion. He just hoped and prayed that those connections to the undesirables Dennis had forged didn't also stretch to Cheryl. Otherwise, despite his former business partner's impending incarceration, life was going to take a significant turn for the worst.

19

2016

Trading Places

The lock appeared intact. If someone had breached my door, they hadn't bust their way in – a professional job, then. For the Broxworth Estate, all seemed eerily quiet, a pre-cursor for what lay in wait, perhaps. Even the flat next door seemed deathly hushed, and I feared what evil deeds that bastard might mete out to my leggy-blonde accomplice.

Perhaps I should have stepped in to help her, be a real man and support the girl who'd taken the time and interest to help me. However, notwithstanding my gratitude for her support, the chances of me tackling Karl and surviving the inevitable altercation were perhaps somewhat on the slim side. Still, it didn't negate the cowardly accusations that my mind suggested I'd let her down.

My four-roomed shithole didn't take long to inspect. The kitchen drawers and that lopsided three-legged chest of drawers all appeared to house the same selection of crap as when I'd last poked around in them. By the time I raked through my collection of suitcases, holdalls and black plastic bags that only a couple of weeks ago I retrieved from the doorstep of Bridget's flat, I concluded that my leggy-blonde friend had got this one wrong. Whatever her mate Deli witnessed, it appeared not to have happened in my flat – nothing missing, and more to the point, nothing added.

Because I'd lived out of a suitcase, to coin a phrase, my flat now resembled a burglary after I'd upended all my meagre possessions searching for what wasn't there, I thought I'd better invest some time and make this dump a home. Now having to rely on, certainly in the short term, state benefits, my rank flat would be the top end of what I could afford.

After investigating how to claim Jobseeker's Allowance, I attempted to input some order into the flat whilst thinking about Terry. Somehow, I needed to find the bloke. However, all I knew was his first name, we had similar facial features, and he'd known my mother. So, I was at a loss to know where to start searching. Also, if he wasn't my unknown caller, that would suggest there were two men keen to impart some information regarding my ex-girlfriend. Notwithstanding this list of issues, if I was to stand any chance of discovering what had happened and who Bridget really was, I had to find at least one of them.

As dusk crept in, my rumbling gut highlighted that I hadn't eaten. Perhaps I should have joined Courteney in scoffing a cream cake. Unfortunately, the fridge only offered a two-pint carton of milk and half a tin of baked beans, which appeared to have grown a disturbingly black coating on the contents and lacked any appetising qualities. Despite my hunger, the lack of beer on offer put a dampener on proceedings.

"Great, I can't even get pissed," I muttered, as I swished away chunks of ice that had detached themselves from the small icebox at the top of the fridge and now lay in the door jamb preventing me from closing the fridge door on its meagre offerings.

As I lobbed the lumps of ice into the sink, I spotted Courteney through the window waving a couple of four-packs of lager at me. So, unless she was some ghostly apparition, it appeared Karl hadn't killed her.

"You ain't been arrested then?" She placed the tins on the worktop, peeling two away from the plastic rings before handing me one.

"No. But are you okay?"

"Yeah," she nonchalantly replied before pulling the ring pull.

"What about—"

"Twat-head?" she interrupted.

"Err … yeah." Now somewhat concerned that the next time I met her boyfriend, he wouldn't feign a headbutt but carry out the attack, leaving me, at best, with a broken nose.

"Nah, don't worry about him. He's all mouth."

As I opened my can and slugged back a few gulps of the unknown branded liquid, I very much doubted the validity of her assessment regarding her druggy boyfriend. Certainly, when he earlier unceremoniously dragged her across the main square of the estate, she appeared to be the mouthy one, and he a silent thug that could put the fear of God into any hard-boiled, gritty characters that my namesake portrayed in those compulsive action thrillers that I'd always been a fan of. In fact, when asked how to spell my surname, I would always say 'as in, Jason', which was enough to answer the question – the actor was that famous.

"You're not hurt? The bastard didn't hit you?" I enquired after wiping my wet lips with my forearm.

Whilst swigging her beer, she shook her head.

"Where is he?"

"Forget him. He's on a bender at Fat Larry's place. He'll be skunked-up to the heavens in a couple of hours. He can disappear for days, then rocks back up when his suppliers want their cash."

I nodded and swigged my beer, relieved not to be afforded an audience with a man who could have starred in *Trainspotting*.

"You certain you ain't found anyfink? You've searched the place proper?"

"No, nothing. I reckon your mate got it wrong."

"Deli can be a bit of a smackhead, but she ain't usually wrong. You sure you've searched everywhere?"

I nodded before taking another swig. "This shithole ain't that big. It didn't take long to turn the place upside down."

"Courteney glanced around the kitchen and smirked. Needs the feminine touch in 'ere."

"I think I've had my fill of that, thanks. Present company excepted, of course."

"Who d'you reckon that geezer was this morning, then?"

"I ain't got a clue."

"Well, he seemed to know you."

"Knew of me. He said he knew my mum."

"She's carked it, that right?"

"Yeah. She died in a car accident a month ago. I never had much to do with her."

"Oh, sorry, mate."

I nonchalantly shrugged. "Don't worry. You know, the really odd thing, that bloke this morning was called Terry which is my real father's name. And twice he called out Deana, which is my mother's name. Spooky, don't you think?"

"Yeah, I guess so. Though somehow you're gonna have to find him." She pointed her can at me, simultaneously giving it a shake, presumably checking how much liquid was left inside. "You want another?"

Courteney glugged down the remainder of her beer, which I reciprocated with mine before she offered up a replacement. Although a seasoned drinker, a complete lack of sustenance had caused the alcohol to fuzz my head.

Good, I could get pissed and obliterate my mind. In fact, the need to forget my situation almost gave rise to suggesting we join Karl at Fat Larry's and get royally off my face.

"That little twat Jordan didn't recognise him, but I reckon I could persuade him to do some diggin'. That gang of his has got fingers in all sorts of pies. What with their drug runnin', they know most people. If they don't, they know who to ask."

"Shouldn't he be at school?"

"Kids like that don't bovver. What's the point? They're set to a life of crime. Learning about the Luddites trashing the cotton mills in the nineteenth century or which way stalagmites point ain't going to change their futures."

I chuckled before taking a swig of beer. Listening to this girl was akin to watching an obscure Open University documentary presented by Eliza Doolittle. Why I thought of that character can only be attributed to my leggy blonde's reference to Professor 'iggins earlier today, when she performed her python impression, after treating me to a seductive licking session along that phallic symbol in the shape of a cream bun.

For sure, Courteney could have stolen a march on Audrey Hepburn or Julie Andrews when any casting director was searching for the right girl. That said, I considered that perhaps Courteney would have been too stunning for the role of a cockney flower seller. The woman could have made it in Hollywood in another life – probably not skinny enough to be a super-model, but you get my drift.

'Err ... hello! Did you just refer to this potty-mouthed porn star as 'my leggy-blonde'? I think, old son, you're a bit deluded. She's a sex worker, and don't you forget it!'

I nodded to my mind talk. Although a little disappointed that my mind judged the girl simply based on her profession.

"Why you helping me?"

"You're cute, remember," she sniggered before taking another rugby-player-type gulp of her beer.

"Oh, yeah," I chuckled, before draining the can and squashing it in my fist. Although I could feel the alcohol shooting around my bloodstream – we were halfway through her stash – and I feared two more cans wouldn't be enough to drop me into a drunken stupor.

"Well, apart from being cute, I dunno, I seem to have a soft spot for the tenants in this place. The last girl who lived here was right down on her luck, and I felt sorry for her." Courteney offered me the remaining four-pack and continued whilst I cracked open another beer. "She got herself in a right mess and even asked about working the streets or making mucky films … she was in that much debt."

"Oh, what happened to her?"

"Some millionaire bloke came and swept her off her feet."

I raised my eyebrows in surprise as I slugged another mouthful. "Bloody hell, regular rags to riches story."

"Pretty Woman."

"Yeah," I chuckled.

"Go on, your turn."

"What?"

"I said Pretty Woman, as in a rags to riches film, which, by the way, always makes me cry. So, come on, you name one. A film with a storyline about rags to riches."

"Oh, err … I don't know." I really couldn't imagine Courteney crying at anything. Apart from radiating beauty, she was as tough as old boots.

"Oh, come on!"

"Alright. Cinderella."

"Slumdog Millionaire."

"Oh, yeah, good one." I gulped some beer, affording myself a moment to think. "Trading Places. Yes!" I triumphantly punched the air.

"Arthur."

"Ah, no, that doesn't count."

"Why not?"

"Well, Arthur was already a billionaire, so that's not strictly true."

"Yeah, but the Liza Minnelli character wasn't."

"Alright, you win."

"Blimey, you give up too easily," she giggled, as she stepped close to me, reaching around to grab another can.

The silly game of naming films demonstrated an innocent, almost child-like side to her. She'd suffered from the day she was born and fought her way through life, overcoming obstacles I couldn't imagine. But she was right, I gave up too easily. Bridget had taken my business. Someone had set a honey trap, and I, like a pathetic wimp, had crawled away to lick my wounds, accepting my fate.

As the odd enigma of Courteney Klein brushed against me, I felt a tingle of excitement. Her t-shirt-covered chest nudged my arm as she plucked her third beer from the second four-pack. Courteney hovered close to me as she yanked back the ring pull.

We locked eyes for a moment, probably longer than was normal for two relative strangers. I glanced away first, finishing my beer and grabbing another.

"What happened with your girlfriend, then? You didn't actually say this morning why she booted you out."

I shrugged. Although there was no good reason not to tell her the story, I'd had enough of relaying the events in that hotel room, especially as no bugger seemed to believe my version of what happened that evening.

"You gonna get back togever?" Courteney held my stare as she took a swig of beer.

"No," I shook my head. "No, we're finished."

"Oh. D'you want her back?"

200

"Christ, no. Bridget took me for a ride. I'm a bit of a gullible idiot, and she definitely saw me coming. Blokes like me don't go out with girls like Bridget. I should have known what would happen, but like a stupid git, I got sucked in."

"What d'you mean, blokes like you?"

"Oh, y'know. She was out of my league, and I should have suspected something was up."

"Don't put yourself down. I think you're a bit of alright," she raised an eyebrow and offered me that impossibly huge smile.

"Thanks," I chuckled, breaking eye contact, taking another slug of my tasteless beer as a distraction from the conversation that now felt a little awkward.

"Guess you couldn't fancy a girl like me?" she whispered.

"Sorry?" I peered at her over the top of the can poised at my lips, surprised by her question.

"Well, y'know … what I do, and being a bit rough, I guess."

"Christ, Courteney! And you reckon I'm the one who's into a bit of self-bashing," I chuckled, before upending the can and glugging down the content.

Courteney flicked her long blonde hair over her shoulder, then placed her can down before tiptoeing up to kiss my cheek. I seemed frozen to the spot, unable to move, but the touch of her lips on my skin sent a rather disturbing wave of desire through me.

"Careful, old son."

I nodded at my inner voice. Could I, with her? Was that what she was suggesting? Was she working? Was this how she pulled in punters? No, she said she doesn't do that anymore – it was all virtual now – sex online. I figured I fancied her. Well, who wouldn't? But paying for sex wasn't something I had ever contemplated.

"Hey, lose the frightened rabbit look. I only kissed your cheek because I like you. I get it … I'm a tart, and you wouldn't be seen with the likes of me."

"No, it's not that—"

"Nah, leave it, Damian. You're a nice guy, and I don't want to force you to lie by saying somefink nice that you don't mean."

"Anyway, why call yourself a tart? I thought you said you don't do that now, what with your films and internet thingy."

"I don't. But I guess once a tart, always a tart. Well, that's what men fink, ain't it? Anyway, if it all goes tits up, I know I can always go back and earn a livin' that way."

I drained my beer. "There's only one left," I nodded to the lonely can on the worktop. "That's yours."

"You have it. I'd better get going. She rubbed my arm before letting her hand rest on my elbow. "You're alright, Damian, you know that?"

"So are you. And just for the record, I don't think of you as a tart."

"Yeah, whatever. Look, I'll leave you to it," she removed her hand from my arm. "If you need any help, you know, wiv finding that geezer, you know where I am," she flashed that smile and stepped away.

I didn't want her to go.

I grabbed her wrist, just as Karl had earlier. Although mine was gentle, gaining her attention and not meting out violence.

"What?" she shot back, glancing down at my hand.

I tugged, pulling her towards me. Although unsure what for or why, for that matter.

Courteney slowly raised her eyes, holding that pose for a few seconds.

"Err … thanks for the beer."

Courteney shrugged, accepting my gratitude. Well, whether she'd actually exchanged cash for the beer was debatable. Anyway, before the moment became awkward, she glanced down to lose eye contact but remained close to me. The girl's body language suggested disappointment that all I was offering was thanks.

"Courteney, I—"

"What?" she interrupted, shooting her head up.

"Err … nothing. As I said, thanks for the beer."

"Hey, you're welcome," she shook her hand free from mine and stepped away towards the front door.

20

Ravel's Boléro

"Deana." Terry lightly tapped on the bathroom door. However, apart from hearing her pathetic sobs, she didn't reply.

Consoling tearful women had never been a skill that Terry mastered. If his wife Sharon had broken down into tears, Terry applied the tactic of making himself scarce. Unfortunately, he'd experienced this dilemma on many occasions at work, usually after tearing a strip off one of his staff or, more often than not, his personnel manager, Penny, who would turn on the sprinklers when he shouted at the woman.

Now living thirty years in the future, Terry struggled to understand the point Deana had made about what was now classed as unacceptable behaviour for management in the workplace. Shouting instructions and bellowing his displeasure at his staff back in the '80s was the tried and tested method to achieve results. So, if she was correct, in that behaviour like that could very well lead to the line manager's suspension or, unbelievably, end up in an industrial tribunal, that was all somewhat difficult to get his head around.

Despite his preference to sprawl out on the sofa and watch a film, leaving Deana to sob, Terry reluctantly persevered. Since making a bolt for it after that thug had threatened him on that odious estate, Deana hadn't spoken much, and Terry was learning when not to push it. Although this sobbing state she'd adopted after locking herself in the bathroom wasn't a Deana that he'd previously witnessed, he guessed their son's verbal assassination of her had become too much to bear.

"Deana, d'you think you could open the door?" he winced, praying she wouldn't so he could avoid the tearful woman. He thought asking twice before giving up and retreating to watch TV could be deemed as showing enough care before leaving her to her own devices.

The bathroom door bolt disengaged.

"Bollocks," muttered Terry.

A teary Deana poked her head out as she creaked open the bathroom door. She sniffed a few times before wiping a scrunched-up tissue across the end of her nose.

"Damian?" he quizzed.

She nodded.

"Come on. I'll put the kettle on.

Taking her hand, Terry led Deana down to the kitchen. Although not too chuffed about comforting a snivelling woman, he knew he would have to do his best. At least she'd stopped crying.

With a well-steeped cuppa in her hand, Deana seemed to return to her normal self.

"You know you can't really blame him, can you?"

Deana shook her head.

"I mean, you weren't exactly part of his life, and if you've not had any contact for over ten years, you can't blame the boy for having that attitude."

Deana shot Terry a disparaging look. "I'm well aware of that. I don't need reminding!"

Terry defensively raised his palm. "Sorry."

Deana huffed before placing her mug on the worktop. "No, I suppose you're right. It just wasn't very easy to hear, that's all. I know I was a lamentable mother. To be honest, I've never found children very easy to converse with."

"He's not a child."

"No, I know. Oddly, he's about your age."

"Yes, that is weird," Terry chuckled. "To think my son is the same age as me is a hell of a thing to get your head around. Although, come to think of it, so is my daughter, Kim."

"That's what you get for dying and coming back thirty-odd years or so later."

"Yes, I suppose so."

"Look, I'm alright. It was just those awful things he said that upset me. And although Sidney and I didn't see eye to eye, it's clear that the man took every opportunity to trash me. So, I suppose it's not too surprising that Damian doesn't hold his mother in high regard."

"And you say he now lives in the States?"

"Sidney?"

"Yes."

"Yes, as I said this morning. After giving up his business to Damian, the bloody idiot ran off with some woman half his age. I can't imagine what the young girl sees in the turgid old git."

"Perhaps they're in love."

"Piffle!"

"If you say so."

"I do so. I'm not one to judge, as you well know. However, a man that age with a woman so young just isn't natural. Now, the other way around would be perfectly acceptable." Deana plucked up her mug and smirked at him.

Terry rolled his shoulders; this wasn't a subject he wanted to get into. "Can we change the subject?"

"Yes, alright. But not Damian. I've had my fill of our boy today. He's really upset me."

Terry nodded, accepting Damian's putdown of his mother, although fair enough, was a lot for Deana to hear. "That eyepatch thing. Can you look up information on that like you can on your telephone?"

Deana frowned as she placed her mug on the worktop.

"That glass plate thing in that folder. You said you would show me how to use it."

"Oh, yes," she chuckled, her demeanour returning her to the Deana that Terry was more used to seeing. "You're not going to watch porn, I hope."

Terry raised his eyebrows. Some of the lads from work shared around the odd mucky VHS tape, but he guessed it was no surprise that Deana owned a collection of porn films loaded on that glass thingy. He was fairly certain that mature women didn't partake in watching mucky movies in his day. That said, Deana was no ordinary mature woman. There were the nude

Twister incidents, for starters. He refused to allow his mind to imagine his parents taking part in such activity.

"I can read your mind, Terry. Anyone can download porn. I don't have a private collection of favourite films."

"Oh. Download?"

"Christ, Terry, pass it over. I'll show you how it works," Deana plucked up her mug and pointed it at the glass plate, as Terry called it, which lay on top of a heap of old newspapers. "Incidentally, it's called an iPad, not eyepatch."

Although he spent most of his waking hours fending off her amorous advances, and when she wasn't berating him or voicing her opinions about the rest of society, which, apart from the Royal Family, Deana saw herself at the pinnacle of, Terry thought this Deana was significantly easier to handle than the teary oh-woe-is-me version he'd encountered after the incident on the Broxworth Estate.

"Now, this is how it works. What do you want to look up? You said about history earlier and the Cold War. Shall I type in that and see what we can find?"

"No. Type in Sidney Statham."

Deana shot Terry a look before tapping out her ex-husband's name as requested. "What are you thinking?"

"I said this morning that the answer to this mission lies in yours or his history. I'm convinced of it. So, can this thing bring up old newspaper articles like a microfiche system they have in a library?"

"Yes, if they're loaded on the web."

"Web?"

Deana raised her eyes at him. "Apart from acting like a cloistered monk, you're exhausting. Having to explain everything is like having a small child in tow ... questions after questions. And we know how I feel about them. So, please do not start your favoured mantra of, why, why, why."

"Yes, I seem to recall your go-to position when faced with a child is to stick your tongue out at them."

"Children should be seen and not heard. Now, be quiet whilst I see what's on here."

Terry peered at the screen as Deana typed in Sidney's name, scanning the information that popped up. Various pictures with text appeared as Deana scrolled down them.

"Hang on. Who are all those people? The screen is moving too fast. Can't you pause it? Can you rewind?"

Deana raised her finger. "Darling, this here," she waved a digit in his face. "Is the pause and play button. Like my phone, I just use my finger to move the screen."

"Oh. Who were all those people?"

"Just people with the same name."

"Blimey, there are quite a few. How many people in Fairfield have the same name?"

"Terry, this is the entire world."

"Wow," Terry let out a low whistle.

"This is his LinkedIn profile," Deana shot him a look, non-verbally instructing him not to expect her to explain LinkedIn. Deana tapped away at the screen whilst Terry, with his cheek nudged to hers, tried to keep up with her lightning-speed finger. "No. Nothing. That's all old stuff. It appears he's not kept his profile up to date since shacking up with that floozy of his."

"He's probably a bit distracted," chuckled Terry.

"I'd rather not think of Sidney in that way. It really doesn't evoke good memories," Deana muttered, as she tapped the screen to close LinkedIn.

"What about newspaper articles?"

"Okay. So, I'm going to give you a quick tutorial and then leave you to it. You can surf away to your heart's content. I, my darling, am going for a long soak in the tub. I feel the need to wash away those dreadful things our boy uttered today."

Terry nodded, and pursed his lips, pleased to be afforded some time alone.

"I really can't imagine what you think you might discover about my ex-husband. The man was so dull he made the old biddies who run the carpet bowls club up at Fairfield Social Centre appear exciting."

"I can imagine."

"Right. Eyes down, Terence, I need to show you have to swipe, tap and scroll."

"Blimey, sounds like a dance routine."

"Nothing like it, I can assure you. Torvill and Dean wouldn't have won gold with this routine."

"Who?"

"Oh, dear. You have been dead for a long time, haven't you, darling."

21

Lady Madonna

Terry soon fell into the swing of how to tap, scroll, and swipe. Although he initially struggled to find a web thingamajig that offered up information without having to subscribe, Terry eventually landed on one that offered a plethora of free information.

He presumed that subscribing was like completing a coupon in a magazine or sending in a postcard with address details with an accompanying cheque or postal order. However, sending off for a subscription would take too long, and perhaps using Deana's postal address may not be a good idea based on the fact they were both fully paid-up members of the walking dead.

The archives of the Fairfield Chronicle, the local rag, allowed Terry to view information that didn't require him to enter personal details and thus negated a trip to the post office. Unfortunately, only the front pages were accessible, but Terry remained patient whilst trawling through just on the off chance something of interest would pop up. Just out of curiosity, he'd started his search in 1983 – the year he died.

A front-page article prior to the general election that year detailed the local MP's decision to step away from politics. Although elected in 1979, Jemma Barrington-Scott had decided that politics wasn't a career path she wanted to continue, stating she intended to return to practising law.

Terry remembered the story well, probably because he recalled Jemma could only be described as a real honey – definitely a woman he'd have liked to woo if the opportunity had arose. He recalled rumours at the time that The Sun newspaper had offered a sizable cheque to the outgoing MP to feature topless on page three. Disappointingly Terry presumed she'd declined, or he'd died and thus missed out on that particular daily delight. Nevertheless, he made a mental note to check it out, hoping this eyepatch thingamajig stored back-catalogues of that publication.

Focusing back on the Fairfield Chronicle, Terry scanned the front page depicted on the iPad, trying to spread his fingers to increase the image size as Deana had shown him. The half-page picture displayed a stock photo of Jemma when opening a branch of Freshcom's Supermarket in 1979. Terry mused about the company he'd worked for before dying at the annual conference. In particular, that shop, which his old friend, Sam Meyer – the man who abused his daughter – had been the branch manager of when the MP resigned her seat.

Terry clicked away from the image of the MP and moved on through the headlines, unsure what he was looking for, but he just had a hunch. Deana presumably would still be enjoying her soak in the bath. Fortunately, Damian's verbal tirade about his mother seemed to have tempered her constant womanly desires, as she put it. A welcome respite, for Terry. Not that he wasn't of a mind to indulge in those sorts of antics – the sort of activity that wild horses couldn't drag him from thirty-three years ago when he was two to three weeks younger.

Although for anyone pinged into 2016 from 1983, being able to understand the technological advances of the age was somewhat head-spinning. However, Terry had now nearly completed three weeks in this new millennium and could honestly say he was starting to enjoy himself. With the news on tap, so to speak, a plethora of TV channels with no need to set up a video recorder to tape your favourite programs, no more rewinding cassette tapes with a pencil when they'd become unwound, and what appeared to be free music at your fingertips, all seemed rather exciting technological advances. That said, the music on the wireless was utterly abhorrent, and Terry really couldn't understand why the youth of today allowed such drivel to assault their eardrums.

Aimlessly swiping through the Fairfield Chronicle headlines, Terry became distracted, with his mind drifting to what could have been if he'd just stayed alive. However, as he swiped through the daily headlines of 1984, his finger hovered on the glass screen before swiping again. One word in the article below the headlines caught his eye – Statham.

Applying the finger-spreading technique that he'd now mastered, Terry read the article about the trial and sentencing of Dennis Hunt in 1984 for human trafficking. It appeared Dennis Hunt was involved in the illegal smuggling of immigrants from the Continent over to the UK via the use of his boat and charging the illegals a hefty fee for the pleasure. Sidney Statham, his business partner, hadn't faced charges but turned Queen's evidence, resulting in Dennis Hunt receiving a ten-year prison sentence – bingo!

Excited with his find, Terry bounded up the stairs heading for the bathroom. Through the steam, he discovered Deana serenely laid out in the bath. Fortunately, the mountain of bubbles covered her naked form.

"Oh, don't mind me. It's polite to knock before entering, you know."

"Blimey, you've changed your tune."

"Well, I've had a rather upsetting morning, in case you've forgotten."

"I know. But listen, we have to move forward with our mission and I've made some rather interesting discoveries," Terry announced as he perched on the side of the bath.

"You do look rather pleased with yourself. What have you found?"

"Now, look. Whilst you've been soaking in here playing with bubbles, I've been busy surfing the inter thingamajig which has thrown up some rather interesting information."

"Not porn I hope."

Terry tutted. "No. Now listen, who is Dennis Hunt?"

"I have no idea."

Terry swivelled the iPad and showed it to Deana, who squinted. "I can't see that. You'll have to read it to me."

"Dennis Hunt was your Sidney's business partner."

"Oh, him. Yes, I only met the man a few times. Odd bloke if I recall. Although I quite liked his wife, whatever her name was."

"Yes, well, presumably, you remember the court case and him being sent to prison?"

Deana played with the bubbles, making cone-shaped points on each breast. "Look," she chuckled. "I look like Madonna."

"What? If you're talking about the song *Lady Madonna,* I really can't see what your breasts smothered in bubbles have to do with a Beatles song. At least you've covered up, I suppose. Also, you and the Virgin Mary have sod-all in common, that much I do know."

"No, darling. Madonna, the queen of pop. Oh, hell, have you been dead for that long? My, my, you have missed out, you poor boy. You'd have liked her; she was the sex symbol icon of the twentieth century. Madonna is a free spirit, embracing love and not inhibited by her sexual desires. Now you seem to have become quite proficient, you should look her up on your iPad."

"Oh, well, yes, I can see you and someone like that would get along like a house on fire. Now, can we focus on Dennis Hunt?"

"Oh, alright. But I don't see the point. What can some old partner of Sidney's have anything to do with the pickle our boy has landed in?"

"I don't know, but it's a start. Remember, we have a mission to complete. You seem to have taken your foot off the gas on this one. I'm assuming the powers that be won't allow us to swan around forever, and presumably, there's some sort of time limit on this?"

"Yes, probably."

"Well, come on then, let's look lively. Start concentrating on the job in hand, and not playing with bubbles making cone shapes on your boobs."

Deana shrugged. "Alright, darling. Keep your hair on."

"So, come on, what happened with this Dennis bloke?"

"Oh, I don't know. It was so long ago, and Sidney and I broke up, remember?"

Terry raised his eyebrows, indicating he expected Deana to make an effort.

Deana dramatically huffed. "So, at the time Mark and I got it together, I recall Sidney landed himself in a spot of bother with the police. Dennis and Sidney owned that second-hand car place, but Dennis was topping up the finances with a spot of people smuggling. He had a boat, fishing-trip type thing that he and Sidney would take out at weekends to indulge in a spot of sea fishing. You see what I mean? The man was so dull. He actually would rather sit out in the middle of the North Sea waiting for some fish to bite than entertain me. You can hardly blame me for running off with Mark, can you?"

Terry ignored the question. "So, the newspaper article suggests Sidney was the principal witness for the prosecution?"

"Probably, I can't remember. We'd split up by then."

"Okay. So, this Dennis Hunt bloke would certainly have a grudge against Sidney. Can you remember what happened when they released him from prison? That would be perhaps around 1990 or thereabouts."

"No, darling. By that time, Sidney and I had minimal contact. He'd found a new woman to look after Damian by then."

"Hmmm."

"Darling, what can Sidney's old business partner possibly have to do with Damian?"

"I don't know. But what if this Dennis bloke is looking for revenge? Perhaps he can't go after Sidney because he's upped sticks and swanned off with that bird in America. So, could he be targeting Damian instead? Dennis presumably lost everything when he got sent down. By all accounts, Sidney's car business, which he gifted to Damian, was pretty lucrative."

"For the sins of my father?"

"Exactly!"

"Oh, darling, you clever boy."

"Well, we don't know that for sure, but it's a start."

"So, what's the plan, then?"

"Well, as I see it, I think after today's debacle, talking to Damian again is out of the question. So, in the morning, we should nip up to that car showroom, sniff about, and see what we can find. We need to know who this woman is who's taken the business from Damian and whether she has any connection to Dennis."

"Oh, good idea. Now, as a little treat for being such a clever boy, you see that tub of body cream on the shelf?"

Terry glanced behind to the plethora of potions regimentally lined up on a shelf below the mirror.

"You can rub that all over my body for me. A woman has to keep her skin hydrated even when dead."

"That's a treat?"

"Of course it is, darling. Rubbing your hands across my naked body is most definitely a treat, and you should be thanking me for the opportunity."

Terry nervously grinned as he passed the tub of cream to Deana. "I think it's best you do it yourself."

Deana grabbed his wrist. "You'll have to do my back, darling. I might very well have a gorgeous body, but I'm not a contortionist."

Terry frowned.

"Oh, please, darling. I've endured a horrid day; you should be grabbing the opportunity to cheer me up."

"Christ, alright, if I must. No funny business, though."

"Me, darling? I have no idea what you're on about," she smirked. "It'll be fun."

"That's what worries me."

22

To The Lighthouse

I watched with a bucket full of regrets as that beautiful girl with the kindest heart stepped away and pulled open my front door.

She was a sex worker-cum-prostitute, dabbling in a sideline in porn films, topping up her income with a mucky website where she presumably performed lewd acts to saddo blokes who sat in front of their laptops with their trousers around their ankles and a box of Kleenex in easy reach. Despite her radiant beauty and kind heart, she wasn't the sort of girl I should get involved with.

"No, absolutely not," I muttered.

Anyway, she had a boyfriend, and so lowering myself to paying my neighbour for sex was a step too far. Christ, I'd sunk low enough by living in this shithole, so contemplating banging the local tart suggested I had nearly hit rock bottom.

As I pulled the ring pull of the last can of beer, I watched her step out onto the landing. Perhaps, if I stayed in position gazing out of my kitchen window, I'd spot her in a few minutes tottering back down the landing in those four-inch stiletto thigh-length boots as she scooted off to star in her next blockbuster. Or maybe tonight she would be online, giving a live performance on Suzzysuck.com to those blokes with a maxed-out credit card and a box of tissues by their side.

Courteney flashed a smile at me through the window and disappeared out of sight. I took a swig of beer, contemplating that she'd said she liked me. Did she say that to all her punters? I guess as they came online and punched in their credit card details, she would have to say she fancied the fella because he was paying to be entertained. I don't think her declaration that I was 'alright' meant anything.

Anyway, there was the thug Karl – she had a boyfriend. She wasn't coming on to me because she fancied me, as a normal couple might flirt in a pub or club. No, she'd suggested she was still up for selling her body if needed. Courteney was performing her well-practised act when encouraging a punter to open his wallet to top up this month's earnings.

Whilst guzzling the tasteless lager, I thought of when I'd met Bridget. The woman flirted with me, giving me the come-on to suck me into her entangled web of lies and deceit. That night when we'd met, I thought I'd won the bloody lottery.

"Idiot," I muttered. A woman like Bridget couldn't fancy a bloke like me.

Despite my somewhat low self-esteem, I allowed my mind to drift and recall how my mates ogled her with their salivating tongues dragging across the floor as Bridget and I flirted whilst the drinks flowed before I escorted her home. Rob couldn't wait to ring me the next day to find out if I'd managed to bang the fit bird, as he put it – he had such a way with words. Even though he was married to that prissy bitch Laura, I could tell he was jealous.

220

Notwithstanding my obsession with her, now we'd split, the blind fog of infatuation had lifted from my mind, allowing me to see her who she really was – a black widow. Although the sex had been frenetic, towards the end of our relationship, before that envelope stuffed full of A4 pictures showing me in that compromising position landed in her hands, she'd started to avoid me. I hadn't noticed at the time, just subconsciously putting it down to the first few months of passion waning, as it does in all relationships. Well, it did in my somewhat limited experience – I hadn't enjoyed many meaningful relationships with the opposite sex.

I'd been blinded by her beauty, although she didn't have the heart that Courteney clearly possessed. Also, although a shallow thought, something that most blokes are guilty of, Courteney was also a few rungs up the gorgeous stakes from Bridget.

"She's a hooker," I muttered before upending the tin to drain the last few dribbles of beer. As I scrunched the can in my fist, I glanced out of the window, where I spotted Courteney leaning on the steel rail of the balcony with her head in a book. I chuckled to myself – there I was, fully expecting the leggy-tart to be feigning an orgasm to some panting bloke through her webcam, but no, she was just reading.

As I allowed the can to emanate that tinny sound whilst I repeatedly bent it back and forth, I leaned against the sink and watched her for a few moments – or was that ogled? How much beer had I drunk? The gentle spring evening breeze lifted her hair, causing it to dance in the fading sunlight that peeked through the gap between the two tower blocks opposite.

"Who are you, Courteney Klein?" I whispered.

221

The girl next door undoubtedly intrigued me. Five tins of lager on an empty stomach dulled my inhibitions, and although I knew it was probably a bad idea, I padded to my front door and quietly pulled it open before leaning against the frame, surveying the girl who appeared lost in her book. Although oblivious to my presence, she occasionally turned the pages or swept her hair around her shoulder after the gentle breeze wafted a few strands in front of her eyes.

"What you reading?"

Courteney glanced towards me, dragging her hair from her face. "A book."

I nodded. "Yup, I guessed as much."

She waved the book cover at me. "To the Lighthouse … Virginia Woolf."

"Never heard of it."

She closed the book and turned around, leaning against the balcony wall. "The book or the author?"

"Oh, both, I guess."

"Heathen."

"Oh."

"It's a classic by one of the greatest modernist authors of the twentieth century."

I shook my head in wonder. "I'll take your word for it," I chuckled.

"You do that."

"You're not working tonight?"

"What d'you mean? Am I getting my kit off in front of my webcam or giving head to one of my co-stars?" she aggressively fired back.

"Sorry."

"It's all too easy to judge a book by its cover, innit?"

I nodded, now embarrassed, and detected more than a hint of annoyance in her tone.

"I've drunk all the beer, but d'you want a coffee? Assuming I'm not dragging you away from your book, that is."

Courteney shrugged.

"Okay, it was just a thought." I presumed her nonchalant shrug suggested she'd prefer to read than enjoy my company. Fair enough, Virginia Woolf was probably more engaging. Anyway, with all that alcohol swilling around my system, perhaps I'd misjudged that moment when we parted a few minutes ago. Also, I quickly reminded myself the girl was not someone with whom I should want to be associated with. Christ, I was already in enough shit without getting embroiled with a local hooker. Before grabbing the door, I took one more lustful alcohol-infused glance at her.

"You sure you want to be seen in my company?"

I stepped back and peered around the door frame at her.

"If you're like most geezers on this shithole of an estate, you fink I'm just some slag whose only use is to give them a hand-job."

I held the door frame and glanced at the piss-stained concrete floor. "I have judged you ... you're right," I glanced up. "I'm lonely, and I like your company. You make me laugh."

"Go on then. You can make me a coffee." Whilst clasping her book to her chest, she stepped forward and followed me back into my flat.

"You get your books from the library, then?"

Courteney placed her paperback on the counter and hopped up onto the kitchen stool, the faux leather pad hissing like a whoopie cushion as the air fired out through the ripped holes where the foam padding poked out – we both burst out laughing. Not that it was in any way amusing, just schoolboy humour, but I guess the beer had loosened us up.

"Nah, I hate second-hand books. I get them from that big bookshop in the High Street."

I glanced at her as I grabbed the jar of coffee.

"No, I pay for them! Jesus, I don't nick everyfink, you know!"

"Sorry."

"You say that a lot, don't you?"

"What?"

"Sorry … you say sorry a lot."

"Oh, maybe. Sorry."

I filled the kettle and flicked it on before swivelling around and leaning my backside against the counter. "What's it about then? Is it shipwrecks, smugglers and a group of kids solving the mystery?"

Courteney dismissively shook her head and raised her eyebrows. "It's not Enid Blyton; five go to an orgy," she sniggered. "It's not a kid's picture book, y'know."

"Right. Well, I'm not big on books, but I can't see that a book about group sex would be something Enid Blyton would have written."

"That was a joke."

"I gathered that much."

"It's about emotions, childhood memories and relationships ... adult relationships."

"Oh, right ... a sort of *Fifty Shades of Grey* type book, then?"

"No, Damian, nuffin of the sort. Have you read that book? You into a bit of erotica, are ya?"

"Oh, no, not me," I chuckled, shaking my head as the kettle came to the boil.

"I take it you're not into bondage or a bit of BDSM, then?"

"Me!" I exclaimed whilst grabbing two mugs from the cupboard. "Jesus, Courteney, I'm not exactly that experienced, to be honest with you." I turned and faced her, blushing at the admittance of my less-than-adventurous sex life but also not wanting her to think I was suggesting anything about hers.

We held each other's stare. Was she annoyed with what I'd just said? Had I again unwittingly intimated that I was judging her because of how she earned a living?

As I stepped over to her, Courteney parted her knees, inviting me to close the space between us. I gently lifted her chin with my finger, holding it there as I lowered my head; our lips hovered inches from each other. "I'm sorry, I didn't mean ... you know," I mumbled.

Courteney closed her eyes. "Sweet and cute," she whispered.

23

All Creatures Great And Small

I awoke to darkness. Whilst waiting for my pupils to expand and allow the shapes in the room to form in my vision, I deduced that my full bladder was the guilty party for the disturbance of my slumber.

Shit! – Spoons.

My God, I was in the spoons position with a prostitute, or ex-prostitute, as she claimed. But whichever, what the hell was I doing? The decision to kiss and then bed my leggy-blonde accomplice after sinking five tins of unnamed lager, probably past its use-by date, of dubious provenance, or both, now took precedence in my mind over the need to pee.

I gently lifted the sleeping bag away and peered down. Courteney's arm lay on my side, with her hand resting on my chest. I could feel the warmth of her body on my back.

Would I have to pay her? If so, how much? I'd kissed her, and she kissed me. So, was this a freebie or a try-before-you-buy sort of scenario?

Karl – bollocks.

I just prayed the human form of a Pitbull was royally skunked-up in that place called Fat Larry's, as she'd suggested.

I gently lifted her arm away and padded towards the bathroom. As I pointed my manhood at the toilet, I became concerned about another potential problem. We hadn't used protection. I might have caught something. Okay, not a hugely charitable thought suggesting Courteney might have unwittingly gifted me some hideous sexually transmitted disease. However, that surely was an occupational hazard in her line of work.

"Shit."

When I'd finished, and after waving it a few times, I wondered if I should rinse my old-chap under the tap. Would that help?

"Fucking hell. What are you like?" I muttered. I wasn't sure if my mutterings were regarding the idea of washing my old chap or the act of having sexual encounters with a lady of the night.

As I padded back to the bedroom, dawn had just broken. During those few minutes, whilst emptying my bladder, the Earth turned, transferring my bedroom from darkness into a greyish glow. Courteney, now on her back with her arms above her head, her mass of blonde hair splayed across the pillow, slept soundly like a beautiful princess depicted in a children's picture book. Although, I doubted any illustrations would show the princess's naked chest, which, in Courteney's case, gently rose and fell as she slept.

The girl was stunning.

I berated my earlier thoughts of disease, payment, freebies and alike. Who was I to have such thoughts?

"You're a twat, Damian," I mumbled.

This girl had tried to help me for no other reason than just wanting to help a fellow human being who'd landed himself in a spot of bother, or *bovver,* as she would say. I snorted a little chuckle as I thought about how she'd corrected my 'yup' statement when she took a break from devouring that cream bun yesterday lunchtime.

Courteney Klein was an enigma. A girl as coarse as low-count-graded sandpaper, who spoke like a toothless navvy digging holes in the road, displayed the diction and clarity of mind of the poet laureate, performed brilliantly as a light-fingered kleptomaniac who Fagin would have been honoured to have on his team, and had a brain that could compete with Stephen Hawking. She offered a caring attitude that could out-trump any Salvation Army soldier, and was simply –
"Stunning," my mouth taking over to complete the list my mind had started.

Whether Karl would castrate me or tip me over the balcony, that was too late to worry about – the deed was done. I nipped back to bed and slipped in beside my enigma. Trying not to wake her, I leaned over and gently lifted her arm towards me. In her semi-conscious state, Courteney cuddled up close, resting her head on my chest. As we quietly lay in the half-light, I gently stroked her hair.

"You shitting yourself about that twat, Karl?"

"Didn't know you were awake," I whispered.

"Well, are you?"

"Err … yeah, probably."

228

"Don't. I bet you're thinking you fucked up, and do you have to pay me now?"

"No, course not," I lied.

"Liar."

I snorted a reply, which seemed a better option than revealing those uncharitable thoughts whilst I'd performed my ablutions.

"Well, you ain't, and I'm not expecting a wad of notes when I leave."

"Are you going, then?"

"You want me to?"

"No. No, I don't."

"Good," she whispered. Although only a smidgen, Courteney tightened her cuddle.

"Just so you know, sex with men I want to have sex with is different. And before you ask, I ain't had sex with any man other than Karl since I was sixteen. Well, if you discount punters and Donk, my partner in the films I make, that is."

"Donk?"

"Yeah. He's the producer, director, and co-star."

"Oh," I continued to run my fingers through her hair.

"I'm clean if you're wondering. I ain't got no disease."

"I'm not."

"You're a shit liar. I can tell in your voice."

Courteney swivelled her head and smirked at me before wrapping those impossibly long legs around my body and resting her head on her folded arms on my chest. She held my gaze, sporting an impish grin throughout this swift manoeuvre.

With her mass of bed-ruffled blonde locks that now draped over her eyes, she wiggled her knees to force my legs apart whilst constantly puffing away wisps of hair to ensure she could maintain eye contact.

"I get the feeling you're pleased to see me, or is that a pool cue between your legs?" she giggled.

I parted her hair. "It's not a pool cue."

Courteney slithered down my torso while playfully grinning and licking her top lip. Her eyes locked on mine through the strands of hair that flopped forward once again. After her performance a few hours earlier, I knew what to expect.

~

"You need to get a bleedin' bottle of bleach. That khazi is enough to make a girl retch. And the mould in your shower is that developed you could grow mushrooms in it," Courteney announced to the whole flat as she stepped out of the bathroom, scantily wrapped in a towel.

I poked my head out of the kitchen to spot her standing in the hall on the threadbare carpet. If Lee's father regarded at least three inches of floorboards showing could be described as wall-to-wall carpeting, then I guess the permanently sticky, cigarette-burn-pock-marked lino in the kitchen could be described as stain-proof.

"I'll bear that in mind. You want a coffee?"

"Yeah."

"Sorry, it's instant."

As she padded into the kitchen, her bare feet met my stain-proof flooring. "Jesus, Damian, what the frigs on this floor? Ain't you got a mop?"

"Sorry. I haven't quite got around to domestic chores just yet. I'll add it to the list," I chuckled.

Courteney hopped onto the whoopie-cushion stool, flicked her untied hair over her shoulder, and waited while I dug out heaps of coffee from the jar.

"What happened last night?" I knew the physical part but was confused regarding the emotional side of things.

"You necked five cans of lager on an empty stomach, kissed me, and took me to bed."

"Yeah, I got that bit."

"You mean, why did I do it since I've already got a boyfriend?"

I turned and nodded as the kettle boiled.

"You're cute."

I poured the water whilst pondering her reasoning. Assuming Karl and I were her only relationships, excluding those involving a financial transaction, I guess being cute wouldn't be her only reason for sleeping with a man because that word couldn't be used to describe her Pitbull boyfriend.

"Any other reason apart from apparent cuteness?"

Courteney exaggeratedly shook her head, causing her hair to sweep around her head, resulting in her face ending up partly obscured. After placing the coffee beside her, I parted her drooping locks with my index finger. Then, I leaned in and peered at her. "Milk?"

She nodded.

"That's a solemn look you have there."

"It won't work, you know that. I'm with Karl whether I like it or not. I work in the sex industry and, although you've somehow landed in a stinkin' puddle of shite, you come from a different world to me."

"D'you want to be with him?"

"Makes no difference whether I do or don't. You and I ain't a fing. As I said, you come from the other side of the tracks. Girls like me don't go out with geezers like you."

I huffed out a lungful of air towards the sticky lino.

"Look, we had some fun, alright? You're in the shit, and I guess a girl like me may seem alright at the moment, but in reality, it ain't going to work. You'll get back on your feet, leave this dump, and that will be that. You ain't gonna want to rock up with me on your arm to one of your swanky suburban BBQs with all your mates."

"Not sure I'm that keen on BBQs."

"You putting any milk in this pig's swill, then?" she nodded to her coffee.

I yanked open the fridge door, only to be greeted by another two lumps of ice that detached from the icebox and jumped out, slithering across the lino. "Not again," I muttered before snatching them up and slinging them in the vague direction of the sink, then grabbed the milk and gave it a good sniff, aware it had resided in the fridge door for nearly a week.

"Damian, what's in your icebox?"

"Nothing. How much milk d'you want?"

"Nothing?"

"I thought you said you wanted—"

Before I could finish, Courteney hopped off the stool and yanked open the fridge door. One tug on the inner icebox door and it flew open.

"Shit me!"

"What's that?" I stretched past it to grab what appeared to be half a pound of butter that the previous tenant had left behind.

"Don't touch it!" Courteney slapped my hand away.

"You alright?" I shot her a look, wondering what all the fuss was about.

"I take it when you checked everywhere yesterday, you didn't check in 'ere?"

I frowned as I shook my head. "No. Why would I? I was checking nothing had been planted, not searching for a pack of fish fingers or half a pound of frozen butter for that matter."

"You idiot."

"Thanks!"

"That's the first place I'd look."

"For what?"

"That ain't butter. I knew Deli was right. I said she was on her toes, didn't I? Whoever entered your flat planted that there and has probably alerted the filth."

"Oh. What is it?"

Courteney swivelled her head as she clung to the fridge door. "It's drugs, Damian. There's enough there to do you for intent to supply. Get caught wiv this in your possession, and you'll have to call Brixton Prison your home."

"Oh, Christ. What the hell do I do with it?" Panic rose in sync with the tone of my voice.

"You got a Tupperware box?"

"What?" My bemused expression probably confirmed I didn't regularly attend Tupperware parties. However, something suggested Courteney didn't either.

"Lunch box, plastic box."

"I know what Tupperware is. I can't see how finding out about my lack of plastic storage collection is going to resolve this."

"Friggin' hell, Damian, we ain't got much time. Get me a box, a bag, or somefink."

"Shit." I dashed into the bedroom, scooped up one of the bin bags Bridget had lobbed some of my clothes in and presented it to Courteney as I bounded back into the kitchen. "Will this do?"

"Bleedin' hell. Couldn't you have found anything bigger?" she sarcastically spat back as she snatched it from me. Then, slotting her arm into the bag, she reached in and grabbed the package – much like a country vet might do when shoving his arm into a cow's nether regions to help the poor thing when calving. Like any responsible dog owner, when retrieving the family pet's offering from the grass verge, Courteney expertly folded over the bag and wrapped it into a tight bundle.

"What happens now?"

"We don't have much time."

"Why?"

"Jesus, Damian, you're like granny's custard."

I bulged my eyes, bemused by what this naked woman wrapped in a towel holding a large poop bag containing drugs was talking about.

"Fick!"

"I don't get it."

"Look, some git planted this 'ere. This ain't yours, right?"

I shook my head. "I still don't get it."

"So, no one dumps this amount in that icebox, just 'cos they fancy hiding a stash in your fridge."

I nodded.

"This has been put there for someone to find."

"Yes. I get that."

"So, it could be the filth, or worse."

"Worse? Bloody hell, what could be worse?"

"Look, I don't know. But the filth ain't gonna rock up here just 'cos some twat tips them off about a stash of drugs. I reckon they get calls like that all the time, rival gangs fittin' each other up, that sort of fing. So, either this stash is nicked, the owner's been given the nod about its location and will come to get their gear back, or some bent copper's been given the tip-off 'cos someone in the know wants you banged up."

"Christ."

"Get my clothes."

"Why?"

"I can't very well waltz out of your gaff wrapped in a bleedin' towel, can I?"

For the second time, I dashed through to the bedroom, now searching for her clothes, all of which I suspected were hooky gear. Scooping them up, I whizzed back and lobbed them on the counter.

"Sorry, can't find your knickers."

Courteney dropped the towel and snatched up her skinny jeans. "I'll just go commando. You can keep 'em as a souvenir."

"Thanks," I smirked as I gawped at her attempt to wiggle her bum into the impossibly tight jeans.

"Oi, this ain't the time for perving. Pass me my bra."

I grabbed the delicate lace garment from the heap and held it out to her. "What are you planning to do with it?"

Now at the latter stages of performing her bum wiggle as she shoehorned her bottom in, Courteney turned and snatched the bra. "Well, I thought I might stick my tits in it! What d'you fink?"

"That!" I exclaimed, ignoring her sarcasm whilst pointing to the oversized poop bag that lay on the countertop.

She grinned at me as she fastened the clasp and grabbed her t-shirt.

"Hilarious."

"I'm gonna stick it in my fridge."

"Why?"

"'Cos it's all I can fink of at the moment." She rammed her feet into her trainers, wiggling them in a similar motion to how she had her bottom, forcing in her heels.

"Oh, right. Good idea."

She snatched the bag, turned and kissed me full on the lips – although initially taken aback, I snogged her back. My potty-mouthed, leggy-blonde accomplice had stolen my heart.

Courteney broke the kiss and offered me that impossibly wonderful smile. "Hang on. I'll be—"

The front door took a fist hammering, thus halting our conversation – not the sort of knock that an Amazon or Deliveroo courier might perform, but more of a pounding from a posse of Viking raiders hauling a battering ram back and forth as they attempted to gain entry whilst on a campaign of rape and pillage.

"Karl?" I whispered.

The colour drained from my street-wise, leggy-blonde.

24

Centrefold

"Police. Open up."

"Fuck," I mouthed to Courteney.

She snatched up the bag. "Stall them," she whispered, before dashing off to the bedroom.

The door received its second thumping. "Open up," repeated the Viking raider.

I approached the front door and hovered with my fingers on the Yale lock, slowly counting to ten.

As the fist on the other side once again landed heavily, causing the door to vibrate in the frame, I turned the lock. With the lock disengaged, the swinging fist on the other side caused the door to shoot inwards.

"Damian Statham?" aggressively asked a chap a few years older than me, flanked by two baby-faced uniformed officers. He held up what I presumed was his warrant card.

I nodded.

"I have here a warrant to search these premises. Can we come in?"

Before he'd given me a chance to answer, the two officers brushed past me and entered the flat.

"What's this about?" I squeaked out.

The plain-clothed officer seemed to smirk and then stepped past, following the other two into the kitchen. As I turned and followed, I heard one of the officers call out.

"Nothing, Guv."

I discovered one officer squatting with his head in the fridge. As the plain-clothed officer turned to face me, he appeared to have lost his smirk.

"Search the place," he ordered whilst holding my stare.

"Err … what are you looking for?"

"We have reasonable cause to believe that you are supplying class-A drugs." He smirked again before allowing his mouth to widen, showing off a gold tooth on the left side. It appeared he attended the same dentist as Jordan.

"No, no way." I involuntarily glanced down the hall, wondering where Courteney had disappeared to.

"We'll find out, won't we?" His eyes followed my furtive glance.

"Guv," called out the other officer from my bedroom.

Gold-tooth bolted down the hall, with me trotting behind him. We all reconvened in the bedroom where Courteney seemed to be embroiled in a tug-of-war with one officer, my sleeping bag acting as the rope. The officer won, leaving a naked Courteney perched on my bed with her back against a pillow, legs pulled up, and her hands and forearms raised in an attempt to cover her chest. Her pose akin to that of a centrefold beauty depicted on the cover of a men's top-shelf magazine.

Although I'm no expert in that area of publications, I doubted many models would sport a look on their face that could kill – as was currently my leggy-blonde accomplice.

"Get out! Fuck off, you pervert," she bellowed.

I presumed Courteney had stripped as a diversion tactic and wasn't offering her wares for viewing in case there was a bit of business to be capitalised upon. Whatever game she was playing, I thought she was better placed than me to conjure up a cunning plan to escape our current somewhat tricky situation. However, as she'd earlier suggested, someone was fitting me up because that officer headed straight to the fridge, expecting to locate the 'pack of butter' which rather conveniently had been placed there.

"Nice," chuckled Gold-tooth.

"Fuck off!"

"She's a tom," announced the officer, who was still of the mind to cuddle my sleeping bag.

"You know from personal experience, do you, Constable?" quipped Gold-tooth.

"No, Guv, I recognise—"

"Right, you tart, stand up and get your kit on," he interrupted his blushing junior officer.

"Fuck off and get out," Courteney fired back, holding her ground and that odd pose.

"Move her," ordered Gold-tooth.

Both officers waded in. Despite receiving a few slaps and a couple of kicks from her wildly flailing arms and the thrashing of her long legs, whilst also being subjected to a string of obscenities, the officers rather unceremoniously dragged Courteney from the bed, leaving a half-pound of butter-shaped package visible in the pillowcase.

"Bollocks," I muttered.

"Stop gawping, you fucking pig." Courteney snatched up her t-shirt from the heap of clothes she'd presumably hurriedly discarded only moments earlier.

The officer, who'd been on the receiving end of this latest torrent of verbal abuse, averted his eyes from where he'd clearly been lecherously taking in the sights whilst his senior officer snapped on a pair of blue nitrile gloves.

"Yeah, look away, you pig. I wouldn't suck your dick, oink, oink."

Gold-tooth pointed a blue finger at Courteney. "Shut that mouth, you little slag." Despite my accomplice's less-than-courteous responses to an officer of the law, he seemed to be enjoying himself.

"Bet you've got a small dick as well," she muttered, whilst making a grab for her jeans.

Gold-tooth ignored Courteney's accusation regarding the man's appendage, instead choosing to turn and grin in my direction whilst encouraging the glove to fit by forcing the thin latex down between his fingers.

I'd seen enough films and TV shows depicting naked prisoners preparing to endure an intrusive orifice-violating strip search to cause my breathing to become laboured. Fortunately for my anus, Gold-tooth didn't instruct me to drop 'em and bend over. Instead, he delivered that grin before stepping towards the bed.

"This is interesting." Gold-tooth shook out the tightly wrapped plastic bag onto the bedsheet. With his blue nitrate gloves applied, he unwrapped the black plastic bag and peered inside.

I glanced at Courteney as she wiggled into those tight jeans again and shook her head at me. Whether that was an instruction to look away, keep quiet, or both, I wasn't sure.

"What's this?" Gold-tooth pointed at the bed sheet where he'd upturned the plastic bag.

My eyes popped out of my head as my jaw dropped.

"Well, you fick twat, I reckon it looks like shower gel," Courteney pointed to the bottle on the bed where Gold-tooth had upended it from the black plastic bag. "Maybe you should get some 'cos it stinks of pig shit in 'ere."

I was reasonably confident I kept my bottle of Lynx in the bathroom and not hidden in my pillowcase. Perhaps the aroma permeating from my skin was the real reason Courteney found me attractive, not my apparent cuteness. Well, those TV adverts suggested their product would make the user irresistible to the opposite sex, so maybe their claims regarding a quick rub down with a handful of their scented gel had turned me into an instant babe magnet.

"Guv?" questioned the officer who'd stopped leching over Courteney now she'd reapplied her clothing, his question dragging me from my thoughts about tongue-in-cheek advertising campaigns and back to our current dilemma.

"Rip this place apart. And shut her up. Gob out anything else, you little tart, we'll be making a note of it and arresting you." Again, he pointed a gloved finger at Courteney, although he didn't appear so cheerful this time.

Like me, I suspected Gold-tooth wasn't expecting shower gel to fall out of that bag. However, where Courteney had hidden the stash in the thirty seconds she had at her disposal, God knows.

"Pigs! Stick that in your fucking notebooks. Oink oink! And if you can't spell that, you fick fuckers, it's O-I-N-K which spells pig."

"Shut it."

Neither officer attempted to quieten Courteney, although I had to agree with Gold-tooth in as much that I didn't think Courteney was helping the situation. Despite her distraction with my shower gel, surely it would only take a moment to locate the drugs. Moreover, the flat was small, lacked furniture, thus affording limited hiding places.

"Get on with it," instructed Gold-tooth to his officers, who'd hovered and hadn't complied with his earlier instruction. They both scuttled out, leaving room for him to reach down and flip up the mattress. "Stand against the wall and don't move. Either of you utter another word, I'll arrest you for assaulting my ears, namely a breach of the peace."

"Oink."

I groaned. Christ, she just had to have the last word.

I shot her a look. Courteney smirked back. There was I, concentrating on ensuring my anus stayed tightly closed whilst she seemed to revel in the experience. Perhaps my potty-mouthed blonde lover had a point – we came from different sides of the track.

After the three officers had regressed my flat to a state worse than prior to my efforts to tidy up the previous evening, they left empty-handed. Gold-tooth appeared somewhat put out, threatening me with violence when out of the earshot of his officers.

Before today, my previous encounters with the police were limited to traffic officers pulling my car over to inform me about excessive speed. Although they had issued me a fixed penalty fine, they performed it with professionalism and, as I recall, were courteous and almost apologetic. However, Gold-tooth's style of policing was somewhat different, a point I raised with Courteney when they'd left.

"Yeah, well, that's 'cos he's bent."

I shook my head, indicating I needed her to elaborate further.

"Jesus, come on, Damian. Work it out."

"He knew the drugs had been planted."

"Yes! He must have organised some snout of his to plant the gear so he could turn up and nick you for it."

"Why?"

"I don't know. But listen, drug raids up 'ere are fairly commonplace. Karl is right careful about how he stores and moves gear about 'cos he knows that lot will occasionally raid the place. Gold-tooth, as you call him, wouldn't have secured a warrant from a tip-off. As I said, that happens all the time. So, for him to bowl up 'ere with the cavalry means it's a set-up job. Either someone is giving him a backhander, or he himself wants you banged up."

"Oh."

"Damian, he's bent."

"I don't get it. Christ, why me? As far as I know, I haven't upset anyone."

"Well, someone wants you taken down, so you've done somefink."

I huffed as I scrubbed my hand over my face. "Anyway, where the hell did you put the drugs?" I whispered the last word as if concerned that I'd be overheard.

Courteney whipped off her t-shirt and flung it on the kitchen worktop, again exposing her naked chest.

"Oh, look, I'm not really in the mood."

"You should be so lucky," she chuckled, as she wiggled her bum and wandered off down the hallway towards the bedroom. "I'm gettin' my bra. When those pigs were 'ere, I didn't have time to fuss around putting it on."

"Oh," I chased after her. "Courteney, the drugs?" I hissed.

"Cleva, ain't I?" she raised her eyebrow as she fastened the bra clasp behind her back.

"Well?"

"I texted Deli when you went to the door. As soon as you let the filth in, she nipped out of her flat, and I passed her the stash through the window."

Relieved, I blew out a heavy sigh. "Wow, that was quick thinking. So why the shower-gel trick?"

"I needed to buy Deli some time. Wrapping up your shower gel meant that pig would take a little longer."

"Right. As I said, quick thinking."

"Yeah, the look on his face was priceless. Anyway, we have a problem."

"What to do with it now? I guess your mate Deli will want shot of it pretty sharpish."

"No, that ain't the issue. Deli would have flushed it down the shitter 'cos I told her to get rid of it."

"Oh, good idea. So, what's the problem, then?"

"I was standing in the nuddy when I passed it to her."

I shook my head, my usual way of indicating I wasn't following the point she was making.

"Look, we all know what I do for a livin', right?"

"Right," I nodded; this was easier to follow.

"Right, but she ain't stupid. Deli gave me a knowing smirk as she grabbed the package. She bloody knows I wasn't working and, as she said in that text, we both think you're peng. She knew I was hittin' on you, so standing in your gaff in the nuddy kinda made it a bit bleedin' obvious. There's a big difference between business and pleasure, and Deli's got a big gob."

"And?"

"Karl!"

"Oh, shit. She'll tell him?"

"Deffo."

I swallowed hard, wondering if I would soon take flight over the balcony when Karl flung me to my death after hearing the news that I'd knobbed his missus on a freebie.

25

Grey Goose

"Shouldn't you be working?" I regretted the question as soon as it left my mouth. Although Courteney's employment status wasn't a secret, after the previous night together and posing that same question as we stood chatting on the landing outside my flat, asking why she wasn't producing her latest cinematic masterpiece with her co-star Donk or panting into her webcam felt rather churlish of me.

"Jesus, Damian! Ain't you got any other topic of conversation rather than constantly enquiring when I'm making my next porn movie? Christ, anyone would fink wiv your obsessive questioning that you want to join in!"

I waved my hands and winced. "Shit, I don't know why I said that. I suppose I was in a roundabout way just asking if I was taking up your time and you would rather be doing something else."

She turned and thumped her hands on her hips. "Christ, men! You're all like granny's custard. Would I rather be lubing-up to take Donk's ten incher or helping the bloke who gently made love to me last night? I'm 'ere, aren't I? So, work it out for yourself where I'd rather be. Anyway, I thought you needed my help?"

"I do. Sorry, that was really crass. You said I gently made love … was that a good thing?" I winced, dreading the reply. Also, slightly concerned because I couldn't match up to Donk's huge offering – maybe Lee had a point.

Courteney tiptoed up and kissed me, cupping the back of my head with her hand to pull me close. Then, breaking the kiss, she kept her hand on my head. "Yes, it was a bleedin' great fing," she whispered.

"Oh, right," I flashed a grin, pleased that apparently size didn't matter.

Courteney smirked, I presume reading my thoughts, as she looked up at me whilst we hovered on the pavement across the road from what used to be Statham Cars. Although the large sign stated as much, the empty forecourt and showroom afforded it a ghostly appearance. And yet, only a few weeks ago, it had been a thriving going concern. Notwithstanding my lack of knowledge of the second-hand car trade, and although I was out of my depth, the business had been booming. Before he'd embarked on his mid-life crisis, my father had built a successful business, and his reputation alone was enough to secure a loyal base of repeat customers.

Now it appeared like many units on the industrial estate, boarded up and derelict, with the weeds already poking up through the tarmac like an army of Triffids sensing the opportunity to rise up and take hold.

"Come on, let's go and see what we can find out."

"I don't see what we can gain from coming up here. Bridget has closed the place up and already moved my stock of cars. Look, the forecourt is empty."

"You want to get back on your feet and away from the Broxworth?"

"Yeah, course."

"Well, we have to start somewhere, then. And 'ere is as good as anywhere."

I nodded. "Why you helping me?"

"As I said, you're cute."

"Apart from that."

"Does there have to be any other reason?"

"No ... I guess not, but—"

"But nuffin. I fink I've made it quite clear that I like you, alright?"

"Blimey! You've gone red," I announced whilst pointing to her cheeks.

"No, I haven't!"

"You have! Courteney Klein, you're embarrassed," I chuckled. "Christ, I didn't have you down as the bashful sort, especially not in your game. You're not exactly the shrinking violet type!"

"What the hell is that supposed to mean?" she spat back, as she aggressively turned on me.

"Err ..."

"Come on? What you saying? 'Cos I'm who I am, I'm not like normal women, and I can't have feelings, is that it?"

"Sorry. I didn't mean—"

"Look, just because I gave you a blow job this morning don't mean I want to marry you and have your children. I just like you, alright!"

"Okay!"

"Well, I did up until a minute ago!"

"Okay, okay." I shot my hands up and grinned at her, replaying in my mind that sexual act she had expertly performed. "Anyway, I think you'd have to attend some BBQs and meet my mates before I propose marriage."

"Yes, very funny. You're starting to lose that cuteness. I prefer the little lost boy look you give off, as opposed to this cocky persona."

"You like a lost cause, then?" I pouted.

"That's better. The oh-woe-is-me Damian is the man I'm starting to love."

"Oh."

"Shit," she muttered.

"Love?"

"I'm blushing, ain't I?" she whispered.

I nodded. "Yes."

"Sorry, forget that. I didn't say it."

"But you did."

"Yeah, well, as I said, that's all kinda Cinderella stuff, not the real world. The world I live in is violent, unpredictable and not somefink I can ever escape."

I slipped a strand of hair from her eyes, only to repeat the action as a gust of wind blew it back. "You help me, and I'll try to help you."

Courteney responded with a tight smile.

What I meant by that statement, I had no idea. However, I think we both knew that I wasn't offering a glass slipper.

My new lover took hold of my hand and squeezed it as she stepped off the pavement before dragging me across the road. Notwithstanding Courteney's somewhat surprising declaration of love, and although losing my business and home was a disaster, the concern of what her druggy boyfriend might do to me was uppermost in my thoughts. Before suggesting nipping up to the car showroom, Courteney visited Deli to ensure she'd successfully flushed the drugs and secure her silence. If the woman gobbed off to Karl, I feared for my health – a lost business would pale into insignificance.

"What are we going to do about Karl?" I asked, letting go of her hand as we reached the other side.

"Don't know. Deli will keep quiet until she's had a few … that's when we need to start worrying."

"Oh, right. So, does she drink much?"

"Deli? Christ, yeah. She's a pisshead. That girl can't get through to lunchtime without half a bottle of vodka."

"Oh, great. Guess we ain't got long before your bloody boyfriend comes looking for me."

"Relax. That twat won't be back for days. I'll just keep bribing Deli with a few bottles, and maybe she'll forget it. It's surprising what the promise of a few bottles of Grey Goose or Belvedere vodka can do when persuading her to keep that mouth of hers shut."

"Right, let's hope so. Look, I'll give you the cash for the vodka. I can't very well expect you to have to bail me out, and I'm guessing that stuff is premium vodka and costs a fair bit."

Courteney, who'd just flipped one of her long legs over the barrier to the car lot, turned and faced me. "Damian, wake up. I ain't paying for the gear. I sent one of the little lads from the estate down to the local supermarket to pinch me a few bottles."

"Oh." I hovered, unsure of what else to say and not knowing whether to be concerned that potentially made me an accessory after the fact. They stole the vodka to order, as in helping me out of a fix – I was complicit.

Courteney, now on the other side of the barrier, leaned back and grabbed my hand. "Don't look so worried. You really are a powder puff, ain't you? The supermarkets build into their prices to account for stuff getting nicked. Those that can afford to pay for the stuff just subsidise the likes of us on that estate that can't. It's how the consumer-led economy works."

I raised my eyebrows.

"Look, we nick the gear ... that puts prices up, right?"

"Yeah, I guess so."

"So, higher prices mean those who pay, as opposed to stealing, demand higher wages to pay for their goods."

I nodded.

"Higher wages means more cash about, and the economy grows, benefiting everyone."

"I see."

"Without the likes of us on the estate nicking gear, the country would be in a right old state, I can tell you. We're helping to keep the wheels of industry moving if you see."

Courteney squeezed my hand and pulled, encouraging me to join her on the other side of the barrier. As I no longer owned the business, I presumed by entering the forecourt, that act could be construed as trespass. However, I decided not to worry too much. Like her take on the economy, I guess she'd have some reasonable argument as to why that was acceptable, citing that breaking and entering somehow supported local jobs and economic growth.

"What's the plan then? The place is all locked up," I whispered, concerned about what illegal act my leggy-blonde accomplice had planned as we headed around the side of the showroom.

"I don't know. But we have to start somewhere, don't we? That bloke on the estate yesterday afternoon ain't the geezer who planted the gear in your flat. Deli said the bloke who broke in was an old git."

"Well, he's not going to be here, is he?" I whispered again, concerned about making any noise that might alert someone of our presence.

I furtively glanced around as she cupped her hands on the glass pane and peered into the now-empty showroom that only two weeks ago held over ninety grands worth of high-class second-hand motors.

Still with her face pushed up against the glass, Courteney mumbled, "Interesting."

"What is?"

"When did it all go tits up?"

"A couple of weeks ago," I hissed. "Courteney, we'd better get going before we get spotted."

"And you say that Bridget disappeared straight after?"

"Yes! Come on, let's get out of here."

Courteney nipped over to the door of the offices, a white UPVC door with an obscured glass top panel.

"What you doing?" I quizzed as I watched her remove her hoodie. Yes, it was a warm spring afternoon, but stripping out of her clothes at the back entrance to my old car showroom didn't seem the place to partake in a bit of alfresco nookie if that was her intention – the low-cut V-neck cropped top drew my eye. I shook my head, realising this wasn't the time to harbour those sorts of thoughts. There was always Suzzysuck.com if I felt the need.

"Christ, Damian," I muttered, disappointed that my mind had drifted to smut now faced with the vision of Courteney's pierced navel and her ample cleavage.

Courteney wrapped her hoodie around her right arm. "So, some bloke who we don't know tricked you by arranging a meet in the park so he could plant the drugs. Then some odd geezer called Terry comes looking for you on the estate. And then this morning, your flat conveniently got busted by some bent copper looking to fit you up."

"Yes. But what are you doing?"

"You need some answers, don't you?"

"Well, yes, but—"

"Pull that bin out so it covers me." Courteney hovered with her back to the door.

"What d'you mean covers you?"

"Damian, just do it."

I kicked down on the wheel locks on the bin and hauled it in front of her. "Courteney, you're not going to—"

Before I could finish my sentence, Courteney swung her hoodie-wrapped elbow back through the frosted glass. For a woman of reasonably slight stature, she amazed me with the momentum and force she could apply. The resulting breaking glass was enough to wake the dead.

"Jesus! What the hell are you doing?" I furtively glanced around the empty forecourt, relieved that only the Triffids appeared to witness her illegal act.

"Helping the local economy."

"What? How the hell does breaking and entering help the economy?"

"A local glazing company will soon have a new contract to replace this glass. See, I'm just greasing the wheels of commerce."

Stunned by her take on the economy, I gawped whilst witnessing my girl reach through the broken pane and flip the thumb lock. "This bleedin' place got an alarm?" she quizzed without turning to look at me.

"Err, sorry. What?"

"Damian!"

"Err …yeah."

"Right, you'd better go first then and disarm it."

"Me?" I incredulously asked, as I pointed to my chest.

"Who else? Come on, Damian, man up!"

"Christ," I huffed, as I again furtively glanced around before gingerly stepping forward and slowly turning the handle of my old office door.

After kicking away a heap of post, I made a beeline for the alarm panel whilst praying Bridget hadn't had the foresight to change the code. As I punched in the four digits, I held my breath before collapsing in my old swivel chair when the alarm sounded its two long beeps indicating I'd successfully deactivated it.

Courteney plucked up the heap of letters and closed the door.

"What now?" I squeaked out, still shitting myself and, for the second time today, desperately trying to hold my anus shut.

"We need to find out where Bridget has disappeared to. Have a rummage through those filing trays and see if there's anything there," Courteney instructed as she ripped open the letters after discarding the flyers and a copy of the Fairfield Chronicle.

"Are we allowed to open that post?" I asked, as I extracted the few sheets of paper from my old filing tray.

"Damian, as we've just committed breaking and entering, I think opening someone else's post ain't too much of a worry."

"Oh."

"Bridget Jones. Fuck me, is that her real name?" she chuckled, turning an envelope around to show me the typed name and address.

"Err … yeah, I assume so. Although I thought the other day that it might not be."

"Why?"

"Well, for the few months we lived together, she never seemed to get any post, and apart from the agreement to put the business in her name, I never saw anything official with her name on it."

Courteney raised an eyebrow as I filled her in about not becoming acquainted with any of Bridget's friends and only meeting Nathan, her brother, when completing the documents to stupidly put my lost business in her name.

"Bleeding hell, Damian, you really are like granny's custard."

"Thanks," I mumbled. That said, she was right.

"So let me get this straight. You met this bird and move in togever, sign over your business because it seemed like a good idea, but you knew nuffin about her."

I nodded.

"And she's disappeared."

I winced.

"What about the brother?"

"Nathan?"

"Nathan Jones, I presume?"

"I guess so … I never knew his last name."

"Jesus, Damian. I just give the impression of being fick, but you actually act it!"

I bowed my head and nodded.

"Well, she ain't that bleedin' cleva because this letter from a solicitor is about selling this place and, at the bottom, it confirms they sent a copy to her financial advisor, Nathan Bragg. So, I'm guessing he ain't her brother."

"Oh."

Courteney swivelled around and glanced at the door, holding her hand up to silence me. She turned and placed the

257

tip of her index finger to her lips as I heard the unmistakable sound of the crunching of broken glass underfoot.

I held my breath, convinced that we'd be arrested or, at best, I would actually crap myself. I pondered; if I had the choice, I'd go for self-defecation as opposed to gaining a criminal record.

Courteney placed her stolen-trainer-clad right foot strategically between the pieces of glass that had fallen inwards and peered through the hole.

"Who's there?" I hissed from the safety of my old desk.

Courteney animatedly waved her hand, indicating I should be quiet, whilst she carefully assessed the forecourt, only to jump back when the crunching of glass became audible once more.

"What?" I hissed.

Courteney swivelled around and shook her head, sporting a bemused expression. Then, she nodded to the main reception area, suggesting we should move through there.

Now fearing the worst, Courteney followed as I tiptoed through the open doorway and crouched behind the reception desk, where we huddled together and waited.

"Who was there?" I whispered.

"No one … I couldn't see anything."

"But … but I heard footsteps."

She shrugged her shoulders.

"Shit! D'you reckon it's the police?"

She raised a finger to her lips as the sound of footsteps padded into the office. I shot her a look, my eyes bulging. Courteney moved her finger from her lips to mine and held it there whilst her eyes pleaded for me to hold my nerve. I guess she could be classed as significantly more street-wise than me, but whether she had previous in this sort of situation remained to be seen.

From our hideout position, we couldn't see into the office but could hear the shuffling feet of at least one person moving around.

Feeling the urgent need to nip to the gents whilst focusing on praying my bladder and sphincter would hold, Courteney poked her head above the reception desk.

26

Brummie Trap

I tugged on the pocket of her jeans, attempting to pull her down behind the counter, fearing that the intruder would spot her. However, Courteney held her stance, resulting in my tugging efforts only achieving to expose the top lacy band of her ill-gotten-gained knickers.

"Courteney!" I hissed, almost pleading. However, my girl held firm, ignoring my request.

After previously witnessing her struggle when shoe-horning her bum in those jeans, so reasonably safe in the knowledge I wouldn't be able to pull them down, I persevered and again yanked on her back pocket. I feared if she remained in position, she would be spotted and thus get us arrested, or worse.

What constituted worse, at this point, I couldn't imagine. However, I guessed if it wasn't the police snooping around, it would be someone who wouldn't be too chuffed about our little breaking-and-entering escapade. I already had Karl, Gold-tooth, the mystery caller, the old git who entered my flat, and that Terry bloke to worry about, so adding to that list seemed like a bad idea.

After a couple of extra tugs on her back pocket, she bobbed back down beside me. "Christ, you getting frisky? You trying to get in my knickers again?" she sniggered.

"What did you see?" I whispered, whilst rolling my eyes.

"Nothing … but weirdly, the office chair appeared to move on its own, but there's no one there."

I screwed my face up, indicating she wasn't making any sense.

Courteney shrugged. Then the unmistakable sound of crunching glass caused us both to hold our breath and lock eyes.

"Darling, stay outside for the moment. I think Damian and that awful girl from the estate are trying to hide in the reception area," Deana hissed out to Terry, who crouched behind the bin in front of the office door.

I raised my palms at Courteney, questioning what the plan was to get out of this mess.

"Stay there," she whispered. Then, before I could offer up any protest, she was up and away, barrelling her way around the counter towards my old office.

"Shit!"

One thing for sure, even though she was clearly street-wise and possessed a viperous tongue, Courteney would be no match for some thug that might be lurking or an opportunistic thief who'd spotted the broken pane of glass and was now rummaging around. Although I thought it would be a stupid move, I couldn't leave Courteney to face a potential assailant alone. So, I took a deep breath, broke cover, and hot-footed back to my office in pursuit of my lacy-knicker-elastic exposed, leggy-blonde accomplice.

Courteney stood by the open door with her hands thrust upon her hips. "Oi, you. You hiding behind the bin. Who are you?"

"Oh, Terry, I said to stay out of sight!"

"Come on. I can see your legs. Who are you?"

I joined Courteney by the door as the odd man I'd met on the estate yesterday afternoon peered around from the bin and stood, appearing to sport a nervous grin.

"You!" I exclaimed.

"Who are you? What you doing 'ere?" Courteney fired out.

"Terry, please don't say anything stupid!"

"I could ask you the same question."

"You could, but we're not lurking behind a bin, are we?" my viperous-tongued assistant spat back.

"Err … well, we're not the ones who've broken into this place, are we?" he quipped, as he stepped forward.

"We?" I quizzed, whilst peering over Courteney's shoulder. "Who's we? Who else is here?"

"Terry! I'm warning you," threatened Deana, whose head appeared from around Damian's arm.

Terry appeared to focus to my left, nodding to the space beside me, much like that odd performance when we met yesterday.

I glanced to my left, following his line of sight, convinced I heard the crunching of broken glass by my side.

"You following us?" Courteney aggressively questioned as she jabbed her finger in Terry's direction. "'Cos listen up, tosser. I know the sort that can rearrange that pretty face of yours, and I'm not referring to a plastic surgeon. That said, you might need the services of one after they're done wiv you."

"Oh my. What a revolting woman! Terry, darling, I know I wasn't there to guide him, but what on earth is our boy doing with this thing? She really is a gutter slut."

"As I was saying yesterday before that thug stepped in, I know … knew your mother. Well, actually, I sort of know your father as well," he chuckled.

"You deffo ain't the filth?" Courteney waved that accusing finger.

"The police?"

"Yeah, pigs. I've had enough of that lot today."

"No, I'm not the police. Look, in case we get spotted, shall we talk inside?"

"Darling, please be careful. We didn't discuss this eventuality. We really can't show our hand too early, and I think after the debacle in that bookies with little Kimmy, trying to convince Damian that you're his dead father might be a mistake."

"Trust me, woman," Terry muttered as he stepped into the office.

"Who you calling woman? I don't know you from Adam, so watch your mouth."

I grabbed Courteney's arm, sensing she was about to lose her shit. However, I, for one, wanted to know who this stranger was and why he seemed to have appeared in my life.

"Look, I wasn't talking to you."

"Who then? I'm the only woman here?"

"Woman! Rough trollop would be a more fitting description! Now, given the opportunity, I'm all for whipping my clothes off, but the amount of unnecessary flesh this girl has on display is close to pornographic. There's a marked difference between nudity and gratuitous porn, and this girl is the latter!"

Terry glanced to his right, then back at Courteney. "Sorry, who are you?"

"Good question! Miss Trollop, I should imagine."

"I asked you that, you twat."

"You did. As I said yesterday, I'm Terry."

"Same name as my real father, then?"

"Yes. But who are you?" Terry turned to Courteney, who I thought appeared about ready to slap the man.

"I'm his girlfriend. But that's got fuck all to do with you, tosser."

"Oh, good God! The boy has sunk to depths so low that I'm not sure we can haul him back!"

I glanced at Courteney and raised an eyebrow. Somewhat surprised that I'd progressed from being cute to casual lover and all the way up to boyfriend in the space of less than twenty-four hours. I wondered where the human form of a Pitbull, Karl, fitted into this equation and doubted he'd be up for a throuple or be willing to indulge in a ménage à trois type of arrangement. And what about her co-worker, Donk? Where did he fit into all this?

"Oh, thank God. By the look on his face, it seems our boy disagrees with this filthy hussy."

Courteney reached out and took my hand. "I'm Courteney, if you must know," she defiantly announced to Terry.

Deana tutted and dismissively shook her head. "Courteney, whatever kind of name is that? Only gutter sludge living on benefit street are called Courteney!"

My apparent newly acquired girlfriend affectionately squeezed my hand. Although she wasn't my girlfriend, apart from Bridget's lies, no one had shown this level of affection to me. Yes, okay, a few in that long line of my father's female acquaintances warmed to me when I was a child – a time I might have been cute – but a woman showing genuine affection was a new experience for me. Also, unlike Bridget, I didn't have Courteney pegged for playing games. However, we'd only just met. Also, I couldn't rid my mind of the fact she was a seasoned sex worker, and there was Karl – I wasn't sure what to make of it all.

For sure, this girl intrigued me. Also, there was no denying it – she was truly stunning. Parking her declaration that we were an item to one side, I focused on the stranger called Terry.

"So come on, mate, who are you? You reckon you know my dad, Sidney?"

"No, Terry Walton."

"What? Don't dick me around. Terry Walton died before you and I were born!"

"Christ darling, I said be careful, and already you've blown it!"

"Look, I'll come back to that. But do you know a Dennis Hunt?"

"No. Should I?"

265

"He was Sidney's business partner, imprisoned for human trafficking just after you were born."

"Excuse me?"

"You weren't aware?"

"Is this a joke?"

"Seems good old Sidney was a bit tight-lipped about the whole affair!" Deana sunk into the swivel office chair, spinning it around to face the three who stood near the open doorway that led through to the reception area.

"That chair just moved again!" Courteney let go of my hand as she pointed to my old chair, which appeared to swivel around of its own volition.

The three of us all stared at the chair, which now appeared to be still.

"Sorry, darling. I'll try to behave. Do carry on. You're doing such a sterling job."

Courteney shook her head as if releasing the vision of a self-swivelling chair from her mind. "So, what's this Hunt bloke got to do with Damian, then?"

"That, I don't know. But it fits that Dennis Hunt would have an issue with Sidney because your stepfather helped put him away."

"What's that got to do with me?"

"Well, I'm led to believe that Sidney has moved to the States, and up until a few weeks ago, you owned this business, correct?"

"I did until Bridget and her brother conned me."

"Oh, our boy isn't the sharpest chisel in the toolbox, is he? I think he must have inherited that stupidity from you, darling. Because I can assure you it didn't come from me!"

Terry glanced at the office chair, appearing to frown, before returning his attention to me. "I think Bridget may have something to do with Dennis."

"Like what, exactly?"

"I don't know. Perhaps she's his daughter or an acquaintance of some sort."

"Her surname is Jones, not Hunt."

"She could be married?"

"What? Married and then lived with me for three months!"

"Divorced?"

"Oh, that's a bit tenuous! I really can't see how my ex-girlfriend can have anything to do with some business partner my dad stiffed thirty-odd years ago."

"Maybe, but you got any better ideas on why this Bridget conned you?"

Courteney, who'd been uncharacteristically quiet, halted her chewing gum swirling motion and fronted Terry up. "You heard of a Nathan Bragg?"

Terry involuntarily leaned back as Courteney entered his personal space. "No, should I? Who is he?"

Courteney waved the solicitor's letter in his face. "Nathan Bragg is working for Bridget. He introduced himself to Damian as her brother, but I'm guessing that is a load of bull."

"What's his part in all this?"

"Oh, no. You tell us what you know first," my newly acquired girlfriend fired back at the stranger, who seemed to know a lot about me.

"Yes, darling. I think you should tell him what we know so far."

Terry appeared to nod to the self-swivelling chair.

"Damian. As I said, I know that your previous girlfriend has conned you. I also believe that she engineered to have you set up in that hotel room in Birmingham, so she could have an excuse to kick you out on your ear and legitimately take your business whilst making you out to look like the one who'd cheated on her. So, as I—"

"Woah! Hang on. How the hell could you know about that?" I blurted, somewhat shocked that a stranger could possibly know anything about that night unless, of course, he'd been part of the set-up.

"I have certain information that an acquaintance supplied."

"What the hell does that mean?"

"Look, it just so happens that I know that information, and my job is to help you get out of this mess."

"Why?"

"Careful, darling. You're doing well up to now, so don't blow it!"

"That doesn't matter. What's important now is we're here to help you recover what's lost."

"We? Who is this we?"

"I mean me."

"I don't get it. Since that night in Birmingham, every bell-end on this planet seems to want to stiff me, and now you turn

268

up claiming to know what happened that night and reckon you're here to help me out."

Courteney retook hold of my hand. I glanced at her, surprised she'd become mute again. Although we'd only very recently made each other's acquaintance, I'd never known her to be this quiet for so long, even though it was probably only sixty seconds.

"Sorry, I wasn't referring to you as a bell-end," I offered her my best smile and squeezed her hand.

"What happened in Birmingham?" she asked with an almost vacant expression.

"That's why Bridget chucked me out. In your kitchen yesterday, when I said Bridget had booted me out, you said I'd stuck it where I shouldn't, remember?"

She nodded.

"Well, as I said, that wasn't the case. But someone set me up by getting some naked woman to pounce on me in my hotel bedroom while some bloke clicked away with their camera, gathering what looked like evidence of my infidelity."

"When … when was this?"

"Oh, a couple of weeks back."

Courteney let go of my hand whilst I refocused on this Terry bloke.

"So, come on, what is it to you? Why do you think it's your place to help me out?" I stepped forward and poked my index finger at him. "Because, pal, apart from Courteney, every tosser I've encountered in the last fortnight seems hell-bent on ruining me. So, you'll forgive my scepticism about your offer of assistance."

269

"Damian."

"Hang on, Courteney. I need this bloke to start talking."

"Babe."

I swivelled around, somewhat surprised that she called me babe, but more so by her tone, which afforded a hint of worry.

"Babe, it was me."

"What was you? What you on about?"

"It was me in Birmingham."

"What was you in Birmingham? Sorry, I might be doing my granny's custard thing, but what are you on about?"

Courteney appeared teary and, if I wasn't mistaken, I detected a slight chin wobble. I turned away from this Terry bloke, sensing a dramatic change in her demeanour. No longer was she the self-confident, brash woman comfortable in her own skin. Instead, she seemed to have taken on my perpetual state of anguish. Uncharacteristically, she chewed her bottom lip as a single tear tipped out of her right eye and careered down her cheek.

"Courteney?"

"I'm sorry, babe. I didn't know. Some geezer paid me eight-hundred quid for the job … I was the honey trap … he said …" she pinched her nose, as more tears flowed.

"Brummie trap might be more the term," chortled Deana.

I gawped at my not-so-confident accomplice. I never got a good look at the woman who flung herself on me that night. She was naked, beautiful, and it lasted for only a few seconds. My mind whirred around.

Were those crocodile tears, or had she unwittingly played a part in my downfall?

"All right, I get it, judging by the fact she seems hell-bent on showing off her knicker elastic and that plunging neckline suggests she's the sort of trollop that would appear in a men's grubby magazine, but I was led to believe the woman in that hotel room was supposed to be gorgeous ... this girl's just some rough slut with big tits from that bloody estate!"

The sound of a car door closing yanked me from my state of shock. The three of us shot each other a look. Despite Courteney's revelation, I had to remember that we were in my old office after performing a spot of breaking and entering. If this new arrival wasn't another guardian angel coming to join the party, Saturday afternoon was about to get a whole lot worse.

27

Where Do I Begin?

"We need to hide!" hissed Courteney, grabbing my hand and yanking me back through the reception area. Terry clearly agreed with her statement and bolted through the doorway, following us to our previous hiding place.

The three of us huddled down in a tight formation. Courteney gripped my hand, I suspected not through fear of what was coming through the door, but I sensed more through the desire to hang on to me after the revelation that she had been the gorgeous woman in the honey trap in that hotel room.

What game she was playing, I couldn't fathom. Had I just been a financial transaction, as she claimed, and it was just a quirk of fate that she was the girl who pounced naked upon me that night? Was she in on this con to ruin me? But why? And why did she say she was my girlfriend? She mentioned the love word earlier – had Courteney fallen for me – surely not.

Whilst I tried to work out who this girl was, Terry, the stranger, nudged in tight to Courteney's side, rendering my teary-eyed lover as the squashed filling in a rather odd man-sandwich – a position in her line of work I thought she might be well accustomed to.

"Get your arm away from my tits!" she hissed, as she pugnaciously jabbed her knuckles into Terry's biceps, the aggression in her voice more the attitude I was used to hearing from her.

"Oh, sorry," Terry winced, then rubbed his arm before squishing it tightly against his stomach to avoid further contact with Courteney's chest and presumably negate the chance of receiving any more violent pokes.

"Shush!" I hissed, as that familiar sound of someone treading broken glass became audible.

"Darling, it's some old chap who's as bald as a coot driving a battered white Transit van. He's hovering by the door and peering in through the broken window."

"I'm sorry," Courteney mouthed to me as I heard footsteps enter the office.

"He's stepped inside and looking around. Darling, he's definitely up to no good because he's wearing gloves. I think he's come to burgle the place. I reckon he must be one of those gyppo types. They drive those awful old vans, don't they?"

Terry swivelled his head towards us. "It's some old chap wearing gloves ... could be a gyppo."

I shot Courteney a look.

"You got x-ray eyes?" she whispered, before glancing at me and shrugging her shoulders. "How does he know that?"

I shook my head with knitted brows. Like her, I couldn't fathom how this Terry geezer could know who was rummaging around in my old office – unless he had x-ray eyes as Courteney suggested – hmmm, maybe not.

Deana sauntered through to reception to stand behind the three, who huddled in an almost scrum formation as they crouched down behind the counter. "I've had to move, darling, because he was about to sit on my lap! Now, as you know, I'm up for a bit of close male contact, but he's not my sort, I can tell you," she chuckled, before her face dropped at the sight of the low waistband of Courteney's jeans as she squatted down on her haunches.

"What's he doing?" Terry whispered into thin air.

Courteney turned to me, her face inches from mine. "Who the frig is he talking to?"

I shrugged, bemused and still wondering who this idiot was.

"The bloke's a frigging nutter!"

I nodded.

"Oh ... blimey, darling. I'm getting a right eyeful from this angle. This awful girl's got her G-string showing! She might as well not have bothered; you could park your bicycle up there!"

"Deana!"

"Sorry, darling, that awful girl's bottom distracted me." Deana stepped sideways and peered back into the office. "Yes, he's riffling through the desk drawers, and he's rammed that heap of post lying on the desk in his jacket pocket. I think I might go and have some fun."

"Christ, not again," muttered Terry.

Courteney raised her eyebrows at me, her eyes popping, non-verbally raising her concerns that this Terry bloke seemed to be talking to himself. I, on the other hand, couldn't shake from my head that, as he had yesterday, this bloke had blurted out my dead mother's name.

The three of us held our position as we listened to whoever rummaged through the desk. They clearly became frustrated when we started hearing loud tuts and the slamming of filing cabinet drawers.

Courteney shook her hand free from mine as she altered her stance and peeked over the top of the reception desk. Again, I tugged at her pocket. However, as per the last time I tried this tactic, it was to no avail.

Deana placed her hands on the back of the swivel chair and shoved it towards the frustrated chap as he barbarously raked through the bottom drawer of the filing cabinet.

"What the fuck!" he muttered, as he staggered backwards whilst bug-eyed watching the chair glide across the lino towards him. His backward stumble only halted as he crashed into the window blinds.

"Oh, darling, I love this! You should see the look on his face!" Deana clapped her hands, hopped up and down, and beamed like a schoolgirl who'd just won the top prize in the school's sports day skipping competition.

"What … the … fuck!" Courteney slowly exclaimed.

"Jesus, get down!" I hissed, tugging on her jeans.

Terry dropped his head in his hands. "Christ."

"Oi!" bellowed Courteney as she stood and purposefully marched towards the office.

"Oh, for God's sake. That bloody girl!"

"You!" blurted the shocked chap as he steadied himself on the windowsill, causing the Venetian blinds to clang like a set of wind chimes caught in the full force of a category-five hurricane.

275

I shot Terry a look, who reciprocated and shrugged before breaking cover and following her. I jumped up to follow but, in my haste, cracked my head on the protruding lip of the reception desk.

"Bollocks!"

Although I'd walloped my head and continued to verbalise my pain with a torrent of expletives, no one turned around. Whilst rubbing the affected area, I witnessed Courteney shimmy her way towards the bald chap, who appeared to have taken on a pale complexion as he fought to extradite himself from the tangle of metal slats.

"Yes, it's me! What the hell are you doing 'ere?" she wagged her finger at him as he appeared to accept that the tangled blind had the better of him. And now, like an exhausted fly trapped in a spider's web, he gave up his fight and accepted his fate as the venomous-tongued black widow in the form of Courteney advanced.

"Why are *you* here?" he fired back.

"I'm not surprised they know each other. They're both a couple of low-life reprobates. What with this tart parading all that unnecessary flesh and his unshaven pasty look, they're like a couple from the great unwashed!"

Terry and I appeared from the reception area and took in the odd scene in front of us.

"This is the bloke who paid me for Birmingham."

"The bloke who took the pictures?" I mumbled, still rubbing my head, expecting any minute now a sizeable red bulge to protrude from my skull, just as they always would in the Tom and Jerry cartoons.

"Yeah, it is!" Courteney swivelled around, her ill-gotten trainers squawking on the lino floor. "Babe? What's up with your head?"

"Jesus, is there a lump?" I glanced upwards, half expecting to see that throbbing protrusion.

"No, babe. You alright?"

"Yeah, I think so. I hit my bloody head on that counter."

"Hang on, what's going on? How come you two are here … together? And who the hell are you?" From his tangled web position, he pointed at Terry, who pulled back the swivel chair and plonked himself down, appearing to bear the weight of the world upon his shoulders.

"I'm Terry. And you are?"

"None of your business, mate."

"You said your name was Fred when we had that little jaunt up to Birmingham. So, is that your real name, then?"

Fred shrugged and nodded, seemingly accepting defeat.

"Right, Fred—"

"Nah, Right Said Fred, although he deffo ain't too sexy for his shirt, that I can tell you!" chuckled Courteney, leaving Terry appearing somewhat bemused.

"Oh, ever the comedian! It's a song from yesteryear, darling. You were dead, and luckily for you, you missed out!"

Spotting no one else seemed amused by her joke Courteney nodded to Terry. "Go on, mate; you were about to say?"

Terry nodded before clearing his throat. "Okay, so, Fred, you'd better start talking. You may think you know this girl," he waved his hand towards Courteney. "But believe me, mate, she's tougher than she looks, and her bite is definitely worse

277

than her bark," he chuckled whilst rubbing his biceps. "Also, unless you come up with some credible answers, self-swishing chairs is going to be the least of your worries," Terry nodded at Courteney, who still held her finger out, pointing at the man tangled in the Venetian-blind web. "The floor is all yours."

"Cheers. But when I've done wiv him, you need to explain how that chair moves on its own."

"Careful, darling. We don't want any silliness, do we now?"

Terry nodded at Courteney, then turned and appeared to nod to the open doorway to the reception area.

I decided he was a nutter.

"What you on about self-swishing chairs?" I quizzed, wondering what Courteney had witnessed when peering over the reception counter.

"Not now. Christ, babe, just be quiet for a minute," she batted back at me, somewhat aggressively.

"Oh, well, thanks!" I belligerently mumbled. "Jesus, it's alright for you, but it's me who's in the shit here, you know. I'm the one who lost everything, got the police trying to fit me up, and not to mention a psychopathic drugged up nutter about to castrate me," I muttered, feeling a bit put out that she'd barked.

Courteney stepped a pace towards the man tangled up in the blind. "Don't move a bleedin' muscle, you hear?" Then, turning to face me, she thumped her hands on her hips. "Look, babe. I know I said I like the little-lost-boy persona you give off but, right now, I need to find out what this twat 'ere knows," she thrust her hand towards the man in the blind, who appeared to be performing a reasonably good impression of a

278

quivering fox facing a pack of bloodthirsty hounds. "I'll be straight up with you. Although it's pretty friggin' obvious, I've had a few geezers in my time, but last night I fink I also made it abundantly clear that I showed you how much I fancy you."

I nodded, then winced, convinced I'd acquired a brain haemorrhage.

"In fact, I've fancied the arse off you since the day you moved in next door, and since yesterday I now know that I think I might be in friggin' love with you, alright?"

"Oh, right," I nodded and offered a nervous grin.

"Good. Because if we're going to get you out of this bleedin' mess, I need to see a little bit more backbone from you. Stop rubbing your naffin' head and man up! I'm sticking myself out on a limb for you, not to mention what the fuck we do about that twat, Karl. But listen up, babe, whether I'm too low down the social ladder for you, or you just couldn't face being seen wiv someone like me, I'm prepared to risk everyfink just on the off chance you might fink I'm worth a go."

"Oh, well. It's not exactly a scene from Love Story, and this girl is no Ali MacGraw, but I'm welling up! Although she really needs to sort her dress sense out and her mouth is like a sewer, I'll give the little slut her due, there's a bit of fight in the girl. I suppose after a trip to a decent lady's outfitters and a bar of soap in her mouth, she might scrub up alright."

After Courteney had laid her cards on the table, silence descended in the room for a few moments. I wasn't sure how I felt about her lifestyle. Without any measure of doubt, I was concerned about Karl. However, apart from Bridget's bull-shit lies, no one had said anything close to that nice to me before – discounting the fuck and twat references.

"Damian?" quizzed Terry.

I glanced at him as he swivelled in my office chair to face me. "What?"

"At the very least, I think the girl deserves an answer."

The blinds rattled as the terrified fox shifted his weight on the windowsill. "Err ... this is all very nice, but—"

"Shut up!" barked Terry and Courteney in unison.

I pointed at her. "You change careers?"

She enthusiastically nodded.

"You give up your acting side-line with Donk?"

She nodded again, this time with a little more vigour.

"The girl's an actress? Christ, I had her pegged as some rough prostitute, not an actress!"

"You close down your Suzzysuck.com website?"

"Oh, my God! She's a porn star! That explains the tits and lack of acceptable attire."

She nodded. "Deffo, babe."

"Karl?"

"I'll leave him."

"Then yes, I think you're worth a go."

"Cool! I fink that's great," she sniggered, flashing her enormous smile, then spun on her heels, which produced another loud squeak, before baring her teeth at the fox. "Right, you better start talking. I wanna know who paid you to set up my man!"

28

Follow The Yellow Brick Road

After my newly acquired girlfriend allowed Fred Hallam to extract himself from the Venetian blind, she verbally and physically made it abundantly clear by expertly applying a torrent of abuse and that wagging finger that he needed to start talking.

So, whilst pondering my new relationship, along with the possibility I may be suffering a life-threatening bleed on the brain, whilst also sporting a gaping mouth, I listened as the private eye recounted his story about the mystery man who appeared hell-bent on ruining my life.

Whoever this man was, he'd gone to great lengths and a considerable financial outlay to ensure those pictures landed in Bridget's lap and then plant drugs in my flat. As my leggy-blonde girl squeezed the information from him, my mind whirred around, trying to think who the hell would go to such extraordinary lengths to ruin me.

Okay, Bridget had clearly conned me. I'm guessing that her brother, Nathan, wasn't her brother but an accomplice who was part of the sting to take my business – the real honey trap had been Bridget, not Courteney.

I'd been so sucked in they probably couldn't believe their luck in discovering such a gullible idiot like me. Christ, they must have laughed their way to the bank with the proceeds of my stock of cars and now this garage. Bridget and Nathan had tricked me out of my fortune, and the pictures of a naked Courteney entangled with me had presumably been the final act in that elaborate con.

However, they had disappeared, so who wanted me caught with a stash of drugs? Who had that kind of cash to throw at this dodgy private investigator? And who wished for me to languish inside Brixton Prison for the next ten years? Nope, I couldn't think of anyone who hated me that much. Well, okay, there was Laura, Rob's wife. Her dislike for me was fairly obvious to spot. However, I hadn't pegged her for this kind of elaborate operation, which would indeed be an overreaction to the debacle at their wedding breakfast.

I considered this Fred guy was just some bloke earning a crust. Whether that line of work was particularly ethical or not, I didn't know, but he wasn't to blame. At least I'd discovered the identity of the bloke on the phone who seemed to sniff a few times. Although this Fred bloke had tricked me, I was relieved that the willy-waver in the park hadn't been the caller. So, although I still had no idea what was going on, at least I didn't have a pervert stalking me – a smidgen of relief in all this chaos.

To add to this odd situation, I still couldn't fathom out what part this Terry bloke was playing. I considered my earlier assessment that he must be some random nutter who liked to repeatedly call out my dead mother's name. Also, it appeared he suffered from that odd tic of constantly offering a nod to thin air as if he'd brought along his imaginary friend to keep him company.

For a young woman, slight in stature, Courteney seemed to afford the presence to persuade Fred to talk. Whether Fred was attentive to her questioning style due to fear of receiving a slap, or he was ogling her exposed pierced navel and the thin elastic of her G-string, I couldn't tell. Maybe the latter, as he looked the sort and probably, with some regularity, paid his subscription to Suzzysuck.com and would now be devastated that avenue of relief would soon close.

However, I figured if she hadn't been forced into a life in the sex industry, Courteney could have made a go of it in the Criminal Investigation Department up at Fairfield nick. I could imagine her putting the fear of God into anyone who threw in too many 'no comment' answers, judging by her constant hostile probing of Fred's story.

"So let me get this straight. Some geezer just rocks up at your gaff and chucks ten grand your way to set Damian up wiv me in that hotel room and then plant a stash of drugs in his freezer."

"Yeah," he nodded as he perched on the windowsill whilst wringing his hands.

"Darling, I wonder if we should involve the police? You know, an anonymous phone call, perhaps?"

I glanced at Terry as he swivelled in that chair and, again, shook his head towards the area near reception. His actions confirmed there was something not right about the bloke. Perhaps, after my leggy-blonde girlfriend had chewed up and spat Fred out, she needed to turn her attentions on Terry and wheedle some sensible answers out of him.

"Babe, what d'you reckon? You believe him?" Courteney glanced over her shoulder whilst maintaining her aggressive stance in front of Fred.

"No idea," I shook my head, bemused by the whole affair.

Whilst Courteney returned her attention to Fred, I pondered the giant puddle of poo that I seemed to be sinking in. Two days ago, I only had a lost business and a breakup with my girlfriend to worry about. Now, I'd just agreed to date a porn star who definitely wasn't the type of girl to take home to mother, not that I had one of those, but you get my drift.

Also, I wasn't quite sure about being called babe. However, chavvy terms of endearment aside, since her declaration of love and intention to dump the Pitbull, I couldn't get it out of my head that Karl may not be too chuffed about that idea. Ignoring the fact that Karl would castrate or kill me, or if I was super lucky, both, there was something alluring about this girl that sucked me in. Could I imagine a future with her? Or had I just leapt from one disaster to the next?

"Hey, look, I'm telling the truth," blurted Fred.

"Okay, but you deffo don't know this geezer? You never met him before?"

"No, never. As I said, he gave me the job, and I employed you to carry out the sting. And I might add you were quite happy to take the cash and whip your kit off."

"Yeah, well, that was then. I didn't know that Damian was my neighbour."

"Hang on, why are you here?" I interjected.

Courteney swivelled her head around and nodded at me before returning her aggressive stance over Fred. "Well?"

Fred held up his hands. "Look, to be honest with you, I had a call from that bloke about an hour ago."

"The geezer who gave you five grand and the drugs?"

"Yeah. He was pissed off because he reckoned the drugs I planted yesterday have gone missing. He said, unless I found out what had happened, I could expect a lengthy stay up at Fairfield General."

"I'll stick you in Fairfield General if you don't get to the bleedin' punch line."

Fred winced, probably because he thought my leggy blonde was capable of such an act. "Look, to be honest with you, I get the feeling he's not the sort to dish out veiled threats. I know Sidney, and then Damian owned this garage, so I thought this place would be as good as any to start sniffing around and see what I could find out."

"Find out what?"

"Hell, Jesus, I don't know. But listen, that bastard is holding me responsible for the lost package and, unless I could get some information, I have no way of finding out how to get it back."

Courteney nodded.

"I don't suppose you know where the drugs are, do you? You'd be doing me one hell of a favour if I could get them back?"

"Are you for real, mate? You plant the drugs in Damian's flat, and now you want them back? Fuck me, you're also like granny's custard."

"What?"

"Fick! You're bleedin' fick if you fink we're just going to hand over a pack of drugs and say, there, no harm done!"

"Yeah, I know, I know. But listen, this git is going to break my legs if—"

"Like we give a shit! Anyway, you're royally stiffed because we flushed the whole lot down the shitter."

"Oh, shit," Fred mumbled as he dropped his head in his hands, presumably pondering what colour plaster casts he could request for his soon-to-be snapped limbs – I'm led to believe that plaster of Paris now comes in a variety of colours other than white.

"So, hang on, you were going to break in here, then?" I threw in.

"Well, no, I thought I'd pick the lock. But it turns out someone had already used a blunter method to gain entry."

"Fred, you ever heard of a Dennis Hunt?" Terry asked, as he rocked back and forth, making himself comfortable in my previously owned office chair.

Fred narrowed his eyes but said nothing.

"Went to prison in the early '80s for people trafficking," Terry added.

"Okay. So, here's the thing. The guy who paid me to set up Damian in Birmingham and then plant the drugs came to me a few months ago and asked me to do a spot of investigating into Sidney Statham."

"Why?" I blurted.

"I don't know. I don't ask those questions. All I do is gather information and get paid. Now, listen, my inquiries did throw up the name Dennis Hunt because he and Sidney were ex-business partners."

"Could this chap who paid you be Dennis Hunt?" Terry quizzed.

"No, Dennis Hunt is dead. He was released from prison in the late '80s and moved to Ireland. He died in a hospice last summer."

I shot Courteney a look whilst Terry performed his usual odd tic by nodding at the empty space by reception.

"Oh. Well, I take it this bloke who employed you wasn't him, then," Terry's shoulders sagged, appearing deflated by the news of this Dennis bloke's demise.

"Unless he's a ghost, no, it ain't. He scares the shit out of me, but he's no ghost. Anyway, as I said, I reckon the chap who you're after is about your age." He nodded to Terry and me.

"What about Nathan Bragg? You heard of him?" Courteney threw in.

Fred, who faced interrogation from all sides, frowned again and shook his head.

"Oh, Jesus, this is getting us nowhere," I threw my hands in the air in frustration. Although I'd solved the mystery of how that strange 'pack of butter' ended up in my fridge, we were careering headlong down a dead end. One thing for certain, I couldn't see how Sidney's ex-business partner had anything to do with this situation.

"Darling, this isn't the answer. I just can't see how Sidney's dead business partner has anything to do with this. It's that Bridget girl we have to track down and force to return the garage and proceeds of the sale of his cars to our boy. Blackmail is our game, not hunting spooks."

"What about Bridget Jones," Terry quizzed.

Fred's eyes flitted back and forth between the three of us. "As I said, this bloke mentioned that name, as he said it would convince Damian to turn up at the pre-arranged time in the park. But, look, honestly, I don't know a Bridget Jones."

"Bit of a bloody useless private investigator if you ask me. Not exactly Jessica Fletcher, is he? I think the criminal fraternity of Cabot Cove could sleep easy at night if they had little sweaty-head Fred investigating. I'd be surprised if he could find his way out of the lavatory, let alone solve this mystery. Anyway, he's only a little fella, more Inch High Private Eye," she chuckled.

"Tell me, Mr Hallam, do you believe in ghosts?" Terry casually asked. His tone suggested it was a typical everyday question that one might ask, like enquiring if Fred fancied a coffee.

The three of us all peered at Terry, who, with his deadpan expression, raised his eyebrows at Fred to affirm he was waiting for his answer.

"Jesus, what the hell are you on about? If this Dennis Hunt is dead, he ain't wandering around Fairfield chucking around ten grand trying to get Damian fitted up," Courteney belligerently batted back at Terry.

"Hear me out," Terry held his index finger aloft, indicating he wanted to make his point.

I shot Courteney a look – we both shrugged.

"Well. Mr Hallam … ghosts?"

"Darling, I might need a heads up on this one. Where are you going with this? Also, please could you ask that girl to hitch her jeans up? Although that G-string is very nice, I'm sure, but Inch-High Private Eye appears to be struggling to concentrate with all that flesh and lace in his eye line."

"I have no idea what you're on about, mate. What the hell have bloody ghosts got to do with this conversation?"

"Oh, no. You're not suggesting ... are you? Darling, please don't expect me to start prancing around the room, flinging objects about like the Wicked Witch of the West!"

29

Action Man

Unsurprisingly, Courteney wasn't of the mind to allow Terry to question Fred regarding his ghostly beliefs.

"Are you for real, mate? This git has been party to setting up Damian, and you want to know if he's into ghost stories or believes that the un-dead are roaming around amongst us. Christ, what are you, some kind of deluded nutter?"

"Well?" I raised my hands, enforcing Courteney's point.

"Okay, as I see it, we need to know who this man is that has set you up, right?"

"Yes!" blurted both I and Courteney in unison.

"Agreed, and this chap here," Terry waved a hand towards Fred. "Needs to find out who he is—"

"You can forget that! I think I've said too much already, mate," Fred interrupted. "The bloke who wanted you set up is a no-good gangster type of psycho. I'm not getting involved in whatever nutty scheme you're cooking up."

"I thought you'd say that," Terry shifted forward in his seat before pointing at Fred. "That's why I asked if you believe in ghosts."

"No, darling. Oh, no, I'm not getting into another fiasco like we did at that bookies," Deana folded her arms and defiantly stuck her nose in the air.

"You are," Terry muttered.

"No! You're just abusing my talents. I won't play your silly games!"

"You are what?" Courteney quizzed.

Terry ignored Courteney and instead continued to mutter. "Don't let me down. I'm out on a limb here."

"Well, you should have pre-warned me you intended to use my rather exclusive skills. I can't just be used and abused at your whim. Of course, if you want to use me in the bedroom, that's another matter, but expecting me to leap around like Elphaba Thropp is not acceptable."

"Babe, I don't know who this twat is, but he's got issues."

Terry ignored Courteney's somewhat accurate assessment, instead choosing to focus on Mr Hallam. "See, this is how it's going to play out. You are going to find the bloke who set Damian up, or I will unleash the power of the dead upon you."

"What the—"

"Filing trays on the floor," commanded Terry as he pointed to the three plastic stacked trays positioned on my old desk.

"No. No, I told you I'm not taking part in this charade!"

"Deana! Now."

I glanced at Courteney, then at Fred. I sensed that none of us knew whether to burst out laughing or should call for the men in white coats to take this poor, deluded nutter to a secure unit for the mentally disturbed. However, Courteney and Fred were probably just wondering why Terry was instructing a set of trays to move of their own volition, whereas I was also bemused why he again spouted my mother's name.

"Filing trays on the floor!" he again commanded, waving his finger at the innocuous plastic trays as if trying to will them with his mind to move like performing some Uri Geller trick.

"Oh, that's it. I'm off." Fred stood, affording Courteney a wide berth as he shimmied around, although giving her the once up and down for good measure. "Look, sorry, Damian, no hard feelings? I was just doing a job," he held out his hand to me.

"Bloody hell, woman. I need you to step up to the plate here; otherwise, the mission is blown. I suspect the powers that be are going to be somewhat miffed!"

We all gawped at Terry as he blustered his demands to the open doorway. Fred held his hand there, waiting for me to shake it; Courteney just shook her head in disbelief.

"Alright, alright. But I don't like being used as a pawn in some game that I'm blissfully unaware we're supposed to be playing." She leaned across the desk and swished the stack of trays to the floor. "There, I hope you know what you're doing!"

I glanced at Fred, who appeared fixated on the heap of trays and paperwork that now lay strewn across the floor. He still held his hand out as if Medusa had turned him to stone.

"What the fu—"

"Plant pot!" Terry interrupted Courteney, as he swivelled around and pointed his finger at a somewhat dilapidated, dehydrated spider plant that drooped in a white ceramic pot on top of the filing cabinet.

"Oh, good grief. If I must!" Deana, releasing her frustration, slapped her hand at the plant, sending it flying over Terry's head.

"Christ, Deana, be careful!"

"Oh, don't fuss! It missed you, didn't it? Now, listen, you might be having fun, but I'm finding this all rather tedious."

"How the bejesus can you do that?" I blurted.

My outburst appeared to release Fred from his trance. Not waiting for my handshake, he made a grab for the door and yanked it open, only for the door to slam shut and rattle in the frame, causing the last few fragments of glass to topple out and land on the lino floor.

"Now that's it! Get this pasty-looking old sod to do what you ask because I've had enough. And for Christ's sake, stop saying my name. I think our boy has cottoned on to the fact you keep blurting out the name of his dead mother."

Fred backed up a pace, his mouth gaping. I glanced at Courteney before we both focused on Terry, who rocked back and forth in my old chair with his arms folded, sporting a rather smug look.

"Babe, this geezer's like Matilda," she whispered, her hand flailing away at her side as she tried to find mine, gripping it when she eventually latched on.

"Mr Hallam. I warned you I could unleash the power of the dead. And a few flying objects will be the least of your worries if you don't start playing ball."

Fred turned and faced Terry, his Adam's apple appearing to perform a hop, skip and jump as it bounced around whilst he swallowed whatever bile had risen in his throat. "Look, this bloke's in his thirties, wears a baseball cap and scares the shit out of me. That's all I know."

I shot Courteney a look whilst Terry continued. My girl shook her head at me. I guess indicating that we shouldn't say anything about that bent copper. However, I had Gold-tooth pegged for at least forty. So, unless Fred was poor at guessing ages, it suggested Nathan was our man. That said, Nathan hadn't come across as scary, so I considered the possibility that there was a third person involved.

"But you don't know how to contact him?"

Like a schoolboy accused of being up to no good, Fred exaggeratedly shook his head. "He rings me. Burner phone, I suspect."

"Well, I suggest you find out, Mr Hallam. We now know who you are and where to find you. Unless you want the vengeance of the dead unleashed upon you, I suggest you do as I ask."

Fred involuntarily nodded. "He's going to ring me tomorrow night. He said I'd better have the drugs by then. If not, I knew the consequences."

"Good, that's settled then. You find out who he is, and let's reconvene on Monday. Shall we say All Saints Church at noon?"

I glanced at Courteney, who shrugged. I thought it an odd place to meet, but it also reminded me I hadn't been up to tend to my real father's parents' grave for some time.

"You want to meet at a church … where they bury dead people?" Fred seemed to pale, probably imagining a scene from the *Evil Dead.*

"Well, I suspect not many alive are buried up there," chuckled Terry, before applying a somewhat sterner demeanour and wagging his finger at the pasty little man. "Turn up with the information, Hallam. Otherwise, you will have visitors from beyond the grave."

Fred nodded, turned and bolted to the door, tentatively checking it wasn't going to slam again before stumbling out and rather chaotically bounding across the Trifid-infused forecourt to where he'd earlier abandoned his Transit van.

"Well, you seem to have become quite cock-sure of yourself, I must say. It's a pity you weren't a bit more forthright during our last mission when trying to help little Kimmy."

"What's going on here? And come to think of it, you still haven't explained who the hell you are," I stammered, still trying to figure out how he could command objects to fly across the room.

Deana propped her bottom on the end of the desk, leaning towards Terry and squeezing his thigh. "I think I quite like this display of authority. Perhaps you could take me home and become all domineering in the bedroom," she pouted.

Terry appeared distracted. Whether he possessed telekinetic powers or some other unexplained reason had caused these odd phenomena that we'd just witnessed, the man could only be described as a bloody fruit loop.

"Damian, as I said yesterday, I knew your mother. I promised if anything happened to her, I would look out for you."

I huffed as I let go of Courteney's hand. "Sorry, mate, I don't get it. My mother couldn't give a flying whatever when

I was alive, so I can't see how she would give two shits when she's dead. So sorry, mate, your story is full of shit."

"No, it's not. She genuinely does. Your mother wants me to help you."

"Oh, okay, is that so?" I sarcastically batted back. "So, you're some medium with spooky powers, are you? What, you gonna whip out your Tarot cards in a minute and tell me I'm gonna meet some gorgeous blonde bird who's going to whisk me off my feet and I'll live happily ever after?" I scoffed.

"You have, babe."

I turned to Courteney.

"I'm your gorgeous blonde," she smirked and grabbed my hand.

"Oh, heavens, how old is she? What does she think this is, a bloody Cinderella pantomime! She's acting like a gooey-eyed nine-year-old who's fallen for a Donny Osmond type, who she has pegged for Prince Charming," chortled Deana, who allowed her hand to continue to stroke Terry's thigh.

Terry removed Deana's hand as it came to rest on his groin, only for her to replace it there and him to repeat the action.

"Oi, you're not playing with yourself, are you?" fired out Courteney.

"No!"

"Why you rubbing your bleedin' balls, then?"

"I wasn't." Then, as he always seemed to perform, he shot a look to his left and hissed. "Get off."

Courteney and I glanced at each other, she was presumably like me, once again somewhat bemused by his outburst. If he was some psychic, I guess their minds worked differently. So, perhaps this odd behaviour was all quite normal for him. That said, Terry didn't dress and act like your average fortune teller, and he didn't appear to have a crystal ball or wear a headscarf. I mused for a second if I should tap him up for this week's Euro Millions lottery numbers – in my current situation, fifty-million quid could come in handy.

"This is more like it, darling. So much more fun than flinging things around the room." Deana sniggered as she replaced her hand on his lap. *"You're so manly when you're in control,"* she growled.

"Look, I'm not a medium, as you put it, but I am in contact with the dead. In more ways than one, you might say," he mumbled whilst peering at his lap.

"Nutter!" scoffed Courteney, before yanking my hand, indicating we should move. "Come on, babe, let's get out of here. We're pushing our luck 'cos some git will notice the broken window, and we'll have the filth down on us if we're not careful."

"I hasten to agree with the girl. She makes a good point, darling. Perhaps we should go too."

"Hang on. Are you in contact with my mother? Is that why you keep saying her name?" Not that I thought for one moment he really was, but hell, I was keen to see what he'd say.

"Babe, we need to go," Courteney tugged my arm.

"Hang on. Just give me a minute." I focused on Terry, who didn't answer me. "Well, come on, is she here? In this room right now?" I dramatically waved my free hand around the office.

"Babe, you alright?"

"Damian, it's complicated."

"Ask her what she brought me for my fourteenth birthday. The only birthday she ever gave me a present, I might add."

"Damian, I not sure—"

"No, go on, ask her," I interrupted him.

"An Action Man," Deana muttered, bowing her head.

"He said fourteenth, not fourth!" Terry performed that oddity of shouting at no one.

"I know, it's embarrassing. I didn't realise he'd grown up that fast. It wasn't my fault. How was I supposed to know what pubescent fourteen-year-old boys like? Anyway, it's the thought that counts, and it was the one with real hair and swivelling eyes … I seem to recall the toy shop assistant saying it was the latest must-have toy."

Courteney stopped tugging and stepped back by my side.

"Your mother bought you an Action Man, apparently."

I held his stare as a solitary tear clouded my vision in my left eye.

My mother arrived at my house on that birthday and handed me the parcel wrapped in Power Rangers paper. She said she hoped I liked it and then left. I can recall nearly every word my mother had said to me because there weren't that many.

"Babe?"

"I'm getting upset again."

"All I wanted was her love … perhaps you could tell her that?"

"I will. But I think your young lady is right. We need to get out of here before someone calls the authorities."

"First sensible fing this twat's said."

"I've proven to you I know things that can't be explained, and I've earned the right to gain your trust, yes?"

I nodded, simply because I didn't know what else to do.

"Oi. You still ain't explained how you moved those fings."

I glanced at Courteney. "I think it was my mother."

30

The Sopranos

After Terry disappeared around the side of the building, we nipped across the road, back to the pavement in the same place we'd stood just half an hour ago when Courteney educated me about her take on fiscal policy and her understanding that shoplifting and breaking and entering were assisting in keeping the wheels of industry turning. An interesting take on crime, I mused.

"How's your head, babe?"

"It's okay, I think. Anyway, as you said, I need to man up."

"Look, babe, I didn't mean anyfink by what I said. But it's a tough world, and unless you're prepared to grab what you want, you'll get nowhere in life. Dog eat dog."

I nodded. "I think I'm starting to learn that."

"So, you got concussion then?"

"No. I'm a hypochondriac. I'm sure it's fine," I mumbled whilst rubbing my head, searching for that lump that wasn't there.

"Okay. So, what was all this shit about your dead mother, then?"

I shook my head, glancing back at the ghostly hollow of the showroom. "I don't know," I mumbled.

For sure, either a poltergeist had taken up residence in my old business, Terry was a medium with ways of contacting the dead, or my deceased mother had actually stood in the office with us.

'Jesus, Damian, what are you suggesting?'

I ignored my mind talk. However, rather than elaborate on what was whirring around my head, I decided to change the subject. "So, what now?"

"Now, babe, we need to get to the train station, and quickly." Courteney grabbed my hand and hauled me forward as she set off at a punchy pace.

"Courteney, why are we heading for the train station?" I tugged her hand, trying to slow her blitzkrieg-type march.

"Babe, trust me, we ain't got much time."

"Time for what?"

"Karl!" she fired back.

"Oh, shit. What, we're going on the run?"

Courteney raised her eyebrows at me. "Come on, babe, just trust me."

I pondered that this would be my new life. Courteney and I would hide away in some remote town before needing to skedaddle every few months when the Pitbull or Gold-tooth started to close the net. I faced an existence of hiding in the shadows, never putting down roots and regarding everyone we met as a potential grass. For sure, if Courteney wanted to become incognito, she'd have to alter her appearance because whether she donned those thigh-high boots or her pink hoodie and stolen trainers, the girl turned heads – she'd turned mine, although I still wasn't quite sure if I'd made the right choice.

As for me, well, yes, she was quite right – I needed to grow a pair. Let's face it, I don't recall Jason Bourne or Richard Hannay wimping out when the pressure was on. Also, I remember they both got their girl. So, if Courteney was sincere about me, I must take control, deal with what lies ahead like a man and just maybe I would earn the right to have my girl too.

'This is it, Damian, thirty-two years of drifting through life ... now it's time to man up!'

I nodded to myself as we zipped our way through the back streets and alleyways towards Fairfield's train station. Anyway, if this girl was smitten enough with me to jeopardise her whole life, then showing a bit of backbone was the very least I could do.

She halted at the end of the alley that led out opposite the station, waving her hand behind her to indicate that I should stop. She parted the overhanging branches of a large laurel hedge and peered through like some amateur sleuth following the killer. "Agatha Raisin, eat your heart out," I muttered, as I moved my head around trying to spot what Courteney was checking out.

"Shush, babe."

"What we stopped for?"

"Babe, I know a few of the girls that work the station area. I'm just checking it's clear."

"Right. And where are we going first? Scotland has always been on my bucket list."

"Bleedin' hell, ever the adventurer!" she chuckled. "Top of my list is Nepal to see the sun rise above Everest. But if

302

chasing the Loch Ness Monster or visiting some drug den in Glasgow is your fing, whatever floats your boat, I guess."

"Nepal?"

"Come on, babe, it's clear. Too early for the girls to be out and about yet."

I trotted along with Courteney, wondering where she planned for us to go tonight. For sure, we wouldn't be catching a train to Nepal because I didn't have my passport with me. Also, I doubted the Orient Express, or the sub-continent equivalent, departed from Fairfield. So, perhaps it was Scotland, then – I'd heard that springtime on the Isle of Skye could be pleasant.

Fairfield station comprises two platforms with a dilapidated, although ornate, Victorian footbridge spanning the lines. The bridge, being the last remaining evidence of a time when rail travel held a certain romantic notion, all of which had now frittered away. The concrete, glass and steel block that replaced the Victorian station building at the time of the millennium condemned the golden age of the railways to history. The flaking-paint bridge and the modern station, now unlikely partners guarding that gateway to escape my previous somewhat humdrum of a life.

Courteney scooted through the glass doors that efficiently swished apart as we approached. However, rather than heading for the ticket machines, instead, she hot-footed to the bank of public pay phones.

"Who you calling? Why don't you just use your mobile?" I quizzed as she grabbed the receiver before extracting a tissue from her jeans pocket and vigorously wiping the mouthpiece. "And where are we going?"

303

Courteney glanced up at me as she scrubbed the handset. "Granny's custard," she chuckled. "We ain't going nowhere. I just need a payphone."

"Oh."

"Filthy fings, God knows what shit you can catch from these bastards."

"You need a phone card to use this. Look, it doesn't take coins."

"Not for nine-nine-nine, you don't." She tapped out the numbers whilst I huddled close to her, leaning my head in to hear the conversation.

"Which emergency service do you require?" asked an apathetic, almost bored female voice.

Courteney placed the tissue over the mouthpiece before she spoke. "Police."

I shot her a look. Was she reporting the break-in at the garage and using the tissue to hide her voice?

"Police. What's your emergency?"

"Listen up and take note. The gun used to kill the Albanian geezer on the Broxworth Estate free weeks ago can be found in a shoe box under the bed in flat 120 Belfast House. Karl Green, a local git who's well known to you lot, used the gun to kill that bloke. You can find him at flat 110 Dublin House."

"Can I have your name, please?"

"A concerned citizen." Courteney replaced the receiver and puffed out an enormous sigh. "What?" she quizzed, as I hovered close whilst sporting a bug-eyed expression with my mouth performing a reasonable impression of a Venus flytrap.

"Is … is that true?" I stammered.

"Yeah. The twat had to kill him, or the Gowers who control the drug gangs were going to stiff Karl."

I shook my head, unable to find my voice. This was a whole new world to me.

"Look, babe, as I said, the Broxworth is a tough place … it's not for the likes of you."

I nodded, knowing never a truer statement had been uttered.

"Karl's a twat. He kept that gun as a souvenir. He thinks he's bleedin' Tony Soprano and reckons he's high up in the echelon of organised crime. I know differently. And the Gowers fink he's a dick, who they just used to clean up a mess."

"Christ." I stepped back a pace.

"Babe, it was the only way. Karl's always getting that bloody thing out and waving it around. His prints will be all over it."

"I take it you're referring to the gun, not his todger?"

Courteney thumped her hands on her hips, shifting her stance whilst sporting a smirk. "Yeah, he likes to wave that around too, but I'm talking about the gun. You're funny; you know that?"

"Hilarious. But Jesus, Courteney, this is heavy shit! Won't they raid your flat, and then you'll be arrested?"

She shook her head, causing her long hair to take flight before coming to rest across her eyes. My girl parted her golden locks and stepped towards me. "The filth know I'm a tom, and they know Karl's in with the Gowers. They'll lift the gun and then take him down."

305

"Why?"

"Why did I grass?"

I nodded.

"Babe, there was no other way."

"To leave him?"

She nonchalantly offered a shrug of her shoulders. "Babe, our relationship is all about me owing him. I can never leave the git. Never. He'd kill me."

"Err …really? He … he would … kill you?" I asked, my staccato voice reaching a high note whilst still sporting those bug eyes, but I managed to stop catching flies.

"Yeah, really. Sake, Damian, I can't just say it's not working for me anymore and suggest me and him have a temporary separation to see where our hearts lie. Jesus, babe, Karl decides what I do, who I see, and where I go. Only when he's on a bloody bender at Fat Larry's gaff do I get any soddin' respite."

"Why? He doesn't own you. If you want out, you just leave him."

"He thinks he does. Normal relationships don't work like that in my world. If Karl ever decided he didn't want me, he'd just kill me."

I slowly shook my head in disbelief. Was this reality? Is this how she lived her life? And more to the point, was I just a convenient get-out-of-jail-free card she'd plucked from the stack of those pink Community Chest cards in the real-life game of Monopoly?

"Babe?"

"Are you using me? You know, a route to get away from him?"

A dark thundercloud crossed her face, her eyes taking on an evil glare.

Out of the corner of my eye, I spotted a guy with pointed shoes, wearing a flashy grey suit and sporting that perfect designer stubble, which all the flashy city types thought was the required look, as he barrelled towards us. Before Courteney could verbalise what was clearly going to be quite abusive in response to my accusation, Pointy-shoes nudged me sideways, feigned a head butt and offered me a waft of his heavily alcohol-infused breath.

"Piss off," he held my stare before turning to Courteney. "Alright, love?" He thumbed out a wad of twenties and rammed them into her jean's front pocket, rubbing his hand across her crotch as he did so. "Come on. I need a decent-looking tart to bounce on my lap for a couple of hours."

"Fuck off!" Courteney shoved him backwards.

He stepped back and smirked. "Come on, I've had you a few times. Nice tits if I remember."

"I ain't working," she spat, shoving him in the chest with both hands.

Although going by the pungent waft of stale alcohol emanating from his mouth suggested he'd been on the piss for a few hours over lunch, he held his ground before barbarously grabbing her wrist and yanking her away. "I've paid you, bitch, so come on."

I glanced around the foyer as he and Courteney fought. She slapping with her free hand, him grappling with her wrists as he tried to control her. The doleful-looking chap in the snack kiosk glanced up at the commotion before bowing his head. An elderly couple who'd just figured out how the ticket machine worked glanced at the two of them fighting, then scowled and shuffled away. This was Saturday afternoon, not a busy time for a provincial train station, and no one else entered or left as Courteney did her level best to blind the man with a few finger jabs to his face.

'*Man up!*'

"Alright!" I belligerently muttered back at my mind talk.

I spun around, searching for an appropriate weapon, knowing the last time I'd punched someone was about twenty-seven years ago when I clattered one of dad's girlfriend's sons. I was five; he was three. However, this was a bit different.

Tearing off a CO_2 fire extinguisher from the wall, I hefted it up and swung it down on the tosser's forearm. The unmistakable sound of cracking bone preceded a silent sucking of air as he collapsed to the floor. As he found his voice and screamed in pain, I grabbed my girl's hand and dragged her through the glass door that obediently swished as we darted towards them.

Hand in hand, we ran – this time, with me taking the lead.

31

World Peace

At the point where my thigh muscles delivered that burning sensation, accompanied by my lungs failing to provide enough oxygen to enable my legs to continue, I halted and let go of her hand, bending over to catch my breath. Courteney, who whipped out her phone from her back pocket, didn't appear to have suffered the same physical pain from our exertions.

We'd managed to put a reasonable distance between the train station and us, now catching our breath in one of the back streets behind the High Street in the centre of Fairfield. Although a few passers-by glanced at me as I panted, bent double with my hand on my knees, it was nothing compared to the looks we'd received as we scooted through the alleyways and streets when trying to put distance between us and Pointy-shoes, who most likely now sported a broken arm. As we dashed hand in hand, I guess those onlookers assumed we were shoplifters fleeing the scene or a young couple running through Fairfield like infatuated lovers gayly prancing across some sandy beach at sundown.

I glanced up at Courteney, who now leaned against the window of a haberdashery store. The sort of place that had existed in its current format since before both world wars or even the Crimean, judging by the décor. With her head down and one trainer sole slapped onto the glass, her thumbs swiftly darted across the screen of her phone. I presumed once she'd finished her message exchange with whoever, we would discuss my accusation that the girl was using me to escape the clutches of the Pitbull.

Of course, apart from the revelations that Fred Hallam had offered earlier, and trying to understand how Gold-tooth fitted into my catastrophe of a life, I still hadn't processed the possibility that my dead mother may be wandering around like some spook on a mission of atonement for her wrong-doings when alive. And now, to add to this exponentially ever-growing list of disasters, I'd committed grievous bodily harm in front of a plethora of security cameras.

Brilliant.

As the girl beside me danced her thumbs across the screen, the spring breeze caught her hair, whisking it around and causing it to float. She expertly swished her head, allowing her long hair to fly over her shoulder as she focused on her screen.

'You're a knob. You know that, don't you? So, she's not the sort of girl to take home to mother. Well, dick-head, you ain't got one of those, irrespective of whether she's now roaming around Fairfield like the White Lady. This girl has done nothing but help you, and all you can do is accuse her of using you. Rob's prissy missus, Laura, has a point, you know ... you're just a tosser!'

Now I'd caught my breath, I nodded in agreement with my mind talk.

I straightened up, took a deep breath and stepped towards her, placing my hand on her phone before gently pushing it down. Her head shot up; those bright blue eyes darkened as she glared at me. I cupped her cheeks in my hands and kissed her. Courteney fought for a second, placing a hand on my chest and pushing me away before turning her head sideways and gobbing her gum on the pavement.

Nice.

Somewhat shocked by her action, I watched the ball of gum as it bounced before coming to rest by the door of the haberdashery store. Courteney turned my cheek with her hand before wrapping her arms around my neck as we progressed to sucking each other's face off. Now caught up in the moment, I grabbed her bottom and gently lifted her, causing her to rise on her tiptoes like a nubile ballet dancer.

"Excuse me! This isn't a knocking shop. This is a respectable establishment, you know. Go on, be off with you."

Cheek to cheek, whilst holding our tight embrace, we glanced around at the point when a middle-aged lady sporting a florid face wearing appropriate attire, accessorised by a set of bifocals on a chain around her neck, stepped out of the doorway, planting her foot on Courteney's pavement offering.

"Go on before I call the police. If you must copulate like a couple of rutting stags, then show some modicum of decency and perform your lewd acts in private!" Now with one sandal glued to the pavement, the woman shooed us with her hand.

"Naff off, you starchy cow. I bet that fanny of yours has all but dried up, it's been that long since it's seen any action."

"Good God! Whatever has the world come to."

"Come on," I whispered, dragging my girl away. Not that I needed reminding but, whatever happens between us, her suggestion regarding the shopkeeper's less-than-active sex life

311

confirmed that although I could take the girl out of the Broxworth, I could never take the Broxworth out of the girl.

'So?' my mind talk screamed at me.

At the street corner, four doors down from the haberdashery store, stood the Nutshell Pub, aptly named due to being a somewhat tiny establishment usually packed to the rafters, which wasn't difficult because the floor area being no larger than a folded napkin. As the lunchtime trade had passed, there appeared to be a free table by the window. Not that I was usually in the mind to partake in alcoholic beverages in the afternoon, but it had been one hell of a day, and I thought perhaps a beer was in order.

With a pint of lager each, we squeezed into our seats. The only other afternoon drinker perched on a bar stool, appearing to have held that position for some hours going by his drooping head and bloodshot eyes. He'd luridly checked Courteney out as we entered and continued his lustful gaze as we settled into our seats.

"No good comes from a woman like that," he slurred, waving a finger at me.

"Excuse me?" I blurted, wondering if this tosser was going to offer a wad of notes – I scanned the bar for a fire extinguisher.

"Beautiful women ruin men. They ruin us," he hiccupped.

"John, that's enough. You've had enough," barked the barman before holding his hand aloft to Courteney. "I'm sorry about that, love."

I stopped searching for an object to inflict blunt force trauma.

"Beautiful," he muttered, his head swaying as he attempted to drag his whisky glass from the bar.

I grabbed her hand, just managing to stop her from hopping up and larruping him one. "Leave it, I hissed."

Bridget often suffered the same depraved treatment from the opposite sex. In a somewhat shallow way, for those few months together, I'd always enjoyed having such a vivacious beauty hanging off my arm whilst revelling in the envy of others. A downright awful male chauvinistic attitude that should be resigned to the days when Miss World contests paraded around young ladies wearing skimpy bikinis whilst they spouted their desire for world peace.

I guess it's just biology. However, just because Courteney was easy-on-the-eye to coin a phrase my father used to trot out with some regularity, I'd come to realise that fifty per cent of the population needed to change their attitude, or we might as well regress to cavemen and drag our women along by their hair.

What had changed my outlook – well, the kindness of another human being who was prepared to risk all for me. And no, I hadn't become all holier than thou because she also just happened to be gorgeous, and I fancied her.

"I'm sorry."

"What for?"

"What I said about you using me. I'm sorry."

"That again."

"What?"

"You spouting that bloody word, *sorry*."

I snorted a chuckle before sipping my much-needed lager.

"You don't fink I'm using you, then?"

I huffed as she leaned forward and noisily sucked up her lager without lifting the glass from the table.

I chuckled as she grinned back, now sporting a frothy white moustache.

"Christ, Courteney. No, no, I don't. I'm just worried that whatever I do, I seem to land myself in even more shit."

"Well, you've got me now."

I didn't respond, just lifting my pint to take a long slug of lager.

"Look, I get it. I'm not exactly the sort of woman you dreamt of being wiv. But I'm putting everyfink on the line for you. If they don't put Karl away, I'm a dead girl."

I leaned forward, folding my arms on the table. "Why are you risking it, then?"

"Granny's custard."

I nodded and smirked. "Care to explain."

"You ever loved anyfink?"

I pondered that thought for a moment. "My Sega Mega Drive."

Courteney rolled her eyes. "No, idiot … anyone, not stuff."

I shook my head. "No … maybe Dad, a bit, when he gave me some attention if he had a spare moment between one of his floozies. And there were my real father's parents … my grandparents, I suppose. They were nice to me."

"Well, I ain't. But you're different." She broke eye contact, bowing her head to noisily slurp her drink.

I waited until she looked up. "What are you saying?"

314

"Sake, Damian. Do I have to spell it out?"

"You actually think you love me? We've only known each other for twenty-four hours, or so."

She nodded. "Yeah, and in that time, I've made love to you twice, grassed up my boyfriend to the filth, which I might add is considered a death sentence where I come from, and agreed to dump the only way I know of how to earn a few quid."

"You said this morning we wouldn't work. We come from different worlds."

"Maybe I was wrong. It's been known to happen on a few rare occasions," she smirked.

"I'm ten years older than you. I have no money, no job, and now face the possibility of being arrested for GBH. I'm not exactly the catch of the century, am I?"

Courteney offered a shrug of her shoulders, dismissing my list of issues. "You said earlier that you fink we could give it a go. And when you kissed me a moment ago, that wasn't just an attempt to get back inside my knickers. That was … well, more than lust, I guess."

"I guess you might be right."

"I am, babe. I've been around long enough to tell the difference, and no one has ever kissed me like that. No one's ever defended me like you did when you smashed that fire extinguisher on that tosser's arm."

I returned a tight smile, not sure how to respond. I wanted to believe the girl. I wanted her. However, notwithstanding those desires, which I wasn't convinced didn't just come from my groin area, would I be just dropping myself in deeper shit?

'Err … hello, butt head,' my mind thumped its metaphorical knuckles down hard on my scalp. 'No one is

315

ever, ever, going to commit to you as this girl has just done. Jesus, Damian, what in God's name is the matter with you? Miss bloody World sitting opposite, slurping her beer, has just 'fessed up to loving you. Not to mention how she's gone out on a rather long limb for you. Can you wake up and smell the coffee, dick-head?'

I took her right hand, holding it between mine, and raised it to my mouth before offering the gentlest of kisses. "I might be in love with you," I whispered.

"Might?"

I rocked my head from side to side. "Am."

She extracted her hand from my grip, plucked up her glass and skilfully sunk half a pint in one gulp like any self-respecting rugby player might do after a particularly tough match.

After wiping her lips on the sleeve of her hoodie, she flashed me that enormous smile. "Right, Mr Statham, before we get married, buy a big house in the country and have at least four babies, we need to sort out this bleedin' mess."

"Four?"

"Hell, yeah. I want two of each."

Whilst momentarily contemplating living in a country manor with Courteney by my side dressed in a long crinoline dress and four children perched around us, like some scene from a Dickensian novel, I glanced up as two men pushed open the pub door.

One of them locked eyes with me.

"You!" I blurted.

32

Tanya The Lotus Eater

"Action Man!" exclaimed Terry. "Christ, up until a few weeks ago, I thought I didn't have any children, but even I know you don't buy a fourteen-year-old boy a bloody Action Man, whether it sported the upgraded real hair and swivelling eyes features or not."

"Alright! Don't shout. You're giving me a migraine," pouted Deana.

"We're dead. Surely, as we no longer breathe air like the rest of the population, we can't feel pain."

"Terry Walton, you'll feel pain if you don't shove a sock in it," Deana batted back as she rhythmically rubbed her temples with her index fingers whilst slumped on the sofa.

"Tetchy!"

"Well, for heaven's sake. I'm not here just so you can use me to play your silly games. I have many more talents than just being able to fling objects around a room."

"Oh, like what?"

Deana opened her eyes and pointed to the ceiling. "Take me to bed, and I'll show you just how finely tuned my talents are."

"Oh, not that again. You've got nothing but sex on the brain, woman."

"Three weeks, Terry. Three long weeks I've waited. Christ, since the age of sixteen, when spotty Thomas Higginbottom at the school disco rather disappointingly popped my cherry in the broom cupboard whilst keeping up to the tempo of a somewhat rather rushed rhythm to the Rubettes' *Sugar Baby Love,* I've never had to go three weeks without a man. My poor pussy thinks it's been put out to pasture."

Terry raised his eyebrows at her outburst. "You want one?" he enquired, waving a bottle of gin he'd plucked from the drinks cabinet.

Deana nodded. "Large one. It's probably the only stiff thing I'll get if you're not going to take me to bed."

"You're relentless, Deana. As you well know, I've been around the block a bit, but I've never met a woman like you. It's normally the man that has constant urges."

"Pity you don't! I want to see a bit more of the man who ravaged me in that hotel room thirty-three years ago, not the pious monk act that you seem to be constantly trotting out now you're alive again."

"Alive? We're dead."

"Yes, alright. It's just a turn of phrase. Christ," she muttered.

Terry focussed on the task in hand, hoping she would relent. Of course, although Deana was now a woman in her fifties, not the nubile little twenty-something minx he'd had the pleasure of bedding a few weeks ago, there was no denying he was still attracted to her.

However, worryingly, since arriving back from a dead state, he just didn't seem to hold the same desires. Anyway, when this mission was over, perhaps he could be reunited with his Sharon in heaven or wherever the walking dead end up after roaming the Earth. Although Sharon may never forgive his transgressions of thirty-odd years ago, and whether from wherever she now was, perhaps perched on some celestial cloud looking down upon him, he wanted to prove to her he'd changed. He missed his wife – he longed for her. So, if behaving himself now afforded him that slim chance of rekindling their love, it was what he intended to do.

"Large G&T, ice and a slice." Terry offered her the drink.

Deana reached out and rubbed his bottom before taking the glass. "It's Sharon, isn't it?"

"What do you mean?" he asked, stepping away from her wandering hands and sipping his drink.

"You think if you refrain from dabbling in a little bit of pleasure, she'll somehow take you back when our mission is complete?"

"Maybe," he muttered, his G&T millimetres from his lips.

"Darling, I think you're hanging on to a thread. Sharon was a good person. We weren't in case you've forgotten all your little indiscretions. There's Penny Pincher, Paula, the little checkout girl, and good old twinset and pearls, Marjory, your old neighbour, to mention just a few."

Terry held his drink to his lips.

"Oh, and me, of course," she chortled.

Without taking an intended sip, Terry lowered his glass. "What? You're saying we're going to hell? The devil already has our souls. Jesus, have I got to spend all eternity living in purgatory whilst you, dressed in a skin-tight leather corset, chase me around waving a whip in the burning fires of the underworld?"

"You don't have to wait for that, darling. I've got all sorts of erotic leather costumery I can shimmy into right now for you if you like," she smirked before seductively licking the rim of her glass.

"Christ. Tanya the Lotus Eater's got nothing on you."

"Sorry, darling?"

"That dominatrix woman with the whip in the *Chinese Nookie Factory* in that funny film *The Revenge of the Pink Panther* that was on at the pictures a couple of years ago."

"Oh, if you say so. But I think the Pink Panther films were forty years ago, darling. You're forgetting you missed thirty-odd years whilst you were playing dead."

"Yes, alright. But I can just see you in a black leather catsuit wielding a whip."

"Hold that thought, darling, hold that thought. Let me go and slip into something tight-fitting and sexy, which I think will bring that vision alive."

"Woah! Hang on there. The vision in my mind is enough. You strutting around whilst clad in a shiny black leather catsuit really will send me to a life of purgatory."

"Oh, if you say so, darling. Let me know if you change your mind. It won't take long to slip on; just a quick rubdown with talcum powder, and it easily slides over my womanly curves."

Terry spluttered a mouthful of his drink back into his glass. "Christ," he muttered.

"Anyway, I think you'll find that purgatory is a state of expiatory purification after death for the wicked. I'm pretty sure with our track records, even the most focused angel of death might think we're way past any redemption."

"You're just saying that to get your way. Aren't you?" Terry added the question to his statement with a little less confidence in his voice.

"You'll find out when we take our final journey. I do hope there's some debauched swingers' club down there. Otherwise, it will all be rather tedious."

"Surely, if we do manage to help our boy back on his feet, that will be two successful missions under our belts. Won't that be enough to demonstrate that we've redeemed ourselves?"

"I don't know, darling. But if we are regarded as recovered souls, I'm a little concerned about what up there will be like. I can't imagine for one moment that heaven offers recreational excursions that involve a hedonistic existence of champagne on tap at all-night erotic parties. I imagine it's more bible study and praying, which I can assure you isn't my thing."

"No, I can quite imagine," Terry nodded at Deana before slugging back his drink and making a beeline for the gin bottle for a refill. "Well, on the off chance I can redeem myself and perhaps see my Sharon again, we need to get this mission back on track."

Deana exaggeratedly huffed. "Alright. What's the plan then?"

Terry slopped in a considerable measure, then added a bit more before making a grab for the bottle of tonic. It was a good job Ziggy over-ordered on the alcohol front for the wake because with Deana's latest revelations about what lay before him, he felt the need to be able to relax, and not in the way Deana would prefer.

"I'll have a top-up, darling," Deana waved her glass in the air and exaggeratedly blew him a kiss. "I'm prepared to drop the subject of sex for a little while so we can focus on Damian. However, you might want to consider the fact that by denying me some pleasure you're being mean, which could also tot up more points against you when it comes to the final decision of where you will end up."

Terry side-eyed her as he snatched her glass from her hand. "Bloody hell, that's a bit of a desperate argument."

"I am desperate. And remember, because I'm invisible to all but you, I can't very well slip on something sexy and trawl around the wine bars trying to pick up some young hunk."

Terry side-eyed her again. Her expression suggested she was seriously suggesting flaunting her wares in some posh drinking establishment would be an activity she would partake in.

He handed her a topped-up drink. "As you said, let's focus on our boy and not your constant desires to ram your hand down my boxer shorts."

"I'll try, darling, but that is a lovely thought. You should see the vision I have right now."

"I dread to think. Right, so we've established that Dennis Hunt is dead. We've also established that this Nathan Bragg bloke may have colluded with this Bridget woman to con our boy."

Deanna nodded and sipped her drink. She patted the sofa seat beside her. "Come on, darling, sit with me. You look like a spare willy in a brothel, hovering there in the middle of the room."

Terry shook his head but relented and flopped down beside her.

"You were very manly today, you know." She seductively rubbed her index finger back and forth along his thigh. "You commanded the meeting in that office with such authority, it made me wet."

"Jesus, Deana! Act your age. You're like a bitch on heat."

She pouted. "Go on. I'm all ears."

Terry huffed before swatting away her finger, which only encouraged her to squeeze her thigh next to his.

"It's nice to cuddle up, isn't it?" she doe-eyed him as she sipped her drink. "You were saying …"

"The chap who paid Hallam could be this Nathan Bragg. What do you think?"

"I think that girl Damian's got himself tangled up with is a right sort. I really can't imagine how he's ended up with her."

"You can talk," scoffed Terry, before taking a mouthful of gin.

"Yes, darling, we know I have desires, but I don't parade cheap knickers on display, and I don't mouth off like some gutter fishwife from the market, do I?"

"I thought she was a pretty little thing … back in the day, I would—"

"Oh, Terry. Per-lease. Well, I have to say I thought she was a right trollop, and our boy can surely do better than that."

"What, like Bridget?"

"Good point. Of course, we've never met the girl, but she really is evil."

"I think that Dennis Hunt blamed your Stanley—"

"Sidney! Remember ISMAAAR. Ian screwed Mark after Adrian analed Richard."

"Yes, quite. How could I forget? Anyway, that doesn't help much because both names begin with the same letter."

"Oh, good point," she chuckled.

"Now, listen, Sidney's evidence sent Dennis to prison. Perhaps Bridget and Nathan knew him and were aware of his history."

"Yes, that's possible, darling, but I can't see why they would then set out to get our boy."

"That Fred chap said he was paid to investigate Sidney. Now, perhaps by that time Stan ... err, Sidney had skedaddled to the States with his young bird. So, rather than pay out for a fly-drive, they focused on enacting their revenge closer to home, as is, on Damian, instead."

"For the sins of his father."

"Exactly. I'm not sure we're getting very far because I seem to remember having this conversation whilst you pretended to be the mother of Christ in the bath."

"Madonna, the sex symbol, not the Virgin Mary, darling. There's quite a difference," she chuckled. "You know, we could slip back in the tub if you like? It might stimulate the little grey cells and perhaps some other parts too," Deana stroked his thigh and purred.

Terry nervously grinned at her as she moved her hand and placed it on his chest. Whilst attempting to ignore the fact Deana seemed intent on climbing all over him, he pushed on. "I think your Wicked-Witch-of-the-West antics were enough to scare Hallam into discovering this chap's identity. So, by Monday, we should know for sure if it is this Bragg bloke who's behind it all. Trouble is, even if it is, how do we find him?"

"We could get Hallam to say he's recovered the drugs and arrange a meet. We turn up, I cause chaos with my witch antics, and then terrify this Bragg chap into returning Damian's assets."

Terry shifted in his seat and raised his eyebrows at her. "Blimey, not just a pretty face, are you?"

"Oh, darling, I'm so much more than that." She ran her long-painted nail down his chest, letting her fingers slide between two buttons of his shirt, offering a deep guttural growl.

Terry slapped his hand on hers, performing the end sequence of the Denim Aftershave adverts.

"Don't stop me, darling. I've been a good girl … now I want my reward."

33

Giant Haystacks

"You've got some bloody explaining to do!" I boomed, rising from my chair whilst he bug-eyed stared at me. I guess his brain whirred around, considering the fight-or-flight options. After dealing with the Pointy-shoes git, I seemed to have gained a sudden surge of confidence in my ability to handle myself. Anyway, Nathan Bragg didn't appear to radiate the same confidence or aggression as had the man now nursing a broken arm, who presumably waited in line up at Fairfield General Hospital.

I shimmied around the table, reaching out to grab his arm. However, Nathan took flight by yanking open the door and bolting up the street, his more confident companion blocking the door, preventing me from giving chase.

"Hey, buddy, hold up," he palmed me back. "I don't know who you are, but you'll have to go through me first."

As I stepped back from his giant palm, I assessed the chap blocking my path. I guess a man in his late fifties, who probably played rugby in his youth. If not, he'd spent a lifetime as a lumberjack in some Canadian forest whilst humping ten-tonne logs about, going by the size of his arms and a North

American accent with that elongated vowel sound. Also, few middle-aged men in the UK wore baseball hats, but this guy's head sported a well-worn Toronto Maple Leafs Ice Hockey Team cap, and I had him pegged for the sort to hold an extensive collection.

Akin to a tornado ripping a path of destruction through a mid-western town, a whirlwind of blonde hair shot past me, leaving a wake of upturned chairs and smashed glasses as Courteney aggressively reached up and jabbed her middle finger into the man-mountain's sternum. "Who the fuck are you?" she barked.

"Oi, what's going on?" bellowed the barman, a tall stack of steaming glasses resembling the Leaning Tower of Pisa finely balanced in his hand, which he'd presumably just plucked from the glass washer. As he glared at the destruction she'd caused, his spectacles slowly fogged, either because of the steam rising from the machine or due to copping an eyeful of my girl's lacey G-string as her hoodie rose to reveal her midriff whilst aggressively berating the colossus Canadian.

I glanced across at the wake of destruction caused by my soon-to-be fiancée – apparently. That said, I didn't recall proposing, but the girl already had me halfway up the aisle.

"Hey. I said, hold up, there." Although Courteney harboured that wild streak, I guess the man, benefiting from his hefty frame, rarely experienced intimidation that he thought he couldn't handle. He grabbed Courteney's finger with one hand and her wrist with the other, forcing her back. Courteney kicked his shins, causing me to wince in sympathy with the guy, although he appeared unperturbed.

"Right feisty one," he chuckled, shoving her away.

"You're going to have to pay for the damage, you know," spouted the barman as he placed the glasses tower down and peered over the top of his spectacles at me.

"Wanker!" she blurted, but chose not to advance, presumably realising moving the lump would require the services of a JCB.

I nodded to the barman, indicating I understood his demands. Then, akin to a tag team of below-par wrestlers taking on Giant Haystacks, I recalled my father's rather impressive collection of old VHS recordings of all his and Big Daddy's bouts, I stepped forward, taking up the fight where Courteney had left off.

However, after assessing that a physical assault would be pointless, I took a somewhat more diplomatic approach. "Look, mate. That bloke you're with was Nathan Bragg, right?"

"What's it to you, buddy?" He nudged his head forward, causing me to take a step back. It seemed every male I encountered over the last few days preferred the feigned head-butt technique. I wasn't too surprised to witness Courteney barrel back into the fray. Although I somewhat doubted she planned on employing an engaging conversation tactic. Cutting my arm across her chest, I held her back.

"Hold on, babe." I pushed on with my questioning whilst trying to ignore the fact that I now appeared to have been infected with her chavvy speak. "Look, mate, I don't want any trouble. God knows I've got enough of that, but I need to speak to Nathan ... it's what you might say quite urgent."

The man offered his arms out wide, his wingspan to rival a Boeing 747. "Hey, buddy, I reckon he ain't too keen on speaking to you."

"No, I guess he's not. But as I said, I need to talk to him and also find an acquaintance of his."

"Sorry, buddy, I can't help you."

"Bridget Jones, ever heard of her?"

I detected a dark cloud float, then hover across his face. Clearly, he knew Bridget, and I suspected he harboured a similar diminutive view of the woman as I did. In that instant, he dropped that bellicose demeanour, his shoulders visibly sagging, causing the man to shrink before my eyes as if he'd just plucked up the *'Drink Me'* bottle and withered to the homuncular size of Alice.

"Hell, what's she gone and done now?" he asked, slowly shaking his head from side to side.

The lugubrious-looking chap perched on the bar stool dragged his eyes away from Courteney's tight jean-clad bottom and looked up. "Bridget Jones?" he slurred.

The three of us all glared at him.

"Did you say Bridget Jones?" he questioned.

I nodded.

"She ruined me … she ruined me," his manta almost at a whisper when repeating the words.

"Sorry? You know Bridget?" I blurted.

He held up his empty whisky glass and drunkenly waved it in the general direction of the barman. "Double … no, make it a triple."

"Sorry, you've had enough."

The poor chap, who I had pegged for some lecherous tosser, flopped his head, allowing it to thump heavily on the bar, his slack hand letting go of the empty glass that rolled around in an arc before coming to a rest next to a beer pump handle.

"Christ, is he alright?" I blurted.

"John will be fine. It's become an everyday event for the last six months. I'll pop him in a taxi like I do most days."

As I attempted to glean more information, I shook the drunk's shoulder, only receiving mumblings back. I shot a look at Courteney. "He knew Bridget."

"Where's this git live?" she aggressively fired out at the barman whilst pointing at the prone drunk, the protruding bar that held his head, the only obstacle stopping him from collapsing to the floor.

"Oh, look, I can't tell you that."

"Hey, buddy, forget him. I can tell you all you want to know about that girl."

Courteney and I swivelled around to assess the shrunken Canadian.

"Let me buy you a drink," I flashed my best smile.

He nodded. "I'll have a large Canadian Club. That's what I prefer," he pointed to the top shelf of spirits behind the bar.

"Course you do," I chuckled.

"Barman, set 'em up. Three doubles of your finest Canadian Club, please," I chirpily sang, swishing my arm around my newly acquired friend's shoulder. "Come take a seat, my friend."

The barman slapped a dustpan and brush on the counter and nodded at Courteney. "Woman's work," he smirked. "You can sweep your mess up, and I want a tenner for the broken glasses."

Fortunately, Courteney only offered a scowl in response as she snatched up the dustpan and assessed the carnage that she'd earlier caused when doing her level best in performing the starring role in *Twister*.

After Courteney expertly wielded the brush before unceremoniously thumping the dustpan back on the counter, and the barman had assisted the heavily inebriated John into a waiting taxi, we settled back into our seats with our large Canadian Club each and our large Canadian for company. No one else entered the bar, probably because it was one of the few pubs in town that didn't feel the need to place a sixty-inch TV screwed to the wall showing Saturday afternoon sport. I suspected as the early evening approached, the Nutshell would soon swell to capacity when three or four more punters would enter.

Our new lumberjack friend gripped his glass of whisky, affording it the appearance of a thimble rather than a Paris goblet in his massive bear paws.

"The floor is yours," I laid my palms out, indicating he should start talking.

He nodded and tipped the whisky down his throat before gently placing the glass down.

"Okay. Look, Nathan is a good guy."

I raised my eyebrow.

Courteney grabbed my hand. "My guy is the good guy. I reckon that Nathan tosser is a right little twat who needs a good slap."

"Babe," I shook her hand to encourage her to reel it in, then rolled my eyes at myself for trotting out the babe word again.

"Look, by the sound of things, the boy's got himself embroiled in one of his sister's stupid games—"

"Sister?"

He nodded. "Bridget."

I slumped back in my seat. "They are brother and sister, then?"

"Why wouldn't they be?"

"Different names, or is Bridget really Bragg, not Jones? Christ, not exactly a well-thought-out pseudonym, is it?"

"No, look, sorry. Bridget is Nathan's half-sister."

"Oh. So, her name is Jones, then?"

"Yes, Hunt is her maiden name."

"Hunt?" I questioned whilst shooting Courteney a look. My girl shook her head, presumably encouraging me to keep my powder dry, so to speak.

"Yeah, so? What's the significance about Hunt?"

"Oh, nothing."

"Okay, now look—"

"Oh, hang on," I interrupted. "She's married?" I blurted, now thinking about my proposal and planned marriage to the girl.

"She was. She married some bloke old enough to be her father. The idiot didn't take out a prenup, and she took him for half of his estate … quite a sum, I'm led to believe."

"Oh."

"Bridget is a con woman. She's a bloody black widow, luring stupid men to hand over their fortunes."

I involuntarily offered a nervous laugh, knowing I was one of those stupid men. Clearly, by the sounds of what my new Canadian friend was suggesting, I didn't hold exclusivity when it came to stupidity.

"Look, sorry, buddy, but who are you? I need to be careful who I'm talking to here."

I nodded and leaned forward again, still holding Courteney's hand. "Fair enough. I'm Damian Statham."

He glanced at my girl.

"Courteney. I'm his fiancée."

"Oh, congratulations. I hope everyone behaves at the wedding."

"Sorry?" I frowned at his somewhat odd statement, which just about trumped Courteney's declaration that we were engaged. In the space of two days, I'd progressed from a casual shag to boyfriend, all the way up to fiancée – fast work. At this rate, I considered I'd be married and divorced before Monday.

He chuckled and rubbed his shin. "I fear for anyone who upsets the bride. My shin will have a bruise the size of a dinner plate before the evening's out."

Courteney shrugged.

"Does this beautiful woman have a family name?" he raised his eyebrow at her.

"That's for me to know. I suggest, if you don't want a matching bruise on the other shin, you reel it in."

He leant back and raised his palm. "Hey, girl, no offence."

I nudged her arm, suggesting this wasn't the time to antagonise this bloke. We were close to gleaning some valuable information, and I couldn't afford to let my fiancée blow it.

'Christ, fiancée? Really, Damian?'

'Slip of the mind talk,' I responded in my head.

'Okay. Although I reckon you could do a lot worse.'

I nodded to myself.

"And you are?"

"Alex Bond, or 007, as many call me," he chuckled.

"Do I know you? Have we met before?"

"I don't think so, but your name is familiar. I'm sure in the back of my mind that Statham rings a bell."

"Jason, the actor."

"Oh, could be. Anyway, look, my long-suffering partner, God rest her soul, unfortunately, had all sorts of trouble with Bridget. That's her daughter, my stepdaughter if you like, not that she will have anything to do with me."

"Right, so you're Nathan's stepfather?"

"Yes, sort of. We're more buddies, really, and he *is* a good guy. My Cheryl was married twice before she met me. She had Bridget with her first husband and Nathan with her second. Now, what has Bridget done to you? Because I made a promise to Cheryl before she died that I'll sort her daughter out, once and for all."

"I'm sorry for your loss."

He offered a slight nod before pursing his lips. "Tragic, you know. I lost my girl to cancer two years back. But hey, she wouldn't want me all maudlin. So, tell me, what's that Bridget done this time?"

"It's a long story, but she's conned me."

He huffed and shook his head. "I'm afraid there is a long line behind you on that front. My Cheryl knew the net was closing on Bridget, and she will get her comeuppance, eventually."

"Bleedin' right. The slag will have me to deal wiv if she shows her mug around 'ere."

"I don't suppose you can put a lead or muzzle on her?"

"Oi, fuck head, who the bollocks do you think you're talking to?"

"Woah," I slapped my hand down, causing the standoff between them to halt, before wagging my finger at him. "Apologise."

Rather than larrup me one, surprisingly, he nodded. "Hey, sorry."

Courteney chewed a wasp, which I guess gave her a break from gum.

"So, as I said, she conned me."

"Well, as I say, I'm sorry to hear that, but what's Nathan got to do with it?"

"He was part of the con."

Now sporting a knitted brow, I wasn't sure if he was about to reach across and crush my head in the palm of one of his giant paws or about to burst into tears. "Nathan, involved with Bridget?"

"Yep. She conned me, and he produced the paperwork as part of that con."

Alex, in a somewhat resigned manner, dismissively shook his head.

"Look, I take it Cheryl's first husband was called Dennis."

"Yes, how would you know that—"

"Lucky guess, mate," Courteney threw in before glancing at me, presumably trying to ensure I was careful about what information I disclosed.

Alex shot Courteney a look before focusing back on me. "Look, by all accounts, Bridget has been a bit of a handful since leaving school, what with shoplifting and then progressing to running cons. Now, apart from her poor husband, it's all been small stuff, a few thousand here and there."

"A few grand?"

"Yeah. Of course, Cheryl, being her mother, couldn't face the thought of Bridget going to jail. So, on the odd occasion, I've stepped in and smoothed the waters when it's all got out of hand."

"Sorry, I don't follow."

"Look, on a couple of occasions, I repaid the money she'd conned out of some poor sod on the proviso she stops these antics, grows up and gets a proper job before she ends up in jail. Trouble is, Cheryl always hoped it would work, but I knew differently. Bridget is a lost cause."

"But—"

"Hang on, son, let me finish," he interrupted, holding up his bear paw to reinforce the point. "Now, if, as you say, she's dragged Nathan into this, then that's a different matter. I won't have that boy dragged down to the gutter."

"He was—"

"If you say so. Look, I'll sort Nathan, then I'll deal with that girl because she's not going to drag him down with her."

"Well, that doesn't help me, does it—"

"Hey, easy tiger, let me get to the punch line. As I said, I can't have the boy in trouble. So, if he confirms your story, I'll reimburse you what you've lost, as long as you don't involve the police."

"You for real, tosser?"

"Yes, ma'am."

"You'll pay me … just like that?"

"I said I would. I'll be true to my word. Now, you can't say fairer than that, can you?"

"Alex, I think you're a bit behind the game. Bridget didn't take me for a couple of grand."

"Oh, hell, I see. Look, buddy, I can probably go to ten, but that's it. How much did she con you out of?"

"About a million quid, give or take the odd penny."

It appeared my new Canadian friend had just slugged his second bottle of *'Drink Me'* potion as he shrunk into his seat whilst simultaneously performing his impression of a carnivorous bug-eating plant.

34

Mr. & Mrs. Smith

Alex left the pub after he'd recovered from the shock of the size of the con. As I watched him go, I'm convinced he appeared at least twelve inches shorter than when he entered. Of course, he didn't whip out his chequebook, and it seemed I was a step up of major league proportions on Bridget's previous little capers.

We exchanged numbers and parted with him agreeing to catch up with his stepson and arrange a meeting between us all.

Neither Nathan nor Bridget had technically committed any crime other than preying on my stupidity. Although, of course, there could be a suggestion of fraudulent activity at play. However, Alex knew, as I did, the chances of the police investigating or the CPS thinking it would be in the public interest to prosecute was somewhere similar to the possibilities of my new fiancée grabbing a teaching career at a debutant school for young ladies – zero.

Three punters entered the bar, thus swelling the pub to capacity. So, not wishing to rub shoulders with three doleful-looking gents, we took our leave.

As we hovered outside, me thinking what next and would the police now be cruising around searching for a madman with a penchant for wielding a fire extinguisher, Courteney whipped out her phone and tapped her thumbs across the screen before glancing up and taking my hand.

"Babe, we need to lie low for a bit."

"What's happened?"

She turned her phone around to show me the text exchange with Deli.

"I texted her earlier to remind her to keep quiet and not to go mouthing off to Karl. What I was really doing was seeing if anyfink was going down on the estate after my anonymous call. All she texted back earlier was that she would keep quiet, which I knew was bollocks." She waved her phone in my face. "She's just texted this."

Deli: *Hey kid. Feds disin U flat. Word that FL gaff busted. K nicked.*

Courteney: *Babe. Cant talk. Check feds lock it up.*

Deli: *Wusup? U wid peng?*

Courteney: *Babe need U to keep that gob shut. Serious Shit.*

Deli: *Defo. Keep cool kid.* Followed by a black thumbs-up emoji.

"It's another language. What does all that mean?" I shook my head, unable to decipher any of it, thinking Egyptian hieroglyphics would be easier to decode.

Despite the serious shit we were knee-deep wallowing around in, Courteney gave a little giggle. "I'll translate for you, babe."

"I think you need to."

"So, basically, the filth have found the gun and arrested Karl at Fat Larry's gaff. Deli knows I'm wiv you, and she promises to keep quiet."

"Will she?"

"No chance," she snorted. "I reckon the entire estate is in turmoil right now. The Albanians will be planning to get Karl, and the Gowers will probably be doing the same to ensure he don't blab. Deli will be telling everyone about the raid and that I've done a runner wiv you."

"Shit."

"Yeah, great stinking heaps of it."

"If the police have arrested Karl, how will the Albanians or Gowers get to him?"

Courteney peered at me. The look presumably would precede a 'granny's custard' comment, but it never came.

"Well?"

"Jesus, Damian, you really that fick?"

I shrugged.

"Babe, when the filth have rattled his cage for a few hours, they'll charge the git and place him on remand. When the twat waltzes onto A-wing in Brixton nick, there'll be a bunch of gits with instructions to do him."

"Oh."

"The only worry we have is if he sings. Then the filth will protect him, but he'll still go down. One way or anover, he's facing a lengthy stretch or a sharpened toothbrush across his carotid artery."

I scrubbed my hands over my face, wondering how the hell I'd ended up in this world.

"Right, babe. We can't return to the estate tonight, so we need another option."

I peered through my fingers at her. "Any ideas?" I mumbled.

She nodded and grabbed my hand, almost dragging me across the road. As we approached the entrance of one of those convenient mini supermarkets, she halted and instructed me to stay put before hot-footing into the store.

From my position on the pavement, I spied her through the floor-to-ceiling window as she whizzed up the aisles whipping off various items from shelves that immediately and somewhat expertly disappeared up her hoodie or squeezed down the front of her impossibly tight-fitting jeans.

"My God," I muttered, whilst witnessing my girl as she assisted the local economy before brazenly sauntering towards the exit, skilfully bypassing the pay point. The apathetic security guard, who seemed more interested in some YouTube video playing on his phone, yawned as she left the store. He had to be the only male I'd encountered today who hadn't visually assessed the body of my newly acquired fiancée.

"Alright, babe? Come on." She tugged my hand as we headed down the High Street. "I got the essentials. I had to get a roll-on deodorant 'cos the spray cans are too big to conceal, although I got us a toothbrush each. I chose a medium bristle for you, hope that's alright. Hey, babe, don't look so shocked. Anyway, I shoved yours down my knickers 'cos I thought you'd like that going by the lengthy munching you gave me last night," she giggled as she skipped along, bouncing up and down, her hair flowing wildly.

Stunned, I struggled to find an appropriate response. "Where we going?"

Still skipping, she waved her hand towards the Maid's Head Hotel. "There, babe. Honeymoon suite if it's free."

"Free, it will cost a fortune! You can't nick a hotel room, and my account is a bit on the low side at the moment. I think we'd better find something cheaper, like a B&B."

She stopped bouncing and wrapped her arms around my neck. "You love me, babe, yeah?"

I smirked. "How could I not when you've thoughtfully placed my new toothbrush inside a pair of stolen knickers you just happen to be wearing."

"Cool. Now listen up. I've got a fair bit put aside. I don't want to disappoint you, but I won't always look this hot, and I've always known that I couldn't earn a crust forever by whipping my boobs out. So, babe, I've been saving."

"Right."

"Come on. Tonight is my treat," she snogged me before dragging me through the revolving doors to the reception of the only five-star hotel in town.

"If you've got a few quid behind you, why did you steal all those toiletries?"

"Got to have a bit of fun, ain't ya. Anyway, as I said, I'm helping the local economy."

"Course you are," I muttered.

Courteney bounced to the reception, folded her arms on the high counter and hauled herself up so her toes lifted from the floor. "Or-right, mate?" she grinned, visually rolling around her chewing gum as the suited middle-aged reception manager assessed her with a heavy heap of disdain.

I clocked his gold-coloured name badge – Stephen, Reception Manager. "Please, for the love of God, don't call him Stevie or babe," I muttered.

"So, Stevie, babe, we want the honeymoon suite for tonight. No, make it free nights. Don't we, babe?" she turned and grinned at me, still offering her concrete mixer impression as her gum rolled around.

Stephen, ever the professional, tapped away at the screen, then huffed. "We do have the honeymoon suite available. However, it's three hundred and forty-nine pounds per night. Therefore, I think we'll be requiring payment up front." He raised his nose and eyebrows before slowly sporting a smug smirk, presumably thinking he'd just put pay to Courteney's request.

"Cool." She slapped a bank card on the counter. "Add a fiver to the bill and get yourself a beer when you knock off."

Clearly disappointed, Stephen plucked up the card and swiped it down the groove on the keyboard. "That's very kind but not necessary."

I detected a slight furrowing of his brow as he passed the card back, presumably surprised the payment went through. "Can I have your name, please?"

"Mr and Mrs Smiff."

"Smith or Smiff?"

"Oi, you gobshite, you taking the piss?"

I tugged her arm, effectively stopping my girl from delivering a torrent of abuse.

"Smith, I presume. We've had a fair few Mr and Mrs Smiths stay here over the years," he smirked.

343

I shook my head, closed my eyes, and tipped my head back.

"There, all done. Two room cards for you." He placed them on the counter and tapped his finger on Courteney's credit card. "Thank you, *Miss Klein*. I hope you enjoy your stay with us."

Courteney blushed. Efficient Stephen had clearly won the verbal battle.

"Would you like me to make a reservation for dinner? We have three restaurants, The Rogan offering the delights from our Michelin acclaimed chef, André Pierre Rogan."

"Babe?" quizzed Courteney.

I shook my head, concerned about how much she was spending.

"Nah, fanks anyway, we'll nip out for a Maccy D's."

"No problem, Mrs Smith. If you let me know when you're ready to dine, I can send out for your food and arrange to have the food delivered to your room."

"Cheers, Stevie."

"You're welcome, Mrs Smith. Now, can I get someone to assist with your luggage?"

"We ain't got no bags." She dropped from the counter and stepped back. "Everyfink we need is 'ere," she tapped the front of her jeans where there could clearly be spotted the outline of a medium bristle toothbrush.

"Quite." He clicked his finger for a bellboy. The well-trained lad instantly appeared, standing at attention with his hands clasped behind his back. "Please, take Mr and Mrs Smith to the honeymoon suite."

Courteney swivelled around. "Just tell us where it is, don't need a bleedin' guide."

"It's all part of the service, Mrs Smith," he delivered that well-trained smile before immediately dropping it in favour of a scowl as he addressed the bell boy. "Order a bottle of champagne on the house, of course, to be delivered to Mr and Mrs Smith's room immediately." Then, re-plastering on his smile as he addressed Courteney. "Mrs Smith, Tom will show you all the room has to offer and assist if you require anything else."

"Cool."

The bell boy nodded, then searched the floor for our bags.

"There's no luggage," Stevie, as my girl liked to call him, informed the embarrassed bellboy.

"Thank you," I mouthed at him.

"You're alright, you know," she flashed a huge smile at Stephen whilst grabbing my hand.

"Thank you, Mrs Smith. I hope you enjoy your stay at Hertfordshire's most prestigious 'otel."

We followed the way indicated by Tom's waving arm. "Was he taking the piss, dropping the 'H' on hotel? I've a good mind to give Stevie a slap."

I shot her a look.

She giggled and grabbed my bum as we entered the lift whilst Tom, clearly trying to contain a smirk that appeared determined to appear, turned to face the wall and pressed the button for the top floor.

"I'm joking, babe."

After Courteney rammed one of Pointy-shoes man's twenty-pound notes in the breast pocket of Tom's waistcoat, she ran around the suite, playing with the gold shower taps, squirting the offensively expensive looking soap pump, rifling through the mini-bar and generally causing mayhem like an errant child tearing up the room at a birthday party.

It certainly wasn't lost on me that I'd previously been in a hotel room with Courteney. Although, at the time, I didn't know and was in somewhat different circumstances.

I accepted the chilled bottle and two flutes from a room service attendant whilst shitting myself about what would happen to me. My girl appeared far better equipped to cope with the pressure of the impending doom than I. Perhaps her upbringing had steeled her to take these sorts of issues in her stride, whereas I, well, prior to a few weeks ago, having my Sega Mega Drive confiscated had been my biggest trauma.

I popped the cork and poured, deciding the best course of action for the short term was to get shitfaced.

When my leggy-blonde thief had finished ransacking the place, devouring a Kit-Kat and bag of nuts, she threw her clothes off, reminding me very clearly that she was no child, before grabbing a champagne flute I'd handed her and hopping onto the bed.

"Come on, babe. Get your kit off. Your new toothbrush can't be the only one to have had some fun."

A little after four in the morning, I padded into the bathroom to take a leak. Whilst pointing my old-chap at Armitage-Shanks, I mused whether I'd developed a prostrate problem, this being the second night in a row that my bladder had demanded I rise early. "Perhaps not," I muttered when spotting the remains of the third bottle that languished in the

346

flutes positioned on the side of the jacuzzi bath where we'd abandoned them after we'd earlier frolicked in the bubbles and jets of water before returning to bed to carry on where we'd started.

After waving my old-chap a few times, not concerned, as I'd been yesterday at about this time, that I needed to rinse him under the tap, I quietly tiptoed back into the bedroom whilst trying not to wake sleeping beauty.

I parted the floor-to-ceiling voile curtains and peered out of the window. The owners of the barges moored up on the river would cop an eyeful if any of them were glancing this way with a pair of binoculars pressed to their eye sockets. I grabbed a chair from the dressing table and plonked down whilst surveying the lights of Fairfield – not exactly Blackpool, but the lamps dotted along both sides of the embankment lit the river, affording the dark water the appearance of a bendy runway.

Courteney laid her hand on my shoulder; I glanced up at her.

"Sorry, did I wake you?" I whispered, for some odd reason.

She wildly shook her head, allowing her hair to flow as she nimbly swished a long leg over me and positioned herself on my lap. The dim light of the table lamp radiating through from the lounge area silhouetted her naked form against the glass backdrop.

"You're gorgeous, you know that?" I whispered.

She leaned forward, allowing her lips to brush mine. "I know."

I cupped her butt cheeks in my hands. "Do you, now?"

She nodded, giving a little snigger, before swishing her hair around her neck and appearing to assess my torso.

"What?"

"We can get out of this mess, babe."

I nodded. Although not convinced.

"Babe, I know, in reality, we ain't getting married and living in the country wiv four babies, but I can help you get out of this shit."

"You don't want to marry me, then?"

She shook her head.

"Oh."

Courteney laid her hands on either side of my head and kissed me, writhing her bottom on my lap as she introduced tongues to our smooch while my mind whirred around wondering what her game was.

After successfully reinvigorating my old-chap, she removed her tongue from my mouth. "I don't fink there's any point to marriage. All that white dress shit is fake. Anyway, I don't like fruitcake."

"You could have some of granny's custard on top."

She snorted a laugh.

"What about the four babies?"

She slowly brushed her hand over my hair and flashed that smile. "I'll have your kids, but you can shove the fruitcake up your arse."

"Deal," I whispered back, gripping her tightly and pulling her closer.

"Oi, watch where your fingers are. Nuffin goes up my arsehole. That's the only part of my body that's exclusively mine."

"Can I claim exclusivity on the rest?"

"Yes, babe. Deffo, it's yours."

Courteney performed what years of training had elevated her to degree level whilst I briefly imagined those boat owners' eyes popping through the lenses of their binoculars. However, that quickly faded as my girl focused my mind elsewhere, a million miles from Gold-tooth, Karl, Bridget, Nathan, Terry, Alex, stolen toothbrushes, and my dead mother's ghost.

Part 3

35

August 2015

Submariner

"Sign in the box where I've marked," stated the Custody Sergeant as he slapped her purse, phone, and keys on the desk.

Bridget plucked up the pen offered, tucked her hair behind her ear and hovered whilst studying the form the officer had placed in front of her. He stabbed his finger at the box to show where he wanted her to sign before huffing and raising his eyebrows at the Detective Inspector, who stood by her side.

Bridget scribbled her signature and plucked up the returned items she'd surrendered three hours earlier when arrested by the man, who now appeared to stand a smidge too close. That said, she'd flirted with him all afternoon, so not totally surprising he thought it acceptable to sidle up all close and personal – men were so gullible.

Although no charges were to be levied against her, Bridget knew she'd sailed far too close to the wind on this one. She needed to take stock and tighten up her operations because she was determined to avoid a repeat of today's somewhat irksome events.

For fifteen years, since the age of sixteen, Bridget enjoyed the spoils of living a life of crime and, until now, she had avoided any sanction – not even a police caution to sully her clean record. From petty shoplifting to running cons, where she could fiddle thousands from stupid gits who fell for her charms, Bridget had made a career out of ruining others.

With a population of nine-odd million people, and plenty of places to hide, London offered endless opportunities and literally thousands of potential marks to target – Bridget had carved out a successful career.

There had been a few issues in the past when cons hadn't quite panned out as planned, and recently that Canadian lump of gristle her mother had taken up with had bailed her out of a couple of tricky situations. That said, with her new partner in crime, it was time to up the stakes. The days of running cons that would only net a few grand were history – they were moving into the big time, where the risks were greater, but the rewards were potentially life-changing.

She'd returned to Fairfield to take revenge. However, despite this minor hiccup of their latest con gone south, she wouldn't allow it to sway her conviction about the man she simply had to destroy.

Sidney Statham was going to pay a heavy price. She, with the help of her new partner, was going to ruin him.

That said, the Detective Inspector had missed a golden opportunity to charge her, so perhaps Lady Luck was on her side today. Also, that seemingly incompetent officer, who she'd spent most of the afternoon with, albeit, him one side of the desk and her the other in a particularly drab interview room, was just the sort of man she would go for – as in for pleasure, not the marks who she expertly singled out to con.

If she'd read the signs correctly, perhaps she could whisk him back to her hotel for a bit of fun – Bridget possessed an insatiable appetite for men, her stock-in-trade in luring her marks, and this man oozed sex appeal.

"I'll show you out, Mrs Jones," Brett Templar flashed her a smile and cupped his hand on the small of her back to usher her away from the counter.

Bridget had been around long enough to know that glint in his eye suggested the Inspector considered her in the same way – well, he'd spent most of the afternoon gawping at her cleavage, so he'd not exactly been subtle.

"In fact, I'm done for the day, so I can drop you back to your hotel if you like?"

She clocked the Custody Sergeant's smirk as they stepped away. Presumably, offering a lift to a good-looking woman was a regular event where Detective Inspector Brett Templar was concerned.

Earlier in the week, Bridget booked into the Maid's Head Hotel for a few nights to be close to her mark as she closed in for the kill – well, a con that would net her at least ten grand. However, her mark smelled a rat, so to speak, resulting in her enjoying the company of Brett Templar for the afternoon.

Bridget smirked while Brett focused on her chest as if the answer would come from her cleavage, not her mouth. However, Bridget was okay with his lecherous gawping because her chest was the mainstay weapon in her arsenal. The weapon she regularly deployed to suck in her marks before blowing bazooka-sized holes in their bank accounts when the gullible idiots fell for her allure and then her sob stories before she disappeared without a trace.

"Look, I have to make a quick call, but then you can buy me a drink if you like?" Bridget needed to update her partner regarding the afternoon's events. After that, well, if he played his cards right, Brett Templar was in for one hell of a ride.

Brett reluctantly raised his eyes from her cleavage and flashed a smile – Bridget detected dilated pupils – he was smitten.

"Sure, let's go," he smirked, before gently laying his hand on her leather-trouser-clad bum as he guided her through the doors of Fairfield Police Station, now confident he'd made the right decision not to charge the woman. Not only was a night under the sheets on offer, he thought there could be some mileage in forming a relationship with Bridget Jones. Although, with the evidence against her, it was abundantly evident she'd cocked up. Nevertheless, Brett harboured a feeling that suggested a relationship with her would satisfy not only his loins but also his wallet.

~

The wine bar, situated at the top of Elm Hill, one of the few go-to places in Fairfield, sported an opulent décor with prices to match. With an exorbitantly priced bottle of Chablis nestled amongst the ice in a silver wine cooler and two glasses, they squeezed into a tiny booth away from the noise and chatter of the bar.

The early evening crowd of drinkers, who appeared to have piled out of their offices some hours ago, judging by the levels of inebriation, swelled the bar area as they laughed and flirted – voices rising whilst hands wandered to places that they probably shouldn't.

Whilst Brett poured the wine, Bridget eyed up a couple who she guessed might regret this evening come the morning – well, he might. A suited, suave-looking forty-something married man and an equally attired woman half his age, not wearing a ring, appeared to have reached that moment of decision. Either an elicit night of sex in some hotel room, or he returns home drunk to his wife. Bridget loved people watching – she'd made a career of it – she excelled – a process she employed to identify her marks.

Brett slid the glass across to her as he nudged his knee against hers. "There you go."

Bridget raised her glass, offered a flirtatious pout, and waited for Brett to clink his glass to hers.

"Cheers."

"So, go on then, tell me, do you take all your suspects for a drink after you've released them?"

"Only the gorgeous ones," he smirked, holding his glass close to his mouth whilst waiting to see her reaction before swilling a mouthful of Chablis. Brett wasn't drinking the wine for the taste – he couldn't be classed as a sommelier – alcohol was alcohol.

"And how many gorgeous women do you let loose?"

"Not many."

"What about a gorgeous woman who you have enough evidence against but choose not to press charges?"

Bridget thought that question might be somewhat risky. However, she hypothesised that Brett Templar wasn't only interested in her physical attributes and suspected there was mileage to be gained in forming a relationship with this man – a bent copper in your pocket could be all the protection she needed. Also, unless he'd holidayed in Turkey and taken advantage of the endless bazaars offering fake goods, she doubted a Detective Inspector's pay would stretch to purchasing a Rolex Submariner. All of which suggested Brett Templar had either won the lottery, enjoying the proceeds of an inheritance from a crusty old aunt or regularly took backhanders from those that dabbled in a spot of organised crime. Bridget suspected the latter.

"Do you have someone in mind?" Brett flirtatiously raised an eyebrow.

Bridget offered a seductive smirk in return before slowly licking her top lip. "I might."

Brett glided his index finger gently across her hand before glancing up as she waited for his reply. "Are you suggesting that I intentionally ignored and discarded incriminating evidence?"

"Perhaps … did you?"

Brett pursed his lips. "Now, why would I do that?"

"Perhaps you sense an opportunity?" she raised an eyebrow before sipping her wine, never losing eye contact.

"An opportunity for what?"

"You tell me?" She rubbed her leather-trousers-clad thigh against his as she wriggled her bum on the velour bench seat.

"What you're suggesting is that I haven't followed the correct procedures and missed an opportunity to arrest you?"

Bridget shrugged whilst maintaining eye contact.

Brett plucked the chilled bottle from the bucket and topped up both glasses. "Are you saying you're guilty?"

As Brett glanced away to nestle the bottle in amongst the rapidly melting cubes of ice, she took the opportunity to undo another button on her blouse, the gap now tantalisingly exposing the top and side of her bra – just enough.

"What do you think?"

He nodded whilst restarting that seductive finger-on-hand stroking routine, although his eyes were firmly on the mainstay of her arsenal. "Yes ... but I'm ... well, let's say, intrigued."

"Is that intrigue regarding what's inside my blouse or something else?"

Brett took a mouthful of wine before answering. "Both."

"So, you want to fuck me?"

Although slightly taken aback by her bluntness, he didn't show it. "I do," he nodded.

Bridget sipped her wine. "And if I was inclined to fuck you ... after that?"

"After that, I will probably want to fuck you again."

"What if I didn't fancy a repeat performance?"

"I think you would. It would be the fuck of the century."

"Maybe. And would you want anything else?"

Brett gave a slight shrug of the shoulders. "Maybe we could ... do a little business together."

"Maybe we could. What sort of business do you have in mind?"

"Well, hypothetically, of course—"

"Of course."

"If my new business partner found herself in an awkward situation. Say, a con gone south, I might be in a position to smooth the way forward."

"As you have today?"

"Maybe."

"And would I have exclusivity?"

Brett shook his head before draining his glass and reaching for the bottle. "You mean, would you have exclusivity regarding my ability to smooth out problems?"

Bridget nodded before swallowing her wine.

"No."

"You fuck all your business partners, then?"

"No … I think you could assume exclusivity in that department."

"Hmmm. Apart from smoothing the ground and gaining a fuck buddy, what other benefits would I gain from such a partnership?"

"I know this town, the people, the opportunities and the pitfalls. I have connections."

"And?"

"The mess you got yourself into was caused by picking the wrong mark."

"Who's suggesting I picked a mark?"

"You did, and I think you would normally show better judgement. But … you don't know the town, and you don't know the people. So, I'm thinking you cocked up … something you wouldn't normally do."

Bridget nodded as she drained her glass. As she held it out, waiting for Brett to top it up, she noticed the couple who would regret their actions in the morning exiting the bar with their arms around each other's waist – a hotel room, it is, then. The idiot had no idea that one night of passion would probably lead to a marriage breakdown, resulting in limited visiting rights to his children being granted, which would only stretch to a Saturday lunchtime in McDonald's. *Idiot.*

Brett emptied the bottle between the two glasses. "Shall I order another?"

Bridget plucked up her glass and shook her head. "No."

"You got somewhere you'd rather be?"

"No … not at all. But I thought you wanted to fuck me."

36

2016

Wacky Races

"Deana, I'm really not comfortable about this. Christ, woman, we could get arrested." Terry hissed whilst following Deana up the clanging steel staircase.

"Darling, we're ghosts. So, unless Venkman, Stantz and Spengler are about to rock up with their *Proton Packs* strapped to their backs whilst waving around a *Neutrona Wand* to zap us, I don't think we need to concern ourselves about PC Plod wandering around waving his truncheon."

"What the blue blazes are you on about?"

Deana halted at the top, swivelled around, and thumped her hands on her hips. "Ghostbusters!"

"Christ, who are they? Jesus, woman, you never divulged that there's a gang of mercenaries running around hunting ghosts!"

"Darling—"

"Don't darling, me. Bloody hell, Deana, why on earth haven't you mentioned before about these Ghostbuster chaps?"

"Terry, darling—"

"I thought a life of purgatory with you in that leather corset sounded bad enough, but this is another level!"

"Darling, keep your voice down," Deana hissed, as she leaned down to where Terry peered up at her from three stair rungs below.

Terry ducked – an involuntary movement caused by the fear that these Ghost Buster chaps may well be close by. "Can they hear us?" he whispered, now furtively glancing around and fully expecting to see some commando types wielding Star Trek-type phasers. He prayed they'd switched them to stun.

"Darling, please put a sock in it. Ghostbusters is a film and not a very good one at that. It's make-believe. They are not real, okay?"

"Oh, right." Terry straightened up and allowed a silly, nervous laugh to escape. "You seem to know a lot about it, considering you don't have a very high opinion of the film," he added, as he nipped up the last few steps and joined her next to a red-painted wooden door on the gantry.

"Oh, it was one of my Dickie's favourites. I endured the silly thing on far too many occasions that I care to remember."

"Right," he huffed.

"I can't believe you've not seen the film, but I suppose playing dead for thirty-odd years is a reasonable excuse."

Terry raised his eyebrows and shook his head. "Look, are you sure this is the place? It looks a bit seedy if you ask me."

"Yes, I looked it up. And before you ask, not in the Yellow Pages, because I'm quite certain that no longer exists. Anyway, this is just the sort of place I would expect that pasty-looking, Inch-High-Private-Eye to work from."

"And what, we're just going to break in and have a snoop around?"

"Yes! Man up, darling. If you're not man enough to quench my womanly desires, grow a pair and help me force this lock."

Terry huffed, frustrated that Deana seemed capable of constantly pulling the conversation back to her desires. "Don't you have a lock-pick, a hairpin, or something like that?" he mumbled.

"Darling, do I look like the sort who'd carry around a lock-pick? What on earth do you take me for? I'm not some low-life tea-leaf like those scummy lot from benefit street, you know."

"So, what do you suggest?"

"Use your shoulder."

Terry huffed again. "Anyway, I explained last night why I can't satisfy your somewhat overactive libido."

"Oh, yes, 'I'm saving myself for little Sharon'," she delivered in a childlike voice whilst dramatically shaking her head. "Pathetic!"

"Christ, you sound like that Bonnie girl with that screechy voice. *'I'll scream and scream until I'm sick!'*. Anyway, you know I'm hoping to see Sharon again."

Deana rolled her eyes. "Oh, turn the record over, for Christ's sake. Now, come on, put your shoulder to that door."

Terry scowled at her as he aligned his shoulder against the wooden door before gritting his teeth, wincing in anticipation of a dislocated shoulder, and taking aim.

"Do you have to pull that face?"

Terry halted mid-launch just before throwing his weight against the door. "What face?"

"That gurning look. You look like Steptoe."

"I'm not gurning!"

"You are so. Come on, get on with it."

Terry slammed his shoulder into the door. "Holy crap, that hurt," he blurted.

"Shush! You're making enough noise to wake the dead," she hissed.

"I'm already awake, and I can definitely feel pain."

"Oi ... is someone there?" a gruff male voice called from the alley below.

Deana and Terry shot each other a look.

"Shit, who's that?" he whispered.

Deana raised a finger to her lips. From their position of the high ground, on the top of the metal gantry, she peered over the railing to the bottom where the steel staircase exited near a row of shabby-looking garages at the back of an equally unsavoury alley, presumably the go-to place for druggies going by the liberally scattered used needles.

"Oh, it's some scummy-looking young chap wearing a pair of filthy baggy joggers and a t-shirt. I can almost smell his repugnant odour from here. The man needs dunking in a vat of disinfectant. Well, at least that disreputable lump of gristle confirms we're in the rough end of town."

"What's he doing?"

"He must be suffering from particularly painful anal piles, or he's got worms because he's inserting those dirty joggers up his backside whilst scratching his arse and pulling a face like you were a moment ago."

"Well, does Crackitch look like he might come up and investigate?"

"No, darling. He's shuffled back to whatever cesspool he just slithered out of." Deana rejoined Terry by the door. "You called him Crackitch. Do you know him?"

"No," Terry whimsically replied, whilst Deana sported a quizzical look.

"Oh, odd name."

"Czechoslovakian goalkeeper," he chuckled.

"Oh, really?"

"No! It's a joke."

"Oh, I don't get it."

"Forget it."

"Well, you should know jokes that may have been acceptable in the '80s are most certainly not these days. Whatever the punchline is, making fun of people from other countries is considered offensive. I never had you down as a xenophobe. You'll be trotting out the Englishman, Irishman, and Scotsman jokes next, I suspect."

"Alright, keep your hair on," he somewhat petulantly replied.

"Anyway, Czechoslovakia no longer exists."

"Oh, where's it gone?"

"Nowhere. It's now two countries. Czech Republic and Slovakia."

"What was the point of that?"

"Darling, I haven't got time to explain the new political landscape of Europe whilst we attempt a spot of breaking and entering. There's a place and time."

Terry nodded. He was already uncomfortable about the whole idea, so the sooner they were away from here, the better.

"Now, come on. Give that door another heave. I think you'll get through with another good shoulder barge."

"What about you-know-who?" Terry nodded down the staircase.

"Oh, forget him. I expect by now he'll have lost his entire arm up his backside by the way he looked to be rummaging around."

"Well, it's alright for you. Being invisible, you don't have to concern yourself with being caught. But if he or someone else hears me barge this door down, I'll have Lieutenant Kojak and Detective Stavros bearing down on me. And just because I'm a ghost, that won't stop the handcuffs from being whipped out."

"I've got a few pairs of those. I like the ones with pink fluff around the clasps."

"Course you have," he muttered.

"That was one of our favourite games at our little parties. I'd chain Dickie to the bedposts, and then us girls would pleasure the boy. I'll show you them later and, if you like, I might even stretch to supplying you a lollipop."

367

"Christ, I dread to think what kind of debauched sex toy that is!"

"A lollipop?"

"Yes, but don't tell me. Some things are better left unsaid."

"I was referring to a sweet, darling. You know, 'Who loves ya baby'," she delivered in an appalling American accent whilst tapping his bottom.

Terry slowly shook his head. "You're unbelievable. You know that?"

Deana sniggered and licked her lips, just at the point the St Giles Church sounded its bells as the campanologists yanked their ropes, breaking the relative quietness of the bright spring Sunday morning.

Terry grabbed the opportunity, hoping the din emanating from those bells would cover his exertions and threw his weight at the door, which splintered next to the flimsy Yale lock before swinging inwards.

"Oh, what a clever boy you are. Come on." Deana crept in, exaggeratingly stepping through, keeping her poise low whilst furtively scanning the room.

Terry swivelled around to assess whether he'd been spotted. Fortunately, the alley appeared clear, and Crackitch hadn't resurfaced.

"What's the plan? What are we looking for?"

Deana, still with her head bowed whilst hovering on her tiptoes, swivelled around, her tennis shoes emanating a loud squeak on the lino floor.

"Why are you creeping around? You look like the Hooded Claw."

"Charming. I always thought I was more Wonder Woman, myself. That was one of Dickie's favoured costumes for me to wear to our little shindigs. He always said how that little red corset accentuated my womanly curves. Something, I might add, that you seem completely oblivious to."

"Christ," Terry huffed, trying not to allow space in his mind for the image of Deana dressed as Wonder Woman whilst cracking a whip with a naked Dickie shackled to the bedposts by way of fluffy pink handcuffs and sucking one of Kojak's lollipops.

"Darling, we're on a stealth mission to uncover information. So, I suggest we try to maintain the poise of church mice," she pointed to the floor. "There are flats below us," she hissed. "Although the tenants probably display a similar repugnant appearance to that awful arse scratching lump of Neanderthal gristle, we can't afford to disturb their Sunday morning hangovers."

Terry returned a po-faced nod.

"You rummage through that battered old desk whilst I rifle through this filing cabinet."

"What are we looking for?"

"Anything that might give us the upper hand."

"Like?"

"Oh, Terry, I don't know," Deana shot over her shoulder as she gingerly pulled out the top drawer and tiptoed up to peek inside. "Oh, dear!" she chuckled.

"What?" Terry glanced up from where he'd been rummaging through the top drawer of Hallam's desk, only discovering a bottle of whisky, a random selection of pens and a pocket-sized notebook.

"Might suggest how Inch-High fills his spare time," she waved a few tatty, presumably well-thumbed copies of *'Hairy Housewives'* publication. The glossy cover of one displaying a well-endowed lady, although fortunately, she'd strategically placed a hand so as not to confirm the first word of the magazine's title.

"Oh, nice!"

"Not really," Deana gave a wheezy snigger as she flicked through a few pages.

"Who d'you think you are? You sound like Muttley. What's funny?"

"Blimey, the man really does have a fetish for the au naturale look," she chuckled, turning the publication sideways to inspect the centrefold before presenting the double-page spread in Terry's direction.

"Oh, wow. That is hairy."

"It's like a forest down there. The woman's got enough pubic hair to stuff a mattress."

"Not a publication you're likely to feature in, then," he muttered, recalling the sauna incident.

"Sorry? You have some opinions regarding pubic hair?"

Terry huffed and yanked open the second drawer before offering an answer. "Deana, I really don't think you've got time to gaze at dirty mags. Anyway, it doesn't feel right a woman your age nosing through that sort of publication."

"What on earth do you mean by a woman of my age?" she hissed.

"Oh, nothing. I'm just suggesting girlie mags shouldn't be your chosen leisure read. Woman's Realm or Family Circle would be more appropriate. My mother used to take them on a regular basis."

"Oh, dear, how dull. Dickie has an extensive collection of porn. We regularly used to flick through them together with a cup of tea in bed on a Sunday morning after we'd read The Sunday Times. Not *Hairy Housewives*, of course," she chortled. "More upmarket sort of publications and a few rather risqué ones when we fancied spicing it up a bit."

"Why am I not surprised," he muttered. "Come on, stop studying Hairy Harriet, or whatever her name is, and focus on what we're here for."

"Quite right, darling." Deana lobbed the mucky publications back in the drawer, plucking out a box of Kleenex and waving them at Terry. "The thing's nearly empty," she smirked. "It appears our pasty Inch-High Private Eye regularly enjoyed choking the chicken."

Again, Terry shook his head in disbelief whilst attempting to pull the handle of the large drawer on the opposite side. He glanced at the wastepaper bin by the side of the desk overflowing with scrunched-up tissues. Terry made a mental note not to sift through Hallam's rubbish. After exerting two hearty tugs on the handle, he only managed to pull it open a few millimetres. "This one's locked."

Deana halted her rummage through the second drawer of the filing cabinet, which only yielded a scratched can of de-icer, a pair of black gloves smothered in some dubious-looking gunk, which Deana tried to put out of her mind, and a set of screwdrivers. Then, whilst carefully avoiding the gloves, she was now somewhat relieved to realise they appeared to be smothered in T-Cut car polish, going by the split tube nestled between them, and plucked up the toolset.

"Voila!" she announced, waving said screwdrivers at Terry before nipping over to where he perched on Hallam's chair.

"Clever girl. Hand them over." Terry snatched up the largest one and rammed it through the gap, forcing the flat end against the lock's flange, resulting in the flimsy lock buckling and allowing the drawer to ping open.

"Oh, well done, darling."

As Deana peered over the desk, Terry delved inside.

"What the devil is that?"

37

Three Lions

After exposing ourselves in front of the large window in our luxury suite, essentially fornicating in public during the early hours of Sunday morning, we lazily awoke to discover we'd missed breakfast despite the hotel's generous five-hour window in which to make it down to the restaurant.

Notwithstanding my concern regarding the humongous amount of cash Courteney appeared to be flashing about, she rang through to Stevie – her new best mate – who organised a substantial breakfast offer to be delivered via room service.

Wrapped in fluffy white monogrammed dressing gowns, we lay in bed munching our way through our feast. I mused the chambermaid may offer a disgruntled tut when having to change the sheets, which now appeared liberally splatted with toast crumbs, jam, grease from the bacon, and blobs of squashed scrambled eggs – amongst other less savoury deposits best left undisclosed.

Courteney held her sausage between her fore and index finger, smoking it like a cigar, as she ravenously picked through the selection of dishes akin to a starving river rat gorging themselves in an all-you-can-eat buffet. She rammed handfuls of bacon in her mouth between puffing out imaginary smoke. As she sucked in each greasy rasher, it added to the harmonisation of chomping and slurping loudly emanating from her open mouth.

I shook my head in disbelief as I carefully buttered a piece of toast.

"Wha'?" she barely audibly replied, momentarily taking a one-second breather from ramming food between her perfect white teeth. Her mass of blonde locks cascaded over her face as she glanced up and grinned before discovering the tiniest gap between her lips to expertly blow a wisp of hair from her eye.

"My god, it's like watching some cave woman," I chuckled whilst pointing a triangular piece of toast at her before taking a bite.

Courteney giggled and snorted before raising her sausage-cigar-holding hand to cover her mouth. Now in mid-chew, expertly containing a mouthful of bacon, she'd forced the mulch sideways, thus causing both cheeks to swell and afford her the chipmunk look. Then, with a wicked grin, she set about seductively licking her 'cigar' – somehow transforming the scene from a repugnant speed-eating contest to something almost pornographic.

Stupefied at the scene before me, my mid-chew spellbound gaze only broken by the short burst of Baddiel and Skinner attempting to harmonise with The Lightning Seeds.

Probably because I could never be bothered, I hadn't changed my ringtone since England capitulated and crashed out of the World Cup over two years ago. Now, only weeks from the commencement of the European Championships, my ringtone could be considered back in vogue. Also, now buoyed, as many others were, by the anticipation of future success and the unwavering belief that football would be coming home this time. With only Russia, Slovakia and Wales to turn over in the group stages, it was almost a foregone conclusion – even England couldn't fail in that piss-easy task.

Alex Bond's name flashed up on the screen. I shot a surprised glance at my cavewoman, then snatched up the phone from where it lay abandoned on the covers. With a butter-covered finger, I stabbed the green button, somewhat surprised to hear from him again. Although he appeared genuine when we'd chatted yesterday, I firmly believed he would disappear in fear of police involvement that could land his stepson in a tight spot, or another verbal mauling from my cavewoman.

Still gripping her sucked sausage between her teeth, Courteney cuddled up so she could hear the conversation – my phone on speaker held out in front of me as if face-timing or copying all those knobs who prefer to shout in public rather than holding the damn thing to their ear.

"Damian?"

"Yes. Hi, Alex, thanks for—"

"Look, I had a chat with Nathan …" he interrupted before falling silent.

"Right." I shot Courteney a look and shrugged, conveying that Alex appeared cagey. She reciprocated whilst devouring the sucked phallic object, offering me a mulched sausage vision as she chomped her way through.

"I'll come straight to the point. I think we should meet."

"Agreed—"

"But listen. Nathan is just a pawn in all this. You're not going to get any recompense from either of us, but we're prepared to talk through what Nathan knows to help you get to Bridget."

"Okay—"

"I'm assuming that's what you still plan to do?"

I nodded, glancing at Courteney for confirmation that was still on the agenda after discovering in the wee hours that marriage was no longer on the cards and I was just being used for sex and maybe for the production of children.

Courteney nodded.

"Damian?"

"Oh, sorry. Yes, yes, that's my plan."

"But listen up, buddy. As we discussed yesterday, there can't be any police involvement. You go down that route, and we're off. You hear me?"

"Yes, that's fine. When are you thinking?"

"Can we do today? Two reasons, I want to get this over with, and I'm worried Nathan may bolt."

I glanced at my watch, noting midday was now imminent.

"As I said, I'm worried about the boy, and I promised my Cheryl I would keep an eye out for him. You know, he's not a bad guy, and I want this sorted, one way or another."

"Okay, do you know the Maid's Head Hotel in town?"

"Sure."

"Meet for coffee in, say, an hour."

"Err … make it two. I've got to pick him up and get there. We can have afternoon tea that you Brits always rave about."

"Yep, two o'clock is fine."

"Okay … oh, before you go. I presume you're aware that Bridget is in cahoots with a bent police officer?"

"Err—"

"Well, she is. So, don't get any idea about the cops. Try and go down that route, son, you'll regret it. That girl has powerful people in her pocket."

"Right."

"Okay, see you in a while. Oh, and you're buying."

"Buying?"

"Tea and cakes."

I stabbed the red button to kill the call after wiping my butter-covered fingers on the sheets. Well, we'd already ruined them, predominantly caused by my cave girl's chimpanzee tea party performance, so, I figured a little extra grease wouldn't make much difference.

"What do you think?"

"I fink that bent copper that slag has got in her pocket has a gold tooth."

"You reckon?"

"Deffo, babe. She's trying to fit you up and using that bent bastard to take you down."

"Because of what my dad did to hers?"

"Maybe, who knows? Whatever the reason, that Terry bloke has some explaining to do tomorrow."

"Look, I get it that she's taken revenge by swindling my old man's business from me, but why ruin me? I'm not the one

377

who sent her father to prison. It's my dad she should be focusing on, not me."

"Dunno, babe. But we have to get one step ahead of the bitch."

"I think I'd better call my dad. Christ, that ain't going to be an easy conversation."

"Why?"

I shot her a look. "Jesus, Courteney, he built a successful business and I, in a matter of months, have managed to lose it!"

"No, why call him?"

"Oh. Well, I guess I'd better come clean and warn him that this Bridget woman will probably come after him."

"When d'you last speak to him?"

"Months ago."

"Well, you ain't close, so I'd just forget it. I reckon that slag is after you 'cos he's naffed off over there."

"Yeah, you're probably right. Anyway, I don't really fancy telling him what a twat I've been."

"Come on, babe. It'll be alright ... we will get this sorted."

"And what are *we* ... as in, you know, our relationship?"

"What d'you want it to be?"

"I don't know ... it's all a bit whirlwind."

"Babe, I said I'd give up my films and website. Ain't that enough for you to be going on wiv?"

"Yeah, course. I guess I'm just not used to someone helping me out like this."

"Babe, what I did yesterday to Karl is somefink I've always known would have to happen at some point. I guess your situation has just given me the nudge to get on wiv it. I've got anuvver, maybe, ten years to earn good money with these babies." She cupped her breasts in her hands. "Then I would have to move on. The older you get, the dodgier stuff you have to perform to get decent money, and as I said, my arse is mine, no one else's."

I nodded.

"Babe … I know I ain't no catch. What wiv my history and all that. But I reckon if you can see past that, you're worth a shot."

My leggy-blonde, sausage-sucking cavegirl could be described as alien when compared to previous girls I'd dated. With a different upbringing, this girl would be in that exclusive league that only film stars, football players, and super-rich guys would date. However, stunning looks aside and trying not to be overly shallow about just focusing on her physical attributes, Courteney cared. She possessed a good heart, something previous girlfriends didn't, or if they did, they hid it well.

Anyway, I fancied the arse off her. So yes, I could see past her history.

"Yeah. I reckon you're worth a shot, too."

Grinning, she flung the covers back, sending the remnants of our feast flying across the plush covers. "Come on, babe. Let's get a shower." She hopped out of bed and wiggled her arse at me as she shimmied out of her dressing gown before turning around and thumping her hands on her hips.

I gawped at the vision of beauty. "You've got some scrambled eggs in your cleavage," I smirked, waving my finger at her boobs before draining my coffee cup.

"That's for laters," she giggled.

"Lovely!"

"Right, babe. We need to get ready to interrogate that tosser, Nathan Bragg. The bastard don't know what's coming his way, 'cos I'm gonna tear his gonads off."

Something in my mind suggested she was capable of such an act.

38

Sweet Child O' Mine

Deana excitedly clapped her hands as she beamed at Terry. "Bingo! That, my darling, is commonly known as a laptop."

"Right. What's one of them, then?"

"Darling, that could just well be the jewel in the crown of this rather debauched collection of somewhat repugnant porn and good-for-nothing useless tat in this sordid den of iniquity which Inch-high dubiously calls an office."

"Bloody hell, Deana, in English if you please."

"It's a computer, my darling. Although a rather knackered-looking old thing, but nevertheless, it might very well offer up just what we're looking for."

"Why didn't you just say that?" muttered Terry, as he plucked the laptop out of the drawer and placed it on the desk.

"Don't get tetchy. Now, step aside, you philistine. This is my area of expertise." Deana muscled past him and dropped into Hallam's chair. Before opening the laptop, she grabbed the cable from the drawer and plugged it into the wall socket behind her.

"Oh, it's like your eyepatch, that swipe, scroll and tap thingy."

Deana swivelled her eyes upwards and peered at a grinning Terry, her mouth gaping.

Clocking her disbelieving look, he dropped the grin. "What happens now?"

"We wait for it to load, darling."

"Course we do," he chuckled.

"Bugger!"

"What?"

"We need the password."

"Oh."

Deana drummed her fingers on the metal desk as her eyes searched around the office.

"What are you looking for?"

"Inspiration."

"Can't you just guess it?"

"Darling, it could be anything! It's a pity Inch-High hasn't written it on a Post-it note." Deana spotted Terry was about to question what that was, so she performed her well-practised, wasp-swatting wave of her hand to stop him, not wishing to elaborate regarding the twenty-first century's essential stationery items. "Don't ask."

"Hang on." Terry whipped open the top drawer on the other side of the desk, grabbed the black notebook, and raked over the pages before flipping to the inside of the back cover. "What about that?" he pointed. "He's written password next to it."

"Good grief," she chortled whilst tapping in the characters spelling out – 'P-u-s-s-y-p-o-r-n-1'.

The laptop slowly loaded, the buffering symbol whirring around before filling the screen with icons. "Christ, it's no wonder the thing takes so long to load." Immediately regretting the comment when detecting Terry was about to bash out that 'why' word – a word he seemed to repeatedly trot out with a somewhat painful regularity over the three weeks they'd been together.

"Darling, please refrain from annoying questions. Just stand there and do what you do best."

Terry frowned. "What's that?"

Deana offered a pout and rubbed his bottom. "Oozing manliness, darling."

"Oh, get off!"

"Ah, here we go. Oh, dear, where on earth do we start?" she muttered, whilst assessing the plethora of options. Deciding to start with the top left icon, she clicked a file titled 'Favpics', which loaded a screen full of thumbnail images. Deana randomly selected one and clicked before shifting in the chair and turning her head sideways, attempting to understand the image that now filled the screen.

"Is that … is that a cucumber?" Terry, sporting a furrowed brow, tilted his head as he squinted at the image.

"I think so … well, I assume it's not a marrow," she sniggered. "That really would make your eyes water!"

"And is it shoved up—"

"Yes, darling."

"Bloody hell. Do you reckon it's a whole one or just a half?"

"Judging by the shock on her face, I'd assume whole."

"It's a bit sick, isn't it?" Terry offered his opinion as he twisted his head the other way to study the picture from a different angle.

"Inch-High pervert-eye, I might suggest," chortled Deana. "Even for my liberal attitudes, that's a bit strong."

"Where would he get pictures like that from?"

"Oh, darling, the internet is awash with stuff like this and probably much worse."

"Really? What on earth could be worse?"

"You wouldn't believe." Deana clicked away from the cucumber image before searching through the plethora of files on the desktop. "Eureka!" She clicked the file named Statham.

The file contained a sub-file of pictures and documents. Deana clicked open the photos, slowly clicking through the carousel. "That dreadful girl and our boy in the hotel room." She tapped the screen before glancing at Terry.

Terry nodded, then pointed to the next image of a middle-aged man walking hand in hand with a woman half his age. "Who are they?"

"Sidney." Deana shifted forward in her seat to study the picture. "I can't say I recognise the woman, but I suspect she must be the young floozy he ran off with. Interestingly, those pictures were taken here in Fairfield because that's the High Street."

"So, Hallam was telling the truth and was investigating Sidney before he left the country, which would suggest that

Nathan Bragg must be the man paying Hallam on behalf of Bridget."

"Revenge for that girl's father. They must be going after Sidney as well as our boy."

"Makes sense. Sidney was the one who turned Queen's evidence against Dennis Hunt. I suppose they're targeting Damian because Sidney gifted the business to our boy after starting their investigations."

Deana clicked away from the pictures, selecting another file. A screen grab from the online version of The Spectator newspaper opened up.

"What's that?"

Once again, Deana leaned towards the screen. "It appears to be an American newspaper."

Palms on the desk like Deana, Terry leaned into the screen, which displayed the article depicting a picture of a lake shoreline surrounded by woodland, with the headline *'Body in the lake identified'* above a brief paragraph below.

Silently they read the story, which stated the body discovered earlier that week had been identified as Sidney Statham, 62, a British national who his wife, Cindy Statham, 34, reported missing whilst honeymooning together in the Ozarks. Hal Kalinowski, a spokesman for Miller County Police Department, stated the death appeared to be a tragic boating accident, and they were not looking for anyone else in connection to the incident. Sidney leaves behind his wife, Cindy, from Monterey, California.

"Oh, poor Sidders!"

"What's the date of that paper?"

Deana clicked to enlarge the image. "March 7th."

"Do you reckon Damian knows?"

Deana shrugged. "Lord knows. I suppose it depends if he's tried to get hold of him or this Cindy woman has made contact."

"So, the poor sod drowned on his honeymoon."

"Sidders was never that lucky when it came to affairs of the heart. I heard on the grapevine that most of his relationships were somewhat brief encounters. I suspect the vast majority with half a brain soon realised what a turgid git the man was. Not to mention how pitifully lacklustre his performances were between the sheets. That's if he ever got them that far, and they hadn't died of boredom."

"I'll take your word for it."

"You do! What that young American girl saw in him, I have no idea. It must have been the size of his wallet because I can assure you it couldn't be attributed to the size of anything else!"

"I'd rather you didn't paint me a picture."

"Oh, darling, it was awful. The man delivered his offerings and whipped up his y-fronts before I'd even had a chance to build up a head of steam. The man was more Ivor the Engine than the Flying Scotsman."

"Do I really need to know all this?"

"I actually suffered some rather unpleasant chafing issues because of him. My poor pussy was as dry as a maiden's minge."

"My God."

"What, darling?"

Terry just dismissively shook his head.

Deana reached around and rubbed his bottom. "I know, darling, I'm unbelievable," she sniggered.

"Yes, you are!" Terry stepped back, removing his backside from within her reach, causing Deana to offer one of her perfected pouts. "Anyway, perhaps they were in love … not every relationship is about what happens in the bedroom."

"Or an electrical services cupboard, as in your case," Deana smirked.

"What?"

"Paula … your checkout floozy who needed comforting."

"Oh, yes."

"Anyway, darling, a pious attitude really doesn't suit you, what with your track record."

"Hmmm. What else is on that computer thingy? I think discovering your less-than-virile ex-husband has popped his clogs doesn't help us much."

"Yes, good point." Deana refocused on the screen and clicked the following document in the 'Statham' file.

Terry pointed at the screen. "That's the same newspaper."

"Yes, darling." Deana enlarged the image. "It's dated 10th March."

As before, both silently read the report, which depicted a picture of The Lakes Hotel below the headline — *Hotel death, linked to body in the lake.* The brief article stated Cindy Statham, 34, from Monterey, California, fell from her fifth-floor balcony in the early hours of Wednesday morning, 9th March. Hal Kalinowski, a spokesman for Miller County Police Department, stated the tragic death of Mrs Statham appears to have been suicide following her husband's boating accident at the weekend. They both read on, the report quoting the night porter's horror at witnessing the body fall to the ground through the front reception windows. A close friend stated she was aware of Cindy's devastation at the loss of her husband a few days earlier and had become concerned about her state of mind.

"Good … God."

Deana glanced at Terry. "How awful. That's true love for you. Throwing herself to her death. Presumably, she must have been besotted with old Sidders and couldn't face life without him."

"Oi, who are you?"

Terry and Deana jumped back at the sight of a thick-set man who'd poked his head around the door frame.

"Oh, hell. Darling, it's that awful Czechoslovakian goalkeeper with an ants' nest stuck up his rectum."

"Err—"

"I'm calling the old bill," the fully paid-up member of the great unwashed interrupted Terry as he delved into his jogging bottoms pocket and whipped out his mobile.

"Hang on, mate. No need to get too hasty," Terry stepped forward, holding his palms up. "I can assure you there's no need to call the police. I can explain."

"Explain … like this broken lock?" Whilst his fingers hovered above his phone, he nodded to the shattered Yale mechanism that hung limply from the door.

"I'll slip into Wonder Woman mode. When I've flattened this stinking lump, make a dash for it, and I'll catch you up." Deana closed the 'Statham' file before slamming shut the laptop's lid.

388

"Wha … what the fu …" Mesmerised by the vision of a floating laptop that now appeared to levitate above the desk, he staggered back a pace before stumbling out of his pool sliders and dropping his mobile, which clattered to the floor.

Spinning her arms around like some whirling dervish whilst gripping Hallam's laptop, Deana pirouetted across the floor. Terry half expected her to appear in full costume, wearing that tight-fitting bustier whilst wielding a golden whip. However, he struggled to visualise her in a pair of star-decorated pants. Not that he wanted to know, but he was fully aware Deana was not the full-brief type of lady, preferring the sheer thong look.

Halfway through her second rotation, Deana slammed the back of the laptop square onto the poor chap's face, causing him to verbalise his displeasure in the form of a cascade of expletives akin to Niagara proportions before shooting his hands up to assess the damage to his nose whilst collapsing against the mucky-mag-filled filing cabinet.

Of course, this action exposed his torso and nether regions to further attack. Unlike any half-sensible football player, when lined up forming a wall, his involuntary movement invited Deana to go for the kill. As she swiftly swivelled the laptop to expose the edge, she hefted it in an arc formation, with considerable force, into the gusset of his jogging pants.

Terry winced, closing one eye, imagining the pain the chap was about to suffer whilst pondering that the man's child-producing days were a nanosecond from coming to a rather abrupt end. As expected, the poor fellow quickly forgot his bloodied nose. Whilst whimpering on the floor where he'd now slithered to, Terry snatched up the dropped mobile and made a bolt for the stairs.

389

"No rush, darling. Old arse-scratcher here doesn't look like he poses any threat now I've pummelled his testicles and sent them on a pinball excursion around that revolting bloated body of his."

Terry glanced at the poor chap who still hadn't managed to breathe ten seconds after the second blow. "Christ, maybe you overdid it a tad. The bloke's turning a rather disturbing deep shade of purple."

"Oh dear, so he has," she chuckled. "What was their song? Not my sort of thing, of course, but my brother used to play it on his old Fidelity record player. Drove my parents nuts, he did."

"Jesus, woman, what the hell are you talking about?"

"Deep Purple! You know all that hair and head banging." Deana turned her attentions from the purple-faced man, who'd puckered his lips and just started to exhale, to face Terry. "Although ... that Axl Rose is a lush, so I'm not totally anti-heavy metal."

"Deana! We have a situation here. What about those below us?" he hissed, nodding to the floor, indicating the flats below.

"Oh, yes, good point. I'm sure he'll recover," she peered down at him. "I think you're making a fuss over nothing, you fat oaf. You should try childbirth, then you might realise a squished testicle is nothing more than a slight discomfort!"

"Deana, come on!"

"Oh, he's not saying anything."

"That's probably because he can't see or hear you."

"Oh, yes, of course," she chortled. "Silly me."

"Anyway, I'll have you know, crushed knackers are a million times more painful than just popping out a baby."

"Err ... hello!" Deana thumped her free hand on her hip whilst waving Hallam's ball-crushing laptop at Terry. "I'd like to see you squeeze out a melon from your redundant manhood!"

"How ... how could that happen," the prone chap wheezed, still clutching his nether regions with one hand, now waving the other at Terry.

Deana peered down at him. "I'm talking hypothetically, you dip-shit. Going by this performance, I expect you're the wimpy type who cries when removing an Elastoplast."

"Deana."

"Yes, darling."

"He's not talking to you or questioning the biological possibility of a man giving birth."

"Oh. Yes, of course." She glanced at Terry, offering a whimsical smile. "I keep forgetting I'm invisible," she chuckled.

"Look, he's breathing, so let's get moving."

Terry and Deana scooted down the metal staircase and along the needle-strewn alley towards the High Street, leaving the purple-faced chap to nurse his testicles and ponder about flying laptops.

With a sufficient distance between them and Hallam's office, they slowed to a more sedate Sunday stroll.

"I didn't know you had a brother?"

"Simon. He died about ten years ago. Cancer."

"Oh, I'm sorry."

391

"You weren't to know, darling."

"Do you see much of him now?"

"Sorry?"

"Well, you know, now you're both dead."

"Oh, I see. No, darling. Simon became a born-again Christian. I suspect we'll end up in very different places."

"Yes, I'm sure you're right. Anyway, to answer your question. It's *Smoke on the Water*."

39

Prima Ballerina Assoluta

"Hiya Stevie," Courteney bounced up on the toes of her ill-gotten trainers, holding that bourrée en pointe position whilst planting her folded arms on the reception desk.

Despite her pose, I couldn't quite picture my girl gracefully choreographing her way across the stage whilst accompanied by a man pirouetting in a pair of tights. Also, I presume, unlike any ballerina at the Bolshoi Ballet company, she flashed a wicked grin while offering an unnecessary vision of her chewing gum that cemented her upper and lower incisors. Then, prising them apart before swirling her gum around, she enquired about the reception manager's day.

"How's it going, babe?"

"Mrs Smith." Stephen glanced up from his keyboard, where he appeared to be one-finger tapping the keys. "How can I help you?" He flashed a better-than-well-practised smile and raised his eyebrows.

"My husband and I would like to order afternoon tea, with cakes, of course." For some reason, unbeknown to me, Courteney attempted to pull off an accent as if auditioning for a part in her favourite TV show – well, she was an actress.

"Absolutely. Would you like to take that in the Orangery or in your suite, perhaps?"

"Well, I won't take it up the arse," she sniggered.

I groaned.

"Quite. I don't blame you, Mrs Smith. Tea and cakes in the rectum would be most uncomfortable, I should imagine."

"You're a real crack. You know that, Stevie."

"I've been called worse," he chuckled.

"Don't let no bastard dis you, babe. Otherwise, they'll have me to deal wiv."

"Very kind. Now, assuming not your posterior, where would you like to take tea?"

"Orangery, please, Stevie."

"Of course, Mrs Smith. And would that be immediately?"

Still holding her position on tiptoes, she glanced around a middle-aged couple standing in line for Stephen's attention to where I hovered whilst surveying the street through the revolving doors.

Since the fire extinguisher incident yesterday, I seemed to have taken on a heightened awareness, constantly assessing my surroundings for potential issues that may lurk at every turn. It wasn't lost on me that this could be how I might have to live my life if the police decided to release Courteney's vicious Pitbull.

"Babe, we want it now?"

I checked my watch. "Err …" I glanced at Stephen. "No, actually, can we book for two o'clock? We have two other guests joining us. So, in about half an hour would be good."

"Of course. Mr Smith, as you're a resident, you don't need to book. Just choose your table, and we'll take care of everything." Although he offered a tight smile in my direction, that false 'I'm happy to help' expression, he saved his true feelings for Courteney, flashing a full grin with dilated pupils – the man was smitten. "Now, Mrs Smith, is there anything else I can assist you with?"

The middle-aged woman behind Courteney huffed before exaggeratedly rechecking her watch. Going by the way she dressed, in what I presumed were high-end designer-labelled clothing and displaying a hoity-toity attitude, I'd venture to suggest she found waiting behind my girl rather irksome. I had her and her husband pegged as those horsey types, suspecting she believed their class should be afforded preferential treatment and not have to queue behind some scummy street trash that appeared to have crawled out from some piss-ridden alley up at the Broxworth.

"Well, now you mention it, the room needs a bit of sortin'. You reckon you can get one of the maids up there? The bleedin' bed's a bit of a mess, and I reckon the sheets need changing."

Stephen raised an eyebrow.

"Oi, Stevie, clear that mucky mind of yours," she sniggered. "I'm talking about the mess we made wiv our breakfast." She halted mid-chew, affording her jaw a two-second break from pulverising her gum whilst flashing her teeth.

"All part of the service, Mrs Smith. I'll have it attended to immediately. Now, anything else?"

"Excuse me. Is this going to take long?" questioned the woman behind Courteney, whose patience had clearly evaporated, her tone displaying palpable frustration with Stephen's persistent cooing over my girl.

Weirdly, her husband seemed to pale. His complexion appeared to flip like a switch, now taking on a rather pasty look. Either the poor chap was about to suffer a stroke or fearing an ugly scene would unfold as his rather highfaluting wife stepped forward.

"Sorry, madam, I'll be with you in a moment," Stephen professionally answered whilst affording the woman the same facial expression he'd offered me a few moments ago – I suspected Stevie didn't like her.

Returning his attention to Courteney, he re-plastered on that almost flirtatious smile. "Now, Mrs Smith, where were we—"

"I'm sorry, but my husband and I are in rather a hurry, I'll have you know," she interrupted, poking her head forward whilst sporting a po-faced expression.

"Oi, fuck off, or you'll get a slap!" My girl lowered herself to the ground before nudging her head in the direction of the woman, who appeared dumbstruck.

"Oh, no," mumbled her husband, now taking on the expression he'd copied from his wife.

"Oh, how revolting," the woman glared at Courteney before turning her attention to Stephen. "Surely you don't allow her sort in a place like this!"

"Madam—"

"Oi, bitch, don't dis me, you slag. Get back in line, or I'll frigging do ya."

Unsurprisingly, the woman hopped back a pace. Although my girl benefited from that Scandinavian ancestry – blonde, blue-eyed, long-legged, femme fatale type – affording her a film star appearance, it all quickly evaporated when she opened her mouth. Contemplating this situation could very well lead to our imminent ejection, I decided to intervene, thus avoiding the curtailment of our mini-break in the honeymoon suite of Hertfordshire's most prestigious hotel.

"Shall we all take a breath?" I offered, flashing my best appeasing expression.

"Helen, I think we should leave," the ashen, pale-faced gent attempted to cup his arm around the small of his wife's back. "I'm not sure we want to be in the company of a woman like this."

Courteney swivelled her attention to him. "Oh, it's you. How you keepin' Dave? You never complained about my company before and Trace said you still do her every Friday. You know I've moved on and don't do that no more?"

I thought his sagging mouth suggested he *was* about to suffer from a cerebral infarction.

Courteney bashed on, despite the fact that the poor sod's knees appeared to buckle. "Well, y'know, I still do it, of course," she thumbed in my direction. "Babe, over there, gets a free ride if you get my drift," she chuckled.

Courteney's chat seemed to drag the woman out of her catatonic state. "Excuse me! Who the hell are you? And who's Dave?"

I stepped closer, fearing this could get out of hand.

"Helen, leave it. Let's just get going."

"No, Graeme," she slapped his hand away as she assessed Courteney with a fair few hefty heaps of disdain. "I'm sorry, but I will not be spoken to in that manner, and certainly not by the likes of you!"

Courteney, rather than carrying out her threat of a slap – what a relief – stepped back and smirked at Dave, or Graeme, whatever his name is, whilst holding her hand aloft in my direction to presumably halt my advance.

"So, it's Graeme, is it? I must admit, when giving you a blow, I never had you pegged as a Dave."

"Graeme, what on earth is this girl talking about?"

I glanced at Stephen, expecting he would intervene and halt my girl from continuing down this marriage-wrecking path she'd decided to traverse. Presumably, that wouldn't be considered good form in the foyer of one of Hertfordshire's most prestigious hotels. However, whilst Courteney revelled in the excitement that this pompous woman was about to learn of her husband's regular Friday night extracurricular activities, Stephen appeared to have sided with my girl. Whilst leaning on the reception counter in his 'front-row seat', Stevie sported a wicked smirk, waiting for the events to unfold.

"Helen … I have," he swallowed hard. "I have no idea who this woman is."

Clearly in her element, Courteney tapped the crotch of Helen's lime green tight-fitting pedal-pushers. Somewhat shocked at my girl's action, Helen flinched but remained in position.

"You all dried up, have ya? Is that why your old man has to bang me or Trace every week, 'cos you ain't servicing him regular like?"

The woman gawped open-mouthed.

"Courteney, come on—"

"Hang on, babe," she interrupted before jabbing a finger at Helen. "Shut your gob, you dried-up old slag. Your breath stinks." Then, keeping her finger pointed at Helen, she turned to address Graeme. "Is that why you preferred to bang me, 'cos you couldn't face humping your missus's dried-up old snatch wiv her panting horse-shit breath at you?"

"Oh … God," Graeme stammered.

"Hey, I got a suggestion for ya. Get a tube of KY to lube up the old prune, then bang your bitch doggy style. It'll save being engulfed by that foul stench."

"Christ, Courteney, leave it," I hissed, grabbing her elbow and attempting to drag her away. The smirk on the reception manager's face suggested Stevie appeared to be about to piss himself.

Courteney grabbed Helen's arm as I attempted to haul her away. "Hey, don't worry if you're a smidge out of practice. He's only got a small cock, and he usually jettisons his load before locking on to the target."

"Christ, come on," I hissed.

Helen appeared to regain some modicum of composure, unlike her husband, whose trembling chin suggested he was close to tears, presumably engulfed with a plethora of regrets. Whether that was for marrying the odious woman in the first place, or his regular Friday night jaunts to the Broxworth, or by all accounts that he suffered from premature ejaculation, who could tell – perhaps all three.

"Helen," shakily whispered Graeme.

"I suggest you take your prostitute someplace else!" she spat at me, ignoring her husband, who I suspected was about to say he loved her and his unfortunate transgressions had meant nothing to him.

I was reasonably confident that in the few moments I'd endured this curmudgeonly woman's company, his impending declaration of undying love for her wasn't going to cut the mustard with Helen.

"Look, I apologise for what's happened. I'm sure there's been some misunderstanding, and I suspect the girl must be high on drugs," I suggested, still trying to hold on to Courteney's arm as she fought to break free.

"What the fuck! Babe, let go."

Not waiting for a reply from Helen or comment on Courteney's outburst, I focused on manhandling my girl towards the Orangery, leaving Graeme either contemplating a visit to the chemist to purchase a tube of personal lubricant or a trip to a firm of solicitors to secure a decent brief to protect his financial portfolio that could well be decimated if Helen wasn't too enamoured about the doggy style suggestion my girl had so kindly offered.

"Oi, tosser, get off!"

I side-eyed her, offering a disapproving glare whilst keeping my hand cupped firmly around her elbow as I almost frog-marched her down a wide flight of carpeted steps that led away from reception.

Courteney halted, planting those trainers firmly on the spongy, hundred-plus quid per-square-yard carpet whilst yanking her arm free from my grip. Although gullible and not brilliant at reading situations, I surmised my girl wasn't overly chuffed.

"Drugs! Fucking drugs?"

"Sorry, that's all I could think of."

"You embarrassed of me?" she spat, before thumping her hands on her hips.

"No, of course not … it's just—"

"I'm an ex-prossy, and that ain't going to change. You know I've serviced a fair percentage of this town's tossers who can't get it for free, so what's the problem wiv you?"

"Yes, I know, but—"

"So, you've changed your mind, have ya?"

"It's not like that."

"What is it then?"

"Well, that couple … did you have to do that?"

"She nosed into my conversation with Stevie, the stuck-up old bitch."

I huffed, expelling enough breath to blow a wisp of her hair.

"I thought you were different … but you're just like every other wanker who looks down on me."

"No, come on, that's not fair."

"You could have said I was your girlfriend. But, oh, no, you had to apologise to that slag and say I was a druggie."

"Alright."

"No, it's not fucking alright! So, every time some stuck-up cow decides to dis me, you gonna claim I'm a druggie?"

I shook my head.

"Babe, this ain't gonna work. If you can't handle my past, I reckon we split right now."

"Courteney—"

401

"Don't fucking Courteney, me. Go fuck yourself."

"Pre-wedding nerves," chuckled Alex, as he approached with Nathan.

Whilst waving that aggressive finger of hers, Courteney addressed the big man. "And you can go fuck yourself as well," she barked her suggestion before stomping back to reception.

"Oh, Christ. Courteney," I called after her.

"I suggest you give her a moment. Anyway, we're here now, and if you still want to hear what Nathan has to say, we need to talk."

I watched my girl barrel away. Whether she would come back, I'd find her in the room when I'd finished with these two, or never see her again, who knows. However, as I contemplated that our short relationship had fizzled out, my mind delivered its well-versed bollocking.

'Twat! I'm not sure if you're aware of this, but you are in love with that girl. Until about ten minutes ago, I'm fairly certain she felt the same about you. But, shit-for-brains, you just let her down. So, you can watch her walk away, enjoy tea and cakes whilst trying to find out about the woman who conned you, or you can go after your girl. So, twat, what's it to be?'

"Alex, Nathan, thanks for coming."

Nathan, appearing rather sheepish, and rightly so, stepped forward. "Look, Damian, I ... I, err—"

"Give me a minute," I interrupted his stammering as I contemplated the bollocking my mind had so eloquently delivered before hot-footing after my potty-mouthed girl.

'Good decision, dickhead.'

40

Both Sides Now

Courteney's stolen trainers appeared to be just the right sort of footwear to enable her to put a reasonable amount of distance between us. As I jogged back up the stairs, my girl seemed to have disappeared into the ether.

Cursing my utter stupidity – a somewhat regular occurrence on my part – I barrelled back through reception to discover Stephen holding court in the foyer whilst employing his calming techniques upon Helen, whose hysterical screaming appeared to have grabbed the attention of residents and visitors alike, thus causing a small crowd to form. By the looks of their gaping mouths, the onlookers appeared to be enjoying the entertainment Helen's histrionics provided as she publicly lambasted her husband for his sexual misdemeanours, namely paying filthy whores from the Broxworth Estate, as she put it.

Whilst Stephen expertly ushered the entertainment towards the exit, he also became a target for Helen's tirade. However, ever the professional, he took it all in his stride. As the efficient reception manager persuaded the couple to leave, the pack of onlookers parted, thus allowing me to spot my girl as she aggressively jabbed the lift's call button.

"Courteney, I'm sorry."

"Fuck off!"

I trotted through the crowd of onlookers. "Excuse me, excuse me," I muttered as I pushed my way through the melee, most of whom now started to drift away once Stephen had shovelled the soon-to-be-divorced couple through those revolving doors.

Courteney jabbed the button again before pointing at me. "I said, fuck off."

"Courteney."

"What?" she barked, turning back to face the lift.

I glanced around, and although pleased to see the melee dispersing, this wasn't a conversation to hold in a public place. "Can we go somewhere private?"

"If you fink I'm up for a bit of that after what you just said, you're deluded."

"No ... you know what I mean. To talk."

"About what?" The lift doors opened with a swish and a ping.

I grabbed her arm to stop her. "You know what about."

"Get the fuck off!"

I whipped my hand away. The aggressive side of Courteney was something to behold, although preferably not as the recipient. I stepped back a pace, fearing a vicious slap was coming my way – that said, I probably deserved it. "Alright, I'm sorry, I'm sorry, but please—"

"Bleedin' hell, that's all you say, ain't it? It's all sorry, sorry, sorry."

404

"Well, I am."

The lift doors swished shut. I assumed a call button had been depressed on a floor above, or the lift itself had lost interest whilst waiting for Courteney to make a decision about entering.

"Too pissin' late."

I thumbed over my shoulder towards the resident's bar. "Just give me a minute to explain. We can go in there."

Courteney repeatedly thrashed her thumb on the call button, demanding its immediate return.

"You can go in there if you want," she glanced at me whilst repeatedly tapping the call button. "I couldn't give a rats-arse where you go, you gob-shite twat."

"Please. I just want …" I squeezed my eyes shut, trying to conjure up a word other than sorry. "Look, I just want to—"

"What?"

"Talk!" I hissed, now noticing a few onlookers appeared to be watching us.

"Talk 'ere," she nonchalantly shrugged. "You've got at least a few seconds before this poxy lift arrives."

Exasperated, I waved my hands around. "It's not exactly private, is it?"

"Like I give a shit."

"Oh, Courteney, don't you get it?"

"What?"

"I frigging love you!" I bellowed.

The loud verbalisation of my inner thoughts was enough for the crowd of onlookers to retake their positions as they formed a semi-circle, with the ones at the back standing on tiptoe to secure a decent view. Although Stephen called time on the previous performance, it appeared Courteney and I were about to provide the encore.

The lift door swished open – Courteney didn't move.

"Courteney, did you hear me?" Although, as I'd unwittingly announced my love for her to the whole hotel and probably a fair few of the surrounding streets, I guess she couldn't fail to have heard.

With her trainers still glued to the spot, she swivelled her teary face towards me.

I took a pace forward. "Courteney, I'm so sorry for what I said, and I promise you I'll never do that to you again." I glanced at the hushed audience, who seemed to hang on to my every word. Although this was embarrassing, I spotted a few encouraging nods from the front row. "I'm in love with you," I whispered, hoping to quietly reinforce what I'd just bellowed.

The crowd held their breath. The sucking of air almost audible as they willed Courteney to stay put – they were rooting for me – the lift doors swished closed.

Courteney thumped the call button – the doors immediately complied with her request.

"Come on, love. I reckon you could do a lot worse than him," suggested a woman about my age as she bounced a baby in her arms. "He looks a damn sight better than my fella," she chuckled whilst playfully nudging the man beside her, causing a ripple of amusement in the crowd.

The lift doors closed.

"Mrs Smith—"

"We ain't married," Courteney fired back, interrupting Stephen as he attempted to intervene. I guess for the Maid's Head Hotel, this morning's events were somewhat unusual. Unsurprisingly, my girl was the centre of it all.

Courteney stabbed the button again. The doors swished open.

"Mrs Smith, I'm fully aware of that fact, but might I suggest—"

"I suggest, Stevie, you shove your suggestion up your arse!"

A collective 'Oooo' reverberated around the foyer as the lift doors closed.

"Courteney?"

"What about that Canadian lump and that twat, Nathan?" she asked, maintaining her gaze at the lift doors.

"What about them?"

"Shouldn't you be pouring tea and questioning them about Bridget?"

"Probably, but you're more important."

Whilst chewing her lip, she shrugged and stabbed the lift button again. "They won't hang around forever."

"So?"

The lift doors opened – Courteney hesitated and glanced at me. "So, they'll piss off, and you'll never know how to find the bitch."

"Reckon he's been caught playing away with this Bridget woman," a bloke suggested. Out of the corner of my eye, I spotted him nudging a woman, presumably his wife, before offering a knowing wink.

The lift doors swished closed.

"Please," I almost begged.

"Bet you a tenner she gets in the lift next time," I heard a chap whisper to his mate, who shrugged, appearing unwilling to wager on a fifty-fifty bet.

Courteney loudly huffed and wiped her eyes with the cuff of her hoodie before thumping the call button.

The lift doors complied with the request, swishing open with an efficient audible hiss.

Stephen, clearly unprepared to receive further advice from Courteney on where to shove his suggestions, raised his eyebrows at me.

"You hurt me again, and I'll cut your knackers off with a rusty saw."

Further murmurings rumbled through the crowd whilst two chaps in my sight line winced.

"I won't."

"You promise?"

I stepped closer as the doors closed – Courteney didn't move. I suspected the chap offering the bet was relieved his mate wasn't up for taking on the wager.

"I promise. Will you give the call button a rest now?"

"Depends."

"Depends on what?"

"Hey, look, get on with it and kiss the girl," bellowed the woman holding the baby.

"Get a room! You're in the right place," shouted a tall chap from the back of the crowd, causing a few 'Ooos' and the odd giggle to ripple amongst the audience.

Courteney twisted her lips and smirked at me.

"Hey, love, if he don't want you, what about me?" suggested a young lad who jumped forward, splaying his arms out wide.

I took her hand and gently tugged. The rather odd enigma, in the shape of Courteney Klein, uprooted her trainers from where they'd been firmly planted for the entire performance and stepped close to me.

"Thank God for that! Now kiss the girl before she changes her mind!"

I complied with the baby-bouncing woman's suggestion. Whilst we snogged, the crowd broke into raucous applause, coupled with a few wolf whistles and cheers of encouragement.

Whilst Courteney proceeded to wash my tonsils, and the crowd cheered, the scene from *Love Actually* formed in my mind. Although Courteney and Natalie held a certain resemblance in the vocabulary department, rank stupidity was the only similar trait I afforded to a British Prime Minister. Also, not that I possessed a particularly extensive repertoire of snazzy dance moves, but I felt sure I could perform slightly better than Hugh Grant if I ever got the chance to strut my stuff around Number Ten.

As the applause abated and the crowd dispersed, I detected the sound of someone close, clearing their throat. We broke our embrace to discover the reception manager hovering beside us.

"Sorry Stevie, I ain't snogging you as well," she giggled.

My effervescent girl was back to her best.

"No, I imagine you wouldn't, Mrs Smith. Now, as lovely as this all is, I thought you should know I just spotted your guests heading through the Orangery and making a rather hasty beeline for the Magdalen Street exit. So, far from it for me to interfere, but I thought you might want to know."

"Shit!" I glanced to where Stephen was pointing, down those steps we had previously traversed and through to the glass atrium. Then, grabbing her hand, I prepared to dash after them. Clearly, Nathan had changed his mind, or Alex had suddenly acquired cold feet. Notwithstanding my delight at saving our relationship, I needed to speak to those two if I was going to hunt that bloody woman down – hunt, an appropriate word, I mused.

Of course, I was well aware that even if I could establish Bridget's whereabouts, I feared I wouldn't know what course of action to take. Bridget was clever – I, on the other hand, had regularly displayed the competence and savvy of many a recent British Prime Minister – it wouldn't be an even contest. However, I had Courteney by my side, and I had a feeling my girl might just have a few aces up her sleeve – cards we may have to play.

For sure, despite that odd man, Terry, and his good Samaritan intentions, I doubted he would show up on Monday as planned. Also, irrespective of his penchant for calling out my dead mother's name and those telekinetic powers, I had Terry pegged for someone I shouldn't be trusting. The fact he knew about Birmingham could only lead to the conclusion that he was someway involved with Bridget and whoever she was in cahoots with in their attempt to ruin me. As for the possibility that Terry enjoyed the company of my mother's ghost – that was too much to contemplate.

As I tugged her hand, Courteney pulled back. She let go of my hand, cupped a shocked-looking reception manager's cheeks and kissed him full on the lips – no tongues, as far as I could see – but a big smackaroonie kiss, causing his eyes to bulge.

"You're alright, Stevie, you know that?" she giggled, before clutching my hand, and together we made a bolt for the stairs.

"Right, babe, let's hunt these fuckers down."

Nicely put, I thought.

41

Pamplona El Encierro

We discovered 'those fuckers' as Courteney had so delicately put it, deep in conversation at the far end of the Orangery by the hotel side entrance where the efficient Stephen suggested. It appeared Alex, employing a wagging finger and hand on Nathan's elbow technique, was doing his level best in persuading Nathan to stay and face the music, so to speak.

Nathan, who appeared to be impersonating a meerkat, nervously scanned around the ornate glass atrium and, going by his bug-eyed expression, spotted us as we entered. I halted at the hostess stand, fearing that muscling our way into their conversation could be the tipping point for a nervy-looking Nathan to take flight once again. Also, although the oversized greenhouse with its art déco inspired decoration appeared to be only at about half capacity, a fair-few diners seemed to be enjoying the delights of early afternoon tea. So, I guessed stepping in and causing a scene wouldn't be considered good form.

However, Courteney, never the one to take the diplomatic route when full-on confrontation was available, appeared to harbour other ideas. She released her hand from mine and stomped forward, bumping into chairs and tables, causing a trail of destruction in her wake. With her trademark diplomacy, as in displaying the savoir-faire of a rutting bull, she stomped her way through. Two guests spilt their tea as she unwittingly elbowed them in the back, and one dropped her dainty cake that unfortunately landed upside down, the cream topping splatting on the tiled floor.

"Courteney, hang on," I hissed, whilst retrieving said cake and offering it up to the somewhat horror-stricken woman. With my index finger, I attempted to smooth the cream back in place, picked off a hair, and placed it back on her plate. "Sorry, I'm sure it will be fine," I muttered, offering a winsome smile.

"Oi, you gob-shite wankers, where the fuck d'you fink you twats are going? We need some answers, you gutless bastards," she bellowed, causing the vast majority of patrons, cakes in hand, to swivel around and gawp at my girl. At the very least, Courteney was nothing but entertaining.

I grinned at an elderly couple as a way of an apology. "Hormones," I offered and shrugged as I tried to conjure up an acceptable excuse as to why she'd uttered an extensive range of expletives – the only saving grace being she avoided the C-word.

A somewhat surprised Alex spun around as my raging-bull girlfriend dropped her head and charged forward, causing the terrified, bug-eyed Nathan to freeze in position whilst appearing to mutter to himself. As Courteney neared her target, I could only assume his mumblings were akin to the benediction prayers offered up by those mad enough to partake in the Pamplona El Encierro bull run.

However, to be fair to the wimp, Courteney's demeanour could be likened to that of the growling Tasmanian Devil, so I

413

wasn't overly surprised to see him shake out of his catatonic state and take flight and thus disappear out into the street and the melee of Sunday shoppers.

Alex caught hold of Courteney's arm as she ripped open the door, appearing intent on giving chase. "Woah, hold up there, pretty thing. No good you bounding along like a rutting grizzly. You're not going to catch him, even in your fancy runners."

With his bear claw holding her arm, Courteney did what she does best in those 'runners' as Alex called them by walloping her trainer-toe into his shin. Then, like any self-respecting cage-fighter, my girl followed it up with a right hook to the chin, resulting in Alex staggering backwards.

"Oh, Jesus. Courteney, hang on," I hissed again. I made up ground by way of weaving my way through the other guests, concerned that she might be contemplating going in for the kill.

"Babe?" she shot me a look whilst repositioning her stance, preparing to fire a well-aimed heel at the big fella's knackers.

"Hellfire! Can't you keep your mongrel on a leash?" Alex stepped away, rubbing his shin, which now probably sported a large bruise to match up with the other one acquired on Saturday. His ruddy complexion complemented the dark-pinkish washed-out colour of the fading maple leaf motif upon his baseball cap.

"Before you ruin the man's sex life, and get us all arrested, let's see what he's got to say, shall we?" I whispered, not wanting to perform an encore to our earlier somewhat embarrassing performance in the foyer.

As Courteney held her stance, although complying with my suggestion, I turned on the big Canadian who now, with one trouser leg rolled up, assessed the damage. "I thought you said Nathan was prepared to talk to me?" I hissed at the man-mountain, now reasonably confident he wouldn't retaliate for fear of another whack from Courteney, who still appeared poised and ready to crush his gonads. For the future preservation of my own testicles, I made a mental note never to upset my girl again.

Alex held his palm aloft. "Look, the boy is worried about what Bridget might do to him or the fact the police could get involved."

"The little twat needs to worry! I'm in a good mind to rip his bollocks off!" Courteney appeared not to harbour any reservations regarding the need to avoid an audience as she barked at the man for all to hear, resulting in those diners that hadn't already to swivel around in our direction. A calm hush descended as the three of us all glanced back into the room.

My leading lady took centre stage as she addressed the gawping audience. "Oi, reel your necks in!"

All but a thirty-something woman nearby instantly complied with her request. The males were probably concerned she was capable of the ripping castration technique she'd threatened to perform on Nathan.

Courteney glared at the woman who'd maintained her open-mouthed gawp. "Shove another cake in your gob. By the looks of that muffin-top gut of yours, your trap is no stranger to a few calories."

From the guests who remained, apart from those still in shock at Courteney's outburst, an almost polite ripple of laughter broke the silence. Buoyed by the titter, my girl, akin to some fast-thinking comic performing at the Edinburgh Festival Fringe, appeared ready to fire out another verbal assassination.

However, before my girl could continue her 'stand-up routine' and offer up any further quips to delight her audience, the maître d'hôtel hastily approached. I presume he intended to ask us to leave or, at the very least, show some respect to the other guests.

"Mrs Smith. Your afternoon tea is ready for you," he dramatically waved his hand towards a nearby table where a waiter had deposited two large three-tiered cake stands presenting desserts and sandwiches arranged neatly upon white doilies.

"Oh, fanks."

"You're welcome. I take it there will only be the three of you dining?"

"No flies on you, are there, mate?" she chuckled.

"There most certainly are not," he offered a calming smile before pulling out a chair and offering my girl a seat – ever the professional.

"Alex, shall we be civilised?" I waved my hand towards the table.

"As long as you stick a muzzle on her," he muttered, as he warily slid into the chair opposite.

"Oi, you dis me again, and these shoes will be pasting your balls," Courteney waved a trainer-clad foot that, from her position, could easily strike the suggested area.

"My God! What did that girl say?" An elderly lady at an adjacent table questioned her husband.

416

"She said she likes the choux pastry balls," I interrupted whilst pointing at the profiteroles delicately balanced in a pyramid formation. I left her to adjust her hearing aid and slotted into the chair next to Courteney, who'd already bypassed the sandwich layer and settled into raiding the top tier.

"So, you're Deana's boy, then?" Alex stated as he poured his tea.

"How on earth do you know my mother?"

"I said your name was familiar, didn't I? Your mother and I were married for a couple of years before Cheryl and I hooked up. Small world, eh?"

"Bloody hell. Which one were you?"

"Husband?"

"Yeah."

"I was her sixth, would you believe? So, technically, I'm your stepfather."

"Join the club. I've got a fair few of them, most of whom I've never had the pleasure of meeting."

"Of course, I knew you existed, but she never wanted to talk about you. I guess there's some bad history between the two of you?"

"Not really. My first stepfather, Sidney, brought me up. My mother wasn't bothered with me. She was only interested in shagging the male population of the south of England … certainly not remotely interested in bringing up her son."

"Yes, I'm fully aware of her penchant for male company. She buggered off with some bloke called Richard we met at a party. Your mother wasn't like any other woman I've ever

417

met. I hope you don't mind me saying so, but Deana was a wanton woman."

"As I said, I'm fully aware."

"Now, I'm a man of the world, and I've been about a bit, but your mother was something else. Can you believe we turned up to a dinner party … well, that's what she said it was, at one of her friend's houses," he paused, glancing left and right before leaning in and whispering. "It was a car-key party … you know what that is?"

I nodded, although not interested in my mother's sordid sex games.

"Well, she plucked out this Richard bloke's key from the pot, and I ended up with the host, some woman called Odette. So, there I was, being dragged to a bedroom by some random woman whilst your mother was doing what she does best with another man!"

"Unfortunately, I can imagine."

"Anyway, I shouldn't denigrate the dead. I'm sorry … you know, for your loss."

"Oh, don't worry. I never knew the woman."

Alex nodded and appeared to blush, probably regretting disclosing details regarding his car-key story.

"Right, what's going on with Nathan, then?"

Alex plucked up a dainty cucumber sandwich, turning it around as he inspected what appeared to be a postage-stamp-sized morsel held between his fingers. "Look, as you said, Bridget got him involved with you. He's a good lad—"

Courteney snorted but offered no comment as she inserted her tongue into the filling oozing out of the sides of a cream slice.

Alex momentarily observed her lizard tongue before continuing. "As I was saying, he regrets getting involved in her little caper."

"There was nothing little about it, I can assure you."

"No, so I've since discovered. But listen, the boy only prepared the documents that Bridget conned you into signing, nothing else."

"He didn't employ a private investigator to set me up, then?"

"Nathan? No. However, he is aware that Bridget and her partner employed a PI, as you suggest."

Courteney and I shot each other a look. As her mouth appeared otherwise occupied with the cake offerings, I took up the probing of Alex's story.

"Partner?"

"Yes, the bloke she's hooked up with. I'm led to believe she's formed an alliance with some evil bastard and upped her game to more elaborate cons."

"You got a name?"

Alex shook his head as he slotted the sandwich in his mouth.

All three of us shot our heads to the left to assess the man who stepped up to our table.

"Lee. His name is Lee."

42

The Thomas Crown Affair

With half a cream slice delicately clamped in her hand, Courteney shot up out of her chair. However, before she leapt into action and restarted her Tasmanian Devil impression, I grabbed her hoodie sleeve, effectively hauling her back down.

"His name is Lee," repeated Nathan, as he slotted onto the vacant chair whilst keeping a wary eye on my cream-devouring blonde terrier.

Alex swallowed his sandwich and grabbed Nathan's arm. "Good lad."

"Damian, I'm sorry. I should never have got involved. But, as you well know, Bridget can be very persuasive."

"I can persuade your bollocks to disappear if you like," Courteney threw at him whilst reaching for the profiteroles pyramid.

I squeezed her free hand, attempting to calm her. Fortunately, the extensive range of cream cakes seemed sufficient to keep her occupied. Also, unlike the woman who was the butt of her earlier joke, Courteney didn't seem to suffer the same issue of 'once on the lips, twice on the hips'. I presumed my girl's stomach must burn like the fires of Hades with her apparent high metabolism.

With Courteney preoccupied, I carried on. "Nathan, thanks for coming back. So, this Lee, who is he?"

Nathan shot a glance at Alex.

"Son, you're here now. So, I guess it's time to spill the beans."

"Look, I've only met him a couple of times, but the bloke's pure evil. All I know is that he and Bridget seemed to have formed some sort of an alliance."

"An alliance?"

"Yeah, they run cons together. Bridget's kind of front-of-house in the operations if you see what I mean. She sucks the mark in whilst Lee performs the behind the scene tasks. They're a couple as well if you get my drift."

I nodded, confirming I understood the meaning. Although an 'item' as in sharing a bed, I presumed they weren't of a mind to spend Saturday mornings in Ikea choosing flatpack furniture or inclined to take in a romantic stroll in the park on Sunday afternoons. I could only assume their relationship was more of a business-type arrangement – friends with benefits – as opposed to a loving relationship. Based on the fact that Lee had pimped her out in order to run the con, or work 'front of house', as Nathan put it, that suggested neither were too concerned that Bridget had taken me to her bed.

A means to an end, I guess. Maybe that's why Bridget seemed to feign many headaches towards the end of our relationship. She'd offered herself up for the purpose of reeling me in. However, in the biblical sense, she harboured no desire to carry on our relationship due to already having a lover in tow – unlike my mother, who, by all accounts, simultaneously preferred to indulge in multiple sexual liaisons if Alex's car-key-party anecdote was anything to go by.

"You know why they targeted you, don't you?" Nathan asked, his question fortunately dragging me from unsolicited visions of my dead mother's riotous merrymaking.

"To swindle me out of my business, I presume. I guess I'm what you might call a soft target."

"Gullible idiot, babe. My idiot, but gullible."

I nodded at Courteney, who smirked at me before expertly slotting into her mouth a cream-filled chocolate ball – a hole-in-one.

"Not really. Although that was the financial aim—"

"Which you brokered," I somewhat belligerently spat back.

"I did, and I'm sorry," he raised his palm, keeping half an eye on my terrier as she devoured her cake. "Bridget bullied me."

"Wimp," she mumbled between chewing.

"Hey, give it a rest. Nathan doesn't have to talk to you," Alex fired back at Courteney, who just shrugged at his request.

"No, she's right. I've let my half-sister bully me my whole life."

"Poison, that girl. Of course, his mother wouldn't hear of it."

"So, what other reason, apart from financial gain?"

"Well, revenge, of course."

"For what? What the hell have I done to her, for Christ's sake? I'd never met the woman until she came on to me in that pub in January."

"Revenge for her father."

"God, damn it. You never said about this," exclaimed Alex, holding his teacup to his lips. "That bloody girl. Cheryl will be turning in her grave."

I shot Courteney a glance. My girl, mouth full of whipped cream and choux pastry, nodded. Although we had both dismissed Terry's suggestion and put it down to a coincidence, clearly the strange man with the odd tic and a penchant for calling out my dead mother's name wasn't a couple of tins short of a six-pack I had him pegged for.

"So, you're telling me that Bridget planned revenge against *me*," I stabbed a finger in my sternum to emphasise the point. "Because of what happened between my stepfather and her father back in God knows when?"

"Yep," he nodded. "That's about the size of it. Bridget offered me a lump sum to help her. Of course, I refused the offer, but in her usual coercive manner, she got her way. She said I had to help her because we were family."

"Damn girl. Someone needs to take a leather strap to her ass," Alex offered up his opinions regarding child obedience techniques whilst slowly shaking his head in dismay.

"She needs shooting!" I added.

"That can be arranged, babe. When we find her, I can have a word wiv a few blokes I know. I reckon I could persuade a couple of them to do the job if we bung 'em a few grand."

"Don't tempt me."

"Hell's bells, who in God's name is this woman?" Alex blurted, sporting a bug-eyed expression whilst pointing his teacup in Courteney's direction.

"This woman, as you call her, is the only sodding person on this planet trying to help me. So, I suggest you watch your tongue."

Alex raised an eyebrow at my suggestion but appeared reluctant to counter.

"Cheers, babe." Courteney gave me a cream-lipped peck on the cheek before returning her attention to the cake stand. "There's only one of those left," she pointed a cerise-pink nail to the depleted selection of cakes, namely the last cream slice. "Anyone mind if I have it?"

The three of us shook our heads – Courteney grinned and snatched up her prize.

"You were saying."

"Oh, yeah. So, her dad, Dennis Hunt, died last year and left his entire estate to Bridget. After he was imprisoned, my mum divorced Dennis and had nothing more to do with him. So, when he was eventually released, Mum refused him access to Bridget. Of course, by that time, my mum had married my father. Anyway, after a bitter court battle that Mum and Dad won, Dennis was left with no choice but to give in."

"That's when he moved to Ireland?"

"Yeah, I believe so. Anyway, after Dennis died, the solicitor acting as the executor of his will tracked Bridget down. Among his effects were papers, diaries and correspondence which detailed what happened in 1984."

"My stepfather turning Queen's evidence against him?"

"Yeah. With the help of some dodgy private investigator, Bridget and this Lee bloke tracked your father down. However, as you know, he moved to the United States. That's when Bridget saw the opportunity to go after you and coerced me into her little scheme."

I thought of that cold Friday evening in January when holed up in a trendy pub in town. I'd recently taken over Statham Cars, so, reasonably well-loaded. Excited by my newly gifted wealth, I'd already started to flash the cash. Basically, amounting to wasting my new fortune on anything that I could lay my hands on.

That particular evening, I insisted on buying a few rounds of drinks, immaturely showing off, thinking it would impress my mates – that's when Bridget appeared. Little did I know at the time this beguiling tight-leather-jean-clan siren would lure me to ruin.

As I stood at the bar ordering another round of blue kamikaze shots, she sidled up to me and flirtatiously suggested I could also buy her a drink. At the time, I thought it was just a cheeky request based on the fact I appeared to be securing a rather large order. However, she rubbed her leg against mine, licked her top lip and said she'd have a large glass of Chablis before making it abundantly clear she wanted more than a free glass of plonk.

Of course, like any stupid bloke, I couldn't resist her. A few hours later, I found myself rolling around on her bed with her naked body wrapped around mine. Although I was clearly minted, I believed Bridget had fallen for my charms, whatever they were, and not the size of my bank account – what an idiot.

Anyway, experience tells me, before my stepfather's gift of the business, women like Bridget wouldn't even glance in my direction, let alone shag my brains out. Notwithstanding the carnal pleasures she offered and my salacious desires, I now realise Bridget was presumably faking it, giving a performance that I suspect Courteney would be proud of when entertaining her clients on Suzzysuck.com.

"This Lee bloke ... he about forty and got a gold tooth?" Courteney asked, when plucking up another cream-filled chocolate ball, poised close to her mouth and ready to be devoured.

Nathan bristled, shuffling back in his seat as my girl pointed her cream-filled ball at him. "No. Well ... not studied him that closely. I'd say he's about Bridget's age, maybe a year or so younger."

"And he's a pig?"

"Sorry?"

"Filth ... you know those tossers with blue helmets, and I ain't talking about their cocks."

"Oh ... no, no." Nathan now sported a red glow, clearly embarrassed by Courteney's description – something I now seemed immune to. "I believe he's done time. Bridget let slip that he's got a few mates he met in Brixton Prison. I can't imagine he's a prison officer, so he must be an ex-con."

Courteney and I exchanged another glance. So, Gold-tooth wasn't Lee, the 'behind-the-scenes' man, orchestrating my downfall. As Alex had insinuated earlier, Lee and Bridget had an inside man on their payroll – a bent copper taking backhanders to perform certain tasks when required.

"What makes you think this Lee has something to do with the police?" Alex interjected.

"Because someone is trying to fit me up. Look, I get the con and her need to take revenge by financially ruining me. That aside, you may not be aware, but this Lee bloke and Bridget haven't stopped there."

"Sorry, I don't follow."

"As you said on the phone earlier, Bridget has connections in the police. They are trying to set me up, so I end up in prison. They're in league with a bent copper and, between the three of them, tried to frame me with a significant stash of drugs. Up until two minutes ago, I assumed this bent copper was the man who hired that private investigator, but now I'm thinking it must have been this Lee bloke."

Alex shot Nathan a look. "Son? Don't tell me you're mixed up in something like this."

"No, absolutely not," Nathan glanced around at the three of us. "I had nothing to do with it … I promise."

"But you know about it?" Courteney momentarily diverted her hand from the shrinking chocolate pyramid to point at Nathan.

Nathan nodded. "Lee's idea. He was a bit pissed about how long Bridget was with you, so he thought he would have some fun. Basically, get you fitted up by way of stashing some drugs in your flat … payback for knobbing his missus, as he put it. Look, I had nothing to do with it. I just overheard them, that's all."

"You damn well better not have, boy. I dread to think what your mother would have said to all this."

"I'm not!" Nathan retorted in a childlike manner whilst petulantly folding his arms and huffing.

"Alright, but who is this police officer Bridget is embroiled with, then?

"Alex, as I said earlier, I don't know who he is! I told you; I had nothing to do with all that drugs and that set-up stuff. Christ, I'm not that stupid. Whoever he is, I'm pretty sure Bridget has got him in her pocket."

"Well, that sister of yours has made her bed. If she's got herself involved with drugs as well as bent cops, she'll come to a sticky end. I sure as hell ain't bailing her out no more. I'm just grateful your mother's not here to witness it all."

After a moment of silence – Nathan sulking, Courteney systematically chomping her way through four generous portions of cream cakes, and me pondering about the fact that we'd achieved bugger all – Alex decided to verbalise his thoughts about his errant stepdaughter.

"That girl has been nothing but trouble her whole life. Like father, like daughter. That Dennis Hunt was bad news, and that damn girl is performing a parody of his life of crime."

"Pastiche, not parody … I fink you've used the wrong word," Courteney corrected him.

"Excuse me," Alex somewhat belligerently fired at Courteney.

"Parody is taking the piss out of somefink. I don't fink Bridget is taking the piss out of her dad. She's more emulating his crimes, so that's like a pastiche … paying homage if you like."

Alex's mouth dropped, presumably stunned by her statement.

"It's a bit like that picture, *The Son of Man*, y'know, the geezer in a bowler hat, with an apple on his face. Loads of artists have pastiche that style."

"There's a lot more to Courteney than meets the eye," I chuckled.

"Yeah, I ain't all tits and teeth, you know. Ain't that right, babe?"

"Definitely."

"I'll take your word for it," mumbled a somewhat stunned Alex.

Now Courteney, like some walking thesaurus, had killed the conversation with her opinion on the correct use of words, I slumped back in my chair, needing a moment to allow this information about Lee to marinate in my mind. Although we now had confirmation for why Bridget and her partner were hell-bent on destroying me, that information wasn't going to help recover my lost fortune or stop that bloody woman before she bestowed another catastrophe upon me.

"You'll have to excuse me. I need the restroom," Alex raised his bulk from the chair before nudging Nathan's arm. "You'll be okay?"

"Bloody hell!" Courteney spat out with a mouth full of cake before swallowing, again performing her python impression. "Piss off and take a leak. What d'you fink we're gonna do, kidnap him?"

Nathan nodded, indicating he thought he'd be okay, despite Courteney's threat.

Now that she'd devoured the vast majority of cakes, Courteney picked up the questioning from where I'd left off. However, despite my conciliatory approach to ensure Nathan didn't take flight, Courteney applied the 'bad cop' persona to her questioning style.

"So, you wimpy git, where do we find that bleedin' sister of yours?"

Alex stepped back to the table, presumably to instruct my girl to temper her questioning style. However, he appeared to change his mind when clocking my raised eyebrow. I guess, after biting back at him earlier, plus fearing Courteney might be inclined to meter out further physical assaults, may be the reason he changed his mind and instead chose to trot off in the direction of the gents.

"Honestly, I don't know where she is."

"That's bollocks!" she scoffed.

"Look, all I know is that she lives in London, but I don't know where."

"T'rrific," I sarcastically muttered.

"Oh, great! That's not exactly a small search area."

Nathan shrugged before reaching for a sandwich from the lower tiers – the top one now devoid of any delicacies apart from four pink macarons. I presumed my girl wasn't a fan of those, or her stomach had indicated no more room was available.

Courteney slapped his hand. "Oi! You can eat when I've got answers."

Nathan whisked his hand back, offering a hurt-child expression.

"So, you got her number?"

"No … she uses burner phones. She rings me. I have to wait for her to call if I need to speak to her."

"Sake! What about this bastard, Lee?"

"No idea," he nonchalantly shrugged, whilst eyeing up a smoked salmon sandwich, probably weighing up if it was worth risking another sortie across the table.

"But you've met him?"

"Yeah, as I said, a couple of times. But that was at that flat she rented in town, which she's not at any more. So, my best guess is she and Lee have pissed off back to London."

"Babe, this is bleedin' hopeless. This twat don't know anyfink."

I grabbed her hand and offered a tight smile. She was right. Although Nathan had taken part in the sting, it was clear he wasn't a willing participant. As she'd said, the man was a wimp, frightened of his own shadow and still too scared to reach across and take a sandwich.

Courteney noticed his hand creep across the table towards the cake stand. Like a well-trained dog, he halted his hand's advance when spotting her glare. My girl gave a slight nod, permitting him to reach out and grab the food – no, this man was no master criminal.

With a mouth full of smoked salmon, Nathan broke the silence. "You could ask the landlord who owns her old flat."

We narrowed our eyes at him. "You know the landlord?" I quizzed, presuming he had some information to impart and wasn't just throwing out pointless suggestions.

He nodded as he swallowed. "Yeah, his name's John Parish, although I don't actually know him. He owns a lot of property in Fairfield."

"You got this git's number?"

"No, sorry."

"Sake! You know feck all, don't you, you prick."

That coin, which had metaphorically wedged itself in the mechanism of this conundrum, finally dislodged – the penny dropped. I closed my eyes and shook my head at my utter stupidity. Why I was surprised, hell knows, because stupidity was my middle name.

Terry, whoever he was, had suggested we meet up tomorrow. A meeting where Fred Hallam would provide the name of who set me up or Terry would unleash the vengeance of the dead upon him, whatever that entailed. However, apart from mild curiosity regarding the odd man who possessed telekinetic powers and knew my mother had bought me an Action Man for my fourteenth birthday, we no longer needed to attend that meeting.

Nathan might know 'feck all' as Courteney put it, but I did – I knew exactly who John Parish was and how to get hold of him.

More to the point, I knew his son.

43

Santo Spirito

"Darling, come on, shake a leg. We're going to be late." Deana bellowed up the stairs before trotting back into the kitchen. She plucked up the burning cigarette from the ashtray positioned on the windowsill and inhaled two hefty lungful's of smoke before stubbing it out and placing the ashtray in the sink.

Due to Terry's insistence that he would rather shower alone, despite her suggestion that together they would save water and could help each other scrub those difficult-to-reach parts, Deana feared they wouldn't make it in time for their meeting with Damian, that rough trollop he insisted dragging around, and Inch-High Private Eye.

Whilst slugging down the dregs of her coffee, she chuckled to herself when imagining the horror on the poor little man's face when discovering his ransacked office. She suspected the crime scene investigators would have a field day when rummaging through the content of his filing cabinet. The only saving grace for the poor man was they wouldn't be able to trawl through his laptop – because if they had, she suspected he would now be answering some difficult questions being thrown at him by an officer regarding the somewhat repugnant collection of porn that the man must have downloaded from the dark web.

Deana was a liberal-minded woman and not easily offended. However, the collection of pictures she and Terry had perused last night when raking through the content of Hallam's laptop, even for her, were beyond the pale. That laptop would be the bargaining chip they needed to ensure Hallam played ball.

Of course, advising Inch-High that they were in possession of the laptop would confirm they were the guilty party. However, that collection of digital porn would stop the little pasty man from squealing to the police.

Despite missing her darling Dickie, and Terry's insistence on leading a celibate dead existence, there were some advantages to being dead. What she'd give to see the police officer's expressions when they discovered a dead woman's fingerprints all over the crime scene. She imagined all sorts of pandemonium would ensue as rechecks were made and questions raised regarding the police's national database's accuracy of stored information.

A couple of summers back, Deana and Dickie decided to take a trip out to a secluded wooded area just north of Fairfield. An acquaintance they'd met at an erotic pool party a few weeks earlier suggested they might enjoy an evening in the woods, as she'd put it. Although 'dogging' was not an activity either thought they would enjoy, preferring orgies with like-minded friends rather than flashing flesh in some layby, their curiosity had been piqued.

Of course, Deana had no intention of whipping her clothes off or grabbing hold of some grubby man's appendage through the car window, but both thought watching from a safe distance might hold some entertainment value.

So, there they were, hunkered down in Dickie's Maserati, taking in the sights of flashing headlights and semi-naked participants huddled around cars with steamed-up windows when two police cars appeared. Unfortunately, it seemed some busybody had reported lewd activity taking place near a public highway, resulting in a police raid and multiple arrests for indecent exposure.

Of course, Deana and Dickie weren't involved – just observing. However, notwithstanding their claims of innocence, when an officer sidled up to their car, they were duly arrested along with the semi-naked troop who'd fled into the bushes. Unfortunately, Deana was caught in a compromising position, namely, using her hand to relieve Dickie, who'd become somewhat excited by the performance of the willing participants. So, the officer who peered through the side window, copping an eyeful of Dickie with his trousers inched down, thought their claims of innocence really didn't cut the mustard – advising Deana that no, she couldn't finish off when she'd enquired because Dickie was nearly there, also instructing her husband to make himself decent.

After an embarrassing couple of hours holed up in Fairfield Police Station, with fingerprints and a somewhat unflattering mug shot taken – the arresting officer not even allowing Deana to reapply her make-up before the camera shutter caught her image – Odette, acting as their solicitor, managed to persuade the officer not to press charges against them.

Anyway, her fingerprints were on file. Deana, a woman who died some weeks back, had yesterday forced entry into the crummy office of a private investigator with a penchant for lowbrow porn.

After securing the laptop in her safe, Deana and Terry took a stroll in the spring sunshine down to the church. Not that a house of God was an ideal meeting place, but back in that redundant car showroom on Saturday, it was all Terry could think of when picking a place to meet up. Anyway, a building surrounded by graves had played into their hands when Terry threatened Fred Hallam with the vengeance of the dead. Also, on a Monday lunchtime, they suspected the church wouldn't be overly busy, with only the possibility of Dreary Drake, her old neighbour, indulging in a spot of flower arranging or Father Wilson fussing about with Bibles whilst counting up the meagre donations in the collection box deposited after the Sunday service.

Terry twisted the heavy iron handle, the latch producing an echoey clunk inside the empty church. "What if Hallam hasn't found out the information we demanded?"

"We resort to blackmail, darling. Although you threatened him with more of my impressions of *The Wicked Witch of the West,* I rather think his missing laptop will focus the mind."

"Hmm, those pictures were horrendous. I can't imagine why any bloke would want to look at that sort of stuff."

"No, quite. The disgusting little man needs locking up. So, if the little pervert hasn't come through with a name, we move to plan B, as in forcing Hallam to arrange a meet with the mystery man claiming he's recovered the drugs."

"Shall we take a seat? Good job the place is empty." Terry waved his hand to the back row of highly polished pews, the patina smoothed by centuries of parishioners' wriggling posteriors.

Deana slipped in first whilst glancing at her watch. "They're all late. We said midday, didn't we?"

"We did. If none of them turns up, I have no idea what we do next."

"We need Odette. She seemed to know what to do when she helped us out with your little Kimmy."

"Christ, we're not very good at this, are we?" he chuckled, sliding in beside her.

Deana shuffled her bum back to close the gap between them, looping her arms through his and resting her head on his shoulder. "We do seem to struggle a bit. I think Odette, with her sharp legal mind, is more suited to this type of work. I'm more for decoration."

"Decoration?"

"Yes, darling, I brighten up the place, wouldn't you say? You know, you decorate to make things look beautiful, like me. I'm what you might call rather easy on the eye," she sniggered.

"Easy … definitely."

"I hope you're not referring to my rather insatiable thirst for sex when you say easy."

"I wouldn't dare."

"No, I should think not."

"If we fail, will the powers that be pull us back, so to speak?"

"You thinking about your little Sharon again?"

Terry shrugged.

Deana gripped his arm a little tighter and nuzzled her face against his polo shirt. "She's gone, darling. Make your peace with that, and let me keep you warm at night … you won't be disappointed, my love."

Terry sucked in a lungful of air through his nose, holding it before loudly exhaling. He wasn't going to comment on that statement, and certainly not in a house of God.

"Do you think Damian knows about Sidney?"

"I doubt it, darling. Well, not unless he's tried calling him."

"But Sidney drowned in that lake weeks ago. Surely, he must know by now."

"I don't know, darling. Although Sidders could bore a sloth to death, I find it rather romantic that Cindy couldn't go on without him."

"Romantic? Christ, it's a bit strong. A few tears at the funeral, perhaps. But to go flinging yourself over a balcony is taking it too far."

"It's a woman thing, darling. Women are more sensitive to affairs of the heart. I certainly wouldn't have wanted to go on if Dickie had died before me."

"I can't imagine you kamikazeing out of a hotel room like some wailing banshee."

"No, probably not. Although half his age, Cindy must have found his tales of fishing exploits riveting. Nowt so queer as folk, as they say. I don't see how anyone can get excited by dragging some poor carp in with a hook in its lip, to then lob it straight back in and then try and catch it again."

"It's a man thing. The hunter-gatherer, it's in our make-up."

438

"If you say so, darling."

The deafening silence of the heavy musty air seemed to quell their conversation. Terry could feel her breath on his arm as he stared at the crucifixion cross positioned at the centre of the altar, which partially blocked the ornate reredos. Nevertheless, the sightless eyes of the carving of the Son of God seemed to hold his gaze. Terry wondered if that inane wooden icon could actually see him. Did that depiction of the crucifixion know he was dead? Was that carved figure now assessing his suitability to enter the celestial paradisiacal empyrean?

The echoing clunk of the door latch caused them both to jump. The door swung inwards, allowing a shard of bright sunlight to flood down the nave and cause the moted dust light to dance. Deana and Terry swivelled around to see who'd entered, but apart from the sunlight, there appeared to be no one there.

"Did you see that?" hissed Deana.

"See what?" Terry whispered.

"I thought I spotted a shadow dart behind that pillar."

Terry and Deana hopped up out of the pew. Deana remained in position as Terry tentatively stepped forward and peered around the pillar to where Deana now pointed. He thought he heard a foot scrape on the stone floor, but as he stealthily crept around, it appeared no one was hiding there.

Had a demon snuck in on a mission to suck him down to the fiery hell of the underworld, or was that angled beam of light that flooded through the open doorway there to guide him to paradise?

As Terry's mouth gaped in wonder, he shimmied forward to stand in the heavenly light. He considered the possibility that the sightless carving had made a decision, and at any moment now, he'd travel through the light and become reunited with his Sharon. He frantically smoothed his hair before tucking his shirt in, determined to look good for his dead wife.

"Terry, what's happening?" she hissed.

"Nothing. There's no one there."

"Oh, how odd." Deana stepped forward, cuddling his arm again before gazing up at him. "Darling, what's the matter?"

"Shush," he hissed.

Although he didn't think strolling through the pearly gates with the diva, Deana, hanging off his arm was the way to present himself to Sharon, who would surely be waiting for him, he wasn't in the mind to shake off Deana's attentions for fear of missing the moment. Presumably, this was the window of opportunity to step into the light and thus enjoy all eternity in salvation.

Deana frowned. "Please don't shush me, darling. I'm not a child."

"Alright. Please, just be quiet," he hissed back.

"Okay, as you said, please, I will. But I must say, you seem a little odd. Is it the dead thing? You know, being dead in a church is all rather spooky," she giggled.

Terry huffed.

"Alright, darling, I'll be quiet," she patronisingly patted his arm.

A minute passed whilst the dust continued to dance in the shard of golden sunlight. Terry held his breath, anticipating the moment whilst Deana rather annoyingly seemed to fidget.

As time ticked past, he became concerned to why he hadn't floated up into the light. Terry tentatively nudged forward half a pace, now contemplating that he may be required to walk into heaven and not be guided in by a winged guardian spirit.

As he waited, eyes closed, head turned up to the heavens, he heard a woman's voice, distant, but the perfect pitch of a beautiful celestial angel – this was it, Sharon had come for him and was here to welcome him into eternal life.

Terry peeked open one eye. Although a little surprised to see an angel wearing what appeared to be knee-high black leather boots, he could only just make out her outline. There she stood, silhouetted against the sunlight on the other side of the open doorway. Her long golden hair gently swayed in the light breeze – an angelic vision of beauty.

"Come on, babe, hurry up. That fucking fruit loop, Terry, is actually 'ere."

44

Dead Ringers

After an eventful afternoon tea taken in the setting of the ornate Orangery of our hotel, where Courteney assaulted the big Canadian, scared his stepson witless, offered calorie consumption advice to other guests and ravaged the top two tiers of our cake stands, we retired to our suite to formulate a plan.

I called my 'mate' Lee and unsurprisingly didn't get an answer. Neither did his father, John Parish, my landlord, pick up. However, I thought his reason for not answering was due to being a Sunday evening and not because he wished to avoid me, as clearly was the case with Lee.

Rob did answer and, for nearly half an hour, I probed him about Lee, specifically how he knew him. Although Rob and Lee were the only two mates to stand by me during this whole debacle, unlike Rob, who I'd known for over twenty-five years, Lee had recently come on the scene – and now I knew why.

However, Rob wasn't much help. He said he met Lee at the back end of last year in his local pub where they'd got chatting, and before we knew it, Lee had become part of the gang.

Although I'd become acquainted with Lee over the past few months, I now realised I knew very little about him. Well, apart from his flatulence and ability to fill my flat with odious gases. I didn't know where he worked, lived, what car he drove – anything. He was a clever operator who'd wormed his way in as part of the con he and Bridget had cooked up. I guess if you're in for the best part of a million quid, then a significant investment of time was worth it. Lee and Bridget invested their time well and reaped the rewards for their efforts.

A couple of months back, a few mates and I enjoyed a Sunday trip out to watch the North London derby – Arsenal versus Tottenham. Lee acquired the tickets through a mate of a mate. I recall we had a great day, which was only marred by a kerfuffle in a pub after the game. Of course, I kept well clear of the flying fists swung by the pissed-up rutting stags wearing opposing replica shirts. However, now I recall how Lee waded in. His happy-go-lucky persona had momentarily dropped, falling out of character into his real self when smashing a bottle on the edge of the bar before threatening some thug with the jagged edge pressed against his jugular – clearly not the first time he had performed this manoeuvre.

Lee Parish was one evil bastard. Whilst that nefarious woman, in the form of Bridget, sucked me into her web of deceit working 'front-of-house', Lee wormed his way into my life, the man behind the scenes, so to speak, as he gathered information and ensured the con stayed on track. In that position, he would know if I was becoming concerned about Bridget. Although I didn't, because I'd been a stupid twat. However, if I had said something about not trusting Bridget or broken through her flimsy backstory, Lee would be one of the first to know, thus allowing them the earliest opportunity to adjust their plan accordingly.

I recall when Laura met Lee one night at the pub, she commented that she didn't like his cut of the jib. Apart from, at the time, not knowing what she'd meant by that comment, perhaps Rob's prissy wife was a good judge of character. Well, she had me pegged for a gullible idiot with a propensity to say the wrong thing at the wrong time and, to be fair to the woman, she made a good point.

My girl made a few calls of her own, the first to her vodka-swilling mate, Deli. Although I could hear Courteney's side of the conversation, I still required a translation due to her conversation being conducted in a whole new language. That said, from text messages over the past few days, I now knew words like *dis, peng, chirps, and mandem*, all of which I picked up when listening in.

"You said peng. What was that about?" I asked over my shoulder, whilst I again studied the snaking river runway as the setting sun glinted off its rippling water.

"That, babe, was when I said about you."

"Oh."

Courteney padded barefoot over to me before wrapping her arms around my back. "Babe, I told her I love you."

"Right. Was that a sensible move? You said she's got a gob on her like the Blackwall Tunnel."

"Probably not. But fuck it, babe, I'm excited."

I pulled her head to my chest as I focused my gaze on the setting sun. "What did Deli have to say?"

"Bleedin' loads, but most of it not worth repeating. The filth have arrested Karl for murder. I reckon he'll be placed on remand in the morning."

I loudly exhaled. Relief that Karl was, for the moment, off that exponentially growing list of issues. "What about you?"

"Nah. They've got him; the filth won't be looking for me."

"They might be looking for me, though. I must have been caught on CCTV waving that fire extinguisher about on Saturday."

"Babe, you worry too much. That CCTV will show that fucker assaulting me, so I reckon he won't be too keen about reporting you."

"Maybe, but someone—"

Courteney whisked her finger to my lips. "Babe, I'm gonna buy you a set of worry beads."

"Buy?" I snorted.

"Yeah, I do buy the odd thing from time to time. Now look, Deli's going to bag me up some gear. You want her to grab some of your stuff as well?"

"Err … how will she get into my flat?"

"Jesus, babe, it's not that hard. Even the little shits in nursery school on that estate can pick a lock. So, I reckon Deli, with half a bottle of vodka inside her, can get through your door in less than a minute."

"Oh. Well, yes, I guess so."

"Right, I'll ping her a WhatsApp. I can't wait to get into some clean gear 'cos I urgently need fresh knickers, and my tit sweat is making my bra stink. Also, I ain't read a book for days, so I asked her to grab a couple for me."

I chuckled at her description regarding the need to change her clothing but refrained from commenting. For sure, I doubt a literary classic by Virginia Woolf and sweaty breasts has ever before been uttered in the same breath.

Now I'd decided Rob's wife may well be a good judge of character, and if I ever managed to rid myself of Lee and Bridget, I wondered what Laura would make of my Courteney. Of course, time would tell, but I didn't give a shit what anyone thought of my girl.

Although I'd lost the business, now meeting Courteney, the need to be surrounded by riches didn't seem that important anymore. Of course, we needed to persuade Lee and Bridget to leave me alone because if they continued with their pursuit to frame me, it would only be a matter of time before they achieved their goal.

So, we had a plan for tomorrow. After catching up with Deli in town, we intended to keep that meeting with Terry and that private investigator. Although we now knew who had set me up, finding the bastard was a whole new ball game. Clearly, Lee and Bridget had both gone to ground. So, the odd man with the same name as my biological father and that shifty PI were as good as any starting place to glean some information regarding Lee's whereabouts.

Contacting my father would also have to be on tomorrow's list. Although we hadn't shared the closest relationship, Sidney had imparted his successful business upon me. So, I thought he had a right to know what I'd done. That said, if he and that Cindy woman were still all gooey-eyed, I presume he wouldn't give two shits what had happened on this side of the pond.

After a frenetic couple of days since meeting Courteney last Thursday, unsurprisingly, we both sunk into a deep slumber within a few minutes of slipping under our clean quilt.

However, unlike the previous morning when we awoke, our bedding appeared to be tucked around us as if neither of us had even twitched a digit, let alone performed somersaults as we ravaged each other's bodies as had been the case the previous two nights – we'd been dead to the world.

While Courteney dozed with her head on my chest, I thought about my mother. Would her ghost be floating around in that church at noon? "Christ," I muttered, and chuckled at my stupid thoughts. Yes, okay, so the weekend had thrown up a rather odd revelation or two, but suggesting to myself that my mother's ghost now roamed around Fairfield impersonating Matilda was a bit of a stretch.

Anyway, I doubted a place of worship for God-fearing folk would be suitable for the ghost of a philandering adulteress, and I presume her ghost wouldn't feel too comfortable visiting. On a sensible note, whilst up at the church, perhaps I should pay my respects at her grave – although, in reality, it was good riddance to bad rubbish.

Deli had come up trumps, hauling two hefty bags of supplies into town. Akin to performing something like a drug deal exchange, she handed them over whilst we grabbed a coffee. Fortunately, Courteney didn't distract the barista and steal any chocolate this time but enjoyed a cream-filled eclair – of course she did. The two girls enjoyed a quick conversation, which, as far as I was concerned, might as well have been conducted in a foreign language before we scurried back to our hotel to freshen up.

Courteney emerged from the bathroom of our opulent suite dressed in clean attire and a pair of four-inch stiletto over-the-knee-length boots, which drew my eye. Previously, I'd only seen her in those 'work clothes' when wearing way too much make-up, her dressing gown and Victoria's Secret knickers or that hoodie and trainers. Now, in a sexy, but not tarty, pair of over-the-knee-length boots and, with her hair down, she blazoned her true beauty. So, as we sashayed through the prestigious hotel, rather than appearing like a couple on the run, we slotted into our surroundings. Her mate Stevie, along with many others, followed her catwalk sway whilst barely able to hold their tongues in.

Not in a saturnalian way, Courteney Klein turned heads as if a famous film star had just waltzed by. I, although in a clean pair of jeans and an ironed shirt, could have been invisible.

"Bleedin' lovely to get my tits in clean underwear, babe. Nothing worse than sweaty boobs hammocked in a smelly bra." Courteney announced, purposefully breaking the illusion as we passed a group of middle-aged residents whose wondrous glances turned to horror – my girl just couldn't help herself.

"I can imagine," I replied, offering a cheesy grin to the onlookers.

~

Courteney paid the taxi driver with another one of the pointy-shoe man's twenty-pound notes. As we traversed through the graveyard, I dragged Courteney over to my biological father's final resting place. Of course, Terry Walton meant nothing to me, and I guess that's the reason I'd never felt the need to tend to his grave. However, I thought I'd show her where my relatives lay at rest. We stopped short due to spotting a couple kneeling by his headstone as they laid flowers and performed a general tidy-up.

From our position some yards away, I could see the newly painted gold lettering on the headstone, gleaming brightly in the morning sunshine. Although, as said, not a grave I usually visited, I recall that lettering had faded, so it appeared someone decided to give the headstone a makeover along with resetting the granite edging stones which had previously laid on the slew where the earth shifted through the passage of time.

Someone had taken great care to return my father's grave to some modicum of respectability – presumably, the couple, whoever they were, now tending to his grave.

"Hiya, babe," Courteney called out before dragging me over to the woman brushing the dirt from her hands. And there was I thinking Stevie and I were the only ones she called babe – silly me.

"Oh, hi Courteney," she flashed a familiar smile, although I had no idea who she was, before giving me the once up and down and warily narrowing her eyes at me.

"What you doing 'ere?"

"Vinny and I thought it's about time we tended my father's grave. I never knew him when he was alive because he died before I was born. But a few weeks ago, I think I met his ghost," she nervously laughed. "Sorry, that's a bit silly, I know."

Courteney, whilst entwining her fingers in mine, shot me a look. I offered the slightest shake of the head, indicating, at this point, I didn't want her to divulge that Terry Walton was also my father. As far as I was aware, my mother didn't bear any other children. Also, as this woman was about my age, that suggested her mother wasn't Deana because, as far as I knew, I didn't have a twin. However, it appeared I'd just met my half-sister.

449

"So, how are you?"

"Yeah, I'm good, girl. This is Damian," Courteney nodded at me as she squeezed my hand. "We gonna get married and have lots of babies," she giggled.

I shot her a look, wondering if the wedding was back on. Would she overlook the fact that she'd stated white weddings were all fake? Perhaps Courteney now decided she might consider stomaching a slice of fruitcake.

"Oh, right. Lovely!" the woman chuckled. "Congratulations!"

"Yeah, Damian's just moved into your old flat."

"You're this Kim woman?" I involuntarily exclaimed.

So, not only had I just acquired a half-sister, but she just happened to be the previous tenant in that shithole of a flat, rented to me by the father of the bastard who set me up. I presumed the quiet man with her must be the millionaire bloke who swept her off her feet. I refrained from asking Kim if she enjoyed Glastonbury in 2004, the location of the missing foot to my chest of drawers and if she could explain the basic plot of James Clavell's hefty Japanese historical fiction novel, which, after the first few chapters, due to lack of concentration, seemed to have eluded me.

"Yes, I'm Kim, and this is Vinny." There was a sharpness to her tongue. Whether she just didn't like the look of me or she suffered from trust issues, I couldn't fathom.

"Damian Statham," I held out my hand.

"Kim Meyer," she offered her hand to me before turning to Vinny. "You remember Courteney? My old neighbour. We had that chat about personal lubricants when we were outside my old flat," she chuckled.

"Sorry?" Vinny shot Kim a confused look.

"Yeah, a month or so back, just before Kimmy left and moved in wiv you. I remember, I was just off for a session with Donk and met you on the landin'.'"

"Err … yup," Vinny offered a slow single nod.

I thought he appeared a smidge embarrassed. The only saving grace to this conversation, it appeared Vinny wasn't one of my girl's ex-clients, irrespective of whatever the reference was regarding personal lubricants.

"Vincenzo Verratti," he somewhat shyly offered his hand.

"Oh, Vinny, have you got any cash on you? We need to pay Courteney, don't we?"

Perhaps I assumed too quickly. That said, although my girl previously worked a few different channels in the sex industry, namely, starring in porn films, live web shows, and a spot of street work, I was surprised that Kim and Vinny had employed her to perform in a ménage à trios type arrangement and now needed to settle up for services rendered.

"Sorry?" quizzed Vinny whilst reaching for his back pocket.

"I promised to pay Courteney back the sixty pounds she lent me."

"Oh, babe, don't worry about that. I'm just glad you didn't end up pimping yourself out. You're way too good for that."

I recall Courteney mentioned that Kim, when living in my flat, had considered prostitution as a route out of her tricky financial situation. However, the look on her boyfriend's face suggested he was blissfully unaware of her previous plans.

"Err ... ha, yes," she nervously laughed before shooting a look at a confused Vinny and quickly changing the subject. "Anyway, I'm so pleased to hear you're no longer with Karl."

"Yeah, dumped that twat at last. I don't do any of that stuff anymore, either. I ain't a prossy no more, and I ain't making no more films with Donk."

"Oh, good," she chuckled, again shooting a nervous glance at Vinny. "Why don't you try modelling? I've always thought you should be on the cover of Vogue."

"Yeah, could do. What d'you reckon, babe?"

I nodded at her, breaking the trance I seemed to have fallen into when studying the facial features of my half-sister. Did we share the same nose? Like mine, her cheeks dimpled when she smiled. I'd always wanted a sibling and momentarily considered blurting it out and hugging her. However, this wasn't the time or place, and I already had a full agenda for the day – another time, perhaps.

"Me and Damian are gonna get out of the Broxworth, so I might try modelling. I think I've got the figure for it."

"Course you have! Blimey, Courteney, you're stunning. I would have thought any modelling agency scout would bite their right arm off to sign you up. Damian, you're a lucky man. This girl is a head-turner, and probably the kindest person I know."

"Aw, fanks, babe."

Vinny handed my girl a few folded notes, which she squeezed into her back pocket. "Cheers Vin. So, next time you fancy watching a bit of porn and having a wank, it won't be me in the film jiggling my jugs at you no more."

"Sorry," stammered a somewhat shocked Vinny.

Kim grabbed his arm. "Jesus, Vinny, she's joking!"

"Oh, right. Sorry," he chuckled. "Sorry."

Kim rolled her eyes. "Sorry, is his favourite word."

"Blimey, you and Damian should hook up 'cos that's your favourite word, too, innit, babe?"

I nodded. "Look, we have to get going. Maybe we could meet up sometime? Go for a pint, perhaps? You have Kim's number?" I quizzed Courteney.

Not for one moment did I believe the four of us would meet for a drink. However, when I'd dealt with my current situation, I wanted to learn more about my newly acquired half-sister.

"Yeah, course, babe."

"That would be lovely. Call me when you're free."

People say that, don't they? 'It will be lovely to meet up', but in reality, they mean the complete opposite. However, I detected a hint of sincerity in Kim's voice, so maybe we would see each other again. I offered a tight smile and turned to leave, aware that we were now late for our rendezvous with Terry.

"Seeya, Kimmy." Courteney joined me as we headed towards the church. "Bleedin' hell, babe. If that's your old man's grave, Kimmy must be your sister."

"I know."

"Why didn't you say somefink, then?"

I halted and turned to face her. "I don't know. I guess it just felt like the wrong time. That was why I asked if you had her number so we can get in contact when I'm ready."

We watched Kim and Vinny as they made their way out of the churchyard. When a few yards from us, Kim halted and turned around. "Courteney, you didn't say why you were up here. Are you going to see the vicar about getting married, 'cos if you are, do I need to buy a hat?"

"No, she doesn't like fruitcake," I threw back.

Kim and Vinny glanced at each other and shrugged, clearly confused by my odd reply. Fair enough, it probably was. So rather than leave them wondering about fruitcake, I thought I'd offer up a sensible answer.

"No, we're here to meet the ghost of my dead father."

45

Mad Dogs And Englishmen

"Come on, babe, hurry up," Courteney called out from where she stood in front of the church door. "That fucking fruit loop, Terry, is actually 'ere."

As we'd weaved our way around the gravel path which circumnavigated the church, I'd hovered by my grandparent's graves – Terry Walton's parents. Whilst Courteney tramped her way towards the entrance, I assessed the two headstones and made a mental note that I needed to remove the rather pitiable bunch of dead flowers and brush off the grass clippings from where the groundsman had splattered green flecks across the headstones whilst wielding his strimmer.

I trotted up to join her, somewhat surprised that Terry had turned up. Of course, like my rather stupid thoughts whilst in bed this morning, what I'd said to Kim a few moments ago couldn't hold any validity.

For sure, this Terry bloke couldn't be my dead father who crawled out of his grave like some samurai-sword-wielding woman wearing a yellow jumpsuit, now risen from the dead to assist his son in times of need. However, despite that ridiculous notion, my newly acquired half-sister had just stated, albeit in a jocular manner, that she'd recently met Terry's ghost, whatever that meant.

I grabbed her hand and marched inside to find Terry positioned in the centre of the aisle as if there to greet us like the parish priest.

"Or-right, nutter?" Courteney asked him in her usual engaging style. "Damian's dead mother tagged along wiv you today, or did you come on your own?" Courteney grinned at Terry, who appeared a little perplexed. "You gonna start flinging gear around again, then?"

"Maybe." I thought Terry appeared a little solemn, as if almost disappointed to see us. "It depends on whether that Hallam bloke turns up with the information we need."

"He ain't shown his face then?" Courteney nudged my arm. "I ain't surprised. Babe, I said this would be a waste of time."

"No, not yet." Terry checked his watch. "I'm a bit concerned that he's not going to show up. Also, there's been some developments over the weekend."

"Like?" Courteney fired at him, thumping her free hand on her hip.

"Careful, darling. I'm not sure blurting out that Sidders has kicked the bucket is the right move at this point. Also, letting on about our little burglary escapade wouldn't be a good idea."

Terry offered a nod to his left. That odd tic he suffered from.

Still clinging to Terry's arm, Deana assessed Courteney, turning up her nose. "At least she ditched the hoodie. I suppose the damn trollop appears a little more presentable today. That said, those over-the-knee, stiletto-heeled hussy

456

boots aren't exactly what you'd call Sunday best. And as for that blouse, there's a little too much cleavage on display that could be considered acceptable for when visiting a church."

"You can talk," he muttered out the side of his mouth.

"Oi, who you whispering to, nutter?" Courteney leant her torso forward, enforcing the question and the need for Terry to start talking.

"See what I mean? That gap doesn't leave much to the imagination. Although, as I always said to Dickie, if you've got it, then why not flaunt it," she chuckled.

"Oi! I'm talking to you. What's the new development, then? You been muckin' about wiv your Ouija board and called up a few of your other spooky mates, have ya?"

"Look, I know this is a little fanciful, but I am in contact with the dead, so to speak."

"What, you chatting with all your mates out there?" Courteney gestured with her hand towards the graveyard. "What is this, spooks reunited?"

Deana squeezed his arm. "Darling, think very carefully before you answer."

As this odd bloke seemed to perform every few seconds, he glanced to his left and nodded.

"Nutter," hissed Courteney, rolling her eyes.

Whilst my girl and Terry batted back to each other about the dead, I became distracted by a rather odious stench. I twitched my nose – I could smell lilies – a reminder of my childhood and one, in a very long line, of my so-called stepmothers. Although I can't remember her name, Sarah or Sally, she insisted on filling the house with those damn flowers that emitted an overpowering, pungent stench.

They say that smell is the most powerful of the senses for evoking childhood memories. I recall this particular one being associated with the woman who, when I was just a wee nipper, suggested I might like to take my toy cars and bugger off to go and play on the M1. Of course, at the age of seven or eight, I thought she was suggesting I could play with my dinky cars with the real ones. However, I later learnt that the woman was suggesting it would be better for her if I'd just got flattened by a truck as it punched along the motorway at sixty miles per hour.

I guess, like the vast majority of the women Sidney brought home, she considered me an unwanted distraction. Whatever her name was, she harboured the maternal skills of my biological mother and therefore wanted nothing to do with a snotty-nosed boy who pined for his stepfather's attention.

After chucking out a volley of sneezes, I waved a finger at Terry. "Who the hell are you?"

Whilst he and Courteney chewed the cud and in between trying to remember the name of that particular stepmother who had a penchant for funeral flowers and praying for my untimely death under the wheels of an articulated lorry, I studied his face again as I had that day on the Broxworth Estate. I deduced he, Kim, and I displayed many similar features.

"Look, as I said a couple of days ago, I'm here to assist you with your little issue. Your mother, God rest her soul, asked me to intervene, so to speak."

Courteney snorted. "Told you, babe. He's a friggin' fruit loop."

Ignoring my girl's presumably accurate assessment, I pushed him on this claim. "So, you expect me to believe that

458

my dead, philandering mother is dishing out instructions from beyond the grave, and you, like some charlatan TV psychic, think you have the inside track?"

"Tricky one, darling, but think you'll just have to trot out the good old 'it's complicated' line. I must say, I'm not overly enamoured with his philandering comment, either."

"Bleedin' hell! What you, some Madame Arcati character, summoning up this Deana woman like Elvira?"

Terry and I both shot Courteney a quizzical look.

"Noel Coward's Blithe Spirit, babe."

"Ooo, very cultured. Who would have thought this trollop would utter the words, Noel Coward! My God, talk about poles apart ... the porn star and the playwright," she chortled. "It's just the sort of idea that would've tickled the man pink!"

"Sorry, is that a song?" Although why I was asking and what relevance this had to our conversation, lord knows.

"Oh, clearly our Damian isn't particularly well-versed in the history of West End shows, unlike his blonde, play-bunny girlfriend."

"Jesus, babe. No, it's a play. A sort of comic farce about a dead woman spook, summoned up by a psychic, who runs around causing havoc."

"Whatever," I muttered, as both Terry and I shrugged our shoulders. Although still surprised by my girl's encyclopaedic knowledge, I refocused on Terry. "Look, I'm sorry, but you claiming to have little chats with my mother really ain't going to cut it with me. However, I need to see that Hallam bloke again. By the looks of it, though, it appears he wasn't too worried about your threat of unleashing the wrath of the dead upon him. Otherwise, he'd have shown." I tugged my thespian-loving girl's hand as I turned to leave Terry, whoever he was, alone with his delusions.

Shaking off Deana's arm, Terry jumped forward. "Damian, hang on, please."

Courteney stepped back and pointed, somewhat aggressively, waving a digit in Terry's direction, which caused him to jolt his head back. "Shut it, nutter. My man's had a friggin' tough week, and you ain't helping much. We don't believe all your shite, despite your ability to make fings fly."

"Before he buggers off with that hussy tottering along in those over-the-knee boots, can you remind our boy that only Sidney and I could possibly know his birth certificate states his surname is Walton?"

Terry slowly swivelled his head to glance back at Deana. "What? What the hell do you mean Damian is really called Walton?" he hissed.

I halted at the door.

"Babe, come on."

"Hang on." As Courteney stepped back half a pace, together we watched as Terry pointed back down the aisle, appearing to have a conversation with thin air.

Deana shrugged. "He took your name. Of course, Sidders changed it to Statham as soon as I was off the scene."

"How come you never told me?"

"Darling, you were dead, remember?"

"Yes, alright, I might have died, but that's no excuse for not telling me our boy took my name, is it?"

"*Terry, you were dead! I could have trotted up to your grave and let you know, I suppose, but until a few weeks ago, I didn't believe in ghosts!*"

"Well, we are ghosts now, and although you're conveniently bloody invisible, you could have divulged this bit of information in the last few weeks whilst we've been haunting our way around Fairfield trying to save Kim and Damian from the evil gits who seem hell-bent on ruining my kid's lives."

"*I know, darling. But why are you getting so het up about it?*"

"My son should have my name … it's a male pride thing if you like. Although, after dying thirty-odd years ago, I guess that may be too much to ask. But, look, now I'm a fully paid-up member of the walking dead and back in the land of the living, so to speak, I thought you'd have told me this little titbit of information about our son."

"*Alright, darling. I'm sorry. However, after I left Sidders, he changed the boy's name. That's all there is to it. I suggest you run after him and use that titbit, as you call it, and get him and that woman in those hussy-boots back here before this operation goes belly up!*"

"Anyway, you're a fine one to talk. His girl might be wearing those hussy boots, as you call them, but I seem to recall you own all sorts of black leather attire, most of which could rival any dominatrix, whip-wielding madam's wardrobe from any seedy Soho club."

"*Yes, alright. I'm just a teeny-weeny bit jealous that the girl can look that good in them. You said you thought she was rather ravishing and, whilst you're not prepared to satisfy my desires, I felt a little put-out, that's all.*"

"Jealous? You're jealous of Damian's girlfriend," Terry smirked.

"Yes, a little. Although I am still rather ravishing, she reminds me of myself thirty-odd years ago. Well, not the potty mouth and sounding like a gutter slut dragged up out of some council estate whilst performing all sorts of lewd acts in some hideous den of iniquity, but rather her youthful beauty is what I mean."

"Well, blow me down. Deana actually admits someone else might be more desirable than herself."

"Terry, you'd do well to remember that I am here and offering myself on a plate to you. Although you have a body of a thirty-two-year-old man, you are actually in your mid-sixties. I am, by far in a way, the best damn offer you are going to get!"

Still smirking, Terry nodded. "If you say so."

"I do so. Now, go and get our boy back before we get hauled over the coals for cocking up this mission."

"Alright, I'll see if I can persuade Damian to come back."

"No need. We're still here."

Terry swivelled around to face Courteney and me as we stepped back into the church.

Deana peered around Terry. "Oh, dear, this could be awkward. Do you think they overheard what you were saying?"

Uncharacteristically, Terry's antics had struck my girl dumb. I, on the other hand, was awash with a plethora of questions.

"How could you know about my original birth certificate?"

462

Terry bowed his head and glanced back down the aisle before holding his hands up as if to impart it was obvious.

"Well?"

He waved his palm, indicating the empty aisle. "Your mother just told me."

"Oh, brilliant! It's all very well claiming I speak to you from beyond the grave, but really, darling, saying I'm actually standing right here is bloody ridiculous!"

46

Jack Oswald White

"Bloody hell, you dickhead. That's ridiculous. My mother is dead!" I belligerently spat at Terry whilst advancing down the aisle, hand in hand with Courteney. Although I'd aggressively bitten back at the man, the thought of my mother's ghost standing in front of me caused a cold shudder and the hairs on the back of my neck to rise.

"See, Damian agrees with me ... ridiculous!"

Terry backed up a few paces, presumably clocking that I didn't appear too chuffed. "She is, but as I've been saying—"

"No." I interrupted, advancing another couple of paces, Courteney keeping in step with me whilst her stiletto heels echoed with a foreboding clang reverberating off the stone walls. "We came here today to see what that Hallam bloke had to say, not listen to your drivel about you claiming to be conversing with my dead mother. And what was all that shit about being my real father?"

"Okay. I know this is a bit of a stretch to believe, but I am Terry Walton, your father—"

"Oh, for God's sake. The man is dead! I just visited his bloody grave out there!" I shot my free hand behind me, waving it in the general direction of where, only a moment ago, we chatted with Kim and Vinny.

That bell clanger, high above in the bell tower, seemed to have floated down and walloped my skull as the words spoken by Kim reverberated around my head.

'Vinny and I thought it's about time we tended my father's grave. I never knew him, but a few weeks ago, I think I met his ghost.'

"Babe?" Courteney shook my hand to bring me back to the present.

"Darling, I know they overheard us, but I'm not sure that was the best move. Stating you have connections with the dead is one thing; informing our boy that you're his real father is another ball game altogether. This is turning into a right old mess!"

"Do you know a Kim Meyer?"

Terry nodded. "My daughter … your half-sister."

"Oh, Terry. For heaven's sake. You've got verbal diarrhoea. We might as well put an announcement on Twitter that we are back from the dead and haunting Fairfield. I must say, you have totally screwed this up!" Deana dismissively shook her head and spun around to face the altar.

"I'm not a twit! This is a somewhat tricky situation here," Terry mumbled out of the side of his mouth.

"Frigging well are, you nutter. Babe, come on, let's go."

"I said Twitter, not twit … and before you ask … don't. This is a complete debacle. God knows how we got ourselves in such a pickle."

"Babe, come on, let's get out of here," softly spoken, Courteney presumably could sense employing her usual tactic of offering this idiot a mouthful was utterly pointless. The man clearly suffered from delusions, and no amount of challenging his story would turn this into anything near to a sensible conversation.

Whilst I contemplated my girl's logical suggestion, Terry spun around on his heels, waving his index finger down the aisle.

"Yes, well, it's alright for you. I'm visible and have to do the damn talking. You … you just stand there trotting out criticism. Any idiot can do that."

"Don't call me an idiot. I'm not the one telling all and sundry that you're dead and now claiming to walk around like the resurrection, am I?"

"Well, our boy overheard us, didn't he? So, what the hell am I supposed to say?"

Deana spun around and pointed past him. "Terry, you're making it worse! Look at their faces. Whilst you're berating me, our son and hussy-boots are probably considering calling the men in white coats. You're about to spend the rest of your eternal life in a padded cell!"

Now sporting an over-exaggerated grin, Terry slowly turned to face us. Whether he was trying to impersonate Jack Nicholson's The Joker character or his delusions were about to take a more menacing stance, who could tell. Notwithstanding my unanswered questions and desire to know how this odd bloke could know what he knew about my past, I thought Courteney was right, we should get the hell out of here.

"Damian … it's not what it looks like. Honestly, I just wanted to help you find the evil git who set you up."

"Well, I now know who that bastard is. I discovered yesterday who paid that bloody PI. We stupidly rocked up here, hoping Hallam might have the inside track on how to find the git."

"I'm right here, mate. No need to go searching."

Still holding hands, Courteney and I swivelled around, releasing and recoupling our hands as we turned around to face the person who, in an ever so familiar voice, had uttered those words.

"Lee! You bastard."

Lee Parish leant against the heavy, wooden arched door. "You owe me, Statham, and I'm here to collect."

"Owe you! Your frigging joking, mate! You owe me about a million quid."

"Nah, you gifted your business to Bridget. We don't owe you jack-shit. Now, regarding what you owe me," smirking and clearly enjoying himself, he placed the palm of his right hand on his chest. "So, according to that little shit, Hallam, you flushed what you owe me down the bog. So, Statham, you prick, you better reimburse me for my out-of-pocket expenses." He hefted his shoulder from the door, folding his arms in the process. "Or face the consequences, mate."

"Mate, who the hell are you calling, mate?"

Courteney shook free from my grip, taking a step forward, although, thankfully, not advancing any further. "Couple of calls to the right people, and you'll find yourself with a bullet lodged in your fat head."

"You're out of your league, girl. You forgotten about my connections in the police? I can get you both fitted up for any crime whenever it takes my fancy."

"That bastard pig with the gold tooth," she muttered.

"I hear he speaks very highly of you, too," he chuckled. Although, like any self-respecting Bond villain, his demeanour changed at the flick of a metaphorical switch – it appeared Lee had flicked his. "So, here's the dilemma we have to sort out. That stash of coke you saw fit to flush down the u-bend came from the evidence locker up at Fairfield nick."

"Well, you shouldn't have hidden it in my bloody fridge," I blurted, although regretted the statement when Lee whipped out a flick knife, pinged open the blade and thrust it into the top of the end post of the first row of pews – the thud of the penetrating blade reverberated around us.

Whilst rubbing the pad of his index finger across the hilt of the five-inch blade, he nodded and frowned. "Fair point, Statham, fair point. But you see, Bridget's got this fixation about you. Now, not in like she wants you," he chuckled. "Of course, no one other than some tart could actually want you. No, Bridget's fixated on ruining you. I take it you know your dead father's evidence sent her father to prison?"

"Oh hell, not the best way for Damian to discover that poor old Sidders is dead. Darling, are we a bit out of the loop here? Who the hell is this awful man?"

"Wha … what do you mean, my father's dead?" I stammered.

"Oh, you didn't know," he chuckled. "Yes, your old man drowned a few months back. Hallam discovered that. You see,

Sidney was the original target. But when he buggered off, you played right into our hands."

"I don't believe you."

"Sorry, Damian, he's telling the truth. Sidney died back in March. A boating accident, apparently."

I shot a look at Terry, then Courteney, who appeared ready to rip Lee a good'un.

"Oi, wanker. I suggest you piss off, or I'll—"

"Or what, you tart?" Lee yanked out his knife from its resting place and stabbed the air in front of Courteney's face.

My girl held her ground, a pace in front of me.

My mind whirred. Not only had I just met my half-sister, Terry reckoned he was my real father back from the dead, and my father, as in Sidney, apparently had lost his life some months back.

"What's the matter, Statham?" Lee raised his eyebrow, clearly enjoying being the one to advise me about Sidney's demise.

"Oi, you git—"

"Shut it—" Lee spat at Courteney before waving his knife in my direction. "Bridget reckoned you were a bloody wimp. So, you hiding behind this tart, now, are you? I seem to remember last week you saying something about this slag being some low-life prossy … changed your tune, have you, Statham?"

"You bastard—"

"Babe," Courteney grabbed my sleeve, halting my advance as the red mist descended whilst attempting to barrel past her.

Lee chuckled, slowly shaking his head. "Jesus, you're like a little lapdog. And this tart now calls you babe! Fuck me, Statham, that's a bit of a comedown after knobbing Bridget." Lee took a pace towards the three of us. "That said, as we discussed last week, Bridget reckons you've only got a little wiener." He wagged his little finger. "So, what d'you reckon, Courteney, that's your name, innit? You want a real man in your bed, 'cos this tit ain't gonna satisfy you."

"Piss off!"

Ignoring her response, Lee nodded his forehead in Terry's direction. "So, who are you?"

"Darling, I think we need to take control of this situation. I'm not sure what exactly, but I'm up for introducing one of my Wicked Witch of the West performances."

Terry glanced back down the aisle and nodded before turning to address Lee. "I'm your worst nightmare, mate."

"Ooo. Look at you, all macho," he chuckled. "Who's this, Statham, your brother? You look just as pathetic as him," Lee nodded in my direction.

Terry stepped around us both. "No, I'm not his brother. Although Damian and I are related."

"Darling, keep him talking. I'm going to have a quick scout around and see if I can't find something to spook him with. Blackmail is off the agenda, so we'll have to scare the despicable git with ghostly acts."

Again, Terry glanced back and nodded down the aisle. "Wave that cross at him. He might think some divine power is present," he hissed.

"Oh, yes, darling. Well spotted. Now give me a moment, and then I'll anoint this disagreeable git with the cross," Deana boomed as she skipped towards the chancel.

Courteney and I exchanged a glance. Whether this Terry bloke was talking to himself, an imaginary friend, the ghost of my dead mother, or just suffered from severe delusions, who knew? But as he appeared to want to take the lead in this conversation, I thought I'd watch and see how it played out. Courteney seemed to harbour the same idea as we both stepped back a pace. Despite my girl's somewhat dubious connections with people I had no desire ever to make their acquaintance, her experience gained by living on the Broxworth Estate had taught her to recognise danger and pure evil when it presented itself.

Now his facade had dropped, it didn't take a genius to see the type of man we were dealing with. Lee Parish, where evil was concerned, was Champions League status – the Real Madrid of the Devil's disciples.

Although Terry, clearly unwell and perhaps schizophrenic, positioned himself in the firing line, that was his choice – his funeral, I guess. I pondered the thought as I glanced around, searching for exits, that perhaps with his misplaced bravado, he might afford us an opportunity to escape. If we found another door that negated the need to get past Lee, that would leave Terry alone with the nefarious bastard. However, as he seemed happy to take one for the team, so to speak, I thought it best to leave him to it.

Only a few minutes ago, I'd wanted to find Lee, then confront him and get back what was rightly mine – well, maybe not rightfully, because Lee and Bridget had the law on their side – but get back what I'd lost when I performed my well-versed gullible idiot performance. However, now I'd realised that was nothing but a pie-in-the-sky notion.

Our limited options now boiled down to either Courteney employing a mate who liked to wave a shooter around, meaning we dabble in a spot of contract killing, or we just go on the run. Despite not wanting to hide out in some remote location for the rest of my days, I felt the latter was the better option. For sure, faced with Lee waving around a five-inch blade, discretion was the better part of valour in these circumstances.

"Darling, cover me. I've got an idea."

Now sporting a furrowed brow, Lee appeared, as we were, somewhat bemused by Terry's odd muttering, "Look, you weirdo, I don't give a shit who you are. Now, unless you're gonna stump up the cash for my lost gear, I suggest you do one, pal," Lee forced his tongue into his lower lip and raised his eyebrows at Terry as he stepped forward.

"Excuse me! This is a house of God. A place of worship, not some back street pub where you can holler obscenities at each other," boomed an authoritative voice from the righthand side of the nave.

We all glanced around to see an elderly gent approach after he'd closed a side door. I'm no expert, but I guess the dog collar suggested this was the parish priest. For sure, if Courteney and I were to get hitched, I guess this wasn't the best way to introduce ourselves, and I thought the ruddy-faced cleric might be reluctant to have our banns read in his church.

Lee retracted the blade and backed away from Terry before pointing at me. "I'll be in touch. You try to wriggle out of your debt, and you know what will happen." Lee backed further up the nave before turning and hot-footing towards the main door as the priest purposely shimmied through the pews.

"I suggest you all take your leave. Otherwise, I shall be calling the police."

Terry held his hand aloft. "Father, please forgive us. We'll leave straight away," he turned and nodded at us both, looking for confirmation that we would comply.

However, Courteney and I were transfixed by the sight of a silver candlestick as it appeared to swing in an arc through the air before colliding with Lee's head as he stepped out of the main entrance. The sickening sound of his cracking skull reverberated back through the church.

Although not a religious man, probably describing myself as agnostic, I considered that some divine intervention had taken place. Large silver candlesticks don't generally swing through the air of their own volition, and Terry hadn't employed his telekinetic powers to command it to do so.

Terry took the lead, followed by the priest, with Courteney and me bringing up the rear as we hot-footed to the prone body of Lee Parish, who now lay half in, half out of the church entrance. The bloodied candlestick lay by his side.

"My good God." The priest bent down and felt Lee's wrist – I held my breath.

"Bleedin' hell, has he carked it?"

The flustered priest glanced up. "Someone, call the police. This man is dead."

If this wasn't God's doing, we had a Cluedo situation. Someone killed Lee with a candlestick in the narthex, and it wasn't the four of us who peered down at his body.

"Deana, where are you?" mumbled Terry.

I glanced at Terry whilst trying to rid the stupid thought that my dead mother's ghost had just murdered Lee Parish.

47

Our Lady Of Paris

Terry scooted up the lane, trying to squeeze in as much distance from himself and the murder scene as possible. Damian and Courteney bolted seconds after the priest announced Lee had passed from this world. Although Terry wasn't in the loop with how these things worked, he was relieved that Lee's ghost hadn't instantly appeared. So, with a drop of good fortune, he rather hoped the Grim Reaper had quickly bundled the nefarious waster down to the burning fires of hell.

At that point, Terry had the presence of mind and good sense to make haste and exit the scene. Not keen on hanging around or relishing the thought of having to explain to the police who he was, avoid mentioning he was dead, and inform them that the killer was an invisible petite fifty-something female ghost with an overactive libido – current location unknown – Terry's quick decision had afforded him ample time to escape.

As he exited the churchyard, the wail of sirens filled the air. Although the Broxworth Estate offered up its fair share of suspicious deaths, Terry surmised the report of a murder at the entrance of a church in a leafy suburb of Fairfield would more than pique the interest of the whole of Hertfordshire Constabulary. Going by the repeated holler of those ever-nearing sirens, it indeed appeared they were attending in some force.

Even from this distance, Terry could hear the cacophony of squealing brakes and banging car doors. Now panting, caused by his exertions, he swivelled around to glance back, hoping not to face a troop of the blue helmet brigade giving chase whilst wielding their truncheons.

To his relief, no officers of the law appeared. However, a somewhat dishevelled Deana huffed and wheezed as she exited the churchyard.

"Bloody hell, don't mind me, will you? You just run off and leave me, why don't you?" Deana belligerently mumbled, as she attempted to hobble up the lane, appearing rather bedraggled. The knees of her baby-pink jeans sporting grass stains, her hair covered in vegetation and sticking out at all angles, offering a look that suggested the poor woman had been dragged through a hedge backwards.

"Oh, there you are."

"Yes! Christ, give me a bloody hand. I think I've sprained my ankle."

Terry trotted back, relieved the police weren't giving chase. However, he suspected the priest would soon point in his direction, indicating where he and Deana had fled. "Where the hell have you been?" Terry crouched in front of her, bent his knees and held his arms back as if preparing to perform a standing jump.

"I hope you're not preparing to break wind!"

Terry peered around whilst still holding his crouched position. "Sorry?"

"You, crouching down like you're about to blow off."

"No, don't be ridiculous! Come on. I'll give you a piggyback."

"Darling, I'm not a five-year-old!"

"Oh, hurry up. Just jump on me unless you want half the flying squad chasing after us."

"Oh, well, that's a first," she muttered as she wrapped her arms around his neck and jumped on his back, Terry catching the back of her knees before hauling her up.

"What's a first?" Terry panted, adjusting his hold to take her weight.

"You, asking me to jump on you. I hope it's the first of many similar requests to come."

Terry groaned. Deana couldn't fathom whether that was a reaction regarding her suggestion or his physical exertions of taking her weight. That said, at a little over eight stone, she really couldn't see how that would trouble him.

"Although, darling, next time you ask me to jump on you, perhaps we could undress first."

"You never stop, do you?" he muttered as he took his first tentative step forward. Then, head down, he powered up the lane.

"Uh-oh. Here come the nosey neighbours."

As they neared the top of the lane, a gaggle of onlookers stood gawping. Above the tree line and from that vantage point, the church came into clear view. Terry nudged through the small crowd, who offered him a wary look. With the invisible Deana clinging to his back, he guessed he probably gave the appearance of some weirdo impersonating the Hunchback of Notre Dame. Fortunately, the scene below appeared far more captivating than Terry's rather odd gait. So, after offering a perfunctory glance in his direction, the rubberneckers all focused back on the unfolding events at the church.

"Come on. Giddy-up, horsey, we're nearly home," Deana giggled.

"Hilarious," he muttered, stepping into Deana's driveway after checking he'd not been spotted. Deana's house was supposed to be unoccupied as the process of probate took its course. So, a man, spotted by a neighbour, impersonating Quasimodo entering her front drive would add more complications to an already tricky situation.

"Right, I'll set you down here. Can you take any weight on that ankle?"

"Yes, darling. Thank you, sweetie. That was very gallant of you." Deana flopped dramatically onto the rattan sofa situated on the rear patio. "Bag of frozen peas for my ankle and an offensively large G&T to dull the pain, please, darling."

"Keys?"

"Handbag."

"And where's that?"

Deana's eyes sprung open. "Oh, God, I've left my bag in that ruddy churchyard."

"Oh, great! I'll guess I'll have to break in then."

"What about my bag? It's a Hermès Birkin! It's my favourite."

478

"What do you want me to do about it?"

"Oh, darling, be a love and nip back and get it, please. Dickie brought me that bag. It holds sentimental value, as well as costing over twenty grand."

"Well, as we have the whole of the local constabulary crawling all over that church and graveyard, I doubt very much if it would be wise to saunter back down there saying I'm just looking for a handbag my ghost friend dropped earlier when bashing some chap over the head with a candlestick."

"I didn't."

"You didn't what?"

"Bash that despicable man with a candlestick."

"Err … hello! That bloke is laid out down there with a crushed skull, probably with some scene of crimes officer marking out his position with white chalk."

"Oh, Terry, this isn't Perry Mason investigates!" she chortled. "Police don't use chalk anymore. Next, you'll be suggesting they're tiptoeing through the graveyard with magnifying glasses."

"You know what I mean."

"Anyway, darling. As I was saying, I snuck through that side door when that grubby little vicar entered and stuck his nose in. I planned to whizz around the outside of the church and sneak up on that awful man from behind—"

"You're invisible, woman. You could have just waltzed up to him and waved that cross in front of his eyes whilst making ghostly moaning noises."

"Hmmm, yes, good point. I didn't think of that. Anyway, as I bolted along whilst carting that damn great lump of wood—"

"The sacred cross of our Lord Jesus Christ."

"Yes, that's it. You've become very pious, haven't you? Perhaps that explains this vow of celibacy thingy you seem to have committed to."

Terry tutted.

"So, I tripped and fell on the grass, ruining these jeans and spraining my ankle in the process. You know, I'll have to soak these because grass stains are a bugger to get out. After Dickie ruined a couple of pairs of expensive chinos, I always insisted he wore shorts when we made hay in the fields."

"Sorry, what on earth are you drivelling on about?"

"Doggy style in the park, darling. Grass stains on knees. Devil to remove."

"My good God."

"Nothing better than a spot of alfresco nookie, darling. You haven't lived until you've done it in public."

"Look, getting back to what's happened. I take it your little tumble happened after you crushed his skull?"

"No, darling. You're not listening. I didn't crush anyone's skull. I was hobbling through the graveyard when I saw you making a bolt for it and, although injured, I hobbled after you."

"I don't get it."

"What don't you get, darling?"

"If you didn't hit that bloke ... who the hell did?"

"Oh ... I see. I presumed you'd walloped him one. No?"

"No!"

"Oh. How odd. Darling, if it wasn't you or me, and presumably not Damian, Hussy-boots or the Vicar, who the hell else could have hit him?"

"What about Hallam? He's got a motive and could have shown up as that bloke was leaving."

"What about the candlestick?"

"What about it?"

"Well, if that little pervert used a candlestick from the altar—"

"Oh, I see what you mean."

"Darling, you don't think whoever murdered that man will come after us, do you?" Deana gave a little shudder.

"We're already dead, so I don't think we need to worry too much if there's a candlestick serial killer on the loose."

"Oh, yes, of course, good point."

Terry flopped down on the rattan sofa beside her. "Deana, we've cocked this one up. Besides the fact that the man who set Damian up is now lying dead, we haven't achieved much. We were supposed to use blackmail or scare him, not be a party to murder."

"No, you're right. I'm not sure the powers that be are going to be too chuffed with our performance. Murder is most certainly not in the brief."

"I imagine it's not. Although he was a nasty piece of work, I'm not sure that his demise has helped us much. Bridget still has Damian's fortune, and we're no closer to finding her."

"Yes, it's a complete disaster, darling. If we're ever going to move on from our state of undead existence, we have to succeed in this mission and the next."

Terry shot her a look. "What? What do you mean, the next?"

"Mission three, darling. Everything comes in threes … omne trium perfectum."

"Is that some spell?"

"Latin … the rule of three. All good things come in threes."

"Oh, no, I don't have a third child, surely not."

"Not that I'm aware of, no. However, my darling, you never know with your record."

"You can talk!"

"Yes, well, whatever."

"So, what's our third mission, then?"

"I'll find out when I report in to confirm that we've successfully completed this one."

"Well, as I was saying, we're not doing too well on that front, are we?"

"No, darling. What do you propose we do next? Because I'm fresh out of ideas."

"Why is it my job to come up with the answers?"

"Because, darling, my job is to act as your guide and look pretty, both of which I demonstrate a high level of competence."

"Do you, now."

"I do so. And, you lucky boy, you get to spend more time with me."

"Oh, great."

"Don't be sarcastic. That's the lowest form of wit. Also, we need to work on this celibacy thing."

Terry nervously glanced at her.

"Yes, okay, maybe that's for another day. My poor ankle might have put me out of action for a few days."

"What a relief," muttered Terry.

Deana tutted. "So, come on then, you'd better get those little grey cells working. What's the plan to sort out this rotten mess we seem to have created."

"Well, first job … I need a stiff drink."

"Shush!" Deana grabbed Terry's arm as she leaned forward. "Did you hear that?" she whispered.

"What?"

"The gate latch, I heard it clunk!"

Terry and Deana froze when again hearing the latch click, now holding their breath in anticipation of who would appear from around the corner.

"Good idea, Walton. Make mine a large one," boomed a voice emanating from somewhere near the back gate.

"Oh, my God," Deana whispered, now gawping bug-eyed at the man who appeared.

"Ah, there you are. Well, Terry, nice to meet you at last. I think you might need my help. Anyway, after today's adventure, I'd better have a large whisky first."

48

White House Ghost

Our somewhat serene swagger out of the hotel foyer when off to attend our meeting with Terry could not have been more different to our panicked flit back after returning from fleeing the events at the church.

I have no idea how, but I guess it must be due to years of practice, or it's just a skill women are born with, but Courteney still managed to put quite a lick on in those boots as we sprinted away from the scene. Occasionally, we'd have to dive into a hedge or behind a parked car to avoid the steady flow of police vehicles, sirens wailing, and tyres screeching, which pelted in the opposite direction from us.

Once we'd put a reasonable distance between the church and us, we attempted to walk calmly, thus avoiding courting any undue attention upon ourselves. However, that vicar would by now have given a complete description of all three of us, so there was still a certain amount of urgency to return to our hotel before some random police officer matched us to the circulated description of the couple fleeing the scene.

Keeping our focus solely on achieving a successful escape, we refrained from discussing the events of flying candlesticks until we were safely back in the honeymoon suite. I leaned my back against the closed door and scrubbed my hands over my face.

Courteney caught my wrists and lowered my hands. "Babe, you okay?"

"Hell knows."

"Your dad."

I huffed and nodded. "I can't believe he's dead. Well, assuming Lee and Terry were telling the truth."

"I'm so sorry, babe."

"Look, it's a shock, but we weren't that close. I can't believe the woman he ran off with hasn't tried to get in contact."

"You got her number? You should call her and see what she's got to say for herself."

"No. I only met her twice."

"What about any relatives? They might know."

"Nah, Dad only had some dotty old aunt who lives near Brighton. She's probably already dead." I plucked my mobile from my pocket, searched the contacts, and tapped the number before placing it to my ear. A few seconds passed before receiving the automated message stating the number was no longer in use. "Bollocks," I mumbled.

"Who you ringing?"

"Dad's mobile. It's no longer in use."

"Oh." Courteney tugged off her boots, hopping on the spot as she grabbed each stiletto heel before flinging them on the sofa.

"You think the police will find us?"

"Nah," Courteney shook her head as she padded back to where I continued to bar the door. "That vicar only saw us for a few seconds. We could have been anyone."

"I hope you're right. Although I am right in saying that whoever hit Lee was invisible, yes?"

Courteney chewed her bottom lip and nodded. "Bleedin' nuts, innit?"

"My mother?" I raised an eyebrow.

"Jesus, babe, are you suggesting that your dead mother's ghost walloped Lee with a ruddy candlestick?"

"I know … I know." I huffed out a sigh, which I blew to the ceiling.

"So, let's just suppose that your dead mother killed Lee, and Terry is your real dad who's come back to life—"

"Courteney!"

"Hang on. Terry can make fings fly, agreed."

"Well, yes, he performed some neat tricks in my office on Saturday."

"And he knows your mother bought you an Action Man for your fourteenth birthday and that your birth certificate states your name was Walton."

I shrugged my shoulders, wondering where she was going with this. "Go on."

"So, by my reckoning, that confirms that either Terry is some cool magician, a psychic with abilities to chat to the dead, or your dead dad has come back to life. All of which are a bit friggin' nuts."

486

"I'll plump for the magician explanation."

"Cool, but how does he know those other fings, then?"

"Alright, magician and a psychic."

"What about what Kimmy said … she met her father's ghost?"

I snorted and shook my head.

"Babe, many sensible people believe in ghosts. Winston Churchill reckoned he spoke to Abraham Lincoln, Arthur Conan Doyle used mediums, and even that brilliant geezer Alan Turing reckoned telepathy exists."

"Christ, you memorised Wikipedia," I chuckled.

"Babe, I read a lot, remember?"

"And not just about the Famous Five guzzling down lashings of ginger beer at the lighthouse," I offered a little smirk, although Courteney ignored it.

"The difference with all these beliefs about ghosts and the paranormal, to what we witnessed, is we both saw the same fing."

"You've lost me."

"People claim to have seen ghosts, yeah?"

I nodded.

"But no one believes these nutters."

"You saying Churchill was a nutter?"

"No, babe. What I'm saying is Churchill reckoned he spotted the ghost of the sixteenth President of the United States standing in his bedchamber. However, research suggests that the mind can play tricks in times of high stress, and it's suggested Churchill had sunk a few too many glasses of brandy after a long soak in a hot bath."

"Is this leading somewhere, or are you auditioning to become a history teacher?"

"Babe!"

"Granny's custard?"

"Spot on."

"You're going to have to explain."

"If these claims of seeing ghosts can be explained away by the theory that the individual who claimed to have seen these apparitions is caused by *their* mind playing tricks, then how come we both witnessed an identical phenomenon? If we both have seen the same fing … it suggests your mother and father are back from the dead." With her theory on the supernatural delivered, she swished her hair over her shoulder, raised her eyebrows, and gazed up at me.

"God, you're sexy."

"I know," she smirked. "Cleva too."

"Christ, Courteney, you've been watching too much of The X-files. So, what, we're now Mulder and Scully investigating government conspiracies about paranormal activity? You're suggesting we're living in the bloody Twilight Zone."

"Babe, that candlestick appeared from nowhere, hovered in the air, and then thumped down on Lee's head. Either you and I both are suffering from delusions, or your dead mother larruped him one."

"Okay, so my dead parents are back from the grave to help me out," I chuckled.

"Maybe."

"Well, I never knew my father, but it seems he's as useless as my mother was because nothing has changed apart from killing Lee. Bridget still conned me out of my fortune, and we have no way of finding the bloody woman."

"We need to forget Bridget."

"You're probably right. I realised when Lee turned up today that I'm out of my depth. Bridget is far too clever for me. Even with Lee out of the picture, I can't see how I could persuade her to hand back my business to me."

"No, I mean, we need to stop looking for Bridget and focus on finding your mother. If anyone is going to be able to convince Bridget to hand back your business, it's your dead parents."

49

A week later

Killing Me Softly

Sidney stretched out on the large king-sized bed and patiently waited. He adjusted the pillow and crossed his ankles before gazing out the window, taking in the view of the Parisian skyline. To his left, Sidney could just make out the central dome of the Basilica of Sacré Coeur positioned high up on the butte of Montmartre. To his right, if he leant forward, he knew he would be able to spot the Eiffel Tower. He didn't bother because he'd just positioned the pillow in the correct position, so forgoing the view of Gustave's wrought-iron lattice masterpiece.

To complement the exceptional views, the hotel suite benefited from a separate lounge area, sporting a collection of reproduction furniture that befitted the suite's opulent décor. Also, Sidney was rather taken by the Louis XIV styled chaise lounge, the centrepiece of the seventh-storey suite in one of Paris's high-end hotels – Bridget had chosen well.

He'd snuck in when the chambermaid entered to perform her duties and patiently waited whilst she changed the bed sheets and busied herself with various bottles of cleaning liquids in the bathroom. Whilst she performed her duties, singing *'Killing Me Softly'*, how apt, thought Sidney, he checked out the drop from the balcony. The pavement below confirmed there would be nothing *'Softly'* about the landing. With his preparations complete, he made himself comfy on top of the quilt and waited for Dennis Hunt's daughter to return.

Before coming to when lying on that damp mat of pine needles on the shore of Lake Ozark, whilst some pot-bellied sheriff assessed his dead body, Sidney had never contemplated murder. Of course, like anyone, he had his fair share of adversaries. However, like most people, contemplating killing those who'd crossed him was not something he would have previously considered. That was then, but now he was dead there were a few he felt needed to be punished.

First up there was Cindy. She'd suggested joining him on that fishing trip out on the lake – nice and romantic, she'd said. So, after slipping a few sleeping pills in his drink to dull his responses, she'd tipped him out of the boat, knowing full well that a gut full of drugs, coupled with a lack of competence where swimming was concerned, would result in his drowning.

He adjusted his pillow, shaking his head at the gall of the woman. She'd tricked him into marriage, ensured his will and life insurance were in order, murdered him, and then claimed to anyone who would listen how devastated she was. Sidney nodded to himself, accepting the saying 'there's no fool like an old fool' could be attributed to him. That said, he'd had the last laugh when tipping her over the balcony of their honeymoon suite and watching with delight as his young wife somersaulted through the air before splatting on the pavement below.

Now he was about to commit his third murder. Again, the same MO, although Bridget would fall seven storeys to her death, whereas Cindy only had to endure five.

The second murder, candlestick in the skull, was more of a spur-of-the-moment thing. However, as he watched that git torment his son, the red mist had clouded his judgement, resulting in Lee Parish becoming his second victim.

Sidney checked his watch, now becoming somewhat bored. He hopped off the bed and strolled out onto the balcony, taking in the sights of Paris on this warm late-spring day – a great day to die.

It had been rather lovely to see Deana again. Of course, they were much older now, but she still had that aura about her. Although the woman walked out on him the day that rotund police officer informed him that no charges were to be levied upon him following their investigations into his business partner, Deana still had to be the most vivacious woman he'd ever been fortunate enough to woo – and he'd wooed a few in his time.

Terry Walton seemed a decent sort, and his few days at Deana's home seemed almost like a mini-break holiday in the company of close friends, as they enjoyed a few bottles of wine whilst he and Deana reminisced about the good old days.

Although he would have loved the opportunity for one more spin around the sheets with that woman, it was clear to him that Deana only had eyes for Terry – well, the dead man was half her age, and he knew Deana couldn't resist a young stud in a pair of tight jeans. Deana and King Louis XIV had both enjoyed many lovers, although, unlike the seventeenth-century French monarch, Deana only sired one child – his adopted son, Damian.

During his time at Deana's house, whilst she busied herself chasing Terry, Sidney conducted a spot of detective work. It hadn't taken him long to discover Bridget's whereabouts after she'd made a hasty retreat following the death of her partner.

When his mind drifted away from Deana, he focused on the street below, where he spotted Bridget scrambling out of a taxi, hauling along a plethora of designer-labelled shopping bags.

"Ha, you ain't going to need those, my girl." That said, he thought he'd watch her shower and change before throwing the woman to her death. A bit pervy – leching over some fit, thirty-two-year-old woman undress and shower? Well, yes, maybe.

But who would know?

He was dead and invisible.

50

New Year's Eve – 2023

Death Becomes Them

"Hi, come in. Kim's just getting ready. She'll be down in a minute. Come through. The others are already here in the kitchen," Vinny cheerfully offered his greeting after he'd swung open the front door.

Over the last few years, Kim and I got to know each other. Not as half-siblings, but just friends who occasionally met up for a meal, liked each other's posts on Facebook, along with the occasional evening whilst taking in a play at the theatre – Courteney was doing her level best to educate me.

Tonight, along with a few mutual friends, Courteney and I were attending a dinner party, which Kim had insisted we attend. Personally, a quiet night in front of the TV would have done me fine, but then, if it weren't for Courteney, I'd probably be classed as a hermit.

Despite my girl's somewhat crazy notion about my dead parents, and the need to enlist their help to exact revenge upon Bridget, we never found them. I, and Courteney, though sharing our ridiculous musings with Kim was not a path we should tread – so we never did.

Whether I would broach the subject regarding our blood relationship with Kim sometime in the future, maybe, but for now, it was a case of letting sleeping dogs lie, as they say.

Anyway, only a week after we'd discussed our plan, following witnessing some invisible force crush Lee Parish's head, Bridget's whereabouts became publicly known. In some quirk of fate, the nefarious bitch had fallen to her death from her hotel balcony after enjoying a spending spree – with my money, I hasten to add – in the boutiques along the Avenue Des Champs-Elysées. Karma for her actions, or my dead mother's ghost embarking on a spot of rampage of murder – who knows – actually, who cares?

Irrespective of whether my dead mother had any involvement, Bridget's death was treated as an unfortunate accident due to a cocktail of drugs and champagne found in her system. An empty bottle of Krug Grande Cuvée Brut on the bedside table and a spilt tube of offensively expensive beauty oil discovered near the balcony where she slipped and fell gave credence to the conclusion that the woman had suffered a fatal accident. The report on the BBC website stated the French authorities suspected Bridget slipped on the oil. Because of her inebriated state, she was unable to steady herself before toppling over the balustrade and thus dropped the seven storeys to her death.

Bridget's will stated one beneficiary, her half-brother Nathan Bragg. Before the August bank holiday weekend, when Courteney and I took our wedding vows on the golden sands of a windswept beach in the Cayman Islands, Nathan signed all my lost assets over to me. Although a wimp, as my

495

wife had called him, the man had done the decent thing. Either that or the threat of a visit from Courteney was enough for Nathan to want rid of my lost fortune.

Later that year, we visited the United States. Although a holiday, we took a detour to visit my father's and his wife's graves. They'd been placed together, a double heart headstone marking their passing. I guess my father finally found true love with his young American bride. Although the circumstances of her death were similar to that of Bridget's, Cindy committed suicide because of a broken heart. A romantic tragedy, like a mash-up of Swan Lake and Madame Butterfly, Courteney said. I bowed to her greater knowledge of the arts.

I sold the garage, as I thought following in my dead adopted father's footsteps was not the route I wanted to tread. Of course, I didn't re-ask *Stinkor* for my old job back, instead investing in property, thus becoming a landlord. However, after my experience when renting that shithole on the Broxworth Estate, I ensured my tenants enjoyed the opportunity to rent decent accommodation, devoid of any mould issues, plus sporting items of furniture which didn't require the application of a rather hefty paperback version of James Clavell's Japanese historical fiction to support their equilibrium.

My experience on that odious estate wasn't all bad. No, far from it, because it's there that I met my leggy-blonde accomplice, who agreed to marry me despite her loathing of fruitcake. Now, seven years on, we were blessed with three children – three blonde-haired girls with Scandinavian heritage, who, when they flourished into womanhood, were going to break some hearts. Notwithstanding our regular practice in the process of procreation, the fourth child that Courteney demanded hadn't yet formed – we'd keep at it.

496

Despite never benefiting from a role model, Courteney took to motherhood as if she'd been born for the position. She never made it to the front cover of Vogue, despite Kim's insistence that she should forge a career in modelling. Three rumbustious girls – I wonder what side of the family they inherited that trait from, hmmm – and her books were more than enough for Courteney.

We followed Vinny through to the open-plan kitchen diner. I hopped up on a stool and gratefully accepted the glass of wine offered whilst placing the brown padded envelope on the counter. Courteney clacked across the tiles in those impossibly high-heeled shoes to catch up with the other guests. When Courteney was in a room, it lit up, and tonight was no different, as our six other friends hung on her every word.

I watched in wonder as my girl held court.

"What's in that, mate?" Vinny nodded to the manilla padded envelope.

"Courteney's new book."

"Oh, brilliant! She's bloody clever, your girl. I have no idea how she comes up with those storylines," he chuckled.

"You're the one with a degree from Cambridge."

"True, but that doesn't provide life experience, does it?"

"No, mate, and my girl has plenty of that," I chuckled.

"Is this another one in her series about that private-eye woman? What's the character's name?"

"Deli Klein."

"Yeah, that's it. Both Kim and I love that series."

"No, this is a new venture. Her publisher reckons it's her best yet."

"Wow, sounds intriguing," he chuckled.

Our group of friends all burst out laughing, something Courteney had said, probably recounting some 'bovver' our eldest had got herself embroiled in at primary school. Katlin Statham, aged six, was nothing short of a handful. Due to her somewhat boisterous antics, we'd had our little bundle of joy assessed for ADHD, only to discover her problem was an exceptionally high IQ – not something that Katlin inherited from her father. The headteacher stated he'd never met a girl like her. I had – her mother.

"Hi, Damian."

I spun on my bar stool and flashed my half-sister my best smile. However, she had no idea of our sibling status. "Oh, hi, Kim. You look great."

"Thanks. I have to make a special effort when Courteney's visiting to avoid looking like some gnarled old witch," she chuckled. "Love her like a sister, but that girl of yours can make the rest of us look somewhat ordinary."

"Hey, you're the sexiest woman on the planet!" Vinny swooned.

"Err … hello," Kim nodded to Courteney. "I don't think so."

"No, alright, second sexiest, then," he smirked.

Kim playfully swatted him on the arm. "On the subject of beauty, I'm concerned about Alessia," her furrowed brow suggested something was on her mind.

"Oh." I could easily concur with that worried look Vinny now sported when concerns were raised about a daughter.

"Yes, oh. Our girl has that imaginary friend, you know, the one she reckons lives in her wardrobe."

"Yeah, it does make me laugh." The relief on Vinny's face was almost palpable, now presumably realising that there was nothing serious to concern himself about his daughter.

"Hmmm, are you aware of this imaginary friend's name?"

"Err … no … no, I don't think so."

"Well, I'm a little concerned. She's up there now hobbling about in my black Jimmy Choo shoes, chatting to her imaginary friend in my walk-in wardrobe, I hasten to add, and she's just called this friend, Deana."

Although I was part of the conversation, I'd turned away, being polite, to avoid participating in what seemed a private discussion regarding Kim and Vinny's daughter. However, my head shot around when Kim uttered that name.

Kim appeared concerned, and Vinny, not a big drinker, swallowed his wine before pouring another large glass and instantly chasing that down after the first.

Coincidence – surely. Christ, was my dead mother up there playing with my half-niece in Kim's wardrobe? "Kim, none of my business, but what's the concern with the name Deana?" I narrowed my eyes, dreading the answer would have anything to do with that woman.

Kim glanced at Vinny, who shook his head as he again filled his glass, his hand shaking as he tried to hold the bottle steady. "Damian, it's difficult to say …but some years ago, I met a ghost called Deana. I know that sounds totally nuts." She offered a nervous laugh.

I glanced across to Courteney, still in full flow recounting her tail, the odd word like 'tosser' and 'twat' causing a ripple of laughter amongst our friends. I knew she'd wanted to show Kim her new book. A book that, if half as successful as any of her others, would financially set us up for life. However, as this conversation seemed to be about an invisible woman called Deana, I thought I'd better show Kim the content of that padded envelope – my girl wouldn't mind.

"Kim, Vinny, I don't think what you said is nuts." I pulled out the book from the envelope and held the cover up to them both. "Many of us experience the supernatural, and Courteney's used just such an experience as the storyline for her new book."

Kim and Vinny, open-mouthed, appeared to be frozen in time by a witch's spell as they gawped at the cover.

"Oi, babe! I was going to show Kimmy that!" Courteney playfully pinched my arm before slinging her arms around my neck and nestling her cheek against mine as she read aloud the cover of her soon-to-be seventh bestselling novel. "Death Becomes Them … Deana, Demon or Diva. Book one in the new psychological ghost thriller series by the international bestselling author Courteney Statham."

"Oh … my good God," stammered Kim, leaving Vinny dumbstruck.

"Bleedin' good, innit!"

~

So, what's next?

Deana and Terry will return in their next adventure, *Dea Goode*, in the summer of 2023. I hope you get a chance to rea that book as well.

Thank you for reading this book. As an independent author, I don't benefit from the support of a large publishing house to promote my work. So, may I ask a small favour to help push me along? If you enjoyed this book, could I invite you to leave a review on Amazon? Just a few lines will help other readers discover my books – I'll hugely appreciate it.

For more information and to sign-up for updates on new releases, please drop onto my website. You can also find my page on Facebook.

www.adriancousins.co.uk

Facebook.com/adriancousinsauthor

~

Author's note

I do hope you weren't offended by some of the vocabulary used by Terry because that wasn't my intention. Unfortunately, Terry came from an era when language was very different from today. Thankfully, education has taken the world on a journey to a more tolerant and inclusive society – although I accept that we still have many miles of that journey to tread. Anyway, I'm quite certain that the diva, Deana, will sort the poor boy out, one way or another.

~

Other titles by Adrian Cousins: -

The Jason Apsley Trilogy

Jason Apsley's Second Chance

Ahead of his Time

Force of Time

Standalone Novels

Eye of Time.

Deana – Demon or Diva Series

It's Payback Time

Death Becomes Them

Dead Goode (Due for release July 2023)

~

Acknowledgements …

Thank you to the following: your feedback and support has been invaluable.

Adele Walpole

Brenda Bennett

Tracy Fisher

Lisa Osborne

Patrick Walpole

Andy Wise

And, of course, Sian Phillips, who makes everything come together, I'm so grateful.

505

Printed in Great Britain
by Amazon